I0668640

A TALE OF TWO COLORS

the
STORM
that
carries me HOME

VOLUME IV

also by
ANTHONY
WOOD

White & Black
Gray & Blue
Peace Before the Second Storm

Up Close and Personal: Embracing the Poor

A TALE OF TWO COLORS

the STORM that carries me HOME

VOLUME IV

ANTHONY WOOD

WILL ROGERS MEDALLION WINNER

HAT CREEK

HAT CREEK

An Imprint of Roan & Weatherford Publishing Associates, LLC
Bentonville, Arkansas
www.roanweatherford.com

Library of Congress Cataloging-in-Publication Data
Names: Wood, Anthony, author.
Title: The Storm That Carries Me Home/Anthony Wood | A Tale of Two Colors #4
Description: First Edition. | Bentonville: Hat Creek, 2023.
Identifiers: LCCN: 2023932448 | ISBN: 978-1-63373-820-1 (hardcover)
ISBN: 978-1-63373-821-8 (trade paperback) | ISBN: 978-1-63373-822-5 (eBook)
Subjects: | BISAC: FICTION/Historical/Civil War Era |
FICTION/War and Military | FICTION/Action/Adventure |
LC record available at: https://lccn.loc.gov/2023932448

Hat Creek trade paperback edition May, 2023

Jacket & Interior Design by Casey W. Cowan
Jacket art by Paul D. Philippoteaux (1846-1923)
Battle of Five Forks, 1885, Oil on canvas
Editing by Bob Giel & Amy Cowan

For Linda McCulloch,
who helped me get to know our shared ancestors.
You are my dear friend.

ACKNOWLEDGEMENTS

HAVING FRIENDS TO walk with on the writing journey has become essential to any success I've enjoyed. This fourth volume in *A Tale of Two Colors* is about Lummy choosing to do what is right when it would be easier to settle for less. My friends at Roan & Weatherford Publishing are committed to making their authors the best writers they can be. They will settle for nothing less. Thank you, Casey Cowan for your masterfully creative soul, unwavering friendship, and relentless encouragement. For your deep insight into stories and not letting me fall short with those pesky commas, Amy Cowan, thank you. Bob Giel, what can I say? You ensure my stories make sense and are historically accurate. You have my deepest thanks. For your guidance and mentorship, Dennis Doty, I am grateful. For your love and willingness to edit my work, thank you, Lisa. And to all those known and unknown galley editors, you are a blessing my writing cannot do without—thank you. You, my friends, have truly become my writing family.

MOUNTED UNION INFANTRY
A period photograph of a Union soldier from an Indiana mounted infantry regiment. The members of the 1st Mississippi Mounted Rifles would have been outfitted in similar fashion.

DRAMATIS PERSONAE

ANNIE FANNY: Lummy's sassy and frisky snuff-dipping friend who cared for his shoulder injury suffered while crossing the Mississippi River from Vicksburg to Desoto, LA in search of Susannah. She was a mess. Lummy crossed paths with Annie at Desoto on his way to enlist in the Confederate Army. She's still a mess.

CAPTAIN TOM FORD: Leader of the outlaw Choctaw County Home Guard who vowed to kill Lummy for killing Lester, Ford's good friend and fellow soldier.

DORCAS TULLOS HAWTHORNE: The wife of Lummy's older brother, Benjamin Franklin "Benny Frank" Tullos, who moved with his family to Winn Parish, Louisiana from Choctaw County, MS in the mid-1850s. After Ben's death, Dorcas married Freddy Hawthorne. Lummy visited Dorcas and the family after leaving Vicksburg.

BIG RED: a large blaze-face fox squirrel that warned Lummy Tullos and the 27th Louisiana Infantry that the Union Army was about to attack in May, 1863. He survived the siege and the cookpot. Lummy saw Big Red again on his way home to Choctaw County when he visited the 27th Louisiana Lunette where Lummy endured the siege of Vicksburg.

COLUMBUS "LUMMY" NATHAN TULLOS: Archibald and Mary Tullos's sixth child born in Holmes County, MS, in 1834. As the main character in this series, Lummy leaves his home in Choctaw Co., Mississippi and begins his adventurous journey in search of his love, a young slave woman named Susannah. They eventually marry, but nearly a year into Lummy's service with the 27th Louisiana Volunteer Infantry in Vicksburg, MS, he receives a devastating letter from Mr. Gilmore informing him of Susannah's death.

DAN CREEKWATER: Lummy's Choctaw friend whom he first met on the road to Winn Parish back in 1859. Dan became a good friend and confidant for Lummy as he sorted out his recent war experiences and made his decision to join the 1st Mississippi Mounted Rifles. Lummy shared a camp with Dan in the haunts of McCurtain Creek Swamp after killing Lester, who tried to rape and kill Lummy's family. Dan helped Lummy find his soul again.

ELIHU TULLOS: Lummy's eccentric older brother who did not go to war, but stayed home to care for the family and farm in Choctaw County. Elihu became Lummy's greatest ally as he made his decision to join the Union Army. Elihu was the first to experience Lummy's trauma due to his war experiences.

ELZEY TULLOS: Lummy's and Susannah's son who was unknown to Lummy until he traveled to Winn Parish after Vicksburg surrendered. Because of his less than stable state of mind and the possibility of re-entering the war, Lummy decided to leave Elzey with a good family in Winn Parish until such a time that he might return.

JASPER NEWTON AND JAMES A. TULLOS: Lummy's two younger brothers who served with the 1st Mississippi Light Artillery,

Company C, during the Siege of Vicksburg. They were stationed just across Glass Bayou from the 27th Louisiana Lunette where Lummy was stationed. They are still fighting in the war.

LESTER: A bully with whom Lummy has had to contend since childhood. Lummy killed Lester who tried to rape and murder Lummy's mother and nieces. This sent Lummy into hiding with Dan Creekwater in McCurtain Creek Swamp.

SERGEANT "SARGE" McGUGARTY: Lummy met Sarge when he received his parole after the surrender of Vicksburg. Lummy spoke about his new oath with Sarge who offered Lummy the opportunity to put his oath into practice. Sarge encouraged Lummy to consider joining a soon-to-be-formed new Union Army regiment, the 1st Mississippi Mounted Rifles.

SETH: A young runaway slave Lummy took under his wing and to the Tullos farm where Seth became part of the family. In working to help Seth, Lummy realizes the good influence that the late Mr. James T. Gilmore had in his life. This aided in his decision to join the Union army.

SUSANNAH: A young slave woman and Lummy's first love, who was taken from Choctaw County, MS to Winn Parish, LA by James T. Gilmore, who won her in a card game. Lummy left his home to go to Winn Parish to find her. Lummy eventually marries Susannah on Christmas Day, 1861. Lummy received a devastating letter on New Year's Day, 1863, informing him that Susannah died of measles. Lummy returned to Winn Parish after the surrender of Vicksburg only to find that Susannah did not die of the measles, but was brutally raped and murdered by Dawg Smith and his outlaw gang. Lummy made things right by ending Smith's reign of terror.

TOM POOLE: Lummy's childhood friend growing up in Choctaw County.

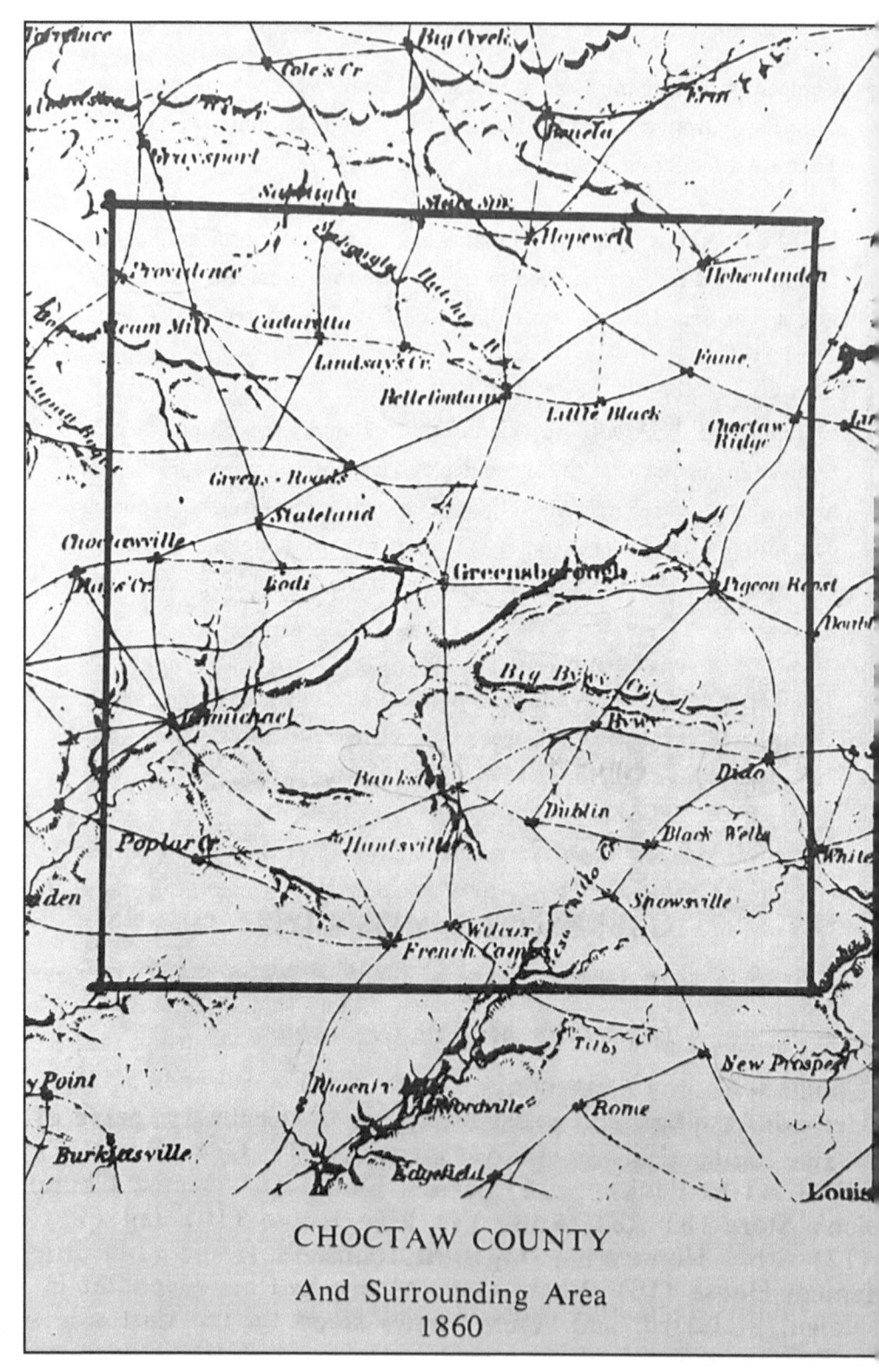

CHOCTAW COUNTY

And Surrounding Area
1860

SCAENA

CHOCTAW COUNTY, MISSISSIPPI: Founded and created in 1833 from lands ceded by the Choctaw Indians and named for them. Lummy's parents, Archibald and Mary Tullos, bought land and settled there as pioneers in 1835. Lummy grew up in Choctaw County and his family helped start one of the county's first Baptist Churches, New Zion, in 1842. With the surrender of Vicksburg, he desperately wants to visit his family and home there.

DESOTO, LOUISIANA: A small but important town at the eastern end of the Vicksburg, Shreveport, & Texas Railroad, which only extended from the Mississippi River to Monroe, LA in 1860. The village serves as a ferry site and railroad depot for travel, goods, and mail just across the river from Vicksburg. Lummy meets Annie Fanny in Desoto after receiving a shoulder injury while crossing the Mississippi River on a ferry. He returns to Desoto to catch a steamer on his way south to New Orleans to enlist in the Confederate Army, where he encounters Annie Fanny again.

PRENTISS (PRENTISE) HOUSE HOTEL: The hotel where Lummy and the 27th Louisiana Infantry were stationed while the regiment served as provost for the city of Vicksburg.

TWENTY-SEVENTH LOUISIANA LUNETTE: an earthworks

fortification given its name for the regiment with whom Lummy Tullos served. The 27th Louisiana Volunteer Infantry received the honor for being the first to arrive to defend Vicksburg and being responsible for having built many defensive earthworks. When the Yankees surrounded Vicksburg, Lummy spent the entire forty-seven day siege in the rifle pits, bombproofs, and behind the parapet that made up the lunette. The Lunette suffered two major attacks, shelling, sniper fire, small skirmishes, and a Union mine that fortunately the Confederate Army countermined and blew up just before the 27th Lunette was lost.

VICKSBURG, MISSISSIPPI: An important river port and railroad town that linked the east and west of the growing United States. Lummy boarded a ferry there in search of Susannah and suffered a shoulder injury while crossing the Mississippi River to Desoto, LA. Lummy saw Vicksburg from across the river as he boarded a steamer to travel south to enlist. He returned to the city after his brief training at Camp Moore near Tangipahoa, Louisiana in early May, 1863. He remained in Vicksburg until the Confederate Army surrendered to the Union Army July 4, 1863. He passed through Vicksburg on his way to Choctaw County from Winn Parish, fall of 1863.

WINN PARISH, LOUISIANA: established in 1852 from lands taken from surrounding parishes. Erroneously nicknamed the "Free State of Winn," young attorney David Pierson was elected to vote "no" to secession at the convention called in Baton Rouge in January, 1861. He, along with a few others, refused to change their "no" votes at the end of the session when asked so as to make the decision unanimous. Though raising eight companies for the Confederate Army, nearly half of the parish's young men hid rather than go fight for "rich men's slaves." Others joined the Union Army. Several Winn Parish slave owners freed their slaves before the war began. James T. Gilmore owned and farmed land not far from Winfield, the parish seat. Lummy had plans to return to Winn Parish after the war where he and Susannah would build a home and family. That was no longer to be when Susannah died. Following the surrender of Vicksburg, Lummy chose to go home to Choctaw County after settling his affairs in Winn Parish.

A TALE OF TWO COLORS

the
STORM
that
carries me HOME

VOLUME IV

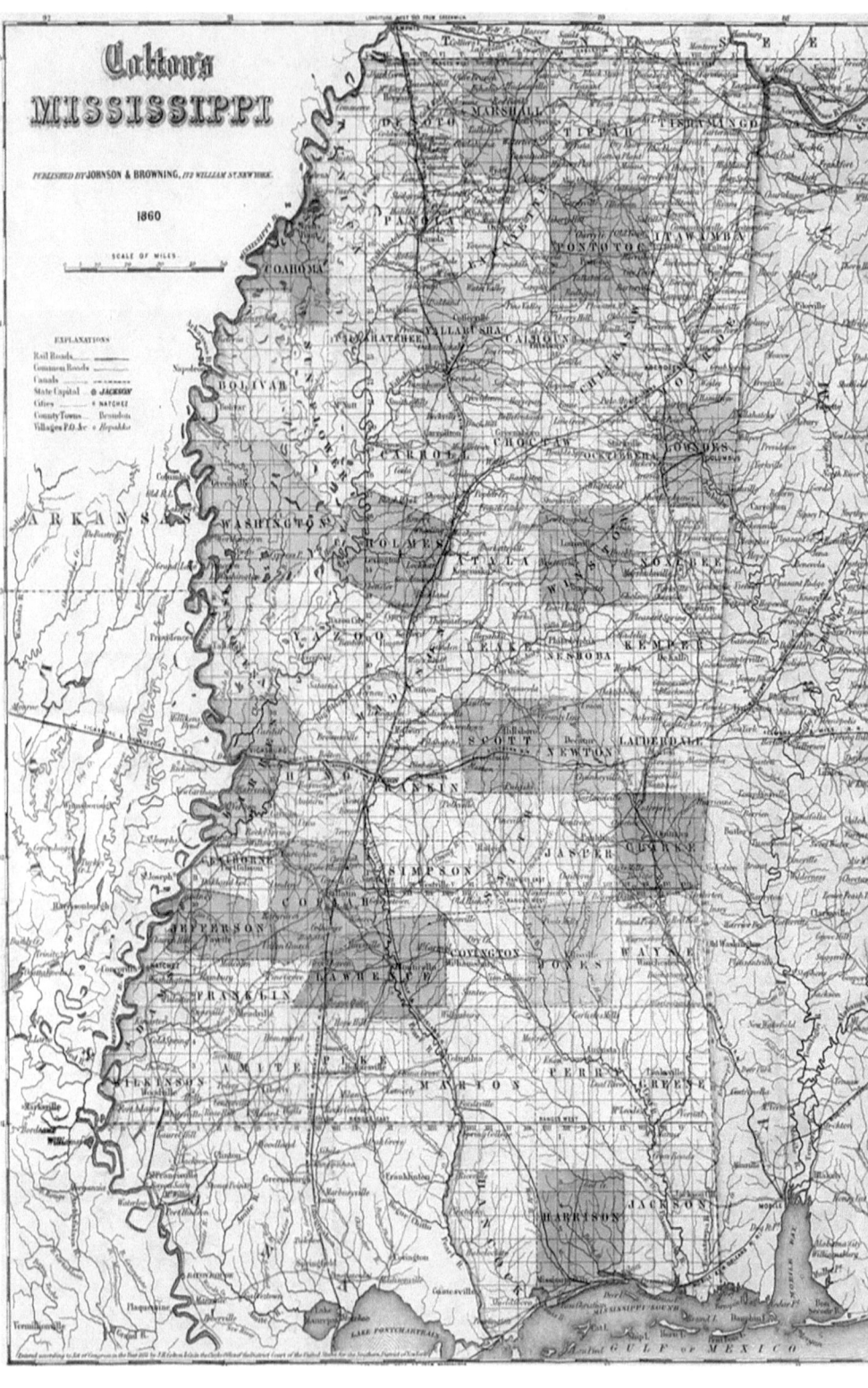

Colton's
MISSISSIPPI

PUBLISHED BY JOHNSON & BROWNING, 172 WILLIAM ST. NEW YORK.

1860

SCALE OF MILES

EXPLANATIONS
Rail Roads
Common Roads
Canals
State Capital ... ⊙ JACKSON
Cities ... ⊛ NATCHEZ
County Towns ... Brandon
Villages P.O. &c ... o Hopahka

CHAPTER 1

LEAVING TO FIGHT FOR THE BLUE

2:00 A.M., NOVEMBER 27, 1864

The best prayers ever prayed were never spoken out loud.

GUNSHOTS PIERCE THE cold night on the other side of the ridge. "Whooowee!" echoes through the pines, unsettling the night birds. Barred owls call to each other from one end of the forest to the other.

Sarge reins his horse up in a skid. "What in the hell was that, Lummy? The Rebel yell?"

"Heck no! That's Choctaw Dan's best war whoop."

Sarge rubs his mount's neck and wipes the sweat on his pants. "That was too damn close!"

"Yeah, I thought Captain Tom Ford and the Home Guard had us for sure."

"Better let our mounts rest a bit."

I hop off my horse. "Ole Cap'n Ford's been tryin' to catch me for several months now. He didn't cotton up to my feedin' Rebel deserters and helpin' out the Union Secret Society. Killin' his best friend, Lester, didn't help none, either."

"You only did what any decent man would do to protect his family."

"It'll take a bullet to end the grudge Ford's holding against me."

"Your man, H.P. Dotson, has done a good job of organizing the true loyalists in Choctaw County."

"Not to mention Pastor Dobbs and my mother."

"Really, your whole family has been good to do their part to help end this war. I know they've risked everything keeping you hidden."

"Sarge, we best get goin' or Captain Tom Ford will figure out he's chasin' the wrong rabbit."

"You think they'll catch your Choctaw friend?"

"Not a chance."

"I hear hounds howling."

"Yeah, Captain Ford is pretty proud of his trackin' dogs. He loves it when his hounds corner a deserter or Unionist and start baying. But Dan's smarter than a few bloodhounds, I think."

"What's he doing? I hear him yelling in one place then in the same place a few minutes later."

"He's runnin' them boys around in circles like a swamp rabbit chased by hounds. He's havin' the time of his life. Don't fret about him. He knows this county better'n I do. He'll give 'em the slip when he's sure we've had time to get away." Keep Dan safe, Lord.

Riders race and scream threats through the hills in the light of a shadowy moon. We rest our mounts as the sound of hooves pounding the earth fade into the wind.

I chuckle. "They'll never catch ole Dan Creekwater. If they don't give up the chase, he'll scalp 'em all by daylight."

Sarge grins. "I should've recruited him as a scout."

"Dan'll be here if we need him."

"Good friends are hard to come by these days."

"God ain't made a better friend than Dan Creekwater... except maybe you, Sarge."

"Well, don't go getting all mushy on me, Lummy."

I laugh and think about the first time I met Sarge when Vicksburg surrendered. He tried to recruit me then at the parole. It took a bit of time, but I guess it worked. I'm riding with him now. For the Union army. Like him, I'm only doing what's needed to be done.

The night is breezy, moving the clouds away from the moon. The sky is clear. And my mind is clear about what I'll do next and with whom. Sarge's new blue 1st Mississippi Mounted Rifles uniform fits his frame rather nicely. One like it will fit my soul even better.

Escaping Captain Tom Ford and his Home Guard outlaws was pretty easy with Dan's help. That old Choctaw warrior is still saving my hide. Captain Ford doesn't like being outwitted and losing his prey in the forest. Dan's smarter than an old buck and strong as seasoned oak. But I fear Ford will take vengeance on my family.

"Sarge, let's circle back around to the farm once more, just in case. Ford might take losin' us out on my family. I've got to know they're all right."

CHAPTER 2

A LAST LOOK AT WHAT MAKES ME LEAVE

3:00 A.M., NOVEMBER 27, 1864

Paintin' a picture of home in my mind will remind me of why I left.

I TAKE ONE last look at the Tullos farm down below the hill where Ma, the girls, and Seth lay sleeping. I draw in the frigid air and shake the frost from my jacket. The starry sky makes me think of how big Creator must be. I clear my mind and still my soul. I pray over my family. Somehow, I will return when the war is over.

Sarge nudges my mount with his. "The best prayers ever prayed were never spoken out loud."

"Yeah, I do believe Jesus said somethin' like that one time."

I trust the Lord knows my heart, thoughts, and feelings. The wind whispers through the pines. I feel Creator's comfort.

"Lummy, don't shoot, it's me." Elihu steps out of the shadows and sits on the ground with Pa and others buried in the family cemetery. I say my last words over the dead and dismount. My brother sings a sorrowful old hymn that reminds me of our upbringing in the New Zion Baptist Church. Elihu's voice is as pure as the night darkness.

I join in. "Shall we gather at the river, where bright angel's feet have trod...."

Sarge pats me on the shoulder. "Time to go, son. We've got another gathering to attend in Vicksburg before we make that one."

"Elihu, I want to—" He's already too transcended heavenward to hear me. He nods. The family is in good hands with my big brother, Seth, and Dan. I mount up.

Elihu stands and slaps my leg. "Don't forget to write." He disappears into a pine thicket.

We avoid the road to Bankston. Captain Tom Ford and his band of outlaw Confederate Home Guard will split up to patrol the roads. His spies will be watching every crossing and side road. He's got eyes and ears everywhere.

Headquartered at Greensborough, Ford's miscreant gang continue to harass good citizens, taking what they want from who they want. They're no better than Dawg Smith's bunch back in Winn Parish. Men bent on the destruction of others for their own profit. But with Lester's body showing up early last spring with my gator tooth necklace found on his person, they only see blood when they think of me. No amount of feeding Reb deserters these past months would ever redeem me in their eyes.

"Nothin' but a bunch of damn hungry porch hounds lookin' for a free biscuit, I say."

I'm thankful Sheriff Platner let my killing Lester go once he learned that bastard tried to rape and murder Ma and the girls. That's because Lester's mother couldn't kick up a fuss. But when she unexpectedly recovered from a fever, she hasn't let up. She won't stop until she gets justice for her dead son and crippled nephew, Kneehigh. Captain Ford is all too eager to help.

Justice my ass. She wants to save face in the midst of everyone knowing what a rascal Lester really was. His squeaky-mouse cousin, Kneehigh, still is. I don't regret killing Lester. He bullied me one time too many. I don't regret picking up Kneehigh over my head in a rage and slamming him down on the street. I do hate that he's a cripple though.

Lester's mother wants my hide nailed to the barn door for all to see. Up to a point, after losing Susannah, I know how she feels.

Anyway, she caught Elihu outside Wesson's mercantile in Bankston last week and chewed on him like a dog working a meaty bone. Just short of attacking him, she did her best to draw a crowd.

Elihu laughed when he told us about it. "She sounded like a squawkin' jaybird flutterin' her boney wings. She should've flown off like the ole buzzard she is, but she kept on shakin' that gator tooth at me. Finally, I grabbed it and slung it up on the rooftop of Wesson's store. She ran to get Sheriff

Platner. I knew it'd take time to find him, so I gave a boy two pennies to fetch it for me. Then I left."

Elihu gave me the tooth on the silver chain last Sunday at church. The good luck charm that saved me at Vicksburg ain't working so good right now.

Sarge and I start down the hill winding through vine covered thickets on lesser used trails. I lead, my head bobbing in rhythm with the plodding. I enjoy the silence of the night and get lost in my thoughts. Time at home with the family has brought some peace before I head into this second storm. It's unavoidable, and I'm running straight at it. Funny thing, there ain't a cloud in the sky as the moon sinks into the west. This storm isn't about thunder, lightning, or rain. It's about fire.

We sneak along the sandy Phoenix Creek bottom that cuts through our farm. My school teacher, Miss Stansbury, once read the Greek myth about how the Phoenix would live five hundred years only to build its own funeral pyre. After setting itself on fire, a new Phoenix would rise from the ashes more radiant and beautiful than before to sing an enchanting song that could even make the sun god stop and listen. Maybe I'll be that Phoenix—rise from the ashes to sing a new song. This funeral pyre has a name. Bankston.

I feel like I've lived five hundred years in my young life already. I'm ready to build my own funeral pyre to end the grief I've experienced. Maybe this final bit of soldiering will do it. I'll certainly have plenty of ashes to rise from.

Sarge whispers, "Let's go this way."

"I thought we were headin' to Vicksburg, Sarge."

"You need to see something first. Then I have the surprise I told you about."

"Tell me."

"You'll find out soon enough. Let's go, soldier." After taking orders in one man's army, it ain't hard taking them in another's—especially if you're finally in the right army.

We walk our horses up the creek bank and follow a woodcutter's trail until we reach the Old Natchez Trace. No one stirs. Night travel makes it easy to avoid people and trouble. We head up Little Mountain, the highest point in Choctaw County.

We crest the hill just before daylight and rest our horses. A cold shiver slithers down my spine like the Devil's crawling down my back with his cold slimy claws. I need reassurance. The last bit of moonlight brightens the land enough I can make out rolling hills covered with dense forests. Individual trees start to take shape. The moon disappears, and the first rays of new hope make the frost glisten.

Memories flood my mind—growing up on the Tullos farm enjoying life with my brothers, living with Pa's anger but also Ma's gentle strength, learning to read at the schoolhouse and learning God ain't only found in a church house, realizing how much I hate bullies and how much I loved Susannah, traveling to Winn Parish to work with Ben and finally marrying Susannah, enlisting in the Reb Army at New Orleans and surviving the siege of Vicksburg, settling my affairs in Winn Parish and ending Dawg Smith's life, coming back home to Ma and living wild as an Indian with Dan Creekwater, killing Lester and helping Mr. Dotson's Unionist cause, and now, only to leave again. When will the storms finally end so I can live in peace?

Sarge dismounts and sits on a log. "Take a good long look."

I scratch my horse's ear and gaze east toward Wood Mountain thinking about the sweet water flowing from Grandpa Aaron Wood's spring that makes the best moonshine. I glance southeast and think about Ma, the girls, Elihu, Seth, Susannah's folks, and the life I leave behind. I look west, and it seems only like only yesterday I took the road to Carrollton chasing after Susannah back in '59. It wasn't that long ago Seth and I passed by here on our way to the farm. But now, my hat is set southwest for Vicksburg where I'll enlist in the 1st Mississippi Mounted Rifles.

"A man needs to know what he's fighting for—what he's willing to die for." The sun peeks over Wood Mountain.

"True, and destroying my hometown has to be part of it?"

"Only the factories and mills in Bankston, Mr. Dotson said. You do want Mississippi back in the Union where it belongs?"

"Yes, I want the twentieth star back on the Union flag."

"Wearing the blue uniform will help make that happen, son."

"I'm willing."

"It won't be easy now, or when you come back home."

"What worth livin' or dyin' forever is?"

The horizon seems so far away and even farther for what life might hold for me.

Granny Thankful told me once when I was twelve, "Lummy, you're becomin' a man, and all of life is ahead of you. Don't look so far ahead that you miss what the Lord puts right in front of you. Be present with your surroundings. Close your eyes. Envision beyond what the eyes can see. You have a gift, grandson. The Lord will lead you to a new world, if you let him."

Sarge pats me on the shoulder. "You ready?"

"A man can almost see forever with the leaves off the trees."

Sarge breathes in deeply. "I've often pondered the honesty of unclothed trees. When a man bares his soul like you have, Lummy, the truth of who he is sprouts new life."

I lean back in my saddle. "I didn't know you were such a poet, Sarge."

He stares into the approaching sunrise. "I'm not, but pondering has kept me sane in this insane world. But enough of that, let's go."

"So what's the big surprise, Sarge? You're killin' me!"

Not really. I just need to think about something else besides leaving home again. Last time, it was nearly more than I could bear. It makes me wonder what I'll become when I rise from the ashes this time.

"You'll get your surprise when we get to French Camp."

CHAPTER 3

OLD FRIENDS BRIGHTEN DARK ROADS

NOVEMBER 27, 1864

Some surprises are worth waiting for.

THE RIDE ON the Old Natchez Trace to French Camp is cold and lonely. We jog our mounts on a deer path, pushing cedar limbs away as we move down the hill to a small clearing.

Sarge dismounts. "Stay here." He draws his sidearm and creeps up to the edge of a small clearing.

A run-down cabin sits off to the side in the trees with a cistern out front. Sarge whistles twice, and out steps a man wearing farmer's clothes holding a Colt's Revolving Rifle like some of the Yanks carried at Vicksburg.

I squint to see underneath the worn-out floppy hat shadowing his face. He waves and walks toward Sarge. I know that familiar gait. He pulls off his hat grinning from ear to ear.

"Poole!" I jump off my horse and hug him. "Where in the hell have you been, boy? How'd Sarge find you?"

"I left home...."

Sarge cuts in, proudly puffing out his chest. "Poole enlisted last spring. When he heard there might be another new recruit from Choctaw County, he knew it had to be you. I couldn't keep him from comin' along."

Poole lays his hands on my shoulders. "Glad to see you, Lummy."

Sarge hands me his reins. "We got two hours 'til sunup. Hide the horses and get something to eat. We'll rest in the shack for the day, and you boys can get reacquainted. We leave at dark."

We laugh ourselves to tears telling old stories from our childhood. If I said, "You remember when...." once, I must've said it twenty times.

Sarge grunts. "If you boys had been mine, I would've beaten the livin' daylights out of you!"

I kick dust at Poole. "Wouldn't have done any good. Our pas tried, but it didn't take!"

I punch Poole in the side, and he backhands my chest. I twist to avoid the lick and he strikes me on my bad shoulder. I wince.

"What happened to you?"

Rubbing my shoulder, I laugh. "When I crossed the Missip back in '59, a big log jumped up like a dragon out of the deep and bit my shoulder pretty hard. It ain't been right since."

I pull out the little cedar cross Poole gave me the night I left to find Susannah. It was the only thing I brought along besides the gater tooth necklace. I hold it up. "In the worst of times, brother, I'd breathe in the sweet smell to remind me of the Lord's goodness."

Poole takes the cross and breathes in the fragrance.

"And, that I've got a friend who sticks closer than a brother."

Poole rubs his thumb over the woodgrain. "My grandpappy carved this cross for my pa when he left to go fight the Mexicans. He said it kept the Lord with him all the time. I wanted the same for you."

"It did me good at Vicksburg."

Poole pokes the fire. "What do you think about people wearin' crosses and such? Some even get religious symbols tattooed on their skin. At the very least, it's gotta hurt, I bet."

I unbutton my shirt and show him the blue ink cross I had etched over my heart.

Poole blinks twice. "Did it hurt?"

"Not really. I didn't feel much when I was starvin', watchin' friends die, and knowin' the breath I was takin' right then could be my last." Susannah's face pops in my mind.

"Why'd you do it?"

I choke and cough. "A man does whatever it takes to keep his soul close to God—cross around your neck or tattoo on your body, don't matter. Especially when he finds out his wife is dead. Anybody wants to judge me for it? They can take their opinion back to Hell where they came from."

Poole pats me on the shoulder. "It's all right."

"But no, it didn't hurt. Sometimes pain reminds you that you're still alive."

Poole stares at the blue cross. "You do it yourself?"

"A Yank prisoner I guarded during the Battle of Chickasaw Bayou showed us how to do it. I borrowed a little ink from my friend, Gunnard, who was always writing in his journal. It may be dumb to some folks, but this tattoo helped me remember the Lord doesn't give up on us."

Poole touches the painted skin. "Ain't it funny how folks fuss about Catholics wearing a cross around their necks but don't mind havin' one put on their grave when they die?"

I laugh sadly. "And then complain about hanging a cross on a chain when they don't mind puttin' chains on Negroes."

Sarge pulls his blanket over his back. "Ain't that the damn truth? You best save them stories for the road. Get some sleep. We got a long ride ahead of us tomorrow."

Poole lies back. "Yes, sir, we won't be long."

Sarge grunts sleepily, "Glad you boys are with us. We got an important mission, and we need you to serve as scouts. Keep that to yourselves."

We know what the mission is, and Sarge knows we know.

Poole frowns. "I'm so sorry about Susannah, brother. I knew you'd marry her eventually."

I brush a tear. "The best wife a man could ever have."

"Tell me what happened?"

"Give me some time. I need to keep my head goin' in the right direction right now. I'll bring up that memory when I need it."

"I don't know what it means to lose the girl God made special just for me. Ain't had that kind of love in my heart yet. I just ain't found the right one, I guess. This damn war sure has put a damper on that fire."

"Don't I know it?"

Poole grins. "But dang if Susannah wasn't the prettiest flower in the garden!"

"God only makes those kind every once in a while. It still hurts somethin' fierce. But like this tattoo, I'll heal in time. And like this cross, she's always on my heart. I'll see her again one day."

Poole looks up into the sky. "You surely will."

I poke the fire. "Marrying a Negro gal, wearin' religious symbols on your body, and puttin' on the blue suit can cause some people to question a man."

"You owe nobody an explanation, Lummy."

"I know. Just because I take a different trail don't mean I'm lost. One person misusing a good thing doesn't make it wrong for another to use it the right way. Puttin' on the blue suit is right for me, no matter who thinks I'm wrong. Why'd you enlist?"

Poole throws a small stick into the smoldering coals in the fireplace. "My folks were Unionists from the beginning. With all those loud mouth Rebels in Bankston gassin' about, they just kept their mouths shut. Pa said a man don't always have to tell a fool what he believes just because he's spoutin' off about his."

"Some people like to hear their own crowin'."

"And some talk to bully people."

"Because that's who they are."

Poole lies down. "You took the words right out of my mouth. Just like old times, boy, finishing each other's sentences. Two minds thinking alike."

I pull my blanket over my aching shoulder. "Not sure if that was always good. You do remember the grief we brought down on ourselves when our two great minds thought alike?"

"Yeah, especially cuttin' up in church and school. My backside nearly got sheared off from the whoopin's my pa gave me."

"And not a one of 'em did you deserve, right?"

Poole laughs. "Nary a one. Remember when you pert near buried that rock in Lester's back?"

"Yeah, and I stayed in Sheriff Platner's jail for a week."

"Couldn't have been too bad. Good food from the café, readin' books, and walkin' patrol with the sheriff."

"I had no complaints."

"Nobody would've wanted to hear 'em, catfish head."

"That's for damn sure, mule butt. My pa thought it was funny."

"And your ma?"

"Do I have to answer that one?"

Poole feeds the fire then crawls under his blanket. "When my pa saw the advertisement about the 1st Mississippi Mounted Rifles in the newspaper, he wanted to join up worse than me, but he was too old. So I enlisted. My folks needed the sign up bounty money pretty bad anyway. Truth be told, I thought about you and your ideas about how the world should be when I signed up."

"I thought about you, too, when I was in the trenches at Vicksburg. I wondered if I'd ever see your slimy, bug eyed catfish face again!"

"Glad we're back together again, Lummy."

"Me, too."

Poole prays, "Lord, I'm better now that Lummy's here. Keep us in your protectin' hand."

"Amen."

A star shines through a crack in the roof. "Lord, carry us yonder, wherever yonder lies this time. Bring us back home to a life of peace."

In my soul, I cross the thin veil between Susannah and me. "Keep us before the Lord every day, my darlin'. I'll see you soon."

CHAPTER 4

VICKSBURG...
AGAIN

DECEMBER 1, 1864

The trail leading back to unpleasant places can bring new memories.

THE RIDE TO Vicksburg is pretty uneventful. I traveled this same road this time last year when I left Winn Parish and found Seth at Brashear's Stand. The Old Trace is remarkably unused for the times—just a few farmers and woodcutters wave as we pass. A small Reb patrol saw us not far out of Kosciusko, but we gave them the slip.

The Rebel Home Guard, a steady concern for any Yank traveling back roads, is not the worst. Men like Captain Tom Ford and his band of miscreant guerillas are. Like Dawg Smith in Winn Parish, they claim Jeff Davis's authority to pillage. Luckily, we don't run into any.

We give a wide berth to Rebel-occupied Jackson, if they still hold it. The capital has changed sides so many times it's just best to avoid it. A fourth capture of the city a few months ago included a black cavalry regiment made up of former slaves. They drove off the Rebel defenders and burned the rebuilt railroad bridge over the Pearl River. I knew it would finally happen. Negros fight as good as any man. Probably better. A man fights harder for freedom and family than for money, land, and politics. I fought with the Rebs because government said I had to. Now I fight because I choose to. It's not the same.

From a hill, we can see Mississippi's state capitol named for the hero of the Battle of New Orleans. Uncle Silas told me about meeting him once and fighting the British in the swamps next to the Mississippi River. That must've been a helluva fight.

Sarge looks out over the war torn town. "Rest your horses, boys."

Poole sips from his canteen. "Bet y'all didn't know Governor Pettus compared Mississippi to Jesus's family goin' down into Egypt while Herod reigned in Judea when Lincoln was elected President. Callin' President Lincoln Herod and slave owners Jesus' family. Ain't that somethin'?"

I take out the last of Ma's biscuits and share them. "Jackson used to be a pretty city."

Poole spits. "They asked for it."

"Yeah, we did."

Sarge adjusts his saddle. "We all did it, boys. Finish up, let's go."

We take the same railroad track trail to Vicksburg I used leaving Louisiana. Winn Parish. Maybe I can visit Dorcas and the family when the war's over. Maybe I'll stay a while, visit Susannah and Ben's graves again. I don't know. That's too far in a future.

We pass Bolton and Edward's Stations and skirt Bovina to finally make Four Mile Bridge. Blue suits are everywhere. Sarge motions for us to stop, and he rides up to the picket guard. He dismounts, shows the guard some papers, and they talk for a bit. They salute, and Sarge motions for us to stay put. We salute and dismount to rest our horses. Poole stretches his back, and I massage my aching shoulder.

I rub my horse's neck and give him a handful of grain. "I spent many a night standin' picket right over there, Poole. In the cold rain, too. Just down the tracks there, Jasper and James slipped and slid pulling a cannon with six other men like mules pulling a plow. That was two years ago, and here I am, right back where I started."

"I forget you got a good taste of army life with the Rebs here in Vicksburg. How bad was the siege? Can you talk about it?"

"It's gettin' easier, but some things are still too touchy, you know, losin' good friends and all. It's pretty bad when you don't care if its rat or squirrel in the pot."

Poole swallows hard. "You ate rat?"

"Like it was your momma's Sunday fried chicken." I punch his shoulder. "Mule meat was the best, though!"

Poole gags like he's gonna puke. "I could never eat our mule Rosie, even if I had to."

"Men died because the mule meat ran out. When you're starvin', there ain't no pets."

"Hope I never have to do that."

"You won't, not in the blue army."

Poole shades his eyes to get a better look. "I'd like to see Vicksburg and talk to a pretty girl."

"*That* we can do."

Sarge marches over. "All right, boys, the rest of the day is yours. Go find a place in town for the night. Get your sweet-talking about growin' up together done so tomorrow you can get about bein' soldiers."

Sarge hands Pool ten dollars. "The quartermaster said make it stretch."

"Lummy served as provost here back before the siege. He knows all the best places."

"Be good soldiers and stay out of trouble."

We straighten up stiffly and salute. "Yes, sir, Sergeant, sir. We see the three stripes you're wearin', sir."

Sarge chuckles. "And I'll be striping your asses if you cut up in town. Poole, get your uniform on. That'll keep you from getting stopped. Watch your step and stay out of the cat houses. Don't want you boys taking any Vicksburg souvenirs with you when we leave."

"No worries there, Sarge."

Poole grins. "I hope I don't, but...." I give Poole a stern look. He sighs. "I'll be good."

Sarge swats the air for us to go. Poole gets his uniform. A group of young lieutenants ride up and dismount.

Sarge wants to make a good impression. "Poole, you and Tullos be back here by roll call in the morning, or there'll be hell to pay."

We salute smartly. "Yes sir!" Sarge returns the salute. I add, "And thank you, sir!"

Poole slips behind a tent to change into his uniform.

Sarge whispers, "So you've learned to talk Yankee. That's good. Some

Yanks don't like southern boys wearing the blue suit. No more "yassuhs" or you'll catch hell."

We walk our horses to the Jackson Road. Wagonloads of sick men wait for hospital care. Assistants run here and there with communications and orders in hand. Several Rebs sit on the ground with their commander. Men yet to be exchanged, I figure. They look sick and exhausted. That was me on this same road not long ago.

A Reb under a shade tree cackles, "Couldn't make it as a Reb, huh, boy?"

I don't say anything. Someone might recognize me, even in civilian clothes. A man six feet six inches tall doesn't hide very well. And my need to chastise bullies isn't as strong this time.

"I made it through the siege with no trouble. I'm finishing this thing on my grandpap's side, boy."

The Reb spits. We mount up. Old feelings well up in my soul. I'll need them to do this.

War. What a useless and terrible thing—cuts to the heart from every damned direction.

CHAPTER 5

FROM GRAY TO BLUE

AFTERNOON, DECEMBER 1, 1864

*Fightin' for the right ain't always what it started out
to be but rather what it ends up bein'. I'm hopin'.*

HUNDREDS OF MEN in blue clog the streets—some stand at attention, others march in formation, and some just lounge around enjoying free time. Each man, each company, each regiment is at the mercy of their commanding officer. And with too much time on their hands, the younger officers tend to take their frustrations out on the enlisted men. Anyway, I hope I have another good officer like Colonel Marks was for the 27th Louisiana, God rest his soul.

The beehive of activity reminds me of the early days in Vicksburg when regiments from all over the South poured in for its defense. It was a sea of gray then.

Blue looks much better.

I recognize a few battalion colors snapping in the river breeze. I probably killed some of their friends. Poole wearing his new uniform puts me more at ease. The Yanks watch every move a man without a uniform makes. They'd all like to capture a Rebel spy to get some fleeting attention from one of their officers. We caught a couple ourselves when we held the city.

Mr. Wiley's advice rings in my ears. "Keep your head down, do what they tell you, don't stand out, keep your mouth shut, and get your ass home quick as you can!" I miss that old man. I miss too many good friends gone on to be with the Lord.

Vicksburg. I never would've thought I'd be back here so soon. I've been here too many times. I bet the Lord makes a man go through Vicksburg to get to Heaven, or Hell, when he dies.

Poole elbows me. "You have to at least one more time to show me around! Still talkin' out loud, ain't you boy? I'm gonna cure you of that if it kills me cause if I don't, it might be the death of me."

I put my arm around his shoulder. "I made it this far, didn't I, bucket head? Watch my back. I'll be watchin' yours."

Vicksburg. Too many memories converge in this place, good and bad—chasing after Susannah and injuring my shoulder on the ferry, meeting Annie Fanny across the river in Desoto twice, enduring the siege, and passing through last year after the Dawg Smith fight. Here I am again—bitter reminders and sweet memories. It won't be the last time pass through here, I'm sure. Vicksburg is a city set upon a hill that can't be hidden from me. But I need new memories.

Fighting for the right ain't always what it starts out to be but rather what it ends up being. That'll be my new memory of Vicksburg—the place where I chose to make things right. One day I'll leave a tribute to the Lord in this place for helping me make this decision, like the ancients did when they piled up rocks to remember a great event in His honor.

We stop in front of the Warren County Courthouse. I give Poole a minute to take it all in. "The Greensborough Courthouse ain't got nothin' on this Greek Parthenon, huh, Poole?"

"I didn't know buildings like this even existed. I've seen 'em in picture books and in the papers, but they ain't real until you see one up close. This one even outdoes the capitol building in Jackson."

"They finished it just before the war. General Pemberton kept Yank prisoners on the grounds to keep Yank gunboats from shelling it to pieces."

"I didn't know there was this many people in the whole world!"

I felt the same at the surrender when gray met blue with the town's people watching. Thousands gathered around the courthouse under the true flag waving in the breeze that day. Mississippi's star was still on it, in principle.

"Let me show you somethin'."

We walk catty corner across the street to a wall. "This is the Warren

County Jail where I guarded Yank prisoners during the Battle of Chickasaw Bayou. I changed my thinkin' that got me here today."

Poole rubs the wall. "Was this where you learned to make a tattoo?"

"Yeah, and other things."

I take Poole to Sky Parlor Hill where I can still hear little Lucy's sweet little bird-like voice and see her curly blonde curls bounce as she danced around. I hope she gets to start her school for Black children someday. We walk down Crawford Street to the river, as I did so many times. We pass Granny O'Neil's home where we ate rooster dumplings. The doors to St. Paul's Catholic Church are still open where I spent many free time hours meditating with the saints and speaking with the priest.

We stop in front of the Prentiss House Hotel. Steamboats dock against the muddy riverbank. People swarm the landing like ants chased out of a burning tree stump. They move here and there like there's no tomorrow—workers loading and unloading, people carrying baggage and walking the riverbank.

One thing's missing though—slaves. There's only freed men and women. If working, they must be receiving a wage or at least room and board for their services. If not, they're cared for by the Yanks. What a sight. It's a new world, and I get to be a part of it.

We tie our horses to the hitching post in front of the hotel. It looks to be almost repaired, but it's not up to its former glory. I can still see Granville giving me the chess set Christmas of '62. Making it for me kept him from deserting the army, but it didn't stop the Minie ball that ended his young life.

"Let's stay here. I lived here a few months when I served as police guard."

Poole shrugs. "Sounds good to me."

We sign in, and the clerk gives us a room on the third floor. The room I once stayed in happened to be available. Wonderful smells tempt us as we carry our belongings up the stairs. Every creak of a step, every turn in a hall brings back memories of the men I roomed, fought, and suffered with.

"This it?" Poole enters the room that has a large bed and coal in the heater for the lighting.

I sit on the soft bed. "Can you believe fifteen men crowded in this fifteen by fifteen foot room and not a stick to light a fire, much less have a bed?"

"I bet you couldn't even roll over." I snicker. "What's funny?"

"Just remembering how my young friend, Edrow, hated getting his undeserved nickname, Hog Fart. How J.A., Isham, and others... seems like just yesterday."

Letters scratched on a baseboard show through a fresh coat of paint.

EDROW WAS HERE DEC 1862.

Besides the epitaph on a beech tree J.A. and I carved after he died on the march out of Vicksburg, this is the only mention of Edrow's life there will ever be. A small reminder of a dear friend I'll never forget.

We trot down the steps and out to the front and untie our horses. We register them with a farrier at a stable near the railroad depot.

Poole rubs his hands together like a squirrel fumbling with a hickory nut he just found. "I'm hungry. Where do you wanna eat?"

The hotel restaurant food wafts over me like a warm blanket. "I stayed at the Prentiss House but never had the money to eat in the dining hall. We cooked our rations on the street and only dreamed of eating that fine food. Let's eat here."

Poole and I sit down to a nicely set table with a view of the river. We order beefsteak with potatoes, peas, and a loaf of fine smelling bread.

I snicker. "Sure beats the mule meat and rat we ate the last time I was in Vicksburg."

"This is the best meal I've had in days. Army rations, well, you know how there are."

We finish and wander the streets to walk off our meal. We find the Recruiter's Office at the corner of Washington and Grove. Tomorrow I put on the blue suit.

Poole throws his arm across my chest. "Can you smell it?"

"What?"

"Fresh brewed coffee, and I bet they'll have some pie to go with it." He closes his eyes to savor the aroma when an Army wagon roars by like the driver is running from the Rebs.

I yank Poole back just before the horses run him over. I swat the back of his head. "You're gonna get us killed before I can get back in this war."

"Nothing to worry about, you had my back."

"Let's get that coffee."

"And pie."

We follow our noses to a café called Handerson's, just a few doors down.

"It must be good. It's full of patrons." I scan the room for familiar faces that might not appreciate a former Reb turned Yank. Folks nod and resume their eating. A well-dressed lady in a Paris style lacy lilac dress off in a corner works receipts and counts money.

We remove our hats and straighten our jackets. A waiter seats us, and we order coffee and pie. This place is a bit more upscale than the Prentiss House eatery and far above these two farm boys' raising. I'd given an eye tooth to have sat here during the siege. That'd been all I could've done. I didn't have two nickels to rub together then for such finery. No one did.

CHAPTER 6

SOME FRIENDS LIVE FOREVER

MID-AFTERNOON, DECEMBER 1, 1864

The dead can be raised, with a little help.

WE SIT BACK, having polished off half a pie, and sip our coffee. Just the smell of the coffee is worth the price.

Poole taps his spoon on the table. "How do you feel about bein' a Yank instead of a Reb?"

"Don't think I'll ever like bein' called a Yank. That's a man from up north. Just call me an American soldier like my old friend Mistuh Wiley back in Winn Parish. I don't want any special names. I just want the twentieth star for Mississippi back on the flag. For good."

"You're helpin' get it there, Lummy."

I hold my cup up for the waiter. The lady in the lacy lilac dress is staring at me. She shakes her head and returns to her figuring.

Does she know me?

Poole whispers, "Do you know her?"

"She looks familiar, but she's got enough paint on her face to make us both look pretty, and that would take some doin'." Poole snickers too loud. She looks our way. I sip my coffee and look out the window.

Poole kicks me under the table. "Oh shit, here she comes. She's gonna kick us out, and I ain't finished my coffee yet."

I keep looking out the window when the lady in the lilac lacy dress clears her throat. "You soldier boys enjoyin' your pie and coffee?"

I snap my head around. "I know that voice."

She leans over and whispers into my ear, "Too bad I ain't got nary a possum for the pot and a little snuff juice to spice it up, Lummy Tullos."

"Why, Annie Fanny, you're a sight for sore eyes." I pull her close, all dolled up with a full set of pearly white teeth. "A cat with nine lives with at least one left!"

Annie scans the room. I didn't mean to, but I just embarrassed her like she did me back in '62 in Desoto on my way to enlist. A few ladies look around like somebody cursed.

Annie whispers, "They don't know me by that name."

I say above the crowd noise, "My mother couldn't make a better pie than this, Mrs. Annie." The customers turn back to their friends satisfied that what they thought they heard was not what they heard.

Annie wraps her arms around me. "Always the gentleman, Lummy, honey. Thanks for savin' my a—, I mean, my hide. What goes around comes around, I reckon." Her lips touch my ear. "You do remember I saved your long lanky ass in Desoto when you came through with them soldiers?"

"Yes, ma'am, you did."

"And you saved a dyin' woman on that riverbank when you came through on your way back to Winn Parish."

"You look really good, Annie."

"The dead can be raised with a little help, but I still ain't used to wearin' fancy duds and talkin' good English. Put a pretty bow on an ugly hawg and you still got an ugly hawg." She turns to Poole, who's fascinated with her. "Now just who is this fine specimen of a man?"

"Same ole Annie. This is Thomas Poole, my best friend since before I can even remember. I keep a very protective eye on him." I squeeze Poole's arm. "Watch yourself, she's a crafty cat."

"Calm down, boy, I'll let him be."

"Poole's not wise to the ways of the world just yet."

Annie flutters her eyelashes like a butterfly. "Maybe I could teach him?"

Poole's face turns red. "I don't know what to say."

Annie laughs. "I noticed you starin' at my mouth, Lummy. What do think about my new set of pearly whites? Cost forty dollars. My hu-u-us-band Beau over there paid for 'em." She bats her eyes at a well-dressed and well-groomed man who smiles and nods.

"Your husband?"

"Yep, me and ole Beau Handerson there got hitched last Christmas. Ain't he the sweetest lookin' thing you ever did see?" Beau smiles bashfully.

"You're a damn good man, Beau, and Annie is a fine catch of a woman." He nods and continues talking with men who look to be bankers or lawyers.

Annie signals the waiter to bring more coffee and begins her story since the last time I saw her. "Beau, come over when you can, dear."

He politely excuses himself and sits with a heavy sigh knowing what's about to transpire. She winks when she tells about me seeing her bathe when J.A. and I crossed the river on our way to Winn Parish.

"I look better than the last time you saw me, don't you think? Why, I was just a sack of bones and naked as a jaybird!" She blushes, hiding her smile behind her Japan fan but not her giggly eyes.

Beau squirms a bit, as do I, and she giggles again. "Aww, Beau, no need to worry. Nothin' happened. He's the faithful type. He accidently seen me bathin' in the river last year when he and his friend...." I barely shake my head. "Were on a business trip."

Beau starts to ask what kind of business, but Annie interrupts, "So no harm done, except I gained some of my fat back."

I smile, sticking my hand out to Beau. "Just more for a good man to love on, huh, Beau?"

"Ain't it so."

Annie winks at Beau. "Don't keep your friends waitin' dear. I won't be long. I just want to catch up with my old friend here."

"Good to meet you two." Beau returns to his friends.

Poole laughs. "You must've been a sight to see, ma'am!"

Annie giggles like a river town whore with twinkling eyes. But now, she's a well-respected lady in town. Still a flirt but a respectable one now.

"Obe left me a spot of land he'd bought years ago in Desoto. After he was murdered by renegade Rebs, the railroad bought some, and the rest I sold to a developer who plans to sell house lots. I'm glad to be on this side of the river."

Beau finishes his meeting and brings his coffee over. We shift to make room for him at the small table. Funny, I have the same strange feeling about Beau marrying Annie as I did about Freddie marrying my brother's wife, Dorcas. Overly protective, like she's my sister.

Beau rubs her arm. She smiles, assuring her love for him. "Beau knows I never really loved Obe, but he did rescue me from livin' on the riverbank like a rat. Still, I should've treated him better. He saved me then, and he's still savin' me now."

Beau consoles her. "Let the past stay where it is."

"Thank you, husband." Annie dries her eyes with a handkerchief trying not to smudge her makeup. "I ain't never had friends like y'all before." She puts her arm around Beau's shoulder and pulls him close. "I've never had a man like you, Beau, and don't want nary another."

Beau's face burns red, but he enjoys every bit of the attention. "You know I love you."

Annie slaps Beau on the knee. "Ain't he somethin'? Ole Beau's so level-headed, why, snuff juice runs out the corners of his mouth the same on both sides!" She doubles over laughing, and we try to hide our snickers.

Beau gives her a peck on the cheek. "Annie Fanny, you're one to talk about snuff drippin', especially when you make possum stew!" They laugh until the tears flow. These two were made for each other.

Annie changes the subject. "So, Mistuh Lummy Tullos, what about that sweet thing you had hawg tied? She must've been somethin' to get you settled down."

I laugh, but it still hurts. Beau shakes my hand firmly again, then goes to greet a couple of patrons who just walked in.

Just for Beau's amusement, Annie belts out, "Yeah, if you ain't hitched, Lummy Tullos, I might let Beau go and take you myself!" She blows a kiss to Beau who winks as he leads his friends to their table.

"Annie, she's gone. I was told the measles took her. A good man tryin' to spare me pain said she caught it from a soldier from the camp where I trained for the army. That wasn't how she died though." I tell her the sordid story of Susannah's death in detail. Tears trickle down Annie's face.

"I ain't been right since, Annie. Don't know if I ever will." We sit quietly.

Poole squeezes my arm and gets up. "It breaks my heart more to hear it a second time than the first. I need some air before I lose my coffee and pie. I'll be right outside."

Annie rubs my shoulder like when she put the ointment on my injury after the tree fell on me. She whispers comfort like a good sister. "That pain you got inside is like this shoulder I doctored up that night. It hurts like the dickens occasionally, but it never really goes away. You keep goin', Lummy. There'll come a day when you won't think about it as much. You have a good and faithful heart, but it'll be empty once the war is over. You'll need someone to help you heal. Is there anybody you're sweet on these days?" Annie bats her eyes like butterfly wings.

"Not ready for that right now."

Annie holds her hands up. "I ain't tryin' to get in your business, but I have a sistuh recently widowed. That puts you two in the same boat. Martha is a sweet girl... and pretty. She was put with a good family named McClure about the time I ran away and Obe found me. I hadn't seen her in years, but she saw my weddin' announcement in the Vicksburg paper and sent me a telegram. She came from Memphis just in time for the weddin'. She was my matron of honor."

Annie breathes in deeply and sighs as she exhales. "Her husband, William Henry Brock, died just last June. He got the pneumonia and expired in the Adams General Hospital in Memphis. Martha and the kids have been livin' here with us since he'd joined the army. He was a Yank from Fulton County Illinois, just north of St. Louis. Martha said he was a hard working farmer and real looker too—five foot ten, dark hair, and gray eyes. He felt poorly when he joined the 1st Mississippi Mounted Rifles, but they took him anyway hopin' he'd get better. He never saw action."

It takes me a moment to catch what she said. "Which regiment did you say?"

"A new outfit called the 1st Mississippi Mounted Rifles, made up of Missip boys who know this country. But they're paddin' the ranks with Yanks for good measure. All the officers are Yanks. I think they're scared of you boys after the hell y'all gave 'em here. Who wouldn't be?"

"Well, I'll be...."

"You'll get knocked off your feet when you see Martha."

"I have no doubt, but I'm here to join that same regiment."

"Columbus Nathan Tullos! I done sent your ass off to war once in '62! I'll be damned if I'll do it again!" She laughs and slaps me on my back. "Waiter, bring these men a drink on the house. Beau, come have a toast with us."

I motion for Poole to come back inside.

"Martha's husband was only thirty-three when he passed. I wish I could've known him. He and Martha had a good life started. She has two fine sons, a daughter, and a baby. It'd be a good family to help a man work a farm when this is all over." I squirm a little. "Just give it some thought, Lummy."

Beau lifts his glass. "Here's to you boys ending this war soon." We finish our whiskey drinks.

"I will give it some consideration. Thank you, Annie. I appreciate you lookin' out for me." I kiss her on the cheek. "I know where you are now, sistuh. I best be goin', my dear friend, but I'll see you again soon."

Poole and I step into the street. "Let me show you somethin'."

We take in the view from Sky Parlor Hill that stretches for miles into Louisiana. We stare out over the river and dream of what a new world could look like.

CHAPTER 7

A VIEW BEYOND WHAT THE EYES CAN SEE

EVENING, DECEMBER 1, 1864

Only from the heights can you can see forever.

SKY PARLOR HILL. Evening fades as the sun sets west in the direction of Winn Parish. I wish I could see Davis Feed and Seed Store in Winnfield and Shiloh Baptist Church on the hill where I first met Mr. Gilmore. It seems such a long time ago.

Across the river in Desoto, soldiers move in all directions yelling and cursing. I'll soon be caught up in the craziness of this war.

"Please keep my family safe, Lord, from blue and gray." I rarely beg, but tonight I do.

Poole sighs. "Amen. Most of the words they're hollerin' over there I ain't never heard."

"My brother, Ben, frequently let out a string of words I'd never heard before if the farm work didn't go well. By the time I surrendered here, I'd cultivated my cursing into a fine work of art."

Just for fun, I lay down a string of words that'd shame my mother. I can hardly get the words out for laughing.

"Dang, I've never heard you speak with such a gracious command of the English language, brother!"

"Eloquent profanity. It rolls right off my tongue like fine poetry."

"What would Pastor Dobbs say?"

"That it's no worse than some sermons he's had to suffer through, I'm sure."

"Dang, boy."

"I know you can't tell it, but I did go to school."

"Did Miss Stansbury teach you that?"

"She was too pretty for that."

We gaze out over the river, taking in the view.

The fun in the cursing doesn't last long, but I want to curse at this war, how it's torn so many lives apart. I know what the Union army has planned for me and what will be required. Burning the factories and mills in Bankston will make people suffer, but it'll help end the war. I don't want to do it. But like I told the Lord in the Tullos cemetery, 'Here am I, send me.' So here I go.

I'm not the same man that stood here last wearing the gray suit. It doesn't matter if anyone else knows that. Some folks want to keep you tethered to the wrongs of the past because it gives them a feeling of control, or at worst, relieves them of the responsibility to change themselves.

A few days before I left for Winn Parish back in '59, Pa blurted out at the supper table, "I've been a mean angry person all these years." All laughter and talking stopped. I thought the world quit spinning. It was like scales fell from Pa's eyes, as if he was seeing us for the first time. His eyes were opened, and his soul gained clarity that night. We didn't know what to say. Those moments are rarely given to people when they realize what they've been for years.

I had compassion on Pa that night. "Pa, all the old wounds are now healed. I just want the bit of time we have left to be good."

It was the first time I saw tears in my daddy's eyes. "That's all I want, son."

When a person like my pa has a moment of awareness like that, he should be allowed to have it. Not only that, he must feel the Lord's mercy from those around him. If not, then we're all the worse for it. I needed his confession to leave in peace. Two days later I left to find Susannah. I'm glad Pa and I worked things out before I left back.

"I'm glad I've changed."

Poole pats my shoulder. "Me, too, brother."

The men across the river still yell and curse. Except for that, Sky Parlor Hill is a peaceful place. We count the lights as far as we can see. I tell the Lord one thing for which I'm thankful for each light counted. It helps.

Poole breaks the silence. "So that Annie Fanny. She's somethin'."

"The Lord broke the mold after makin' that one."

Poole elbows me. "Anythin' else I need to know y'all talked about when I went outside?"

I try to hide my grin. "Nothin' really, except she's got a sistuh she's tryin' to pawn off on me." That didn't sound very good. "I shouldn't have said that. She has a sistuh whose husband died in Memphis earlier this year. He was in the Rifles, too. Fanny's just lookin' out for me. You know how women are, always wantin' to get a man hitched. She means well."

"What's her name?"

"Martha Brock. She's got kids already, but that's not a problem. I want kids someday." I wish I could've had more children with Susannah.

"Susannah would want you to be happy. You do know that, right?"

I say nothing.

Poole leaves it alone, and we return to our own thoughts.

CHAPTER 8

MY SECOND ENLISTMENT

MORNING, DECEMBER 2, 1864

It's kind of strange signin' up for the same thing twice.

SPARKLING RIPPLES FLICKER in the early morning sunlight breaking over the lazy river. We finish our breakfast of ham and eggs, red eye gravy and biscuits, blackberry jam, and fresh butter. It doesn't get any better than this, except if I was eating it at home.

I take my coffee to the front porch of the hotel. A flock of geese sail low over the rolling Mississippi as men along the riverbank start their daily routines of work and cursing. I sip my coffee focusing on the geese and peaceful waters, not the men.

Living with Dan Creekwater taught me that silence and stillness are virtues few in this world understand or enjoy. I've learned to accept the noise of human beings but also how to retreat from it as well, even in a crowd. I find sanctuary away from the world where men worry about life more than trusting the One who gave it. It's a church made not with human hands. My soul.

Pastor Dobbs back home chided, "I've never known anybody who sits with the Lord alone in the woods. I ain't even heard of anybody doing that." A man can't have in his soul what he doesn't understand.

Poole clears his throat. "It's too early to be givin' a long-winded sermon, preacher."

"Talking out loud again?"

"Yep. Maybe you'll take Pastor Dobb's place after the war. You've got the words for it."

"Not a chance in Hell, but thanks. Please don't call me preacher. I don't want the title or the nickname."

We gather our things and walk to the recruiting office near the Post Office. I drop off a short letter at the Post Office to let the family know I made it here all right.

Two neatly dressed soldiers come at us like hungry hounds at feeding time trying to get to me first without looking too undignified.

Poole holds up his hand. "Down, boys, he's already spoken for. Sergeant McGugarty brought him in. He's joining the 1st Battalion Mississippi Mounted Rifles this morning."

The two army recruiters nod but have the look of a couple of dogs that just had the bones they were gnawing snatched out of their mouths.

A sergeant marches up quickly. "Put your stuff down, recruit. Don't worry, nobody'll touch it."

His tone shocks me, but that's because it's been a while since I was in the army. I throw up a smart salute. "Yes, sir, Sergeant."

Surprised, he grins. "Comin' over to God's side, son?"

I carefully word my response. "No, sir, comin' over to the right side. Like President Lincoln once said, sir, it's up to us to get on God's side, not expecting he's already on ours."

He shakes my hand. "Well said, son. Give me your stuff and go inside. See one of the subscribers. He'll fix you up."

A group of privates grumble as they march to the steamer landing. They mumble something about turncoat and bounty money. I pay them no mind.

The sergeant barks out, "Move along and keep your teeth together."

They hold their noses like they're passing a hog farm. I laugh it off. Poole, still standing at attention, relaxes as the sergeant puts my things on a bench in front of the recruiter's office.

Poole sits. "Don't worry about them bastards. I'll wait here for you. You won't be long."

My eyes take a minute to adjust from the bright sun in the dimly lit room. A gray haired second lieutenant is furiously writing and shifting papers. He doesn't notice I've come in. I stand at attention. He looks vaguely familiar.

I clear my throat. "I'm a new recruit ready to enlist, Lieutenant, sir."

He glances over his spectacles without moving his head, leans back in his chair, and strokes his long gray mustache.

He breaks into a grin. "Well, I'll be. You don't remember me, do you, son? Last time I saw you, you were nothing but a rag tag, skin and bones, long and tall, lanky scarecrow at my parole table trying to figure out what in the hell he was going to do next."

"My goodness, you're him?"

The second lieutenant stands to shake my hand with a firm grip. "Glad you came back, son."

"Good to see you too, sir. Sergeant McGugarty brought me here."

The second lieutenant shifts papers around trying to get things in order, mumbling to himself.

"You're a big reason I'm here today. Could I know your name, please sir?"

"Still being a good soldier, Columbus Nathan Tullos?"

"How'd you remember my name?"

He laughs. "Who could forget a hundred dollar handle like that? Explorer and a prophet all wrapped up in one, not to mention with height of Goliath. That's a dangerous combination."

"An old Mexican War veteran said the same thing years ago. He gave me good advice, too."

The officer stares at me for moment. "Good advice is only good if you take it. I'm glad you're taking it. Last time you saw me, I was a corporal. They made me a staff sergeant when I volunteered for action after Vicksburg surrendered. I got shot in the leg at Allatoona Pass, Georgia. Wasn't much there, just a supply depot, but General Corse thought it worth defending against General Hood. I remember it too well. Back in October, I caught a pistol slug in my leg. I saw the man who shot me just before a cannon ball took his head off."

His words trail off into a whisper, and he stares off into space like other men who've seen action and relive their story.

Finally, he comes back to himself. "So anyway, they gave me a big promotion and put me at this desk signing up new recruits for the army. I'm not complaining. I've had enough excitement for one war."

He rubs his leg, then stands up, stretches his back, and sticks out his hand. "Second Lieutenant Walter Octavius Hynson, Fourth Illinois Cavalry, at your service." He turns my hand loose and takes a bow. "But my friends just call me W.O."

Oh no, not another Mr. Gilmore who acts he's playing Shakespeare.

"You're not the only one with a hundred dollar handle, Mister Tullos!' W.O. sits back down to his papers, looking smug. "Enough of that, though. Let's get you enlisted."

He sorts through a pile of papers to find those pertaining to me. "Sergeant McGugarty brought you in for a special mission, but that's all I know. It must be important because they told me to expedite you through the process."

"Expe... *what?*"

"Put a rush on it. You have to enlist for three years just like everybody else, understand?"

"Yes, sir."

Three years. The amount of time sticks out to me.

That's what I signed up for in New Orleans with the Confederate Army. Funny thing, I didn't finish that commitment, but here I am, signing up for another three years. Taking the oath not to take up arms against the Union at the parole relieved me of the first one. I'm doing the right thing without any doubts this time. Susannah's smiling face pops into my head.

Yes, this is the right thing to do.

"First, sign this Declaration of Recruit form and go to the surgeon's tent." He writes my name in big letters on the top line, asks my age, and then pushes the paper to me.

I take the pen and dip it in the ink, looking up before I sign. "Surgeon's tent, for my physical?" He nods.

I sign my name carefully, mostly because ole W.O. spelled my last name wrong at the top. I want it right, but don't want to make a fuss about it.

I sign then read it.

DECLARATION OF RECRUIT

I, *Columbus N. Tullis*, desiring
to VOLUNTEER as a soldier in the Army of the United States, for the term of THREE YEARS, Do De-
clare, That I am *Thirty* years and _____/____
_____ months of age; that I have never been discharged from the United States service on account of
disability or by sentence of court martial, be by order before the expiration of a term of enlistment; and
I know of no impediment to my serving honestly and
faithfully for three years.

Given at *Vicksburg, Miss*
the *2 nd* day of *December 1864*

Columbus Tullos

Witness:

W. O. Hynson

I lay the pen down. "It's strange signin' up for the same thing twice."

W.O. checks my signature and hands me a copy. "You're doin' now what
you should have done in the first place, you think?" I nod. "It was pretty con-
fusing for a lot of folks when the war first started. Not now. A war that was
supposed to be over in a few months wasn't. Death and blood on a hundred
battlefields has cleared up any confusion. You sure about doing this, son?"

"I'm joinin' with no doubt or hesitation. What I was told I was fightin' for
back in '62 changed. So I did."

W.O. sticks out his hand. "Good."

I look at the paper. "Who's Lieutenant Colonel Eli C. Kinsly, my new
commanding officer?"

"No, he's the Provost Marshal in charge of Vicksburg under martial law."

"Yes, sir, I see that now. My old regiment, the 27th Louisiana, was provost for several months here before the siege. We lived in the Prentiss House Hotel and guarded the city to make the good citizens feel safe. We mostly broke up fights, guarded Yank prisoners, and caught spies."

"You'll have lots of stories tell the grandkids, then. If you pass the doctor's test—which I have no doubt you will—come back, and we'll get your enlistment papers signed. After that, I'll send you to the quartermaster for your new uniform and equipment. Then you'll be off to get more stories for the grandkids."

"Yes, sir, Lieutenant, be back in a bit."

CHAPTER 9

FIT FOR SERVICE

MORNING, DECEMBER 2, 1864

Fit for service includes heart, mind, body, and soul.
The army mostly wants just the body.

I STEP OUT into the bright sunlight. It takes a moment for my eyes to adjust. Poole dozes on the bench where I'd left him.

"I'll be right back. I just have to go see the doctor." He tips his hat.

The sergeant on duty barks, "Oh, hell no, that ain't happenin'. You there, make sure he gets back and at the double quick."

We salute and trot a block down the street to where the doctor conducts fitness for duty tests. I hand my recruitment slip to the orderly. A pale man with downcast eyes buttons his shirt walking out from behind a curtain.

He frowns. "Hope you get in, friend. I didn't." You'd think his mother just died.

"Next." I slide between the curtains that offer little privacy. The doctor takes my paper and looks me over. "Damn, son, what'd your momma feed you to grow you so tall?"

"Everythin' the Lord and a good farm could provide, sir."

He sits on a stool. "You don't have to call me sir. I'm local, not an army doctor." He writes my name on a chart. Without looking up, he says, "Take your clothes off, soldier."

"All of them?"

He slowly looks up from the papers. "It's standard procedure, son, nothing personal to you or anybody. The army says I have to check you head to toe, or you don't get in. We clear? This certainly hurts me more than it does you."

I don't want to make this man mad. He's my ticket to get in. I peel off my clothes.

"Not trying to be testy, son, but I get all kinds here. Some come sicker than a dog but trying to get the sign-up bounty for their families. Many will be dead in a month. I'm surprised a few even made it to my office. I hate to send them away, but I have a job to do."

I nod, feeling a bit vulnerable and not wanting this to last any longer than it has to. This certainly isn't the quick fitness test I took when I enlisted in the Confederate Army.

"Let's get started. Do what I ask."

I jump, bend over, kick, receive thumps on my chest and back in several places, have my teeth checked, and then my eyes. This must be how a slave feels at an auction, except I'm free. They will be, too, if I have anything to do with it.

The doctor hands me a paper. "You're healthy as a horse, son. You pass. Get your clothes on and send in the next recruit, please."

"Thank you, sir." I dress, take my paper, and get out the door.

Poole and I head back to the recruiting office, my fitness test certificate in hand. He salutes several officers who look us up and down as they pass. The worst thing in the world is an officer with nothing to do. It leaves him free to dream up things to harass the rank and file just to flaunt his authority.

One can't resist. "You there, stand at attention. What's your business, Private?" The other officers stop and snicker.

Poole salutes. "I'm assisting this new recruit to get enlisted as ordered, sir."

"That's good, Private, but do you boys always walk like two schoolgirls holding hands?"

"No schoolgirls here, sir. Just two men who want to do our part in this war."

The officer steps closer but has to look up. We're both a foot taller than he. He struts like a rooster circling us. "Well, one of you is. Who's this? He looks to be a shit shoveling pig farmer from backwoods nowhere Mississippi."

Poole starts to answer, but I cut in. "Little man with a big mouth, I ain't in this army yet. I may not volunteer if the quality of the officers is of your piss poor character."

He bristles knowing that until I put on the blue uniform, there's nothing he can do. His ranking officer calls for him to go, but he has to have the last word, which I don't let him have.

He snickers, trying to save face, "Yeah, well, it wasn't that way when we stomped your asses like the rats you Rebs ate for supper every night, huh, turnip eater?"

The hair on my neck stands up, my ears pin back, and my eyes narrow.

Poole whispers under his breath, "Oh hell."

I step forward. "Yeah, we ate mule meat for supper the night we buried your dead after Sherman failed twice to take our defenses. We ate rat the morning Grant left his wounded in the field under the hot summer sun. I don't expect you were there, or you wouldn't show such damn little respect for either side, you trumped up little shit-faced peacock."

"Why, I'll—'"

My voice becomes a whispery growl. "You won't do a damn thing, boy."

"Oh yeah, I'll—"

"Shut up, I'm not finished. If you're interested, I'll wait a day to enlist if you'd like to discuss this further, say in that alley over there." I take a step closer, making him look up even more to look in my eyes.

A captain orders the lieutenant, "That's enough, Lieutenant, let's go. You men go on about your business."

The lieutenant glares at me for a moment, knowing he lost this battle. "You men carry on. I'll keep an eye out for you two."

I spit at his feet. "Carry your ass on away from here, right now."

The lieutenant rejoins his fellow officers. The captain grins and slaps him on the shoulder. "You're gonna get your ass kicked one day. You weren't even at Vicksburg, you dern fool."

"Yeah, but they don't know that."

The captain grabs the lieutenant by his collar. "The tallest one does. I saw it in his eyes. He was there. He'd cut you for fish bait then eat the fish, you dumb half-pint bastard. You don't disrespect men who endured a siege like he did. You best wise up. Some things rank and privilege can't protect, especially your back in battle if you treat men like that."

As we enter the recruiter's office, I laugh. "This army surely is shaping up. I think I'll enlist!"

"Yeah, after seein' that, you're fit for service." Poole stops me before I open the door. "Lummy, I'm serious. You've changed. That wasn't the same shy, quiet, peace lovin' boy who took beatin's and mean talk from his pa without a word or who picked Kneehigh up over his head and slammed him on the street in Bankston. There was a time when you'd either back down like it was your pa yellin' at you or in a rage stand up to Lester, not remembering what you did. You ain't the same, and that's a good thing. You're calm and smooth but firm and direct. You take shit from nobody. You'll do well in this man's army."

"I hope so." I hate the anger that just rose up in me. Bullies like him still do that to me. "At least I don't lose my mind over it like I used to. Now that I'm putting on a new blue suit, I'll have to be a good soldier."

He slaps my shoulder. "I'm not so sure you can do it, hawg slop bucket."

As I reach for the door handle, I thump Poole's ear. "But you know I can still take you down any time, any place, you toad frog."

Poole yanks his head away. "When you get to feelin' froggie, catfish head, you hop."

Who could have a better friend than Poole? J.A.'s face pops into my mind. I'm a blessed man. We step inside to get me signed up.

CHAPTER 10

ENLISTED... AGAIN

MID-MORNING, DECEMBER 2, 1864

Old friends often know the best trail to follow.

LIEUTENANT W.O. STANDS up to stretch. "How'd it go, son?"

I wave my paper in the air, grinning. "Passed without a hitch, sir."

"Well, get over here, I forgot to get your description." W.O. points to a wall with measuring marks. "Six foot, six. Damn, I knew you were tall. I was right. You aren't much shorter than ole Goliath himself." He looks at Poole. "And you're not too far behind him, are you?"

"No, sir. He's only got me by a couple inches."

W.O. looks me over. "Let's see, dark complexion, black hair, and what color are your eyes?"

I shrug. "I don't know."

"Bend down here." He looks carefully into my eyes. "Hazel, wouldn't you say, Poole?"

"I guess I've never really looked into them that deeply. We ain't that friendly, sir."

"Is he as much of a smart ass as you, Lummy?"

"We're cut from the same cloth, sir."

"I assume you are a farmer?"

"Yes, sir."

"Let's see here, oh yeah, what county were you born?"

"Holmes County, Mississippi, sir."

W.O. straightens his spectacles. "But you live in Choctaw County, right?"

"'That's right, sir."

"Well, I need to write that down as your residence. I remember you telling me that at the parole. Anyway, have a seat over there, and I'll finish your Volunteer Enlistment form, and you can be on your way, Private."

"Yes, sir, thank you, sir." Poole and I sit near the window and watch men in blue marching up the street from the river and down to board steamers. Two guards walk a string of five Rebel prisoners who look like death warmed over. At least they ain't dead. W.O. waves me back over and hands me a copy of my Volunteer Enlistment form.

"Now, Lummy, you will be paid at the new rate of sixteen dollars per month. You can thank President Lincoln for the raise from thirteen dollars. You're also entitled to a three hundred dollar enlistment bounty. I'm sure Poole's told you that you don't get it all at one time. You'll receive the first hundred soon. Be patient, the army is a bit slow."

"It can't be any slower than gettin' paid by the Confederate government. Come to think of it, they still owe me three month's wages."

"Don't think you'll be cashing in on that. You'll get the rest of your bounty later, probably when you muster out. For most men, that's a good thing. You'll have money to get started on. Be careful with your equipment. They put stoppages on your pay and sign up bounty if it's stolen, lost, or damaged, especially if you're irresponsible or try to keep it."

"Yes, sir, I'll make sure all is taken care of and returned when I don't need it no more."

W.O. stands up, salutes, and speaks in a proper military tone. "Good enough then, soldier." He walks around his desk to the front counter. He shakes my hand and holds it. "Welcome to the United States Army, Private Columbus Nathan Tullos."

He stiffens his grip and gives me my first order, "Report to Sergeant McGugarty of Company C, 1st Battalion Mississippi Mounted Rifles at Four Mile Bridge camp. I assume Private Poole here is in the same Company?"

Poole salutes. "Yes, sir, I am."

I start to turn loose W.O.'s hand, but he grips it more firmly. "Lummy, let me say this, and I'll let you go. You're a man of peace who wants everyone to be free to do what the Good Lord has for them. But you know in this world, there are plenty of jackasses walking around on two legs. Yeah, I heard that lieutenant try you through the windows.

"You've gone through enough troubles for ten lifetimes. You're pretty quick to protect the peace you hold dear when it gets challenged or disturbed. That works okay for a man who works his farm away from everybody but his family. Not here. These boys are tired of this war and hate it. They didn't start it but have lost friends and brothers fighting in it. This is a good time to set things right in this world, but you don't have to do that with everyone you meet. Not everyone is out to hurt you, son. Set things right within yourself. You'll go home a better man if you do."

I wipe a tear from my eye like I something's in it. "Best advice I've received in a long time."

"Good then. Go to the quartermaster's warehouse across the street. He'll get you fixed up. I hope to see you again, Lummy Tullos."

"Yes, sir, Lieutenant Hynson!"

Poole and I snap to attention and salute smartly. He returns to a stance of attention in the smooth grace of a seasoned soldier and returns the favor. W.O. snaps his hand back down to his side and grins. "Now get the hell out of my office."

Poole and I comically fall over each like two boys trying be the first to get out the door when the school bell rings. We step out on the boardwalk. My world just changed. I look at the Volunteer Enlistment paper I just signed. *Do hereby acknowledge to have volunteered this second day of December, 1864, to serve as a soldier in the Army of the United States of America.*

I look up at the stars and stripes waving over the Vicksburg courthouse. I just put the twentieth star back on the stars and stripes. For me it'll stay.

"Twentieth star, huh, Lummy? I like the sound of that."

"Dang it, talkin' out loud again?"

"So, how does it feel being a bluecoat now?"

I knock his hat off. "That's what I was before all this started. It's what I've always been. I just had to re-learn it."

CHAPTER 11

FITTED FOR SERVICE

JUST BEFORE NOON, DECEMBER 2, 1864

The way some men deal with their own business is to get into someone else's.

POOLE AND I wait for a string of wagons to pass on Washington Street before we cross. He asks lots of questions about my Confederate Army service, where I fought and what it was like. And how many men I've killed.

"Since you have to know, let's take the Graveyard Road and visit the 27th Louisiana Lunette on our way to camp at Four Mile Bridge."

We step off the boardwalk. A detail of men with weapons and full packs stand in the shade waiting to catch their steamer. They've heard our every word. Some smile, knowing I'm a Mississippi man ready to end the war in my home state. A couple men snarl like dogs protecting their food.

One smirks, "Damn turn coat just wants the bounty and the equipment. Then he'll run off to God knows where. A little jingle makes mice run for the cheese, huh boys? Rat eater."

I lock eyes with the mouthy one letting him know I can be as mean as he'll need me to be. I keep my mouth shut. No, I can't.

"Yeah, I ate rats. Good enough to keep you sisters from takin' Vicksburg." Poole and I start across Washington Street. "And I know a rat bastard when I see one, too."

Poole elbows me. "Don't forget what the lieutenant said. Besides, the only way some men deal with their own business is to get in somebody else's."

I shrug it off.

"C'mon, let's get your new uniform and shoes. That'll stop most of the dumbasses braying at you. Bunch of damned lop-eared, swayback mules, anyway. Don't know their asses from a hole in the ground and for damn sure ain't got the sense God gave a goose."

I slap his chest. "Dang, boy, do I need to preach a revival sermon to stop your cussin'?"

Poole laughs. "Just makes me mad to hear ignert-ass folks talk."

As we cross Washington Street toward the river, I think about all the boys wearing gray that I fought with. I can see the faces of men who died in my arms for a doomed cause. What a waste.

Truth is, with Amariah dead, I'm not sure how many of my brothers will be left when this thing is over—George fighting somewhere with the 15th Mississippi Infantry, Jasper and James in the 1st Mississippi Light Artillery, and God only knows where I'll wind up. This could be pretty hard on Ma. I rub my shoulder. The pain reminds me of why I left home in the first place. Still, wearing the blue suit is the right course. We walk up to the double doors of the quartermaster's warehouse.

Poole holds the door open. "In here they'll fit you with a new uniform and shoes then issue your new gear and a horse."

I start to enter, but he stops me. "When you try on your new uniform, jes leave it on. Save your farm clothes. You'll need them when we go sneakin' about."

We enter a large neatly organized room with items laid out on tables and stacked on shelves. Poole stands at attention by the door.

The Quartermaster gets up from reading a newspaper and holds out his hand. "Your enlistment papers, Private."

I pull them from inside my shirt. He reads my description then looks at me. "It's a good thing we got a new shipment of uniforms yesterday, or I'd have trouble getting you fitted."

"Yes, sir, thank you, sir."

The quartermaster takes my measurements. "Damn, son, six feet six? Give me a minute." He rubs his chin and mutters, "Now I know I laid those tall men's uniforms over here somewhere." He disappears behind some shelves. I look around at so many different items we surely could've used in the trenches not far from here.

The Quartermaster comes back smiling. "You're in luck! I've got two sets, and you get one. We don't get many like you, except for maybe your friend over there. If the pants are too short, this other pair is a few inches longer. You can always have them taken up."

He hands me dark blue, nearly black pants, a belt, and shirt, a fitted blue jacket with brass buttons just a shade lighter than the pants, an overcoat, socks, and a cavalry style hat with a tassel on it. I step behind a curtain, and everything fits perfectly. It feels good but strange. I killed many a man wearing a uniform just like this one. The grandfatherly old quartermaster hears me talking.

"Don't say such things, son. There are boys here who lost friends and family in those hills you defended. I see remorse in your eyes, but some might mistake it for weakness. Best keep your trap shut, meaning no harm."

"Good advice. Thank you, sir."

He squints his eyes. "Just because you've come over to the right side don't mean there ain't any snakes wearin' blue. Be careful."

Poole turns. "He's right, Lummy. I done witnessed it."

"Let's get your weapons." The quartermaster breathes takes a deep breath. He reaches for my clothes, but I take them.

"I was told I might need these where I'm going."

I pack my old clothes in my new haversack. I straighten my new uniform and hat. The silver haired quartermaster peers over his spectacles from his scribblings in a ledger. "It must be tough puttin' on the same suit you shot at not long ago. But know this, when the Good Lord calls you, it ain't about color of uniform but about makin' things right with him. You're puttin' Mississippi back on the right flag. That's worth fightin' for, ain't it?" The quartermaster hands me a brand new Sharps carbine.

"Can't let you have this one. It's just for show. Get a good look at it so you know what you're supposed to receive. Those boys at the arms stockroom don't like handing out new guns to former Rebs."

"I'll keep that in mind."

The silver-haired man leans up. "Meaning no harm, but why did you switch horses in the middle of the creek, anyway? Why not just hide out in the swamps like them boys down in Jones County until this blows over? It can't last forever. The South has lost too much to win now."

I need to be clear about my reasons. Now is as good time as any. I study the weapon for a moment gathering my thoughts.

It's not about bounty money, though Yankee dollars are best. It's not just about slavery or state's rights, like some Rebs still holler about. That argument is like an old threadbare work shirt—you can see right through it. And it ain't about righting the wrongs I've done in this life. It is about Susannah and what this country stands for—that if you come here, no matter how you got here, or what your standing was when you did, you should be free.

I lay the weapon down. "No two ways about it, sir, it's just the right damn thing to do, that's all."

He chuckles then breaks into a loud laugh. At first I think he's laughing at me, but he stops. He solemnly sticks out his hand, and I take it. "I'll be damned, I've finally met one—a true blue Union soldier who knows exactly why he's in this man's army! You, sir, have made my day!"

"Thank you, sir."

He jerks his hand out of mine smiling. "Now get your ass on down to the weapons stock room, and they'll issue you a brand new Sharps carbine just like this one. Here, take this paper with my name on it, and don't let them give you a hard time. Treat your weapon like you would a sweetheart. She costs thirty dollars. If you return it when this war is over, they won't take it out of your bounty. Make sure they give you sixty rounds of ammunition, a cartridge belt, and box, too. God bless you, son, and be strong. The Lord's with you."

Yeah, I've heard that before from another man about his age wearing the gray suit. This ain't about the Lord's work. It's about men who can't get along. We ain't changed, and when this war's over, men won't change much. Bullets and cannon balls don't change a man's heart no more than spears and swords in Jesus' day. Weapons men fight with just put one sinner on top of another, that's all—on a pile of dead bodies. I just want it over.

I listen to the old man's word for me though. How can he know my heart? The Lord can send messages through whomever He chooses. It reminds me of who's really in charge, and it surely ain't Columbus Nathan Tullos. I nod for Poole to go with me down the hall to get my new rifle.

He elbows me as we walk up to the weapons counter. "You best be done with your preachin' because I ain't puttin' no money in the collection plate."

I laugh. A small man about my age takes my voucher and scurries into the back room and returns with a brand new Sharps carbine. He signs some forms as I look over the fine weapon.

Poole rubs the stock. "You don't use a ramrod with this one."

The clerk hands me ammunition. "Right. I wish we could get you boys the new Spencer repeaters that shoot seven times. Start shootin' it now, and you don't have to quit 'til sundown!"

I aim the weapon at an empty wall.

The clerk picks up his pencil. "Read me that serial number."

Poole points under the stock near the saddle ring. I call out the number.

The weapons stock clerk laments, "What a wonderful and terrible time we live in—inventin' more ways to kill a man... and quicker, too."

I look over my brand new Sharps Military Carbine breech-loader that shoots a .52 caliber cartridge. The date stamped on the barrel is 1863—the year I left the Confederate Army.

The clerk points at the gun stock after he shows me how to load and clean the weapon.

"Best weapon produced yet, well, maybe the most reliable one anyway. Here's an invention you'll like. It's a grinder. Most men think it's for grinding coffee. It'll work for that, but it only makes coarse grounds. The real purpose is to grind corn or wheat, for both you and your horse. Pretty ingenious if you ask me."

Poole scratches his head, "Ingen-you *what?*"

I elbow him and whisper, "Talk about ignert asses."

Poole swells his chest. "I've got me a Colts Revolving Rifle .56 caliber. It shoots five times to this one. So why does the Army think the Sharp's better?"

"When you fire those five shots, what do you do with that thing?"

Poole grins and admits, "Put it down."

"That's right, because yours is a percussion rifle. You have to load those five holes in that cylinder once you're done shootin'!" He looks at me. "You can only shoot one at a time with this one, but you'll still be shootin' when he's loadin'."

"Tell you what, Poole, you keep 'em off me as I shoot 'em one at a time, and I'll keep 'em off of you while you reload!"

"That's a deal."

The clerk hangs his head. "Anyway, it won't be long before every soldier will have a Spencer or some other repeater if this war keeps going. Here's your sling with a swivel. You know how to put that on your rifle?"

"Yes, sir."

"Here's your cartridge box to put your sixty rounds of ammunition in, and take this." He hands me a shiny new sabre with a belt and sabre knot.

I admire its edge and ask if it's hard to sharpen.

The clerk feels the edge of the sabre. "Not really. Buy a piece of broken whetstone from a butcher for a nickel and you'll have that blade singing when it cuts through the air."

"Thanks. Oh, also, I have this pistol. It's mine. Can I carry it with me?"

"You sure can. I'll write down you came in with it so they won't take it when you muster out. We'll supply ammunition for it since we don't have to furnish the gun." He hands me fifty pistol rounds.

I look at the weapon Rainy Mills gave me that saved my life many times during the siege and served me well when we went after Dawg Smith's gang. "Thanks. This'll work for now."

"You boys take care of yourselves."

"Thank you, sir." I gather my gear and new weapon and start out the door.

Poole slaps my shoulder. "How's it feel puttin' on the blue suit?"

"A hell of a lot better than those shit shoveling pig farmer clothes!"

He steps off the porch laughing. "Next stop is the livery to get our horses."

CHAPTER 12

WOULD YOU LOOK AT THAT?

EARLY AFTERNOON, DECEMBER 2, 1864

A doubtful heart takes longer to heal.

I WAVE TO the quartermaster as we exit the weapons stock room. I think about what the clerk said about humans getting better at killing each other quicker and more efficiently. It is a shame men believe that killing solves problems. There ain't no solving, just surviving. I think about Dawg Smith and Lester. They brought their deaths on themselves.

I hate what I've done, but with each passing day I become more at peace with it. The killing, I mean. Hopefully, after this last hitch with the Union Army, I'll be done with it all. Then maybe I can let it all go—the anger, violence, and killing. *Help me, Lord.*

Poole elbows me. "Me, too, Lord. Let's get our horses, and I'll tell you what we're gonna do next."

We mount up. "Get everything you want off, personal and army issues."

"Why?"

"We're gonna sell her. The army's payin' a hundert fifty Union dollars for any half-way decent mount."

"Not this horse."

"If you show up with that horse in camp, they'll press it into service. They'll promise to pay you for it, and you'll see the money next year some time. *If* you live, that is. Do what I did. Sell the horse and saddle, and then the army will have to issue you a horse. You'll get top dollar now, put money in your pocket, and ride a horse you don't own." He makes sense.

I get the deal Poole said I would. The buyer counts out greenbacks just shy of one hundred and forty. He throws in a ten dollar gold piece and some silver to square the deal. I tip my hat to the buyer and toss Poole the gold piece.

"Let's go eat at the hotel one more time before we head to camp, what do you say? I'm buyin'."

"You ain't gotta twist this boy's arm! Let's go get your horse first."

Poole leads his horse while I carry my new equipment to the Army stable. I hand a sergeant the voucher W.O. gave me, and he gathers equipment for a mounted infantryman.

A private calls out each piece of equipment as the sergeant writes it down. "One saddle with a blanket, one bridle, a pair spurs with straps, a halter with strap, curry comb, and horse brush. Everything I need to ride well and care for my mount.

The sergeant looks up. "It's all here. Go out in the stable and pick one out on the left side and saddle her."

Poole follows me into the stable. "There's plenty to choose from. Which one tickles your fancy?"

"We both know there's one condition that rises above any other—tall enough so my feet don't drag the ground."

We wander down the row to a dark colored animal. She seems gentle enough though springy in her step.

"Looks to be a good one, Lummy."

The sergeant yells, "She's a three-year-old that goes seventeen hands."

Poole whistles. "That's a damn big horse. But heck, you're a big man."

I rub her neck and scratch her ears. She breathes well and has no trouble with her hooves. She shakes her head and swats me in the face with her mane.

"This one." I get her saddled and walk her back to the sergeant.

"Sign here, and you're free to go."

I sign my name for what seems like the tenth time today.

The private takes a small brush and paint to a wall of names. "What's the name?"

I answer without looking up, concentrating on writing a good signature. "His name is Poole."

"Not him, you dern fool, the horse's. You have to name the animal. You'll spend more time with that animal than you ever did your wife."

That wouldn't take long. I only had a couple of months with Susannah. I turn to Poole.

He shrugs. "Don't look at me. I had to name my own horse. I call her Patty after my Aunt Patricia who made me pies all the years I was growin' up." The sergeant points at the boards behind his desk, and Poole explains, "You could choose from those names or come up with an original. Either way, he'll write it on the wall. Hell, it just gives us stable boys somethin' to do. So what's it gonna be?"

I look through a window and see white pillowy clouds floating in the blue sky. "Cloud."

The sergeant laughs. "Like a cloud in the sky? Hell, boy, this nag won't ride that soft for your long skinny ass!"

"No, sir. That was my great, great grandpappy's nickname. His real name was Claudius, but he didn't like bein' named for a Roman emperor."

Poole laughs. "You namin' a girl after a man?"

"Works for both, I say."

"She's your horse, but...."

The sergeant barks, "All right, enough of the horseshit. Cloud it is." The private paints the name on the board along with other "originals."

"Here's your ticket, son. Come get her when you're ready to leave."

"Thank you, sir." We salute and walk along the river in the muddy sand. My new boots are dirty already. "Dang, the shine didn't last long on these new cavalry boots, and I like 'em a lot."

Poole slaps my shoulder. "Don't worry. You'll be keepin' 'em shined up for the brass when you're loafin' around the fire."

We walk to the plank road near the landing, and Poole stops me. "Here, let me get that off." He pulls a dirty rag from his pocket and wipes the mud from my boots like Jesus washing the disciple's feet. I'm uncomfortable. He isn't. I don't say anything. Poole finishes and slaps the tall part of my boot. "Now you'll look good for the ladies." He thinks nothing of it. What a brother.

Just as Poole opens the door into the Prentiss House Hotel, I bump into a lady wearing a pretty blue skirt with a hat that shades her face.

"Excuse me, ma'am, I didn't...."

She nestles an infant against her breast as her two boys and a girl step out on the hotel porch. I look past them to see Annie Fanny grinning like a possum.

"Well, butter my backside and call me a biscuit if it ain't long tall handsome Lummy Tullos."

"My goodness, I didn't expect the royalty of Vicksburg to roll out just to greet us, Annie."

I give Annie a hug and peck on the cheek.

She grabs my cheeks and plants a kiss on my lips. "No snuff juice, brother, I promise."

"Good to see you, Annie."

Poole ever so slightly nods his head at the lady with the blue skirt.

The lady in the blue skirt lifts her head and smiles embarrassingly. "Good afternoon." Her face glows like an angel's.

I whisper, "My goodness, would you look at that?"

Annie giggles like a schoolgirl lets go of me. "This is my sister, Martha Brock, the one I told you about. And this is her gaggle of geese!" She laughs, and the children honk like snow geese.

Martha quiets them down, and Annie continues, "This is John A. who's nine, Margaret, named for our mother who's seven, James not quite two, and the baby there with Martha is William, named for his daddy."

I tip my new hat. "Pleased to meet you, Missus Brock. I'm Columbus Nathan Tullos. I'm sorry about your husband. I heard he took sick in Memphis but not before giving himself in service to the United States Army. He must've been a good man, a fine husband and father to these nice lookin' children."

Martha smiles weakly. "He was. It's been such a blow to us all. Thank you for your sympathy. Annie has told me about you. I appreciate your kindness to my sister in her time of need." Martha lowers her head again. She's still grieving.

Annie puts an arm around her and tries to lighten the mood. "That there's

Poole. Don't know if he's got another name or not." She makes a funny face at the kids, and they all laugh.

Poole, who's always been a bit shy, especially with women, politely says, "My name is Thomas Poole from Choctaw County. I grew up with Lummy."

Annie slaps his shoulder and starts up a conversation with him, motioning for the kids to follow her. "C'mon, children, I got a piece of lemon candy for each of you, and I need to ask this good lookin' man a question or two." They trail off down the porch toward the river.

I gently lift Martha's bonnet. She tearfully looks up. "I apologize, Mistuh Columbus, but I believe my sister has been somewhat of a matchmaker here, setting up this chance meeting."

"I'm afraid so."

"She has a very special place in her heart for you. I can tell already, Mistuh Columbus, you're a fine man. I understand you've had a similar experience."

My chest tightens. "I have."

"Not to assume anything, but you must know I still miss my William Henry. He passed just last June in Memphis. It's taken me a while to take off the black robes. I only put on a skirt with color when we left Memphis to come here. I didn't want any questions. Some folks can't help but ask nosey questions at the worst times."

"Miss Martha, I've heard good things about you from Annie, but I had no idea that I'd nearly knock you over this morning."

She smiles and bounces the baby in a little dance. "Maybe it was fate?"

"I still grieve for my wife who passed two years ago. It ain't been easy. But the Lord is a mender of hearts. He closes wounds, and when it's healed, the pain leaves. There may be a scar, but even that can bring back a good memory."

"Thank you for that, Mistuh Columbus. I do say you look right smart in your new uniform."

"Yes, ma'am, thank you. I joined up with the same regiment as your William but in Company C. I want this war over and to get on about the life the Good Lord has waitin' for me back in Choctaw County."

Martha's eyes light up. "Choctaw County, Mississippi? I hear it's beautiful in that part of the state. What do you do there, if you don't mind me asking?"

"Not at all. Our family has a fine creek bottom farm that grows good corn and cotton. We cut timber and have a few hogs and chickens—at least up until the war. Now, we're just tryin' to make it like everybody else. But when this is over, there'll be crops to plant and timber to cut."

"You should see your eyes light up when you talk about your farm. You're like a little kid at his birthday party." She lays her hand on mine. "Like you said, the Lord can heal the wounds of the heart. If he can do that, then he can heal the wounds of this land."

For a moment the faces of Pa, Ben, Amariah, Amanda, Mr. Gilmore, Susannah, Granville, Hog Fart, all flash before my eyes. Part of the healing is the dying, I reckon.

She squeezes my hand. "We both got a lot of mending to be done in us, don't you think?"

A single tear rolls down my cheek. I can't answer.

She smiles and lifts her hand. "You are a good man. It's easy to see you want the simple life that God has for every man. I appreciate that in you."

I look out over the steamboats on the river. "Miss Martha, I don't know what's about to happen, joinin' up with the Rifles and all. But I have to set some things right for our country, Mississippi, for people who need to be free, and for my own soul. If I don't, I won't be able to come home. Really come home, if you know what I mean. But if I make it through what's before me, would it be all right to call on you?" I can't believe what I'm saying, but it feels right.

"Why Mistuh Columbus, we just met." She pauses and rubs the baby's nose. "But then again, it's like I've known you all my life. Isn't that strange?"

"Not in this world, Miss Martha."

She looks up with her sky blue eyes that pierce my soul. "We both have learned that life can be cut short without notice, haven't we?"

"Yes, ma'am."

"Then who are we, not to take the Lord's gift when he offers?"

"May I write you in the meantime?"

"I would like that." Her stare is unnerving but in a good way.

"When I come back, maybe we'll know if there's feelin's between us."

"I don't read and write, but I'll find someone to help me with the letters. We just arrived here this week to take up residence in Vicksburg. When you write, send your posts to Annie. Annie is such a good soul, and the children love her already. I start as a cook at her café tomorrow. We'll stay with Annie and Beau above the café until we figure something out. My oldest two will have a chance at some schooling, too. Maybe I can learn to read and write with them."

My heart leaps. Her words unsettle me for a second. She sees it.

"Are you all right, Mistuh Columbus?"

I'm embarrassed and hurt a little that I'm so excited about a woman other than Susannah. Something's happening, and I can't stop it. I'm not sure what I'm supposed to do or say.

"I'm fine, just a little healin' comin' my way right now."

Martha blushes. I'm embarrassed, like a schoolboy falling in love for the first time.

"So, you're not goin' back to Memphis?" She shakes her head. "Well, not to be too forward, but I may be in and out of Vicksburg with my army duties. If I pass through, may I call on you?"

She tucks her chin into her neck, turning red again. "Much the gentleman, just like Annie said. That'll be fine, Mistuh Columbus."

"And one other thing, Miss Martha. Would you please consider just calling me Lummy? All my friends do, and I'd feel much better if you did."

Martha stares into my eyes for what seems like an eternity. She smiles ever so softly. "All right, Columbus."

She doesn't call me Lummy, but my heart beats like a steamer engine in a strong river current. Love tickles my empty soul. Granny Thankful always said, "A doubtful heart takes longer to heal." I turn loose of the doubt. I have a hopeful heart.

I kiss Martha's hand.

CHAPTER 13

A PLANNED CHANCE MEETING

MID-AFTERNOON, DECEMBER 2, 1864

Two ships passing in the night is just a line in a storybook.
This is no storybook.

I'M LOST IN Martha's eyes. Our gaze is broken only by the sound of laughter and children scampering about. Annie, Poole, and the children are making their way up from the riverbank. I walk Martha down the steps of the hotel to meet them.

"Momma, Momma," John and Margaret call as they run to the hotel. "Mistuh Poole taught us how to skip rocks and whistle bird calls. He even made a little boat out of driftwood that floated on the river." They hug their mother as Annie trails behind. Poole carries James on his shoulders, grinning ear to ear. This looks like family. Peace lands in my heart like a dove lighting in a tree.

Annie blurts out, "Well, I hope you two love birds got all your sweet talkin' done cause, Martha, if we don't get on up to the café, Beau's gonna think I done run off."

Martha and I both blush at Annie's indiscretion.

John asks, "Is Mistuh Lummy gonna be our new...."

Martha responds quickly but not harshly. "Hush, child! Annie, I'll deal with you later. Children, let's go. Maybe I can teach your bucket mouth auntie to put a lid on her butter churn sized mouth. I apologize, Columbus, children don't always know when to keep their little beaks closed." Martha gives me the sweetest smile then scowls at Annie.

Annie shrugs and takes little James, who has become so sleepy he can barely hold his head up. She winks at me. "Told you, Lummy, sweet as honey!" She giggles as long as she knows I can hear her as they walk away. I watch Martha until they turn the corner on Washington Street.

Poole puts his arm on my shoulder. "As fine an example of Eve God ever made."

"I didn't know you took such a liking to ole Annie Fanny!" Poole jerks his arm off my shoulder and punches me in the ribs playfully. I laugh. "I'm just kiddin', Thomas."

"You're a lucky man, Lummy."

"Yep, she's as fine as Creator ever shaped from clay, inside and out."

Not long ago I wondered which way the Lord would take me. I asked him for new reasons to live. I believe he just gave me one.

Poole sniffs the air. "Smell that?"

I laugh. "What, Martha's perfume?"

"No, you sweet talkin' lover boy. The restaurant!"

Poole and I enter the Prentiss House Hotel for an early supper.

CHAPTER 14

LIVIN' OLD WOUNDS BRINGS NEW HEALING

LATE AFTERNOON, DECEMBER 2, 1864

Men can be healed in the remembering.

WE STEP OUT onto the porch of the hotel and stretch having had our last best meal for a while. We have a couple of hours left before roll call, and I head to St. Paul's Catholic Church. Susannah is on my mind, and I need to think about everything that's happening. I ask Poole to wait outside for a moment. I study the saints painted on the walls and the beautiful architecture along the ceiling and behind the altar. What a beautiful place.

I close my eyes and clear my mind.

I know what I want, but if I force my will, that's all I'll get—my will. No, I'll seek God, then his will, will be revealed. I fight against my own thoughts and those the Evil One sends to disrupt me. A light shines in the distance like a sun ray flickering through willow leaves. It closes the gap between us quickly, and a hand extends from the light holding a gold ring.

The sound of a gentle breeze blowing through pines surrounds me. I don't hear the words being spoken. I just know them. "This circle is no longer what binds us together. There is so much more. Be free, my love."

The flickering light fades back to where it came. The chain that holds the alligator tooth and Susannah's wedding ring suddenly falls from my neck. The chain is broken. I put the gator tooth in my pocket and rub the small gold wedding band Mr. Gilmore gave me for Susannah. She wore it for such a short time. A door creaks, and I snap back from my waking dream.

The old priest steps out of his study. "I'm sorry to disturb you, my son. I thought someone had come for confession."

"I did, and I have already, to the Lord. Do you remember me?"

The priest squints through brightly colored beams of light shining through the stained glass windows. "Lummy Tullos, how in the world are you?"

I like this man, always jolly and glad to see me. "Better than I deserve, I reckon, but I'll take what the Good Lord gives me!"

He comes at me with outstretched arms, and I hug this man who listened to me many hours when I served as provost before the siege.

He folds his hands together like he's about to pray. "Have you finally come back to become a good Catholic?"

"I've always been a good Catholic, father. I just didn't know it."

He chuckles. "I know that's right. Wearing the blue suit now I see. Good choice, but don't tell my parishioners you heard me say that. I'd be looking for a new parish in a heartbeat. What can I do for you, son?"

I'm reluctant, but I trust this man. I tell him about my undying love for Susannah but also about Martha. I talk about the wounds and the pain I can't seem to turn loose. "How can I turn my love from one passed on to one who lives?"

"I'm not sure I have the answer, my son, but I do know this. God does not allow one good thing to be taken away without giving another, if you let Him. That says nothing about the first, only that God wants good things for his children. Sometimes we get comfortable with a certain pain because we at least know how it feels. If we keep it, then we judge other life experiences by that pain. Creator did say that it's not good for man to be alone."

"He did, but why are you alone? Were you ever married?"

"As a very young man, yes, I was. But like Susannah, she died young. We were only married two years. Her loss nearly took my soul in liquor. I decided to give my heart, mind, body, and soul to the Lord for the rest of my days. I don't regret it. I guess you can say I've been married to Creator's spirit all these years."

"What's it like givin' all your love and devotion to someone you can't see?"

"You should know that better than me."

"What do you mean?"

"Is that not what you're doing with Susannah?"

"You've got me there."

"Oh, my son, I see Creator every day, and I never feel alone." The priest straightens his habit and adjusts a chain with a cross dangling. "Not every man can do what I do. The Lord does not require it, and it doesn't make me a better man in his eyes. It's my calling to shepherd the hurting, give strength to the fallen, and to help a fellow traveler get to where he's supposed to go. You were made to expand God's kingdom through a loving family. I believe God and Susannah have both given you their blessing. Just give it some time."

I hand the gold band to the priest. "I want you to have this for your work."

The priest taps his chin with his finger. "This'll buy books for the Negro children's school."

"Perfect." I thank the priest and hug him close.

I drop five dollars in the collection box and step out into the sunshine. Poole is talking with two nicely dressed girls. I'm amazed. I wait until he sees me. When his eyes meet mine, his face turns red as a dewberry before it ripens. He politely bows and says his goodbyes. He proudly waves a dainty handkerchief at me. He breathes the perfume in deeply.

"You ain't the only one who can talk pretty to the girls. Dang, they were so beautiful and sweet. They made my heart wanna jump right out of my chest!"

"I do know what you mean, old friend. I do know what you mean."

We ride out to the 27th Louisiana Lunette where I fought during the siege before we join C Company in camp for the night. The place holds a lot of meaning for me—maybe too much.

As we crest the hill on Graveyard Road, the sun casts shadows long and solemn. The veil between this life and the next is thin in this place. Granny Thankful said I had a knack for finding places like this—where the dead are yet to be settled and the resurrection waits impatiently for the trumpet. This one found me.

I scan the dusty hills and hollows that ran wet with blood, sweat, and rain. I study the trenches where Yankee cannon fired ceaselessly, and I waved to a man in blue and he at me. I imagine what it would've been like if I'd been on the other side of Mint Springs Bayou when the great blue snake attacked. Too many good boys in blue were taken before their time. I stare into the sunny sky. "Blue is my color now."

Poole sits still. And quiet. Then he breaks the silence. I need him to, for where my mind wants to go. "So this is it, the 27th Louisiana Lunette?" He frowns. "I should've been here with you."

I hold my hand up for him to be quiet. The hustle and bustle of Vicksburg reminds me that I'll miss the long periods of quiet I enjoyed back in Choctaw County. The breeze has stilled, and the air is thick with the presence of so many wandering souls but also that of the One who lets this go on. "How long, oh Lord, will men need to kill each other?"

"What was it like, Lummy?"

"The Yanks attacked us twice right here when they first arrived. They thought we'd run without firing a shot. My young friend, Hog Fart, wet his britches when the big blue snake came at us. You should've seen Jasper and James's faces as they lit and tossed hand grenades in the heat of an attack. Blue suited bodies covered that field out there. It took Grant a few days to finally let us clear the battlefield of the dead after Pemberton shamed him. The buzzards had a feast."

I'd like to hear one more of Gunnard's stories and chat with the Yanks who were just feet away the last days of the siege. I can't remember the names of the men who died next to me now, but I pray for them. I close my eyes and see the eyes of the Yank I shot off that gunboat down by the river. Some things I will never forget.

I climb the rotting log wall that once formed our rifle line. I peer over into the deep pit I fell into during the seige. I close my eyes. I hear the moaning of the wounded, see the blank stares of the dead, feel the whimpering shuddering of the frightened, but the rest singing "Oh! Susannah" with me. I pray like I did before I climbed out of that abyss of blood and death. "Help them find rest, Lord, and peace."

"Amen," Poole whispers.

"People won't ever really know what happened here."

"Maybe they will, someday."

I stand in the spot where the minie ball struck the brass button on my chest. "No, only the men who lived and died here will and be healed in the remembering."

CHAPTER 15

FOUR MILE BRIDGE CAMP, UNION ARMY

EVENING ROLL CALL, DECEMBER 2, 1864

The Lord giveth, and the Lord taketh away. Today he gives me new brothers.

FOUR MILE BRIDGE camp is just that, a camp four miles from the river. The Union Army controls the railroad trestle spanning a creek bottom several hundred yards wide. Steep banks on both sides descend into a creek. It was outside our lines during the siege. Before the Yanks came, I spent a lot of time here. Now it serves as an exchange site for swapping prisoners. Remnants of the little cabins we built for winter quarters have been left to crumble. The old shacks that we commandeered from the Negroes when we served picket guard still stand. I hated doing that. It was wrong, but I had no choice. Taking up for Negroes and being in the Confederate Army didn't mix well back then. Still, I feel a bit of shame about it.

We tie our horses to the line and remove our saddles. We carry our gear to a tent where Poole stays. Men speak, calling Poole's name.

"Most of these men are raw recruits with no training. Hardly any have seen action. We won't be here long. We'll board a steamer for Memphis when they have enough men to justify a run."

I lay my bedroll out and store my few belongings in Poole's tent.

Poole whistles. "Let's get some coffee, and you can meet the boys."

"Sounds good." I won't get close with these men. I lost too many friends in the siege. Some won't make it. Maybe I won't.

We start to sit on a couple of hogshead barrels when Sarge marches over. We stand back up before our backsides touch the barrels.

"Good, you boys got here just in time!" He looks me up and down and straightens a few things on my new uniform and then backhands Poole on the shoulder. "You did well, Poole. Now before you get your gear settled, grab your weapons. We have an inspection at roll call. Hurry it up and follow me."

Poole salutes. "We're all set, Sergeant, sir. We'll grab our guns and be right there."

"Good, make it snappy."

We line up like good soldiers do. I've done this so many times I could do it in my sleep.

I whisper to Poole, "A good friend from Winn Parish and I stood in this same spot two years ago. He could stand at attention fast asleep with his dang eyes open. Ain't that somethin'?"

Poole elbows me. "Shut the hell up, Lummy. They'll kick your ass out of here just as fast as they put you in if you don't."

As our names are called off, it turns out that only three of us are in Company C of the 1st Mississippi Mounted Rifles. The rest will serve in other companies and regiments.

A smartly uniformed captain with a red feather plume in his hat strolls down the line checking weapons and uniforms. The feather reminds me of the story about Uncle Silas fighting Mike Fink at Natchez-Under-the-Hill. He and Pa went there when they were young men to sell hides and whiskey not long after Uncle Silas fought at New Orleans. I wish I could have seen Uncle Silas fight Fink to a draw. Fink gave Silas his black hat with the red feather. It seems arrogance and pride go with a red feather like that. Uncle Silas never wore Fink's hat, but he was damn proud to tell the story.

The captain stops to inspect my weapon with a smirk. "What's this, handing out brand new Sharps carbines to men who once shot at us? What's this world comin' to?" He yanks on the sleeve of my uniform coat. "And how are those new clothes workin' for you there, pig farmer?"

I'm thinking there ain't nobody on earth who smells more like pig shit than a man whose authority rests solely in his uniform. Sarge, trailing behind the officer, slowly shakes his head at me.

"Fine and dandy, sir. They fit just right for this pig shit shoveling farmer from Mississippi."

The captain knows he's been made fun of. If he responds, he'll look even more stupid. Instead, he turns to Poole. "You didn't get a Sharps carbine?"

"No, sir. I was issued this revolving rifle that fires five .56 caliber shots, sir! When it's done shootin', I'll pull this Navy Colt .36 caliber to continue the fight, sir."

With another smirk, the captain turns to Sarge then back to Poole. "You know your weapons, Private, but completely ignorant of your unimportance to the war effort. Continue the fight? Is that what you think? Major Beaumont already reported that the 1st Mississippi Mounted Rifles isn't worth spit. Going out to fight? You'll be lucky to do latrine duty in this army."

The self-important ass looks around to get the attention he seeks. He finds none except from his staff who follow him around like puppies begging scraps. He likes performing for an audience, apparently.

I feel the heat in my face.

From the corner of my eye, Sarge mouths, "Let it go."

But I can't. "If doing latrine duty helps end this war of aggression, sir, then we'll do it to the best of our abilities. No difference shoveling pig shit and human shit, Captain. *Sir.*"

The captain stares me down for what seems like an eternity, trying to decide if he's been disrespected. Poole's breathing increases. Sarge drops his head.

The officer steps closer. "If you men weren't bound for Memphis in the morning, you'd sure smell like an outhouse by tomorrow evening."

I look straight ahead and breathe calmly. "Yes, sir, and be proud to serve my country, sir."

The captain moves down the line, giving hell where it really won't stick if a man can make it run off him like water on a duck's back. He leaves with his staff trailing behind him to the next company, like ducklings chasing after their momma.

Sarge announces, "Dismissed, return to camp."

Poole sighs. "You really know how to be a smart ass, don't you?"

"Yeah, I guess, and get away with it, too. What that brass peacock said means little to a man who lived in a latrine forty seven days. I wanted to ask where he served to know how bad latrine duty is."

Sarge walks up. "Nowhere. That bastard was gunning for somebody, and he usually picks the tallest and calmest to undo him because he is a little man with an undeserved and untested rank. For a minute there, Lummy, I thought you were gonna lose it. I see you have your wits about you better than I thought. Good job, both of you, and he's right. We leave tomorrow on a noon steamer for Memphis."

The older man backs away and yells, "Gather around, men of the First Mississippi Mounted Rifles, all companies. At ease. You did well in the inspection. Despite what the captain said, he was impressed with how well you formed up and presented arms. He doesn't know that most of you have had more experience than he'll ever see. The rest of you did a good job faking it." The men relax and laugh.

"We board a steamer tomorrow for Memphis. There you'll join the rest of the battalion at White Station Depot. Our job is to protect the Federal base at Memphis and join expeditions into Mississippi, Arkansas, and Missouri as needed. Most of you will only serve as guard, freeing up others to go fight. We're tryin' to keep the Reb Cavalry commanded by General Nathan Bedford Forrest and Wirt Adams busy so they can't join General Hood at Nashville. Some of you may see action. Be happy with what the Army gives you."

Sarge straightens up. "Pack everything. Don't leave anything. We won't be back this way once we board the steamer. Eat your rations and get some rest. Dismissed."

We stand at attention and salute, yelling a collective, "Yes, sir!"

Sarge returns the salute and turns to walk away but stops. "Oh, yeah, be at the dock waiting to board the steamer at 11:30 a.m. sharp. I'm givin' half day passes to anyone wantin' to go to town in the morning before we leave."

A small "hurrah" rises from the men.

Poole slaps me on the back. "Looks like you can go see your girl again before you leave."

He and I walk to the horse line to care for our mounts. I take the brush from my bag and work my way down the long body of this beautiful animal. I feed her a couple of carrots and an apple I took from the cook when he wasn't looking.

"Here you go, Cloud. Good girl. You best enjoy these. They'll be your last for a while."

I rub her neck and scratch her forehead. She shakes her head and bumps my shoulder playfully. After giving Cloud grain and water, I drop her an armload of hay. Poole and I go back to our coffee by the cook fire.

CHAPTER 16

SET FREE BY ONE NEWLY FREED

JUST BEFORE MIDNIGHT, DECEMBER 2, 1864

Sometimes it takes a person once bound, to set another free.

I WRAP UP in my new blanket and roll over to face the tent wall. It's a peaceful night, and I think about seeing Susannah in my soul today at the Catholic Church. She freed me for someone new the Lord may bring. I guess the best person to set another free is one who knows what it's like to be bound. I'm thankful for the time we had. Like she said today in my vision, there's more that binds us together now than a simple gold wedding band.

Annie may have set up my encounter with Martha, but the Lord was in it somewhere. Not sure if she'll be the one, but I wasn't looking for anyone either. She's pretty as the sun coming up over a field of wildflowers. She must have strength to take on raising four children and work in Annie's cafe kitchen. It speaks well of her character.

The hurts and the pains I still wrestle with need to be shed like a snakeskin. No one else can do that for me. The priest is right. I hold on to my pains because I've grown too comfortable with them. Sometimes I justify my actions by them.

"That's not fair to me, my friends, and surely won't be to a wife and kids."

Poole rolls over. "What ain't fair, Lummy?"

"Nothin'. You know me, just talkin' out loud again. Get some sleep. I'll shut up." My mind races like a blue-tailed lizard after a beetle bug. I close my eyes, and Martha's face appears.

I WAKE TO cook-fire pans clanging, men talking around the fire, and orders shouted off in the distance. Morning in camp comes too early too often with bugles blowing and men yelling. It's a far cry from Dan Creekwater's camp in McCurtain Creek swamp back home. I get my gear together, saddle my horse, grab breakfast with Poole, and we head to town with our half day passes. There's something I have to see.

Poole snorts and swats me on the shoulder. "You mean, some*one* you have to see!"

"Damn straight!" The iron horseshoes of our mounts clickety-clack down the cobblestone street as we pass Handerson's café. I want to stop, but orders are that soldiers have to park their mounts at the army horse barn and corral.

"How about a cup of coffee, Poole?"

"Only if I get to buy." I know better than to argue.

We quick step over to the café and find a seat where I can see into the kitchen. A waiter swings the door open to deliver patrons' food, and I catch a glimpse of Martha.

Annie yells, "Two coffees please, and bring a couple sweetcakes if we have any left." She has the smirk of a lady who is about to tell me in no uncertain terms I told you so. I wouldn't mind.

The door to the kitchen swings open, and I see Martha in a long white apron with her hair put up. She leans back from a pie crust she rolls out just far enough to let me see her smile. Our eyes lock for a moment before the door swings closed.

Annie puts her hand on mine. "She's a good woman, you know that. It's a lot right now, for both of you, but you two are made for each other. It'd be a lot to take on four children, Lummy."

I cut her off softly. "That ain't what bothers me."

She leans closer. "Well, boy, spit it out!"

I stammer and stutter. "I just, don't know, well... I'm just not sure if...."

Annie squeezes my hand hard. "What?"

"If I measure up to a sweet woman like Martha with all that I've done!" I sound pitiful.

"Lummy Tullos! You're as fine a man ever walked this earth and good as any in the Bible who did things a lot worse than you. You didn't do half of their meanness, and God called them men after his own heart. So how do you figure God don't love you the same? Measurin' up, what the hell are you thinkin', boy? Talkin' from experience, nobody measures up! Somebody put that in your head. Just look at me! Livin' proof God can work with just about anythin'!"

I turn to Poole. "I have clearly stirred this woman up like a wasp nest!"

Poole sips his coffee calmly. "You asked for it, brother."

Annie calms down and apologizes to the customers. "Sorry folks, this here's my good friend, and I'm tryin' to keep him from messin' up his life." They go back to eating and conversations.

The waiter pours our coffee and places a sweetcake in front of each of us. The warm bread that smells of cinnamon laced with a frosty white icing goes so well with the rich flavorful coffee. Annie lets us eat our treat. I keep my eyes fixed on the kitchen door to catch every glimpse of Martha I can. I finish my cake and sip my steaming coffee.

Annie smiles at me. "You're bit... and bad." My face is hot.

Poole laughs with his mouth full of sweetcake. "I didn't know you had so much red in that dark complected face of yours, Lummy. Makes you look a little like a wild-ass red man!"

"Shut the hell up, boy."

He doubles over, laughing hard enough to shake the table. A little coffee sloshes out of my cup, and Poole tries to stop. I start laughing too. It feels good to be human again.

Annie dabs up the brown liquid with a napkin. "Nothin' wrong with callin' it for what it is. You're in love, boy! Ain't no denyin'."

"Do you have to announce it all over creation?"

"Don't have to, because the only one it really matters to is right over there." She points to the kitchen door where Martha wipes her hands on a towel and stares at me. I turn five shades of red, knowing I'm busted and at the mercy of this woman. Martha straightens her apron and pushes her sandy blonde hair over her ears before she walks to our table.

"I must look a fright, Columbus, but I did want to come speak."

Annie blurts out, "Well set yourself down here girl and talk a minute. You've got time."

"No, I best not. I have a bread coming out of the oven any minute." She looks into my eyes deeply. "Columbus, I do look forward to seein' you again, you hear?" My heart wants to frog leap out of my chest. I gather myself quickly and stand up.

"Yes, ma'am, I want to see you again too, real soon." I take her hand and kiss it softly. Martha blushes, and the older women in the café "ooh" and "ahh." Now I'm really embarrassed.

Just before I turn her hand loose, Martha gently kisses me on the cheek. Our eyes lock for a second, but an eternity of meaning passes between us. I forget all that's around me—the patrons, the noisy kitchen, even Annie and Poole. I let her hand go and sit back down. I watch Martha walk back into the kitchen.

Annie pinches me. "Dang, boy, you got it bad!" She giggles like a schoolgirl. "And the best part? She's got it as bad as you do."

CHAPTER 17

A GAMBLE WORTH THE RISK

NOON, DECEMBER 3, 1864

With the old left behind, surely only the new can be found just around the next bend.

"WE'VE GOT ONE more thing to do before we leave." We say our goodbyes, and I take Poole up to Sky Parlor Hill again, where a man can see for fifty miles on a clear day. We couldn't see much in the dark last night. He's amazed at the view. I'm amazed at myself for being in this place.

New boots and socks, new shirt, pants and under drawers, a well-fitting blue jacket, and the finest Sharps weapon a soldier could ever hold. If I had shaved and cut my hair, I'd surely be a sight to see. I didn't. It'll help keep me from being recognized on the mission to Bankston.

I stand taller and straighter today, feeling good about what I'm fighting for. I pull my new cavalry hat off to feel the warm morning sun. The Mississippi looks so wide. Memories flood my mind—some warm my heart, some test my soul.

Our steamer signals boarding will begin soon. Poole and I hustle to the army livery stable to get our horses. Sarge checks off the names of men as they show up at the landing. We march briskly, leading our horses to the livestock gangplank. Other men who signed up with the 1st Mississippi Mounted Rifles mill around, talking.

"Tullos, Poole, get your horses on the *Sultana* and report back to me."

Poole's jaw drops at her magnificence. "Biggest steamer I've ever seen."

Sarge looks up from his clipboard. "She's two hundred and sixty feet long with a speed of over eight knots. She'll take you to the biggest city you've ever seen, too. Now go on now, get those nags on board and get back here on the double."

We don't move, still marveling at the boat.

"I said, *now!*"

Sarge is clearly aggravated about something, but not at us. We hustle our mounts to the holding pen on board with other horses and mules. The attending private helps get the saddles off and our gear stored away for the trip north.

Sarge stations us halfway up the bank to watch for other men enlisted in the Rifles. Five gangplanks lead up to this boat—one for horses, one for soldiers, another for supplies, a plain one for regular passengers, and a very fancy one for rich folks who quarter in the front of the boat along with officers. We rate lower than regular passengers, somewhere between supplies and livery stock. We'll sleep out on the deck.

A soft bed in a cabin like I had on the steamer *Dime* from Greenwood would be nice. Sleeping out in the fresh air is fine though. I've slept on the deck of a steamer before. Besides, a soldier is expected to live without much comfort. A slow ride up the Mississippi will give me time to write Martha a letter, maybe even a poem.

The whistle blows, and Sarge yells almost as loud. "Damn, I knew it. Those two men from Vicksburg ain't gonna show! Probably ran off with the bounty, Colts Revolving Rifles, horses, and accoutrements. I'm a damned dumbass worthless mule for trustin' them rascals. Well, that's just wonderful. B Company will be short two men. I'm puttin' them down as deserters. Thievin' bastards, anyway."

I've never heard Sarge curse like that.

"Lummy, say a prayer for this angry old Irishman."

"Will do, sir." We start up the soldier's gangplank with our haversacks, weapons, and bedrolls. Poole and I stake out a spot under the cover of a wide awning to avoid rain or dew in the mornings.

"Hey Poole, when I get to Memphis, I'll have traveled the entire stretch of river between Memphis and New Orleans. On somebody else's nickel, too."

Poole shakes with excitement. "This is my first steamboat ride."

I ask a deck hand carrying rope. "How long to Memphis, sir?"

"Sir? Hell, no need to call me that. It's three hundred miles, give or take. This boat runs ten miles an hour loaded. She's got some stout mules pullin' in the engine room. With wood and water stops and barring gettin' stuck on a sandbar, we should dock at Memphis in two days, maybe less."

Poole and I walk the lower deck, getting our bearings for where we'll eat and spend our daytime hours. A small group of men huddle in a corner rolling dice.

One says with a toothy grin. "Come join us, friend. You can't lose."

"Somebody always loses, friend."

Poole keeps his hands in his pockets. "Ain't that the damn truth? I got suckered into a dice game once in Bucksnort and lost three dollars before I got turned around good. That broke me from ever gambling again."

"Yeah, I never thought I had enough money to lose it gambling."

I may not gamble with money, but I'm doing it with my life. This gamble is worth the risk.

CHAPTER 18

STEAMBOAT RIDE TO THE FUTURE

DECEMBER 3, 1864

The calm surface of a rolling river hides well the turbulence underneath.

POOLE AND I lean against the rail as the Sultana backs away from the landing. The nose of the steamer turns upstream. Her sternwheeler paddles plow the dark waters like a mule working soft spring dirt.

Poole is in awe. "How in heck do these boats run so low in the water and not get swamped?"

"Somebody smarter than us figured that out."

Black smoke boils out of the stacks, and the captain toots the horn three times. Men cheer. The paddles churn a rooster tail high into the air as we dash into the main current. In minutes we're traveling in the middle of the stream. I like the wide expanse of water. It reminds me of how big and powerful Creator is. My soul finds peace in this gentle stream so wide, so deep. I study the slow moving eddies, back flows, whirlpools, and the short choppy waves that reveal a sandbar just under the surface. I close my eyes and become part of the river, getting lost in its depth, but finding myself in its flowing.

I lean on the rail just above the waterline. Ripples break away from the boat. I concentrate on the soft sound until all noise fades. The expanse of the broad river draws in my soul, and I'm lost in a place that I know so well. A place strangely familiar but new at the same time. My spirit rises, as if I'm floating across the broad waters. Maybe I am. I'm carried to a place of rest and union with all that surrounds me. The Lord is here. I drift away. A jerk in the churning motion of the paddle wheeler jolts me back.

Poole yells, "We hit a big log."

An old cottonwood trunk banks off the side of the hull and flops like a fish thrown in a bucket—like the log that dislocated my shoulder near this same spot back in '59. I start for the back of the boat.

Poole gives me a friendly push as I walk away. I see his lips moving, but I don't hear his words. He repeats the words. "Look, it's a half-sunk gunboat stuck on that sandbar."

I shake my head and don't stop. I've seen enough gunboats sunk for a lifetime. Barnyard odors of horses and mules remind me of home. I walk to where Cloud is tied. My stiff new uniform reminds me of why I'm here. War.

I killed a man on that very boat that now lies dead in the water. I rub Cloud's nose and scratch her ears. The life in this animal gives me hope. She nods her head up and down. I grab a handful of feed corn. She munches slowly, savoring the taste like we did eating mule meat during the siege. I don't plan to eat this horse.

The Warren County Courthouse with the Union flag flapping lazily in the breeze looms proudly over a city still getting back on its feet. I shield my eyes to spy a lady in a blue skirt running to the landing edge and waving. It's Martha! Poole grabs my belt and pulls me back before I plunge headlong into the muddy water waving back. Martha covers her mouth with her hands. I throw my hands into the air like a circus performer.

My heart aches like it did when I left Susannah to join the Confederate Army. Warmth covers my body to fill my soul. The city set upon a hill becomes smaller and smaller, but my heart swells bigger and bigger. I have a new reason to live. "I have hope."

Poole slaps me on the back. "Damn straight. You got lots to look forward to, but you won't if you do that again." He walks away slowly, mumbling something about always having to watch over me "like a damn kid" and keeping my mind on what I'm doing. He knows me too well.

The blue skirt becomes a small speck on the riverbank. Martha throws me a kiss. I wave big one more time as we make the bend. I will come back... and soon.

We easily make the hairpin Desoto Bend and round the next turn where

J.A. and I crossed the river a year and a half ago. A couple of gunboats lay anchored there now. They provide all the security needed now that the Mississippi River is completely in Union hands.

The *Sultana* glides as easily through the current as spreading butter on a hot biscuit. I take in the sights—passing boats, fishermen, deer, and water birds along the shore. Half-mile long sandbars have gravel beds I'd love to search for agates and other pretty rocks. Willows bend in the wind like dancers swaying to the rhythm of unheard music—music only those who blend with their surroundings can hear, being one with the universe. I close my eyes and soak in the sunshine.

The hum of the steam engine is powerful but soothing. If man can build such power, what can Creator do? Anything. No, everything. Even heal a devastated heart that couldn't fathom being offered new love, or be willing to receive it. I pull paper from my haversack to pen a letter and poem for Martha. It comes as easily as the breeze cooling my face and sunshine warming my back.

The Steamer Sultana, *December 3, 1864*
My dearest Martha, words cannot describe the feeling I have seeing you at the river landing as my boat left Vicksburg. But I will try in this feeble effort to write you a poem.

A Fairytale Chance Meeting
I walk the streets of a war torn town,
Deeds done here leave my soul cast down.
Yet in one bright moment your eyes of sky blue,
Brought love so quickly and forever true.

I honor my oath to return the twentieth star,
To the flag whose truth and freedom travels far.
My ship has sailed yet not before I see,
An angel in blue waving to me.

My heart aches for the doll in skirt of blue,
You must know that I have come to love you.
Some might say such love is fleeting,
Not when God plans a fairytale chance meeting.

Martha, I will not apologize for being so bold. Our time together was short, but I have so little to lose and so much to gain. If the Lord has made our meeting so, then I will follow the path He chooses for me. I will return to you quickly I hope and pray the Lord keeps us both safe for that sweet return.

With great affection, Columbus

I put the short letter in an envelope. I'll put it in the post when I get to Memphis. I close my eyes and picture Martha's face.

Love is a mix of hardship and pain when a man can't be with the flower of his heart. I open my eyes to see a flock of white water birds lift from the shallows. One carries a small fish, another with a small snake striking the crane's long beak.

Life gives good and dangerous blessings. Martha is the good. The blue suit I wear is the dangerous.

The evening sun sets low over the paddles of the sternwheeler. Rainbows from the straining light dance in the shifting spray. Finally, the fiery red ball sinks into the southwest, painting shades of orange and red to make the sky above a deep blue that rivals our uniforms. Will this blue uniform rise above the fire I'll walk through to get back home?

"Lord, let this be the storm that finally brings me home."

Poole puts an arm on my shoulder. "Amen, brother."

CHAPTER 19

FIRE
IN THE NIGHT

3:00 A.M., DECEMBER 4, 1864

Like fireworks on the 4th of July, the night is filled with fire and sound.

I AWAKEN TO men shouting. I grab my rifle, load a cartridge, and run to the rail ready to fire. Poole stumbles up, wiping the sleep from his eyes and aiming his rifle at the shore. I lower the barrel of his gun.

"We're stopping for wood and water, that's all."

"What time is it?"

The big clock tolls three times. "Damn, too early to be doin' all this for nothin'. Now, I won't get back to sleep good before they wake us for roll call at six. I'm goin' back to my bedroll. You comin'?"

I stare at the woods around the wood cutter's camp. "Be there in a bit."

Shots sound from across a small creek where men load wood. One man from our steamer gets hit in the shoulder. Poole rushes back to the rail, and I point to where Rebel rifles flash.

"Pour it on 'em. I'll take aim at fixed targets."

He cocks and fires his rifle that works like my pistol. I never thought as kids we'd be shooting at men together with the intent to kill.

Poole yells, "This sure ain't like shootin' gar in a creek!" He fires four of his five shots. The Rebs alternate taking shots at us and the wood gatherers.

Bullets strike the wall above our heads spraying splinters in all directions.

Poole's mad now. "Enough of this shit." He fires his last shot and wings a Reb in the leg. The wounded man crawls into the willows howling like a bit dog. Poole takes a small object from his cartridge box.

"What's that?"

"My secret weapon." In a moment, he's ready to fire again.

"I keep an extra cylinder loaded at all times!" He looks for a Rebel.

"Always prepared. That's why you made better grades than me in school. You studied. I didn't. But heck, you can't shoot like me. Watch this."

A Reb sticks his head up. I could easily take it off with one shot, but I made a vow not to kill another man unless completely unavoidable. I squeeze the trigger.

"Son of biscuit eatin' suck egg dawg! You took the hat right off his head. It flew twenty feet in the air, and he ran like a chicken at pluckin' time."

A soldier from G Company shouts, "They're runnin' like swamp rabbits!"

Sarge trots to where we crouch. "Just local boys probably trying to kick up a fuss."

Poole yells at the retreating Rebs, "Ain't no turkey shoot here!" He swats my arm. "Ole Lummy made 'em think twice about tryin' that again."

Sarge pats me on the shoulder. "Stayin' true to your oath to the Union."

"And to my God to not kill anybody unless I can't help it."

Poole stares at me. "You really take an oath not to kill anybody?" He studies on that for a moment. "I don't have to either, I guess, if I can avoid it."

"Trust me. You don't want to kill a man. His eyes will haunt you the rest of your life."

He rubs his neck. "It was like fireworks on the 4th of July... and almost as pretty."

"Not if you had a bullet in your shoulder."

The wood gatherers return to the boat. Only one man was slightly wounded. The steamer captain calls, "Lights out. That means everybody. Don't even light a cigar until I say we're clear. Pass the word."

He steps back to the wheelhouse, and the engine puffs smoke blacker than the night. The steamer backs away from the riverbank. We disappear into the night with only the sound of engines pumping in the darkness.

CHAPTER 20

THE BIGGEST CITY I NEVER NEEDED TO SEE

NOON, DECEMBER 5, 1864

If a place doesn't have a good feel, don't stay.

THE WHISTLE BLOWS, and we rush to the side of the steamer. Memphis is just ahead. We pass by less imposing bluffs than those at Vicksburg.

Sarge leans on the rail. "That's Fort Pickering over there and General Sherman's lookout tower. They say you can see for miles upriver and across into Arkansas a long ways."

Greenwood on the Yazoo, Jackson on the Pearl, Vicksburg and Desoto on the Mississippi, Winnfield on the Dugdemona, New Orleans from a distance, and now Memphis? River towns cross my path everywhere I go.

I point to the Arkansas side. "What's that?"

Sarge snickers. "Hope Field, much like that worthless shanty town, Desoto. It's got nothing going for it except railroad business. Probably won't ever amount to much."

Sarge stretches his arm out like a statue. "Get a good look, boys, that's Memphis, Tennessee. Over twenty-two thousand souls, some happy with us being here and others mad as hornets that the stars and bars flag was taken down from the Post Office. Lots of beautiful buildings and the tallest you've ever seen. Fine mansions and city streets with every kind of sundry you can imagine. Watch your dollars, boys. They can slip away fast."

Poole whispers, "I don't mean no harm, Sarge, but there's a whole lot of Negroes around. There were a bunch in Vicksburg, but this is amazing."

"With all the newly freed slaves, nearly half the town is black and growing. Most of the Negroes live south of Beale Street in contraband camps named Dixie, Shiloh, and New Africa. They might just get a chance at a real life now that the war is turning. They take jobs poor whites think are beneath them. They have a fine wood frame Baptist church on Beale Street with plans to build a brick one. Grant headquartered on the end of the street in the Hunt-Phelan mansion."

I take in a deep breath. "It truly is becoming a new world."

Sarge slaps the rail. "Told you so up on that big hill in Choctaw County, didn't I?"

Poole slaps me on the shoulder. "Sure wish Susannah could've seen this."

I smile. "She does."

Sarge shields his eyes from the sunlight. "It's a beautiful town with anything a man could ever want, and prostitution is legal. There are plenty of pretty girls who'll satisfy you for a moment but keep you comin' back for more. You best think twice about all that, boys."

I straighten my uniform. "Yeah, my Reb sergeant told us the same thing. 'Lose your money and catch a disease you can't get to go away.'"

Poole stares at the city. "You mean you can pay a gal and the law won't come after you?"

Sarge tips his hat. "Nope, but anyway, a funny thing happened at the Memphis Post Office after the Battle of Memphis. Our boys had just lowered the Confederate flag and raised the stars and stripes when they heard a clanging sound. Some Reb sympathizers shut the trapdoor and locked our men on the roof. The general kindly informed the good citizens of Memphis that if they didn't completely surrender, and soon, he would shell the city. The trapdoor opened in a hurry."

Poole laughs. "I wish I could've seen that!"

Sarge grins solemnly. "You will soon enough. But for now, take it all in, cause Memphis is a sight to see!"

CHAPTER 21

FIRST STEPS TOWARD HOME

1:00 P.M., DECEMBER 5, 1864

In times past, I was useless. Now I can be useful.

THE *SULTANA* SLIDES up to the landing smooth and sweet like a church lady sitting down at her piano to begin the opening hymn. Gangplanks and moorings are secured by Negroes and white men—working side by side. People stream off the boat, the rich first—men with canes and ladies with parasols trying to look their best for the crowd of spectators who've gathered. We're ordered to wait until the regular passengers disembark, then we can saddle our horses.

Memphis doesn't sit as high above the water as Vicksburg, but it carries on like there's no war. I thought I'd seen a lot of loading and unloading in Vicksburg. This place is busy as termites eating up our old cotton house back home.

Poole elbows me. "Look at that cobblestone landing."

"There's not one like this at any river town I've ever seen. I've seen cobblestone streets, but at a river landing?" A mass of tightly laid cobblestones spread across a once unusable river front. I see why the Yanks wanted Memphis—a steamer can load and unload in any weather, even when the water's high. I want to be as useful as these cobblestones. I've wasted enough time in this fool war.

Sarge taps the rail with his knuckle. "You won't get your feet wet or muddy. Watch out for horse manure. It makes the stones slick, and it'll put you on your backside in a heartbeat!"

We gather our gear and walk our horses down the gangplank slowly so as to not excite them. My horse's shoes barely hit the cobblestones when a whistle from the steamer blows. Poole's horse rears up and jumps into the water and Poole with it. Fortunately, the water is only waist deep. He bobs up like a fishing cork before the horse breaks loose. Men crowd around with their horses to help Poole's settle down.

Poole chokes and spits out a stream of brown river water. "That had the grace of a possum shot out of a tree. I got shucked like an ear of corn and soakin' wet to boot."

I stomp my feet on the cobblestones—every step forward brings me back home. I run my boot across the stones on this once useless muddy riverbank. Now it's a point of departure for soldiers set on ending this war. They want to go home, just like me.

I'm not much different than this landing. The Lord has laid a few cobblestones in my life. They just came at such a high price. But I need more cobblestones. Like the Apostle said, 'I'm putting the past behind and pressing on towards the prize.' But I ain't forgetting. I'm just setting my eyes on the prize.

I breathe in the thick river air. Small waves break on the cobblestones—the line dividing nature creating and man destroying. This river has become part of my soul. Someday I'll sit alone on a sandbar bare, body and soul, before the Lord so I can sort all this out. I crave the silence that awaits me there, the freedom to just be me, and time to release things never intended to be a part of my life in the first place. I'll leave all pain out there—my angry pa, my hateful brother, Ben, Amariah dying, the siege of Vicksburg, Susannah dying, Ben and Mr. Gilmore murdered, killing that gunboat sailor, Granville and Edrow robbed of young lives, killing Dawg Smith, leaving Winn Parish, killing Lester....

"Lord, let me live long enough to go to there."

Poole laughs. "Go where? Hell, you survived Vicksburg. It can't get much worse than that."

"You're right."

What new heartaches must I endure as I step away from this river of peace? Whatever they are, I want them to be steps toward Martha.

Poole reminds me of J.A. back in Winn Parish with his wife and children. I envy him, in a good way. Tom Poole. We're as close as any two men can be, save being brothers. And here we are, going on some crazy mission that'll probably get us killed. I'm not ready for another close friend to die. Enough of this. There's too much good ahead to be moaning about the past and regretting a future that ain't even happened.

Sarge yells, "Mount up. Let's go. We're takin' the German Town Road some call State Line Road if you get lost. Keep up and be mindful. You're about to ride through town. I want columns of two in good straight lines. Look sharp and make me proud. We're stationed at Camp Karge, named for your commanding officer. It's near White Station Depot on the Memphis Charleston Railroad."

A lieutenant at the front of the line waves his arm. "Forward, ho-o-o!"

Men cheer as our horses snort and dance around. They're ready to move. Sparks fly from their shoes striking the cobblestones. So that's why they keep horses and barrels of powder far apart.

We trail up the river-landing road. I'm bound for a new battleground wearing blue instead of gray but still on my way to kill or be killed. My horse strikes a spark on a cobblestone. There'll be more sparks of fire before I'm done.

I try to find some humor in it all. White fights against black. Gray turns blue. Now, white fights for black wearing blue. It's not funny.

Poole kicks my leg. "The Lord never meant for it to be."

CHAPTER 22

MEMPHIS

DECEMBER 5, 1864

Familiar and new both bring hope to a man who's lost much.

AT THE CREST of the bluff, we can see for miles over into Arkansas. Uncle Burrell and his family crossed the river here back in '55 to find new land in the west. Too bad he died somewhere over there. I'd like to have known him better. His daughters, Mary and Emaline, came to live with us after their mother died shortly upon returning to Choctaw County. I'm glad Pa and Ma took them in. Death comes too soon for folks who deserve longer lives. I wonder if Uncle Burrell's grave is marked somewhere. Many buried at Vicksburg have no marker.

A gravestone never tells the best parts of a man's life. Better no marker as a good person than a wicked rich man's fancy shrine. Both will be forgotten. I won't soon forget friends and family who've passed since '59. God has replaced them—Seth, Annie Fanny, and Poole and now Martha and her children. Mr. Dotson and Sarge, Susannah's mother, Sophie, and Mr. Allrice all help fill the empty space in my heart that still aches. Somewhere it says, He restoreth my soul. Creator sent old friends back into my life and added new ones. The familiar and the new both bring hope to a man who has lost much.

We slowly move into town, making a show of it for the brass and townspeople. The streets are busy like squirrels building nests in the fall. Wagons and carriages roll everywhere, people walk here and there. Telegraph poles line sidewalks with lights so people can walk the streets at night. It's marvelous to behold—buildings like I've seen only in picture books of Europe. I want to come back and see the sights.

The Union flag waves proudly over the Post Office. The twentieth star, representing Mississippi, is there. I straighten up in my saddle and feel a bit of pride in myself. It's been a while. Ladies and children wave as men tip their hats, but southern sympathizers also line these streets with scowls. We march quietly and keep our eyes forward.

Sarge motions Company C to rein up to him. "Boys, take notice. This is Irving Block Prison, a place you don't want to visit. We keep Reb prisoners here but also deserters. Don't be one of the dumb bastards who runs off with the bounty money, army issued horse, rifle, and equipment. If you're caught, you will sit in a cell with the Rebs. There are several men of the 1st Mississippi Mounted Rifles in there now. Fair warnin', General Grierson doesn't put up with desertion."

We pass the Beale Street Baptist Church a few streets over. I bet Susannah's mother would be beside herself singing a solo in a church built by Negroes.

CHAPTER 23

UNEASY RIDE TO CAMP

LATE AFTERNOON, DECEMBER 5, 1864

A gently plodding horse can be the stage for uneasy conversations.

ONCE OUT OF town, farmland lays like a soft quilt blanket on my rope bed with the cotton filled mattress back home but with one thing missing—slaves.

I wonder how freed slaves fare with former masters still enraged about having to pay for labor rather than getting it for free, or nearly so. How could buying and selling humans, treating them like animals, ever be good business in the long run? Helping every man stand on his own two feet makes the world a better place.

A troop train passes, headed east to who knows where. I shade my eyes from the low lying winter sun.

"Would you look at that? Black soldiers goin' off to fight. What a sight."

"Wonder where they're headed? Probably to a battle somewhere. I wonder how they'll do when the fightin' starts."

I shrug. "Don't matter. When the bullets fly, it doesn't matter what color your skin is. We all bleed red, and I'm in the same boat with them when it comes to the Rebs."

Poole pops me on the chest. "Yes, you are. The Rebs would skin you alive if they caught a former Reb wearing blue. Did you hear what they did at Fort Pillow?"

I shift in my saddle to avoid rubbing a blister on my backside. "No."

"Saddle wearin' on your ass?"

"This new army saddle isn't like ours back home. It just needs some oil and breakin' in. I'll be all right. What happened at Fort Pillow, wherever that is?"

"Back in April, General Forrest attacked Fort Pillow just north of here and demanded its surrender, several times. When Major Booth didn't, the Rebs swarmed the fort. The major was killed, and they massacred four hundred of the six hundred soldiers garrisoned there. They shot, bayonetted, and slashed men with their sabers. They even killed women and children when they tried to surrender. April 12 will always be remembered as a sad day, for both sides. What brings a man to kill like a madman?"

I wince at the story. "Anger put in a young boy who was never taught how to handle it, like me. If it wasn't for the demon rage I conjured up in the trenches at Vicksburg, I'd be dead. Hell, we were so crazy-headed, we had to tell each other what we did after an attack. The blood lettin' was so fierce, we couldn't remember all the killin' we'd done."

Poole swallows hard. "Killin' can make men go mad."

I take in the fading sunlight. "No. The problem is what makes men kill like that. It's the madness they brought into this war. Forgive us all, Lord."

"Amen, brother. But what got both sides attention about Fort Pillow was that of the four hundred massacred, three hundred were Negro soldiers. The Rebs piled up the bodies and burned them. Even the Confederate authorities called it a massacre, not a battle. There's a pretty bad place reserved for people who do such things."

I grind my teeth at the loss of humanity—for those massacred and men who do such things.

"Poole, every man will give an account, and there's plenty room in Hell for all of us."

Poole slaps me on the shoulder. "Didn't you learn anything from Pastor Dobbs about the lovin' grace and forgiveness of Jesus?"

"All I have to fall back on for the things I've done is the grace of the Good Lord. If that's not enough, then we're all dead in the water." I hum "Amazing Grace."

Poole stands up in his stirrups. "Wonder how far we got to go?"

"Doesn't matter, tater head. A private only knows where he's going when he's told where he's going. Most times, you don't know 'til you get there. For me, every step forward is a step toward home."

I just have to survive the storm that'll carry me home.

CHAPTER 24

CAMP KARGE

EVENING, DECEMBER 5, 1864

Familiar sights and sounds make for new experiences.

I'M RIGHT AT home in Camp Karge near White Station Depot. The land lays beautiful with rolling hills, tall trees, and clear creeks away from the noise of the city. I'll just have to endure the noise of rowdy soldiers who hopefully will calm down when ordered to settle into their tents for the night. Otherwise, this light sleeper won't get any rest. It can't be worse than sleeping in the rifle pits of Vicksburg for forty-seven days.

We care for our horses, then find Sarge who directs us to our tent. "Get to know the other men of Company C. They're friendly enough."

I lift the flap on a tent that's far better than any I ever had in the Confederate Army. The sides are waist high, and a man can stand up in it. The tents at Camp Moore were short, and a man had to crawl over seven men to get out. With only four men to a tent, this is better than the Prentiss House Hotel. There's even a cot for each of us left by the men who were here before. This is getting better all the time.

We settle in and wait to meet our bunkmates. Sarge strides over with two men in tow.

"Privates Poole and Tullos, meet your bunk mates, Privates Benjamin Ainsworth and Seneca Bleake. Don't let the Injun name fool you. He's tough as nails and won't let you make fun of his name. You boys get acquainted and make roll call in fifteen minutes."

We all turn and salute Sarge. "Yes, sir."

Ainsworth shakes his head, smiling as he and Seneca stick out their hands. "Just call me Ainsworth. There's already too many Ben's in this army."

"Call me Bleake."

Ainsworth, about my age and ruddy looking, stands five feet seven with a mop of auburn hair. He's from Simpson County, Mississippi. He knew some of my kin there and carries a rifle like Poole's. His fiery eyes constantly dart about like he's expecting trouble any moment.

Seneca, on the other hand, is a quiet, mild mannered blonde haired eighteen-year-old from, of all places, Winn Parish. He's fresh off the farm and innocent as a babe. He enlisted in the Rifles a month to the day before I did in Vicksburg. We'll have lots to talk about. When you lose a young soldier brother like Granville, the Lord provides a new one. I'm not sure about getting too close. But I do know me. I'll watch after him.

After roll call, we settle by the fire to cook our food. Confederate rations don't even compare.

Ainsworth decided to enlist after Forrest's massacre at Fort Pillow. "They cut down women and children and killed soldiers just because they were black. I had to do somethin'. I hope to run into that rotten bastard some day. I almost got my chance when Forrest raided Memphis just before I enlisted. Damn him."

The story reminds me of Dawg Smith. "What happened on the Memphis raid?"

Ainsworth's eyes flash. He's getting worked up. "They call it a Confederate victory, but that's bullshit. Forrest rode in with two thousand horse soldiers to free Reb prisoners from Irving Block Prison. I'm sure you passed it on your way here. Forrest tried to capture three of our generals, but he failed. He got away with five hundred Yankee prisoners, besides the killed and wounded. He cut telegraph wires and stole supplies and horses. How he gave our boys the slip, I'll never know."

Poole scratches the back of his head. "Well, he snuck in about four o'clock in the morning and surprised the daylights out of our men, especially General Washburn."

Ainsworth barks, "That's right. Forrest came in under a thick river fog posing as a Union patrol with Reb prisoners. They took out the sentries and galloped through the streets of Memphis like wild men taking pot shots at our boys. Forrest split up his force so our troops couldn't keep up with them. Always two steps behind them. Damn, I wish I'd been there."

Poole laughs. "Me, too. Must've been pure comical to watch General Washburn run like a swamp rabbit down an alley in his nightshirt when Forrest's men rode their horses into the Gayoso House Hotel. They high-tailed it out of there quick but not before Forrest took General Washburn's uniform. Forrest had it cleaned, pressed, and returned to Washburn under a flag of truce the very next day."

I laugh. "Somebody ought to write that down."

Ainsworth pulls out a crumpled Memphis newspaper. "They did. General Hurlbut says he can't do his job because Washburn can't keep Forrest out of his bedroom."

Poole asks, "Did he free the prisoners at the prison?"

"Nope, our boys blocked them at the State Female College. It was a well-executed raid, but I still got no respect for Forrest—not after the Fort Pillow massacre."

He'll always be tainted as far as I'm concerned.

CHAPTER 25

COMPANY C, 1ST MISSISSIPPI MOUNTED RIFLES

DECEMBER 6-11, 1864

Foot soldier or mounted infantry, my orders still sound the same.

I'M NOW A uniformed, fully outfitted member of the 1st Battalion Mississippi Mounted Rifles Company C and proud of it. We're under General Grierson's command that includes several cavalry regiments. Our regiment is assigned to the 1st Brigade under Colonel Karge's command, along with the 2nd New Jersey, 7th Indiana, and 4th Missouri. I'm more proud to serve alongside the 3rd U.S. Colored Cavalry. Together, we're a formidable force of thirty-five hundred men, ready for action.

Between training for horse maneuvers and how to fight from horseback, I hear the stories of how the Rifles came to be. Men started volunteering December of '63, but the battalion wasn't organized until last March. The Rifles mostly did defense duty until they joined an expedition to Grand Gulf, south of Vicksburg, back in July. They traveled to Bolivar, Port Gibson, and Grand Gulf then joined General Smith on an expedition to the university town of Oxford. The battalion fought well in skirmishes and small battles at the Tallahatchie River, Hurricane Creek, and at Oxford. Since then, the Rifles have defended Memphis, sometimes joining short patrols and scouting parties.

Ainsworth is the best talking unofficial historian of C Company. He's been on every expedition the Rifles have joined in so far. He reminds me of Gunnard in Vicksburg, the best story teller I'd ever heard. Ainsworth runs a close second. He hasn't got Gunnard's education, but no matter, a good story is a good story.

After evening roll call and supper, I bring Ainsworth a cup of coffee to his picket duty post. He takes the steaming cup. I keep my rifle at the ready.

Sarge makes his rounds. "Private Tullos, what are you doin' out here?"

"I brought my tent-mate coffee to make the cold evenin' go easier. If you don't mind, I'd like to hear what the Rifles have been up to these past months."

Ainsworth nods. "It'll make the time pass quicker."

Sarge rubs his chin. "All right, just know that Reb guerillas have been known to snatch men from the picket line and send them straight to Andersonville. You don't want to go to that hellhole. Private Tullos, consider yourself on double picket duty with Ainsworth until midnight then get your ass back to your tent."

I salute. "Yes sir, and thanks."

Ainsworth blows on his hot coffee then takes a quick sip. "We started off doing patrols and scouting for the general defense of Memphis, riding down into North Mississippi on short 30-75 mile trips. When we joined the other regiments under Colonel Karge, we attacked Wirt Adams's 1st Mississippi Confederate Cavalry at Grand Gulf. We weren't even close to full strength. A few who went AWOL returned, and the few who were sick got well. By the time we started out, we had only 468 good men ready for a scrap.

He pulls out a small book and finds the place he's looking for. "On July 4, 1863, I surrendered and marched into Vicksburg. One year later, I boarded a steamer in a blue suit bound for Vicksburg. The Lord does have a sense of humor."

Something moves in the bushes, and we both raise our rifles, ready to shoot. Out walks a young Negro girl with a baby in her arms. "Don't shoot, please, suh."

Ainsworth yells, "Halt, who else is with you?" He whispers, "Sometimes Rebs will bait guards with contraband Negroes and try to capture us." We step forward, and he barks louder, "I asked, who else is with you?"

The frightened young mother stumbles out of the shadows. Ainsworth cocks his rifle. "I will shoot you!"

"No one, suh. Please let me come in your lines. My baby's hungry, and I ain't ate for two days. I promise, ain't nobody else with me." She faints.

I catch the baby but miss the mother. "Can't you see she's scared out of her mind?"

"Look, Tullos, several boys have been snatched from picket lines. I'm taking no chances. She'll be all right when she gets by the fire and we feed her and the baby."

Satisfied there aren't any Rebs, Ainsworth sends me with the girl and her baby back to camp.

The young mother comes to, and I chastise her gently, "Why'd you sneak up on us like that in the dark? You could have been shot! Your baby, too."

She rubs her face. "I was just so scared. I been seein' Rebs dressed like farmers all day. My massuh done run off. Field hands, too. They told me I couldn't come with them cause I'd slow them down with my baby. They said go hide in Fayette County. I don't know where that is, suh. I didn't know what else to do."

She wobbles, and I steady her as we walk. The surgeon steps out of his tent. "What do we have here, Private?"

"She just walked into our picket line, sir." I seat her with the baby in her arms on a cot inside the surgeon's tent.

He scratches the back of his neck. "Who are you, soldier?"

"I'm Private Columbus Nathan Tullos, Company C, First Mississippi Mounted Rifles, sir."

He pats me on the shoulder. "I'm the Assistant Surgeon for your regiment, Dr. Samuel J. Bell. I appreciate your kindness. She might not have made it to my tent had you not helped. The Lord will reward you for your kindness, son." I return to my post.

Ainsworth drinks the last of his coffee and hands me the cup. "Thanks. Did you get that girl squared away, Tullos?" I nod. "Good, I like the way you took her in gently. Sorry I was a bit harsh, but we're all still alive, and she's gettin' the help she needs. I don't like treatin' people bad who've already been treated worse. Anyway, the Rifles arrived at Vicksburg July 7 and marched to Clear Creek. We met up with a Major Slocum close to the Black River on the Jackson Road. He said our expedition was impractical. So we turned around and marched all those miles back to Four Mile Bridge. I'm sure you know where that is."

"Everybody does. I do believe if you want to go to Heaven, or sent to Hell, you gotta go through Four Mile Bridge camp. So what happened next?"

"On the thirteenth, we were leading the column headed for Port Gibson when two hundred Rebs came at us like a tornado. They pushed us back. Our lieutenant, Colonel Shorey, was shot off his horse. We thought he was dead. We killed several Rebs and took a few prisoners. We looked for Shorey's body on the field after, but he was gone. We found out later he was grazed on the temple by a musket ball and got captured. He was exchanged at the end of the month, but we ain't seen him since."

"Bet y'all were happy he lived. Did you make Port Gibson? I've always wanted to see...."

Ainsworth cuts in. "The golden hand with the finger pointing to heaven on top of the Presbyterian Church?"

"Yeah, is it made of gold?"

"Naaah, the first pastor stabbed at the sky when he preached saying, "Good Christians ought to always keep their eyes on the Good Lord. People liked it so much they mounted a big gold painted wooden hand with that finger pointing to heaven instead of a cross.

"The next day, we led the column into Port Gibson. The Rebs kept takin' pot shots at us, and we'd stop to shoot back. We had one, hour long skirmish but had no losses. Just as we were leaving Port Gibson the next day, the Rebs rang a church bell in town and attacked. The Rebs came at us pretty hard at Bayou Pierre but a bunch of Negro soldiers surprised them."

"I bet they ran with their tails between their legs, seein' former slaves comin' after them."

"You know they did. The Rebs tried us again the next mornin', but we formed up like a real army, and within an hour, they'd skeedaddled out of there. Our boys are shooters. After they left, we found thirty Rebs who'd been shot right between the eyes."

"Damnation, what shootin'!" Reminds me of the Yanks we buried at Vicksburg during one of the truces. We found eighty caps with bullet holes through the front.

"Yep, a Reb prisoner told us General Wirt Adams himself led the attack.

He thought most of us had gone back to Vicksburg. He got confused and got his ass whooped."

Ainsworth takes a deep breath. "Tullos, have I bent your ear too long, or are you up for more?" He pulls out his pocket watch. "Damn, this thing usually keeps good time."

"It helps if you wind it, huh?"

"Another cup of hot coffee sounds good. Maybe you can find out what time it is when you get more coffee. If you want to hear the rest, I'm goin' nowhere."

CHAPTER 26

THE REST OF THE STORY

AN HOUR BEFORE MIDNIGHT, DECEMBER 11, 1864

If you want to know the whole Bible, you gotta read both Testaments.

I BRING US both another steaming cup of coffee. It breaks the chill on this breezy December night. A little sugar sure makes it go down better.

"And the rest?"

Ainsworth laughs. "I can't get it all in, but like my old preacher said back home, 'If you want to know the Bible, you gotta read both Testaments.'"

"Well, get to story tellin'. I only have an hour left."

He slurps his coffee too fast and spits it out. "Damn, burnt my tongue!"

"Cool air will bring it down, then you'll holler about it bein' too cold."

His coffee has cooled, and Ainsworth takes a long draw from his cup. "That's good. Thanks for puttin' in the sugar. It's just the way I like it. The next expedition took us into northeast Mississippi to keep General Forrest's cavalry tied up. Some of us worked on bridges crossin' the Tallahatchie. Some of the Rifles accompanied Colonel Winslow to guard the wagon train and artillery he was movin' to Holly Springs.

"Reb sharpshooters climbed trees at night and took pot shots at us when we started work every morning. A Reb would shoot, then holler, 'How's that Yank?' We'd yell back, 'Can't you do no better than that?' Then we got a spotter to watch for the smoke after a Reb shot. Soon as he fired, we'd throw lead at him. Then we'd yell, 'How'd you like that Reb?' He'd usually holler back, 'Damn, that's good shootin'!'"

Ainsworth hangs his head. "We lost George Reynolds there. He was just seventeen. Guerillas shot him and dragged him off like a deer carcass. They got his horse and equipment, his revolving rifle and accoutrements, and the small revolver his daddy gave him when he enlisted."

Ainsworth stomps his feet to shake off the cold. "Sure wish they'd let us have a fire, but that'd make us easy targets."

I throw up my hand for Ainsworth to be quiet. It's just a possum slipping through the woods.

Ainsworth throws a rock at the possum but misses. "Anyway, Smith sent the cavalry and the Rifles back to Holly Springs to repair telegraph lines. Talk about boring work, but at least we weren't gettin' shot at like at Tallahatchie Bridge. We finished the telegraph lines and headed back to Memphis with only three men from the Rifles missing. Not too bad for a month in the saddle."

Ainsworth drains the last of his cup and sets it on a fencepost. "By then we only had 367 men fit for duty. We've been in Memphis ever since. Word is we're headin' out on another mission into Mississippi somewhere, somethin' about the Mobile and Ohio Railroad."

I know exactly where we're going. "Tell me about Colonel Karge. He sounds like a pretty good commander."

"He is. He was in some revolution in Poland. They actually put a death sentence on him. He fled the country and became a teacher over here before he enlisted. He was wounded at Second Bull Run, but he carries on."

Ainsworth sighs. "Well, Tullos, that's all I got. But hey, the rest is yet to be written."

"What will you do with all those notes?"

He flips through the pages and stuffs the little book into his shirt. "I don't know, maybe write a book someday?"

I slap him on the shoulder as I turn to go back to camp. "Well, I'll be the first to buy a copy."

"Buy it? Hell, you're gonna be in it now."

"I don't need my name in a book. I just want to walk through life not hearin' my own footsteps."

Ainsworth scratches his ear. "I like that. What does it mean?"

"Just give it some thought, and we'll talk about it later. I'm goin' to bed. Stay alert."

He pulls his book back out and writes down my words. "I'll quote you on that."

I wave. I've made enough noise where I've walked, and it ain't all been good. I won't dwell on all that tonight. I know who I am and why I'm here.

CHAPTER *27*

THE COMMITTED AND THE PROMOTED

6:00 A.M., DECEMBER 12, 1864

*Some commit to stayin', some to leavin',
and some are promoted but don't know why.*

IN A WEEK, I have this mounted infantry way of going to war down pat. We're not cavalry in the truest sense of the word, but we travel by horse everywhere we go. We're trained to race into battle, dismount, form a line, and engage the enemy. The second part I have experienced before, but engaging the enemy on horseback is new.

Besides the Colts Revolving Rifles and Sharps carbines, some men also keep a shotgun strapped to their saddles for close fighting. My ten gauge shotgun would've come in handy. With the barrel sawed off, it'd be like a small double barreled cannon shooting grapeshot. Sarge told me I'd be issued a shotgun, but they must've been out of them.

WE HIT THE line for roll call early this morning. Things are stirring. We're told that soon we'll go on expedition. I'm excited to finally be made useful for this new cause. I think about the young Negro mother and her baby running through dark woods just trying to stay alive. And who does she run to? The blue, not the gray. That's one reason I'm here. The other? This damn war just needs to be over.

We're dismissed but told there'll be a formal dress parade at 5:00 p.m. sharp. The rest of the day we eat, care for our horses, tidy up our gear, make sure our weapons are in good order, and enjoy a few hours free in the afternoon. Early afternoon, Poole and I wander through other companies to see if we recognize anyone. Someone said there's a man from Choctaw County. I'd like to find him.

The Union army is a well-organized outfit. I like that, and I don't. I like that I don't have to decide what I'm doing next, where my food is coming from, or where I'll sleep at night. I don't like being cooped up with several hundred men, not being able to wander into the woods when I want to, and that I have to suffer through the boredom of doing the same thing most every day. At Vicksburg, at least there was some variety—building earthworks, serving as provost, manning the rifle pits... what am I thinking? This is much better.

Anyway, we'll head out somewhere soon.

I overhear a soldier in Company D telling a story. He laughs and yells, "That boy went thirty feet up in the air. I don't mean no harm, but I ain't never seen a darkie fly."

They all laugh. One asks, "Did he sprout wings?"

"If he did, they sprouted on his ankles like the Greek god, Mercury, haulin' ass to the Yankee lines." He doubles over, laughing.

"Poole, I need to speak with this man."

I warm my hands by the fire. "You saw the mine explode at the Third Louisiana Redan, sir?" He's a sergeant, so I salute.

He rubs his chin. "Yeah, I saw it from the artillery position close to Glass Bayou. I was visitin' another company in our regiment when it exploded."

"Company C, Turner's boys from Choctaw County, First Mississippi Light Artillery, right?"

"Sure was. How'd you know that?"

I breathe in deeply. "Sorry to bother you, sir, but my friend and I overheard your conversation, and well, long story short, my two brothers, Jasper and James Tullos, are in Company C, sir. They were there when the mine went off. You must've known 'em. I was with the Twenty-Seventh Louisiana stationed at the lunette next to the Stockade Redan."

"You don't say. I'm Joseph Sietzler. I was in the First Mississippi Light

Artillery, Company D. I knew Jasper and James, both good men. That Jimmy is a character, a bit of a daredevil, too."

I fidget trying to be respectful that I'm speaking with a sergeant. "I'm Private Lummy Tullos in Company C of the Rifles, sir."

"I can see you're just about to bust wantin' to ask if I know anythin' about them."

"Yes, sir. Y'all must've started callin' him Jimmy after we left Vicksburg. We never did at home." The sergeant shrugs. "I saw them before the parole but haven't heard from them since. They ain't too good about writin' home. Oh by the way, sorry, sir, this is Private Thomas Poole. He's in the same company with me and my best friend growin' up back in Choctaw County."

Seitzler shakes our hands. "Sit down before you wet your britches, and I'll tell you what I know. I know how important news about family is." He stares into the fire for a moment.

A private hands me and Poole a cup of coffee. Sergeant Seitzler takes another sip of his, looks around at the others, mostly new recruits and men from up north.

"The First Mississippi Light Artillery surrendered and paroled out like the rest of the army at Vicksburg. We marched to Enterprise, Mississippi, where two hundred and ninety one men of the regiment reported present in November. We were exchanged in February and reported to General Polk in Demopolis, Alabama. One company, I don't remember which, was sent off to serve as horse-drawn artillery with General Stephen D. Lee. The rest, men from Companies B, C, D, I, and K, were supposed to be sent to Mobile on provost duty. That's when I left. I'd had enough and never should've joined up with the Rebs in the first place. But everybody back home did, so I did too. And now look at me, a sergeant in the Union army."

I'm trying to be patient and hope he'll get to what I really want to know.

Seitzler lays his hand on my shoulder. "Yeah, I met your brothers. Didn't know them well, but they're good men. They'll finish the war true to the stars and bars. They were sent to Mobile with the rest of Company C. That's all I know. When we started south, I slipped away. I did hate runnin' out on them boys, but my heart just wouldn't let me stay."

"I do understand."

He asks, and I give him the short version of my story. We talk a couple of hours before we walk around the rest of Camp Karge.

I'm glad my brothers were all right, at least up until last May. "Thank you, Lord."

Poole adds, "Amen."

We return in time for dress parade at 5:00 p.m. Two of our officers are talking with Sarge when we get in line for inspection.

Sarge yells, "A-tten-*tion!* For those of you who are new to the First Mississippi Mounted Rifles, let me introduce you to first lieutenant for C Company, Thomas White, formerly of the Seventy-Seventh Illinois Infantry, and second lieutenant for C Company, Edward Holman. These men lead Company C. Give them a fine welcome."

We cheer three times as 1st Lieutenant White steps up. "Men of Company C, it is our privilege as well as our pleasure to lead you in the upcoming expedition. We will now inform you as to the nature of the task at hand. But first, will the following men step forward to be recognized? Sergeant McGugarty."

He steps forward and salutes. "Sir."

"Please have Corporals Hiram W. Goodwin and William C. Wheeler fall out front and center. Also, have Private Henry Hardy join them as well." They form a line in front of the lieutenants, salute, and stand at ease.

In a loud, deep voice, 1st Lieutenant White speaks, "In view of our upcoming expedition into hostile territory and for your continued dedication to excellent and meritorious service with the 1st Battalion Mississippi Mounted Rifles, by the authority given me by the President of these United States of America, Abraham Lincoln, I now confer upon you two men the rank of sergeant in Company C. Thank you for accepting the responsibility and privileges of this all important rank."

2nd Lieutenant Holman steps forward and presents them with their stripes. Goodwin and Wheeler salute and step back.

1st Lieutenant White then faces Private Hardy. "Sergeants Goodwin and Wheeler, it is always appreciated when men of age rise to meet the challenge of rank and duty. We thank you. But you would agree that when a young man distinguishes himself, he sets a course for greater things early in life that will bring great reward and satisfaction. Private Henry Hardy, for continued distinguished service with the 1st Battalion Mississippi Rifles, I confer upon you the rank of corporal."

2nd Lieutenant Holman hands Hardy his stripes, and he steps back in line. 1st Lieutenant White raises his hand, and we give three cheers.

I remember Mr. Wiley back in Winn Parish telling me before I left to enlist in the Confederate Army, "Do nothin' to make yourself stand out too much. That'll get you a medal and a coffin. Just do your job, and if you distinguish yourself, they'll let you know." I'm happy for them but happier to be just a buck private.

1st Lieutenant White holds up his hand to quiet us down. "Now, for a bit of unpleasant business. Lieutenant Holman."

Holman steps up and strikes a pose. "Sir." He's been to school somewhere.

In a shrill voice that hurts the ears, Holman says, "Men, I have been asked to present to you the standing of the First Battalion Mississippi Mounted Rifles. Currently, we have three hundred fifty men commanded by fourteen officers. In the first year of this regiment, over six hundred men enlisted for duty, eleven of which have been captured, five remain missing, fifty-four died, sixteen have been discharged, nine are in Irving Block Prison, and sadly, over one hundred and sixty have deserted. It is of this last group I need to comment."

Men shift around looking at each other.

Sarge yells, "Attention in the ranks!"

The men stiffen up and stop their chatter.

Holman reads from a small piece of paper. "It has come to our attention that Private Peter Thompson forsook his oath and deserted this camp in the wee morning hours of this day absconding with...." He describes what all was taken.

Poole whispers, "Ab- what"

"It means ran off with."

Poole snickers. "Hell, why don't he just say that?"

I elbow him to shut up.

Holman continues. "His home being just across the river in Crittenden County, I suggest that Private Thompson do his best to leave this part of the country for some time or he soon will become the newest inmate at Irving Block Prison. And besides this disgrace, his life will soon become extremely unpleasant. You can count on that."

Holman steps back, and Sarge steps up. *"Attention!"*

A bearded general with no mustache arrives. He's accompanied by several officers and a couple of newspapermen.

Lieutenant White announces, "Men, I have the pleasure of introducing to you our beloved General Benjamin Grierson of great fame due to his heroic and highly successful, well-executed raid from La Grange, Tennessee to Baton Rouge during the Vicksburg campaign. He now...."

Grierson holds up his hand. "Enough of the horseshit, Lieutenant. These men don't care about all that. They just want to know what's comin' next." I like Grierson already.

White steps back, embarrassed. It's a general's prerogative to make his junior officers look like jackasses if he wants to, just like the lieutenants and sergeants who wreak havoc on the enlisted men. I just keep my head down and mouth shut.

Grierson asks, "Am I right, men?" We cheer, but Grierson throws up his hands to quiet us down. "I want to visit as many of the companies in this fine battalion as I can to personally thank you for volunteering, especially you men who once fought for the gray and realize your grave mistake."

We laugh, and he continues. "It cannot be easy fighting in your own home state, possibly against neighbors you once farmed alongside or cousins you used to fish with, maybe parents of sweethearts you left behind. At any rate, I'm proud to have you with us, no matter what other officers have said about the First Battalion Mississippi Mounted Rifles. Hell, what do they know?"

We cheer again. Sarge yells, "Soldiers! Present *arms!*" We stand even straighter and hold our weapons out before us as the general walks the line. It's interesting how junior officers do everything they can to impress generals but the enlisted men like Sarge just do their jobs.

Poole shakes as General Grierson walks closer. Grierson looks each man in the eye on the front line, passing Poole and me, as he did the others. Poole sighs, and Grierson turns on a dime.

"Private, are you scared?"

Poole stutters, "Uh, no, uh, no, sir! Just ain't never been this close to a general before, sir."

Grierson laughs. "You were shaking as I walked by, then I heard your sigh of relief. Have no fear here, son. We're on the same side. I ain't your momma or your daddy, but I will do everything I can to get your ass back home to them in one piece quick as I can. How's that?"

"Yes, sir, better'n biscuits and gravy, sir."

Grierson turns to me. "What about you, son? You scared?"

"Hell, no, sir, I ain't scared. My daddy beat the fear out of me, and I'm ready to do the same to anybody you put in front of me. I'm ready to get in this thing and get it over with so I can get back to my farmin' in Choctaw County, sir."

Grierson grins and steps back so he doesn't have to look up to see my eyes. "I bet you are, you long legged, ridge runnin' son of a...."

He catches himself and laughs. "You men hear that? Get in this thing, get it over with, and get back to his farming. That's why you men are here. I expect every one of you to follow this man's lead."

The men bark out a collective, "Yes, sir."

Grierson turns back to me. "You've been in the presence of a general before, haven't you?"

"Yes, sir, in Vicksburg. I was there May of '62 'til the surrender, sorry to say, wearin' gray."

Grierson looks me dead in the eye. "Don't ever apologize, son, for doin' what you think is right at the time. Some of the best men in this war lie buried in those hills. You may believe you were wrong then, but it was with sincerity of heart. That's why you're here now. You're a man unafraid to search his heart. I like that."

Grierson grins. "Who'd you see, son?"

I kick at the ground. "General Pemberton, of course, a couple of times, but in December of '62, President Jefferson Davis and General Joseph

Johnston inspected our regiment down by the river landing. They were the most famous. Oh, yeah, sir, General Grant spoke to us when we surrendered and marched."

"And famous they are. We sure kept ole Pemberton worried and Joe guessing with that fool raid we made. Too bad we didn't catch ole hawk-nosed Davis himself! What regiment were you with, son?"

"The Twenty-Seventh Louisiana Volunteer Infantry with the Winn Rebels out of Winnfield, Louisiana."

Grierson shakes his head. "Stockade Redan and the lunette next to it?" I nod. "Terrible place. Sherman told us he got a big surprise coming down Graveyard Road when you men didn't just up and run. He should've known better. Terrible losses. Sorry you boys had to go through that, but you did as ordered. Think you can do that now wearing the blue suit, son?"

This is my chance to truly speak my soul. "Sir, if it costs me my life, I want that twentieth star representin' Mississippi back on the right flag, the Union flag. For good, sir."

Grierson rubs his beard. "Choctaw County?" I nod. "So you know where Bankston is?"

"I do, sir. Poole and me here both call it our hometown."

Grierson smiles. "Bet you boys know every deer trail and woodcutter's lane in the county."

"Yes, sir."

Grierson barks, "Lieutenant White."

He steps up quickly. "Sir!"

"Take note these two men are from Choctaw County and remember to bring them up when we hold briefing next week for the upcoming mission."

Poole and I look at each other knowing exactly what he's talking about.

Grierson pats me on the shoulder and moves on down the line. "Now you can be scared. I'll see you both shortly. Stay sharp and committed."

General Grierson finishes his brief inspection and hurries away to the next company. He reminds me of Colonel Shoup at Vicksburg. Grierson's right, too many good men lie buried in the hallowed grounds of Vicksburg. All the more reason for me to be here, wearing the blue suit.

1st Lieutenant White briefs us on the upcoming mission. We'll destroy the Mobile and Ohio Railroad which still serves the Confederate Army. We leave December 21, expecting to return sometime after New Year's Day. We're restricted to camp, so word of the mission stays a secret.

Maybe 1865 will be a better year.

Maybe the war will end, and I can go home.

CHAPTER 28

MOUNTED INFANTRY

DECEMBER 13-19, 1864

Never knew a horse could be a man's best friend.

FOR A WEEK, we train and tidy up camp. The Yanks keep things looking good and professional—a far cry from the rifle pits in Vicksburg. Sometimes it was all I could do to keep my head up ready to fight. What a filthy mess that was. It's a wonder we all didn't die of disease, if not by shell or sniper's bullet. We all died a little in that siege. Camp Karge is different.

The food is good, camp is clean, discipline's better, medical attention is available, and the men know they're going to win. But they also know they may not make it home. I believe I will. I don't deserve to live any more than the next man. I just feel in my soul that the Lord has something for me before I leave this world. I'm hoping it involves a blue skirt with a sack full of children down in Vicksburg. Anyway, if this is army life, then what I had as a Reb was hell.

Sarge barks, "Listen up! Your horse is your best friend next to your weapon. Treat 'em both like a sweetheart. Your horse and your rifle will get you back home to your girls."

Company C raises a collective, "Yes, sir."

Sarge stands on a barrel. "You old heads know the drill. You new recruits heard this when you first arrived. I want no mistakes on this expedition. You are not cavalry, though you may fight on horseback. This week you'll learn how to travel as a unit. You are mounted infantry. You travel by horseback or mule, arrive at the battle, dismount, form a line, and fight as an infantry unit. Under no circumstances do you charge on horseback unless so ordered. You plug gaps, engage guerilals, and fight regulars wherever you meet them. You will scout, forage, and participate in raiding expeditions. Is that clear?"

We stand at attention.

"I said, is that clear?"

"Yes, sir, Sergeant McGugarty!"

"At ease in the ranks. Get your breakfast, tidy up your tent, and tend to your horses. Drill and tactics begin in thirty minutes! Di-i-ismissed."

Sarge looks up in the sky, and a raindrop hits him square in the eye. The pitter patter of big raindrops hit the hard ground.

"Go to your tents. I'll call when the rain stops."

We choke down bacon and bread with steaming hot cups of coffee. We straighten up our tents in case there's an inspection. The rain doesn't let up. In fact, it pours.

Seneca finishes first and leans on the tent pole at the opening. "Did y'all know the First Mississippi Mounted Rifles is the only white Yankee battalion made of Mississippi men? Henry Hardy, who made sergeant, said only a hundred men from the state enlisted. I can't say anything. I'm from Winn Parish, Louisiana."

Poole elbows me. "You gonna tell him you used to live there? He'll figure out what you did soon enough."

"Yeah, just holdin' off until I'm ready to dredge up old memories, good and bad."

The rain lets up long enough that we currycomb our horses while the farrier spreads out hay and fills the water troughs. We fall out for drill and tactics, but it starts to rain again.

Sarge marches over, his rain slicker pulled tight. Corporal Henry Hardy follows him and gives the order, "In fifteen minutes, Lieutenant Holman will start drill and tactics. Have your slickers ready in case the rain returns."

Men light up smokes or stuff plugs of tobacco in their mouths. Corporal Hardy visits each gathering of men, chatting and laughing. He wants the men to know that though he carries two stripes, he's still just a man trying to get back home alive.

He stops to pat my horse on the neck. "You've got a good one here, Private Tullos. She's a big joker."

"Yes, sir, a good one so far. I picked a tall one for my long legs. I like her color. Reminds me of good shoe leather."

He scratches Cloud's ears. "Wouldn't do to send her to the tanner. No, sir. She'll serve the army much better than being made into a razor strap or a pair of boots."

I look up from checking a horseshoe. "You know your leather, sir?"

"Before the war, I was a shoemaker. It's not nearly as exciting as this, but it's a living."

"Well, you might be interested to know that I named my horse after my great, great grandfather from Scotland named Cloud back in 1665. He was a tanner and a shoemaker, too."

"Is that right?"

"Yes, sir. He started as an indentured servant and worked his way free to become a cobbler. Did very well and took on apprentices, too. I had an uncle who worked in the tannery at Bankston and sometimes in the shoe factory there."

Corporal Hardy and I chat, but he says nothing about the upcoming raid that will include a fiery visit to the tannery and shoe factory at Bankston. Ainsworth and Seneca have been listening as they finish caring for their horses. Hardy moves to the next bunch of men.

I'm in a talkative mood. "Seneca, I lived in Winn Parish not long ago. I thought you might like to know that."

Seneca starts shaking. "Tell the truth and shame the devil. You from back home, really? Where about?"

I give him the short version about my life there. I don't tell him about Susannah, but I do talk about working with Mr. Gilmore and Ben.

"We have two hundred forty acres near Sikes. We do pretty well."

Sikes, close to where Ben and Mr. Gilmore were killed and where Dorcas, Freddy, and the kids live. I don't want to talk about that just yet.

He rubs his chin. "Since the war started, nobody has any money. Havin' land, folks can survive. We sold corn and hogs, butter and ducks for the things we needed."

I don't want any more talk about Sikes. "Did you ever go to Davis's store in Winfield?"

"Only at Christmastime with my pa. I liked that store, except Missus Davis wasn't very nice."

"I worked there. Missus Davis, she's a sweet soul who just doesn't know how to show it."

"Then I saw you. We made catalog orders and got sweets to celebrate Jesus's birthday."

"If you came Christmas week of '62, I was there."

"Ain't it a small world?" I nod. "I liked Mistuh Wiley who lived across the street. He told the best stories out on his porch. I'd give him lemon drops while he talked."

"Yeah, I was with him when he died."

Seneca's eyes widen. *"That's* where I know you. You're Lummy Tullos! You did—"

"Did Mistuh Wiley's funeral. I was proud to help that old soldier go home. He was like a father to me."

"My father fought in the small skirmish called the Battle of Sikes, when the secessionist and pro-Union folks clashed. That's why I joined up. Pa was wounded fighting to free the Negroes."

He puts his hand over his mouth. "You're Lummy Tullos."

"You said that already, bucket head."

"No, you're the Lummy Tullos who killed Dawg Smith and his gang."

Poole and Ainsworth stop what they're doing and stare at me with jaws dropped.

"Well, I didn't do it by myself, you see I...."

Poole asks, "Did what?" He feigns ignorance to keep Seneca from asking more questions. It doesn't work. Seneca shivers like a kid opening a gift on Christmas morning.

"I can't believe it. You're him. Will you tell me what happened?"

Sarge yells "Time for drill."

I punch Seneca. "Maybe later."

I'll tell him at the right time. Maybe it'll stir the anger I'll need to survive this raid. I get in line, shoulder my weapon, and straighten my posture. I feel Seneca's eyes on me, like a kid who's met the President.

CHAPTER 29

A MAIL CALL THAT CALLS ME OUT

EARLY EVENING, DECEMBER 19, 1864

Hearin' from home brings it closer and a deep longing to be there.

THE RAIN HASN'T let up, making roads into rivers of mud. It's the worst some have ever seen.

Poole laughs. "Maybe we should build an ark?"

I smile but grumble inside that we can't seem to get dry, even in our tents. But still, we train.

When drill and tactics are over, I ease away from the crowd. I don't want to talk about Winn Parish with Seneca right now.

A clerk yells, "Mail call!" He drags several bags to the end of a covered wagon to call names and keep letters and packages dry.

I've received no mail since I left home, but I haven't been gone two weeks. As Granny Thankful used to say, when it rains it pours. The mail clerk rattles off a list starting with the As. Finally, he gets to the Ts.

"Tullos!" The mail clerk, a small beady-eyed but friendly man, laughs, "Dang boy, who are you sweet on back home?" He holds one of my two letters to his nose and breathes in deeply. "Ahh, this reminds me of my pretty wife back home."

I snatch the letters from his hand jokingly. "You better have saved some of that sweet smellin' perfume for me or you won't make it home to your pretty wife." The clerk chuckles.

Poole elbows me as he opens a letter from his folks in Choctaw County. "Bet that rosy fragrance floated all the way up here from Vicksburg."

I can't help but grin as I put Martha's letter inside my shirt. "Damn straight, son. I'm savin' it for later when you buzzards ain't hangin' around."

He slaps me on the back, happy that I've heard from her. Seneca and Ainsworth wander over with their mail in hand.

"Let's share our letters when we sit down to eat. What do you say?"

I open the other letter from Ma, careful to not tear the pages. Mary has the prettiest handwriting. This reminds me of those few precious times when we shared letters during the siege. I laid in my bombproof alone many times reading those letters over and over. Ma's letters kept me sane, especially after Susannah died. I get a sick feeling in my stomach remembering the letters about my brother, Amariah, and his wife's death. I shudder, thinking about when I read Susannah had died. I hold the opened letter for a moment. Finally, I stare down at the page. I read it silently first, in case there's news of a private nature. For some reason, I feel there will be bad news.

Bankston, Mississippi December 5, 1864
Dearest Lummy,

I hope this letter finds you well and in good spirits. Everyone here is doing well. Elihu manages the farm with Seth's help. They work so well together and sing to us every night. It's always a treat and gives us hope for better days when you come home after the war. Mary and Emaline continue their schooling. Mary continues to teach Seth the three "Rs."

We're doing fine with a good harvest and the help from Uncle Rube. Thanks again for taking care of the family. Not much has happened here since you left. We still hide Seth when anyone comes around. People know we don't have the means to keep a slave, so he hides in the barn.

I have some unpleasant news, son. Your brother, George Washington, is dead. They posted his name on the Post Office wall in Bankston with others of the 15th Mississippi Infantry who died near Nashville. He was killed November 30, right before you left. That's two of my boys who gave their lives for a lost cause. My heart is broken. His wife Sarah is inconsolable. I'm not sure she will survive the loss. I'm not sure I will.

Please lift up Jasper and James to the Lord. I haven't heard from them in some time now. Confederate mail doesn't run very often. Elihu caught a mail rider on his way out of Bankston so no one would know this letter was addressed to you.

I'm sorry to end this letter on such a sad note, son, but know that I love you. I pray for you every night and look down the road everyday expecting to see you. Mary and Emaline say hello as do Elihu and Seth. Take good care of yourself son.

Your loving Ma

I walk away without a word. No one says anything. They know what it means.

I'm stunned that my brother, George, is dead. That news cuts to the bone. I find little solace that he died for his beliefs. Beliefs are luxuries held by men who do little to no fighting in this war but are all too happy to spit out theirs on men who have no choice but to fight. When this is done, those men will rock back in their chairs, sipping fine brandy by warm fires with grandchildren playing at their feet, while my two brothers lie dead in the cold ground. They never will have grandchildren to remember them.

I look up into the sky. "Lord, why?" I drop my head and whisper, "Lord, I know why."

I walk through camp into a field that lays unbroken for planting. Grass and briars have taken over the hard clods. That's my life. I've walked on too many clods of hardness and received too many scratches busting through life's briars to find peace. I breathe in the fresh air. A sweet odor captures my attention. I reach inside my shirt for Martha's letter.

I draw in the flowery fragrance and hold it in. I sit under an oak tree and open the letter. She wrote this the same day I left for Memphis. The letter and poem I mailed in Memphis must be in her hands by now. They passed each other on the way to their destinations. I fidget like a schoolboy just before the last day of class ends for summer break.

Vicksburg Mississippi December 3, 1864

My Dear Columbus,

I hope the Lord has kept you well and safe from all harm. He cares for His own, but please do your part to remain safe. This must seem forward of me to write only knowing you for such a short time. But I feel in my heart that the few moments that passed between us spoke eternal volumes that could fill many books. I want you to know my heart. Columbus, I'm no spring chicken anymore, but I have a heart full of love that wants to be shared with the man God sends me. I will be so bold as to say, I believe that man is you.

You possess a strength shaped by difficult times with hard men. But I also see kindness and gentleness that wants peace to reign in your soul. We have both suffered terrible loss. You more than me, but our wounds can be healed in new found love. Taking on four children not your own is a tall order for any man. But please believe, they are good and respectful, willing to be taught. I have spoken to them about you. Healing will come to their tender hearts about their father in time. It is a hard thing when we experience the pain this world so gladly offers, but children suffer even more. There, I have laid out my intentions for you to consider. I will love you Columbus Nathan Tullos for the rest of my life. I will comfort and care for you as I believe you would me. I hope to hear from you soon. I've opened my heart for you to see. Don't let the wind take it away.

With deep affection and growing love, Martha Brock

I lay the letter on the log where I sit with my eyes filled with tears. I didn't expect Martha to be so free with her feelings. I don't know why. I should have. I feel exactly the same. Warmth falls over me like soothing hot bathwater and hope of new life chases George's death into the shadows for a moment.

My friend Old Bart once told me to hold onto Susannah until the Lord brought another. "When that happens, Susannah will be the first to bless it."

The Lord has sent *another.* She just arrived in my heart.

CHAPTER 30

LETTERS, BITTER AND SWEET

JUST AFTER DARK, DECEMBER 19, 1864

Some say no news is good news. Not today.

HOW DO I respond to Martha's letter? She wants us to consider marriage. I meant what I said in the letter and poem. She understands my intentions and I hers. It's strange how this war has made time precious and decisions easier.

George's face takes my thoughts. Then his sweet wife, Sarah, appears. Too much conflict in one moment—a dead brother leaving a widow behind at the same time I'm offered a new opportunity at being a husband and new father. It reminds me of the day I found out Susannah was dead and my brothers, Jasper and James, showing up almost in the same moment. My heart beats like a locomotive engine pumping her wheels to get started on the tracks. My heart aches for George and Sarah. I push death and sorrow from my mind. My heart thumps for Martha like a train engine running full steam down the tracks.

I go back over to where Poole, Seneca, and Ainsworth read their letters aloud. My turn comes. I announce that I'll read one of two letters and maybe give a hint about the second. I prepare the men for the bad news I received from Ma.

Poole puts his arm on my shoulder. "I remember George to be a good man, quiet and headstrong because of your daddy but determined to make his mark in this world. He was one of the first to sign up with the Choctaw Guards in Bankston, June of '61, ready to march and fight. I'm sorry, Lummy. George was as good a man as there is."

I grind my teeth. "It's a damn shame he'll be under the dirt on some lonesome battlefield soon to be forgotten. Hell, there won't even be markers for Reb soldiers when the Yankees win this thing." No one says anything.

Poole starts "Amazing Grace," and men at other campfires join in. I'm not the only one who received unwanted news of the loss of loved ones. I want to scream, but my soul calms, knowing I'm in the right place doing the right thing.

Poole tries to lighten the mood. "I want to hear what's in that other letter if it ain't too sticky from all the honey dripping off of it. I bet it could cover Company C's entire ration of biscuits in the morning."

I slap him across the chest. "I ain't readin' it, but I will announce that I do believe I have begun to court one, Miss Martha Brock, late of St. Louis but now residin' in Vicksburg, Missip."

Poole's jaw drops. "Well slap me sideways and kiss your granny. You didn't waste no time, did you, hound dog?"

Seneca and Ainsworth shake my hand and wish me well.

Poole shoulder hugs me. "No better man deserves such a blessin'. You got somethin' more to pray about than just keepin' our asses alive."

I take a deep draw of the perfumed letter. "I sure as hell do."

CHAPTER 31

A MISSION THAT TAKES ME HOME BUT NOT FOR GOOD

MORNING, DECEMBER 20, 1864

Sometimes you gotta go around the world just to get back home.

I SLEEP WELL until just after midnight. Life, good and bad, always seems to leave a bittersweet taste in my mouth like they're stuck together and can't be separated. I can't have one without the other—a hard-ass pa but a loving mother, a good older brother, Elihu, but not so in Ben. The same day I'm reunited with my brothers, Jasper and James, I find out Susannah is dead. Why can't things just be sweet for a little while? Why not just good with no bad? I'm whining now. Why ain't the question. How I handle it, is.

The morning sun breaks through the trees in the east as I finish my last sip of coffee grown cold. Sarge marches over to our campfire. Poole and I stand up. Seneca and Ainsworth come out of our tent, and we stand at attention.

"At ease, men. Tullos and Poole, come with me." I look at Seneca and Ainsworth. They shrug their shoulders.

Sarge whispers on our way to brigade headquarters. "General Grierson requested you two himself. I told you about this when we started out. You both know it involves Bankston. The brass didn't tell General Grierson about you. They let him size you two up himself. It worked."

"Yes, sir."

"Just agree to follow orders."

We whisper, "We will."

Headquarters is at full buzz for such an early hour. We salute 1st Lieutenant White who nods as we wait to enter General Grierson's tent. White is from Mississippi and proud of our battalion.

"Stand tall, speak little, and show enthusiasm when General Grierson gives you orders."

We ease into the smoky tent room filled with officers of various ranks.

Lieutenant barks, "A-tten-tion!"

Poole and I stiffen up with our arms straight down the seam of our pants as Grierson enters with a tin cup of coffee.

Sarge announces, "Privates Poole and Tullos at your service, sir."

Grierson sips his coffee, staring at us. "At ease, boys. I have just one question for you. Is it true what Sergeant McGugarty just said, that you are at my service?"

Poole looks at me to answer. "Yes, sir, that's why we're here."

Grierson stroked his beard, then scratched where his mustache would be, but he has none. A wiry built man nearly forty with deep-set serious eyes, Grierson stands six feet. Sherman recommended him to General Grant as the best cavalry officer he had. Grierson proved true, chasing General Van Dorn after he destroyed Grant's million dollar supply depot in Holly Springs back in '62. But it was that 600-mile wild ride with 1700 cavalrymen from La Grange, Tennessee to Baton Rouge that got everyone's attention.

In less than two weeks, Grierson wreaked havoc on railroad and telegraph lines, burning supply depots along the way. He confused our General Pemberton long enough for Grant to cross the Mississippi River without firing a shot on his way to Vicksburg. I'm in the presence of a fighting man's General. I'm in the right place to do the right thing.

"You both are from Mississippi, correct?" We nod. "Choctaw County?"

Poole's finds the courage to speak. "All of our lives, sir."

"You men plan to go back when this war is over?"

"Yes, sir."

Grierson lights a cigar. "I don't agree with Lieutenant Noyes's report that the First Mississippi Mounted Rifles amount to little. He's a little man making big judgments about men he's never seen and never will, hiding behind a wooden desk. I met him once. Spit and polish but full of horse shit, excusing my saloon language."

Poole and I snicker. Sarge gives us a look, and we quiet down. "Thank you, sir. These two men will serve you well in the upcoming expedition."

Grierson hasn't taken his eyes off me. "I do believe they will, Sergeant."

I don't break eye contact.

Grierson smiles and unfolds a map. "Here's the deal. You'll ride with your company at first. Then you'll be attached to the 4th Iowa Cavalry with Captain Warren Beckwith once we get past Egypt Station. You'll serve as scouts for a small raiding party to your hometown of Bankston. Show them the best way to get there safely and where to set the fires to burn the town. Wesson's stepped up his efforts to help General Hood. That must stop. We've destroyed the other manufactories in this state which leaves only Bankston. Will you men commit to doing that?"

I fidget around and kick the dirt. "Meaning no harm, sir, but may I?"

"Ask away, Private Tullos. I know what I'm asking of you isn't easy."

"I volunteered for this because it's the right thing to do. Is this a Sherman raid to burn everything, take everything, and leave the people in worse shape than they already are? I know what's goin' on. I worked with Mistuh Dotson who provided the information about Wesson before I joined up with the Rifles. I'm just askin' if we can only take down the factories and mills and bring no harm to the good folks. There's many who'll welcome your efforts and are willin' to pay the price of losin' their jobs to help put Mississippi's star back on the right flag, sir."

Grierson stands up. "What did you just say, Private?"

I look at Sarge and then around the room, "You mean about the folks welcomin' your efforts?"

"No, son, about the star. I heard that somewhere once before."

I stand straight and in my best English, "That was me in the parade line, sir, when you inspected Company C of the 1st Mississippi Mounted Rifles, sir. I told you that I'm fightin' with you to put the star representin' Mississippi back on the Union flag where it started out and for me will always be."

I'm getting loud, and Sarge signals me to lower my volume.

"Leave him be, Sergeant. We need more passion in this man's army." Grierson walks around the room. "Well said, Private. You're right on target. I order you and Private Poole to scout for the 4th Iowa Cavalry and burn the factories and mills at Bankston in the upcoming raid. Can you get us in and out to the least amount of damage to civilians and protect our men? You know that Wesson has a small army with a couple of cannons?"

Poole braves a word. "They're mostly old men and wastrels, sir."

"Well, let's just hope he decides not to use them."

I point at Bankston on the map. "Sir, if we take this road and catch them at night, maybe New Year's Eve around midnight, we'll surprise them and be gone before they get out of bed."

"Sounds like a good plan, Private. 1st Lieutenant White, take note of that suggestion and get these men ready for the march."

Poole salutes. "Thank you, sir, proud to serve."

Sarge barks, "A-tten-tion!"

We salute and leave the tent. I overhear Grierson say as we leave, "Can we pull that off, Major? We'll keep our word not to harm civilians or their property, but so help me God, if Wesson brings out his cannons, I'll blow him and his wastrels all the way to hell."

I look at Poole. "What did I just agree to back there?"

Poole shivers in the cold. "Givin' up livin' in Choctaw County ever again, that's for sure."

Sarge asks, "Can you boys do this? You know if it goes sour, and it can in a heartbeat, he'll burn the town to the ground and keep ridin'."

Poole paws at the mud with his boot. "You knew they could burn the whole town, sir?"

I take a deep breath. "Why didn't you tell us it was a possibility he might burn the whole town?"

Sarge lays his hands on our shoulders. "I knew you wouldn't have come."

My face is hot. They both wait me out.

I spit. "Nobody said anythin' about burnin' down the whole damn place."

"We didn't know that for certain until it was reported by your man, Dotson, that Wesson took orders from President Davis to send cloth, blankets, boots, and flour to General Hood. He's supposed to have it ready within the month. That's why we're going now."

It hits me what I just agreed to in Grierson's tent. "You realize that burnin' the mills and factories at Bankston will kill any hope of Choctaw County being able to survive after the war?"

"I also know if those supplies get to Hood, it'll extend the war another six months or more. Wesson will keep producin' what Hood needs to keep his army goin'." Sarge takes my arm. "We've got to stop him. And we need you to get us there."

Poole whispers, "Nobody knows McCurtain Creek swamp like you do, Lummy. Hell, we all fished and hunted there when we were kids, but you told me you lived there with Dan Creekwater. You know all the best ways to get in and out of Bankston."

I clench my teeth. "A lot of people depend on Bankston for their livin'. Wesson employs over five hundred people."

"I told you about all of this at the hotel in Bankston. Most of the workers were pressed into service, like your man, Dotson, and gettin' paid worthless Confederate dollars for their trouble."

I can't argue with that. It's true. "Poole, my Uncle Burrell worked in the tannery down by the creek below town."

Poole kicks the dust. "And my pa still works in the flour mill, and Ma was pressed into service back in July to make cloth. You know how her hands don't work so good with the rheumatoid. When Dotson told them Wesson went back to makin' stuff for the Reb Army, they said I needed to do my part. I couldn't go it alone, not for what they asked me to do. I knew I didn't have to, brother. I knew you would come with me."

I poke the fire with a stick. "Just the mills and factories?" Sarge nods. "No burnin' civilian property, no killin' for no reason?" He nods twice. "Damn, I hate this."

He removes his hat to scratch his balding head. "Me too, son. We'll honor your request as best we can. This is no Sherman march. Grierson calls it surgery—cutting out the bad and leaving the rest alone. Bankston won't be the only place we hit. If we can bring the Rebs to their knees, then maybe we can start closin' the curtains on this awful play."

I straighten my uniform. "I told you at the parole in Vicksburg I wanted to help end this war. I never thought it would mean leadin' a raid on my home. Bankston's just a mile from our farm as the crow flies."

Poole hangs his head. "You're right."

I have to get it all out. I glare at him. "You know I've got family close by, boy."

He doesn't move.

Sarge smiles solemnly. "Yeah, we both know. But you didn't know this war would take another one of your brothers either, did you?"

"If you was any other man, I'd hit you in the mouth."

"Son, Poole told me about your brother, George, gettin' killed at Franklin. He was in General Hood's army. I'm sorry he was killed." Sarge stops. He knows I've already figured out the rest. I just need some time.

The war has come to this—my hometown. Good people caught between doing the right thing and trying to survive in a war they didn't start. So herein lies the next big test of my life. Hurt the people I grew up with and care for so that in the long run they might be saved.

I ponder the idea and remember the oath I took at Vicksburg. I did sign my enlistment papers to faithfully serve these United States. I also knew this was part of the deal.

Sarge hands me a piece of cloth. I unroll the small Union flag. "It's the newest one with thirty-five stars. Part of Virginia became a new state in the Union not long ago."

Poole feels the cloth. "Imagine that, they done seceded from the secesh in Richmond."

"A little old lady handed me this one at one of our parade marches."

I point to the stars. "Which one is it?"

He points at the twentieth star representing Mississippi.

"They never took it off, did they?"

"Nope."

Poole takes the little flag. "Some of us never really left."

I take a deep breath. "Burn only the factories and mills and leave civilians be? How can Grierson promise that?"

"He can't. That's why he has you and Poole. You just have to make sure they get in and out of Bankston and do it right, son."

I pull my hat down and straighten my sabre. "All right, let's do what's got to be done and get it the hell over with."

CHAPTER 32

TRAVELING LIGHT

6:45 A.M., DECEMBER 21, 1864

Cleaning up the rest of the world starts at home.

A SLIGHT, BUT very cold, breeze rustles through empty limbs of great oaks waiting for the first rays of light to warm the earth. The constant rain has turned to sleet and snow, and the roads have frozen. The order is given for the expedition to march.

Our horses stamp their hooves and snort, sensing our excitement and uneasiness. For now, Poole and I ride column with the eighty-four men and four officers of the 1st Mississippi Mounted Rifles. I'm glad Company C was ordered to come along. Ainsworth and Seneca at my back eases some of my concern. Still, I have mixed emotions about doing this.

Poole leans over. "You gotta adjust your feelings to the facts, boy. We're movin' out, and you're comin'."

Today I take the first steps to invade my own home state—steps leading home, for good.

We leave White Station traveling light. No artillery, no supply wagons— just 28 day's rations on mules and what each man can carry for himself. I take extra ammunition for my pistol and shells for my Sharps carbine.

I grip my rifle and feel for my pistol. The new sabre bounces on my hip. I'm anxious. I sense the coming fray. I'll do well if I keep my head, heart, and soul together. I know what I'm capable of doing. My close comrades in the 1st Mississippi Mounted Rifles do too. Seneca has spread the word about what we did in Winn Parish. I wish he hadn't done that.

Our battalion is looked down upon by the cavalry units we follow. Some pissant Lieutenant Henry Noyes wrote to a Major Beaumont that as far as he is concerned the 1st Mississippi Mounted Rifles amount to but little. Other officers call us a failed experiment, but they weren't there when our battalion engaged the enemy at Grand Gulf and Port Gibson. Hell, what do they know? Arm chair soldiers are just bullies with pens. They should trade those pens for fists. We'd change their minds.

Though some of us have more experience than the officers, we don't expect much action. They won't put us in the heat of battle. Maybe they don't trust us because some of us are Mississippians and ex-Confederates. I'd think that after the regiment proved itself in battle, doubts would have been laid to rest. But with all the desertions, we must be a sight hardly worth seeing to officers who command full regiments. We'll just have to prove them wrong.

At 7:00 a.m. sharp, the bugle blares. *"Move out!"* 1,166 men of the 3500 total force move out on Colonel Joseph Karge's command—1,101 effectives with sixty-five men to manage a pack train of ninety animals bearing supplies and ammunition. The 7th Indiana, 4th Missouri, 2nd New Jersey Cavalries, and the Rifles take State Line Road to Collierville. We catch up to the First Brigade and go into camp together three miles east of the town.

Poole is a like a kid at a circus. "I've never seen so many men on horses. It's a sight."

Night passes quickly once we care for the horses and lay out bedrolls. Ainsworth and Seneca catch the first watch for Company C, and then Poole and I relieve them at midnight until morning. We won't sleep much until we get back to Memphis.

We leave before daylight. At 2:00 p.m., our column turns on Early Grove Road. Colonel Karge sends Captain Hencke ahead with his 4th Missouri Cavalry to guard the Wolf River at Moscow. We catch them at sunset but go seven miles further to camp southwest of La Grange. We made only nineteen miles today but for good reason.

Late afternoon, Sarge barrels down the line looking for Poole and me. "Want to get your feet wet and your hands dirty?"

Poole says, "Hell, yeah." We follow Sarge with five other men from Company C. It's my first opportunity for action as a private in the Union Army. My heart beats like a battle drum.

We rein up near an old farm house, dismount, and ready our weapons. Sarge splits me and Poole up. "Maybe only one of you'll get killed if they go to shootin'."

We ease up to the batten board shack on hands and knees. I slip up close to the only window and listen. Men whisper plans on how to blow the bridge at Moscow. They don't know we've already secured it. Maybe we can save these men's lives if they come along peaceably.

Sarge calls call out to the Rebels. "Give it up, boys, we gotcha surrounded!" They stop talking.

Two Rebs fire just above my head, but Sarge signals our men to hold our fire. He nods, hoping my thick southern accent might calm these men down.

"Ain't no call for all that, dammit! There ain't no way out except the front door if you want to live. We can smoke your asses out or let you come out like gentlemen who've fought well but know when to quit. Personally, I'd rather you give up, and we'll take you fightin' men back to camp. We've got good food and warm fires. What do you say?"

We give them time to think it over.

Finally, a hoarse voice barks out, "You ain't gonna shoot us, is you?"

"God as my judge, we won't. Makes no sense you men dyin' for nothin'. Heck, if you act right, you'll get exchanged and be back fightin' soon anyway." Not true.

President Lincoln suspended prisoner exchange because the Confederate government wouldn't treat black prisoners the same as white. President Davis proclaimed black soldiers taken prisoner would not be exchanged at all. I'm lying, but these men don't know it. Righteous deception. The door creaks, and three muskets are shoved out across the porch.

"That all you got?"

"Yeah!"

"Better be, or we'll shoot every last one of you!"

After a slight pause, three long knives, two short swords, and three pistols are tossed out. With our backs to the wall of the small house, we order the Rebs to march out with their hands up. They obey, and we tie their hands.

Sarge asks about their plan, but they refuse to answer. You'd never know these men were soldiers in the Confederate Army. They don't have a full uniform between the three of them, and the rags they wear are threadbare. I'm embarrassed for them. I've been in their shoes.

Sarge spits. "Damn guerillas. They do more damage than men who fight on battlefields." I'd be doing the same thing if I was in their shoes.

The youngest of the three politely asks, "Got anythin' to eat? We ain't had nary a biscuit for three days." The biggest of the three slaps him across the chest.

"Shut the hell up. We ain't askin' shit from these damn Yanks."

We pull food from our saddlebags. "Ain't no call for all that. You're honorable fightin' men who had the misfortune of gettin' caught. Once that happens, treatin' each other like human beings is what the Good Lord expects, don't you think?"

The biggest one kicks the dust. "Dammit! We'd had that bridge burnt, but we saw y'all comin'. We should've left here right off instead of waitin' 'til dark."

He scratches the back of his neck. "Hell, I got no call to be an ignert ass about it. We're caught and done for now. I'll take a biscuit if you don't mind."

We share our rations. We march them to camp with their hands tied and roped to each other. We become the talk of Company C and the Rifles, for that matter. Only two days out and we come back with three Rebel prisoners. And not a shot was fired by us. I'm still keeping my promise not to kill another human being in this war—so far, so good.

CHAPTER 33

LIGHTNING SPEED

DECEMBER 24, 1864

If my horse, Cloud, had wings, she'd be the daughter of Pegasus!

WE'RE UP AND off at 6:00 a.m. this frosty Christmas Eve morning. Poole wipes sleep out of his eyes. "It seems like I just got off this nag a few minutes ago."

We marched thirty miles yesterday to camp east of Salem. We'll be in Mississippi by day's end. My backside's never seen so much riding. Sarge said it'd take four days for the soreness to go away even for a man who regularly rides.

I try to be cheerful about it. "Dang, we ride long, hard, and fast. If Cloud had wings, she'd be the daughter of Pegasus."

Poole rubs his horse's neck. "If it didn't make me look like a sister boy, I'd put a pillow under my behind."

Seneca walks his horse over. "I've got decent food and coffee, a good horse, and regular army pay. I got no complaints. Hell, nobody'd want to hear 'em anyway."

"No they don't."

Poole never complains either, no matter how much rain or cold we face. In fact, none of the other men in C Company do either, unlike some in the Vicksburg trenches. Anyone would whine thrown into that mess. The gray suit is becoming a fading memory. The three men we captured yesterday proved that. Destroying the cloth factory at Bankston that makes uniform material will do that, too.

We take the Ripley Road south, and Colonel Karge detaches one battalion of the 2nd New Jersey Cavalry, commanded by Major Van Renssalaer, to take his men to Booneville. They're ordered to destroy the Mobile and Ohio Railroad there. The rest of us cross the Tallahatchie River at Kelley's Mills and make camp for the night—another twenty-seven miles behind us. I expected the bridge to be burned, but Colonel Karge is swift to send out scouts to secure crossings. Except for the three prisoners we captured, this has been an uneventful expedition. I expect that'll change any time. We're in Mississippi now.

CHRISTMAS MORNING AND no time for holiday cheer. I saddle my horse after having bacon and bread washed down with hot coffee. Christmas three years ago, I was standing on Mr. Gilmore's porch on my wedding day. Susannah never looked prettier. She was so dolled up I wasn't sure if she was supposed to be mine.

The laughter and joy that day, the feast and gifts, and especially good people like Old Bart, Mr. Gilmore, the Davises, and Mr. Wiley bring my tired mind good and peaceful memories. I'll never forget those few sweet days of my life. I shake my head. I have to look to what's ahead. Still, a tear forms in my eye.

COLONEL KARGE AND 1st Brigade take the lead moving out at 6:00 a.m. sharp. Among other things that impress me about the colonel, if he orders us to move out at a certain time, we do. Few things stay the same on a raid, but I like it. Sure beats the boredom of living in a filthy rat infested rifle pit.

Back then, I could see the invaders across Mint Springs Bayou. Now I'm the invader. I'm wearing the blue suit. I'm part of the big blue snake that slithers into my own home state. But I'm here for a different reason—to put the twentieth star back on that flag. I'm here to end this war.

CHAPTER 34

A SACK FULL OF CHRISTMAS GIFTS

DECEMBER 25, 1864

Sometimes it takes a bullet to open a Christmas gift.

WE MAKE OLD Town Creek, and General Grierson orders Colonel Karge to cross the stream and head toward Harrisburg.

Sarge trots down the line. "We're going to Verona to attack a Rebel camp. Keep sharp."

We stop for a short time at Harrisburg to let the column close up. It's dark as the black of my boots. I'm antsy. Everyone is.

Poole laments, "So this is what it's like to be in enemy territory. It ain't right, my home state bein' the enemy."

"Mississippi ain't your enemy. We're takin' back what was ours in the first place and make it free for everybody. Don't forget the twentieth star. It's what we fight for."

Poole cups his ears. "Shush, you hear it?"

I catch a slight movement of men hiding behind trees on a ridge. "They've got eyes on us already. We best move on or there'll be the Devil to pay."

I've felt them for a mile now. It's the same feeling I have when hunting. I know when there's a deer nearby watching me from the cover of brush. I'm blessed with the gift of being able to blend in with my surroundings. I can sense a presence before I see or hear it. I sense it now. Besides, there are too many ridge runners in these woods for the Rebs not to be watching a column this size.

The 7th Indiana Cavalry strikes the Rebel picket guard not two miles from Verona. The rest of First Brigade follows up. After the fight, Colonel Karge orders us to destroy all military property in town. A couple of men from the 7th Indiana tell us how the advance guard drove the pickets back in a hail of fire, and they charged into town with guns blazing and sabers waving. It must've been a sight. We could hear them yelling and firing weapons. The Rebel soldiers must have escaped into the dark forest.

We gather 450 English carbines, 500 Austrian rifles, 200 boxes of ammunition for rifles and carbines, a large number of fixed ammunition or artillery, and shells. We cover our ears at the massive explosion when we set fire to the pile of munitions. I bet the Rebs hear it miles away. We destroy 200 army wagons marked "U.S.," a railroad train of twenty cars, a large number of saddles, and quartermaster's and commissary stores found in eight large warehouse buildings. While the weaponry continues to explode and the warehouses burn, we finish up cutting telegraph wires and tearing up rails and ties. The exploding ordinance finally ends just before daylight.

I watch, sitting on Cloud. "So that's our work."

Poole shakes his head. "Ole Saint Nick did show up for Christmas after all."

"Sometimes it takes a bullet to open a Christmas gift, I reckon."

He scratches his scraggly beard. "What a sack full of Christmas gifts for the Union Army though. No fancy wrapping paper or pretty bows, but we did get fireworks."

"I understand destroying the guns and ammunition. But it's a damn shame to burn all that food when families are hungry. Good folks will come out of the woods to dig through the ashes hoping to find a tin can of somethin' to eat."

Poole shivers. "And Bankston's turn is comin' soon."

We make Harrisburg by daylight, December 26, and Colonel Karge gives us a few hours to rest. I catch Poole falling out of his saddle, snoring. He's like J.A. who could sleep standing up pulling guard duty. I could never do that. I can't sleep, so I write Ma a short letter. I'll date it Christmas Day. She'll like that even though it's the day after. I can't mail it until we get back to Camp Karge, anyway.

North Mississippi, December 25, 1864

Merry Christmas, Ma. Not much time to write. We're destroying Rebel supplies and fighting anywhere we can. We fought on Christmas, of all days. We surprised them at a town I can't mention and ran them off. We did a lot of damage they won't soon forget. I can't say much now while we're still in enemy territory, but I will later. It sounds funny callin Mississippi enemy territory. Our beloved state will remain so until the twentieth star is placed permanently back on the flag of the Union where it should be. I do hope that day comes soon. Anyway, I'm well, in body and spirit, hopeful and believe without question I'm doing the right thing. That's a good enough gift for Christmas for me. Many a man wishes he had what I have. A good family, good friends, good health, and regular army pay. Enclosed is half of the first part of my sign up bounty, fifty dollars. I'll send more when I can. Not to let the cat out of the bag too soon, but I've met a nice lady who is the widowed sister of my good friend Annie Fanny I told you about. Don't get too excited, we're just talkin right now. But somethin good just might come of it. Keep up the prayers, hug the girls for me, and tell Elihu and Seth I miss them.

Your affectionate son, Lummy

I stuff the letter into my shirt and turn to adjust my saddle. As I tighten the girth, I know now what I'm going to write Martha Brock.

CHAPTER 35

LITTLE REST

11:00 A.M., DECEMBER 26, 1864

Little rest now, greater rest later. It all works out in the end.

WE'RE IN THE saddle and formed up ready for the next objective on this expedition. We made good time traveling light and fast, crossing the Tombigbee River and camping on the Okolona Road at 9:00 p.m. We've had little rest since Verona. Our horses are spent from the fifty mile march, and so are we. But off we go.

Poole laughs. "Heck, I'll still have the calluses on my butt if I live to be a hundred."

The 2nd New Jersey Cavalry rejoins First Brigade this evening and tells glowing stories of destroying the railroad and telegraph lines at Booneville, ripping up a mile of track, burning two large buildings filled with quartermaster's and commissary stores, as well as a caboose filled with arms, ammunition, and railroad tools. They finished by destroying the 150 foot bridge across Twenty-mile Swamp and eight or ten culverts as well. I bet President Davis has heard about us up in Richmond by now. We tell of the havoc we wreaked on the rebel camp and driving out three hundred soldiers to parts unknown.

1st Lieutenant White stops by after the officer's briefing. "Men, General Grierson is so delighted with the destruction of enemy property and the minimal loss to the expedition, he has decided to let us keep going."

We all laugh and cheer. The General treats us to a full night's sleep for our efforts.

I feed Cloud a good portion of grain and make sure she has plenty of water. She's tired and needs rest more than I do. As I comb her down, the smell of good food overpowers barnyard odors. I finish with Cloud and settle down to my first cooked meal in three days.

I sip coffee and lean against my saddle with my bedroll laid out underneath. I take paper and pencil and sit up to catch the flickering camp fire light. I think for a while about the words that will set my path in a new direction. I don't want to overdo it, but my feelings for her are clear. I read Martha's letter again. There's no mistake in what she says. I do my best to match her words with my own.

North Mississippi, December 26, 1864

Merry Christmas, Martha. I do wish I was with you to celebrate our Lord's birth. Your letter brought joyful surprise to my heart. Please receive my letter with equal affection. If you consider yourself too bold, forgive my anxious heart for not speaking to you the same words before now. When I saw your sky blue eyes underneath your bonnet the day we met, I hoped the Lord had brought me a gift. I prayed that if the gift was for me, you would feel the same.

I see in you a devoted wife who loved her husband, and a caring mother whose children already walk in the ways of the Lord because of her faithful example. Bein blessed with such a woman from the Lord has been my dream since I was a young boy. I pray you will be that fine woman of God for my life.

We both lost the loves of our lives, but I believe that your Henry would speak the same words as did my Susannah in a dream I had not long ago. We must open our hearts to the gift God sends. I am of the same mind as you. I was not looking for anyone, so to meet you has caused a stir in my heart that will not be calmed until I see you again. Though I have not been a father before, I have no fear that I can help raise your children into godly men and women. I will happily walk by your side on such a venture. I too, have laid open my heart. I hope God blesses us in this as soon as this war is over.

Please pray for me and the 1st Mississippi Mounted Rifles. We have seen action already, and soon I will have to do a difficult thing to help end this war. Tell your children I pray for them and to love and obey their mother. Also, tell Annie and Beau hello and thank you. Tell Annie that she was right about you.

Much affection, Columbus Tullos

I fold the letter neatly and seal it in an envelope. I've not written a letter quite like this one before. I've never signed my name "Columbus" either, except on the parole slip at Vicksburg and my enlistment papers to join the Rifles. But that's what she calls me, and it's all right by me. Columbus, an explorer who found the New World. It wasn't easy for him to get where he was going. But when he finally made it, I'm sure he believed he'd found paradise.

Poole slaps me on the back. "Good words, lover boy."

"What, you readin' over my shoulder? I'll whoop your ass into the middle of next week, lookin' both ways for Sunday."

"Oh, hell no, Lummy. You talked that whole letter out loud as you wrote it. You out loud talkin' dumbass son of a...."

Sarge barks out, "Son of a... what did you say?"

"Oh, nothin', Sarge, I was just funnin' with Lummy. He's got a steady girl now and writes the sweetest words you ever did hear. It's drippin' like honeycomb just pulled from the hive. Heck, that letter's so stuck to his shirt he'll have to peel it off with that big knife his daddy made him."

Sarge puts his foot up on a hogshead barrel and leans close. "That pretty gal with the blue skirt who came runnin' down to the river landing when we left Vicksburg?"

"You saw Martha?"

"I don't miss much, son. You got a real looker there. And the makin's of a good wife."

"Thanks, Sarge, I just hope I get back to Vicksburg to see her. Don't know when that'll be."

"Well, you're in luck. At the officer's briefing, General Grierson said we'll end up in Vicksburg when this expedition is over. Should be around the 5th or 6th of January. How's that?"

"Couldn't be any better for what we're out here doin'."

"I figured that'd put a little spring in your step. I'll do my best to get you leave time when we get there. Follow orders, keep your head down, and get there in one piece."

I want to jump up and run off in all directions I'm so happy.

Poole shakes his head. "Damn, if you ain't the lucky one, boy. But I got a request."

"What?"

"That you pray God sends me a pretty gal to be my wife. Would you do that for me?"

"What the hell do you think I've been doin' these past few days?"

CHAPTER 36

THE GOLDEN RULE RETURNED

DECEMBER 27-28, 1864

Turnaround. Showing God's mercy and compassion to an enemy.

COLONEL KARGE LETS us sleep longer this morning. Rested men are better prepared to meet what's coming. Grandpa Temple used say, "You gotta get through the conflict in front of you so you'll be ready for the next one. And there's always another one comin'." Extra sleep helps.

The column starts moving at 8 a.m. sharp, stopping at Okolona to eat and care for our horses. We make camp four miles south of the town, having marched twenty miles today. Riding is getting easier and complaining never enters my mind. Poole and I are assigned midnight watch, so we try to sleep soon after supper.

Sarge wakes us for our three hour shift. We stand picket guard on the edge of camp. Poole stomps his feet to shake off the cold and rubs his hands together before putting them into his pockets. His rifle rests in the crook of his arm.

"Can you get your hands out fast enough if guerillas jump us? It could happen anytime." I hand him a piece of cloth to wrap his hand. "This will help warm your hands, but you can still keep your thumb on the hammer ready to cock it."

We stand in the shadows of a great old hickory tree for about an hour when the hairs on the back of my neck stand up. The bushes shake not fifty feet away.

I whisper so as not to startle Poole, "Somebody's comin'."

Out steps a group of men with their hands up. "Don't shoot, we give up!"

We cock our rifles in case it's an ambush. Poole crouches with his rifle aimed at the man's chest. "On your knees and hands on your heads! I've got plenty of reasons in this rifle to make you do what we say."

They drop to their knees. Poole keeps a bead on them while I check the bushes for more.

The Reb corporal clears his throat. "Ain't nobody else, friend. We just want to surrender."

Satisfied this is no trick, Poole checks them for weapons.

I cock my pistol. They shrink back at the clicking sounds. "Corporal, try anything and you'll be the first to get a bullet right between the eyes."

"Suh, we're done with this war and just want to go home. There's nobody else out in them woods, except Gabriel Marks, who crossed River Jordan yesterday. He was just too weak to get here. We been runnin' for two weeks thinkin' we could dodge patrols. Sneakin' between two armies ain't as easy as you might think, you understand?"

"That I do, friend."

The corporal fakes a smile. "Thanks for callin' me friend. We surely need one." I find no deceit in this man. His men shake from lack of clothing and look to be starving.

"Poole, I ain't your boss, but would you let Sarge know what we've got here? Bring a few more men. Some of these boys can't walk to camp."

Poole hands me his Colts Revolving Rifle and takes mine. "I don't think you'll need the extra shots but just in case."

"Bring whatever food you can scare up and blankets, too."

The corporal rises from his knees. "Bless you, suh. Your kindness won't be forgotten." He sits down on the ground, and his men do the same. I have compassion on these men like the Yanks did me at Vicksburg. I understand that better now.

Poole races off, and I release the hammer on my pistol. The Rebs sigh in relief. We've all heard stories about overzealous soldiers faking a fight with men who surrender just so they can get away with murder.

I assure the corporal, "Do what we say. No harm will come to you."

"Thank you, suh."

I count fifteen exhausted men. I must've looked worse sitting in Vicksburg when we surrendered. My view of Yankee soldiers changed that day. They honored us as fighting men and shared their food. Turnaround demands God's mercy and compassion on an enemy. It does much to heal the soul. My soul.

Poole returns with Sarge and six armed privates. They give the surrendered Rebs hot coffee and leftover biscuits with fried salt pork. The Rebs burn their tongues drinking too fast and only half-taste their food choking it down so fast.

As Poole watches the road and surrounding woods, we get the prisoners on their feet. They hobble and wobble their way into camp. Sarge assigns two privates our place on the picket line. We get the honor of leading these prisoners into camp.

I whisper to Poole, "Sarge has good intentions lettin' everybody see that we captured these men, but there's no honor in it."

"I reckon we just have to play the game."

Our comrades give a muffled cheer as we walk the Rebs into camp. Sarge's face glows like a father cradling his newborn. We take the prisoners to a holding tent where they're wrapped in blankets. Most fall fast asleep as soon as their heads hit the ground. I know the feeling—heart whipped, mind disoriented, body worn-out, and soul lost.

Two men from another company stroll by with smirks on their faces. "Ain't whistlin' Dixie now, are you, boys?"

The corporal bows his head. This is the price of surrender. But this isn't the treatment I received in Vicksburg.

I step their way. "Shut the hell up before I turn one of these fightin' men loose on you. Just one of these beaten, weak, and sickly men could rip your asses into fish bait in a snap. Show some respect for these fightin' men, or I'll make sure you leave with none." I can't believe I rile so easily, but I'm in it now.

The biggest one bows up at me but stops when Sarge and Poole step up behind me.

"Is there a problem here, Private Tullos?"

"No problem here 'til this shit kicker brought one. He'll take it on down the line with him now, sir." Then I notice the mouthy one has two stripes on his sleeve.

"You gonna let this private talk to his superior that way, Sergeant?"

"I don't see his superior anywhere around here, Corporal. And as far as takin' on Private Tullos, I hope you ate your biscuits this mornin', cause when you're done, there'll be a helluva lot left over. But if you'd like to lose the formalities, I'll shed this jacket with three stripes and do it for him."

The corporal shakes his head, embarrassed.

Sarge isn't satisfied. "Apologize to the gentleman in gray, Corporal." He hesitates. "Now, damn you!"

Now it's the corporal who hangs his head. "I apologize for my disrespect."

Sarge barks, "To him, damn it!"

The corporal takes a deep breath and looks at the Reb corporal. "I apologize for my behavior, sir."

Sarge waves at the corporal like he's swatting a fly. "Now get the hell out of my camp."

They leave without saying a word. I walk back over to the tent where the Reb prisoners sleep.

"What else I can do for you, sir?"

He offers his hand. "The Lord has taken note of your mercy and will reward you richly for your grace and protection in our time of need. If I may ask, what is your name, please, suh?"

"Columbus Nathan Tullos from Choctaw County Mississippi and yours?"

His eyes light up. "Choctaw County Missip, you say?"

"Yes, have you been there?"

"No, suh, but have you got a brother or cousin named George Washington Tullos who fought with the Fifteenth Mississippi Infantry?"

My heart jumps like a grasshopper chased by a mockingbird. "You knew him?"

"Like a brother. He saved my life once."

I'm stunned beyond words. I can't even muster up a sentence.

"To tell the truth, when you yelled as we came out of the woods, I thought it was George's ghost. You sound just like him. Y'all favor a lot, but you look to be a head taller."

I choke on my words, "How, when?"

He turns to Sarge. "Would it be all right if I tell this good man how his brother bravely lived and died, suh?"

"Lummy, you and Poole did good tonight bringin' in these prisoners and treatin' them with respect. You're done for the night. Get you're talkin' done. These men will be out of here in less than an hour. Then get some rest. We've got a long ride tomorrow."

"Thank you, sir."

The Rebel corporal recounts his adventures with the 15th Mississippi Volunteer Infantry Company I, from the time he joined the Choctaw Guards in June of 1861 at Corinth. Most men came from around Bankston. They fought from Fishing Creek to Shiloh and from Shiloh to Corinth, served near Vicksburg, and then at Port Hudson where they survived on burnt molasses and cow peas.

"The hickory shad were the worst. The most worthless fish God ever made. Must have a thousand bones to the inch. We ate 'em, though."

"Yeah, we only use 'em for baitin' traps and such."

He blows on his steaming coffee. "Boy, that's good. We couldn't stop Sherman's advance on Vicksburg, and we backed off Jackson when the city surrendered. Just too many Yanks, besides Johnston bein' scared to attack. Lots of men went home after Champion Hill when President Davis changed their one year enlistments to three more without askin'. They didn't even give us leave to see about our families. So some us just up and un-volunteered."

He stares into the darkness. "George took off the end of June just before Vicksburg fell. Said he needed to see about his ma and nieces back home. He promised to return after he helped his brother, Elihu I think was his name, get the crop in."

"George always kept his word."

"Then General Johnston offered amnesty for men who went AWOL or deserted and a chance to return without repercussions, is that the word? Yeah, that's right. George did just that at the end of August after corn pullin'. He rejoined us at Newton Station."

The corporal sips his cooling coffee. "Damn, that George was a man to be admired. He must've had a good upbringin'." Ma and Pa would be proud. The corporal wipes his teary eyes.

"Last winter some of the boys got furloughs. Some begged but got no pass, and some took their chances in a lottery. George picked the right number to receive a pass home but gave it to me sayin' he'd already had his furlough. He wanted somebody else to get the same chance to go home. That's how he saved my life. I went home and found my family safe. I'll always thank George for that, especially since I'll be enjoying the company of the Union Army for a while."

It hits me that had George come home then, I would have seen him. Damn!

The corporal swirls the last of his now cold coffee and drains the cup. "We fought at New Hope Church, Kennesaw Mountain, and Peachtree Creek where we lost forty men, including Lieutenant Hugh Montgomery from Company I."

"We tried to hold Atlanta. but Sherman's army nearly got us trapped in a circle. After three dozen men deserted, we had maybe two hundred men left. George was one of the brave two hundred."

Sarge taps me on the shoulder. "Make it quick. Guards are comin'."

"Hood got the hair brained idea he'd force his way to Nashville. We found the Yanks dug in on high ground near Franklin. Despite protests from his best commanders, Hood ordered a frontal attack anyway. That's where George fell, gallantly charging a hill next to the Harpeth River. The Yanks burned us down like dry grass. He was shot through the chest near the Carter gin house. Private George Washington Tullos passed from this earth in defense of his country November 30, 1864. Brother, I am very sorry for your loss."

I want to scream, but I hold it in. "Sounds like he died in a worthless battle conjured up by a dumbass general. I'd give my right arm to take the knife my pa made for me and gut that son of a...." I catch myself and repent. "I'm sorry, Corporal. My anger got the best of me."

"It's all right. I lost a brother in this fool war, too."

"Did you see George fall?"

"Yes."

"You get to him before he died?"

"I did."

"Any last words?"

"He said to tell his wife, Sarah, that he's sorry for bein' a stubborn jackass for a worthless cause and not comin' home to her. He wanted your ma to know he loved her and to tell his brothers he will meet them in the air with Jesus one day."

I cry with him for a few moments.

He leans over to whisper so his men can't hear. "I shouldn't tell you this, but our troop trains are on their way to Egypt Station to reinforce the stockade earthworks there. They already have twelve hundred to two thousand men waitin' for you. They just don't know when you'll get there. Reinforcements should arrive around 11:00 a.m."

"Why are you tellin' me this?"

He scratches his ear. "For the same reason you're wearin' blue and not gray. I want this damn war over. I never had a slave and never wanted one. It's all been a waste of good human flesh, and I want no part of it anymore."

I bow my head. "Lord, safely carry these men home soon."

Sarge steps into the tent. "Time to go. Lummy, escort these men to the edge of camp and see this good man off."

"Yes, sir, and thanks."

I walk the corporal to where the prisoner detail takes charge. "Thanks for telling me about my brother, George."

He shakes my hand and marches away without a word. All has been said that can be said. But not all has been done that can be done. Not yet.

CHAPTER 37

RUNNING STRAIGHT AT TROUBLE

DECEMBER 28, 1864

I've never run straight at trouble and not see it until it was over.

"SARGE, THE REBEL corporal gave me some information the general will surely want."

"Come with me."

We find Grierson pouring over maps and messages. "What is it?"

"Private Tullos has information."

Grierson leans back in his chair. "Spit it out, Private."

I tell him what the Reb corporal said.

"That confirms the rumors in the telegraph wires. Reb reinforcements are coming from Mobile. Get some rest. We attack Egypt Station tomorrow. That's all, and good work, Private."

We salute. "Yes, sir, General Grierson, sir." I just wanted to say that.

"Wait. You're the Tullos man who'll scout when we get close to Bankston."

"I am, sir."

"I like a trustworthy man who keeps his ears open. Dismissed."

Sarge holds the tent flap open for me. "Sorry to say, Lieutenant White said we won't be part of the attack. We'll be the reserve and guard the pack trains. Get some sleep."

Sarge rousts us out of our four hour sleep. "Boots and saddles! Be ready to mount up at 7:00 a.m." I slept fitfully after hearing about George. Another brother gone. Dead. I'm tired.

We take the West Point Road. Two miles out from Egypt Station, the lead column runs into the Reb cavalry. Colonel Karge orders a charge, but when our men get within a half mile of the town, they find the enemy in strong position. Colonel Karge orders a second charge. The 2nd New Jersey Cavalry breaks the center of the Rebel line. Captain Gallagher just crests the earthworks when he's shot off his horse. We watch from a distance. What bravery. It's hard not be a part of this battle.

Colonel Karge forms up the line of attack before the Rebs get back on their feet. He moves Lieutenant Colonel Yorke and the 2nd New Jersey to the center, with Captain Hencke of the 4th Missouri Cavalry to the left and the 7th Indiana Cavalry, commanded by Captain Elliot, to the right. The Rebs put up a strong fight but are driven back. Colonel Karge sends Captain Elliot to capture a train raining shot and shell from a four gun battery mounted on a flatbed rail car.

General Grierson rides by, waving to lead the capture of the train. I've never seen anything like it. A fighting man's general leading a charge.

The 1st Mississippi Mounted Rifles are ordered to continue guarding the pack train to our great disappointment that we have to forego the pleasure of battle. We pace and shout with all our might. Men fall on both sides—brave men willing to bleed and die for what they believe.

Even after the punishment we bring, the Rebs still hold the stockade on the left and center on the east side of the railroad. Colonel Karge orders another charge. Two mounted squadrons attack the left while three companies dismount on the right. They pour out such a terrible field of fire that the Rebs surrender almost immediately. Five hundred prisoners are taken.

A rider comes yelling, "General Grierson earned his pay today! Two trains of reinforcements was haulin' ass up the tracks. He threw up a defense and captured a whole train. He tore up the tracks south of town and prevented the rest from making it to the Reb fort."

The losses to the brigade are pretty heavy—105 men killed and wounded with three officers dead, two wounded, and one captured. Rebel losses are much worse than ours.

General Grierson rides through. "We have met the enemy, and he is defeated."

After the wounded are cared for, we cross the Houlka River and camp near Houston. Tired from the fourteen mile march, we rest and listen to glory stories of the men who lived to tell about the battle. I find no pride in the telling. Still, it was a marvel to see the battle unfold.

Sarge hands me a cup of coffee. "That's the first time I've seen how mounted infantry can be used to successfully dislodge and defeat a well-entrenched enemy. I had my doubts when the charge began. But it's not the first time I've seen men run straight at trouble without thinking about it."

As I lay my head on my bedroll, I see eyes. Hundreds of eyes of men in blue who didn't want to run straight at trouble waiting behind stockades and lunettes in Vicksburg. I witnessed the fear that took the light of the souls of the Yanks who charged up the hill, only to have a long gray snake rise up and rain down fire from a thousand muskets.

I can hear the screams and calls for mothers. I can see them wrench and wretch, gasping for air, squirming like helpless nightcrawler worms thrown into a fire. I blink, but I can still see them. Something grabs my arm like a snake bite. I jerk, but it squeezes tighter.

Poole whispers, "Think about somethin' else, brother. You're one day closer to bein' back with Martha. You'll see her again. God's done told me."

I roll over chasing away war thoughts with love thoughts.

After today's excitement and learning of George's death, thinking about better things only works so well.

That's not the only thing keeping me awake. Tomorrow Poole and I lead Colonel Beckwith and the 4th Iowa Cavalry to Bankston.

I whisper so as not to startle Poole, "Somebody's comin'."

CHAPTER 38

DETACHED TO THE 4TH IOWA CAVALRY

7:00 A.M., DECEMBER 29, 1864

Too much change in too little time.

W E'RE IN THE saddle early, heading west to Houston after crossing the Sookatanuchie and Houlka Rivers. Grierson is ahead of the Rebs on every turn, securing bridges and crossings so we can move swiftly through enemy territory and not get wet crossing the rivers.

He sends out what he calls demonstrations in every direction—some to do damage, others to deceive the enemy about his real objectives. Pontotoc, West Point, and Winona take the brunt. The 7th Indiana Cavalry burns a large bridge crossing the Houlka River on the Pontotoc Road. We march on the Bellefontaine Road and make camp at 5:00 p.m., having completed a sixteen mile trek. I'm getting close to home. I can feel it.

DECEMBER 30. WE ride slowly, saving our horses in case of an attack.

I punch Poole, who's dozing in his saddle. "We just crossed into Choctaw County."

He rubs his eyes. "We're home."

We've moved through north Mississippi at lightning speed. That's what General Grierson is known for. My life has moved like lightning since I traveled this very road back in '59.

I still believe enlisting in the Rifles was one of the best decisions I've ever made even though I'm about to do the hardest thing I've had to do, in either army. But it made meeting Martha possible and has given me reason to live. It's almost 1865. I'm tired, body and soul. I just want to go home but not like this. I want the life God has planned for me, but burning Bankston to get it? Too much change in too little time. Too many hard decisions. When this is over, I'll take time to sort all this out. Maybe I'll write it down in a book, like Gunnard. Heck, who'd read it?

Poole slaps my chest. "I would, and I better be in it."

"You'll be front and center, catfish head."

I daydream about Martha's pretty smile and sky blue eyes. It's like God dropped her from heaven just for me. I breathe in deeply and let it out slowly, finishing those musings on a sweet note. The cold air feels good in my chest.

Poole clears his throat. "You still think we're doin' the right thing?"

"Yeah, but give me a few minutes. I ain't done thinking about Martha."

We ride through the small village of Hopewell, arriving in Bellefontaine by noon. General Grierson and the rest of the First Brigade move west to strike the Mississippi Central Railroad at Winona. He sends a demonstration east to Starkville to threaten the Mobile and Ohio Railroad and confuse the enemy as to our whereabouts. We move so fast the Rebels can't keep up with us. That's the plan, and it's working.

We stop for the night. Sarge trots over as I brush Cloud. "Poole, Tullos! Quick, come with me. It's time for you men to do your duty."

I can't help myself. "Oh, damn, here we go."

Ainsworth and Seneca wave as we march to Captain Beckwith's headquarters. The 4th Iowa Cavalry colors fly over the tent where he sips coffee out of the drizzling rain.

Sarge salutes. "Privates Tullos and Poole, reporting for duty, sir!" He turns to us. "Privates, this is Captain Beckwith, commander of the Hawkeyes of the 4th Iowa Cavalry."

Poole and I salute. Beckwith waves his hand to let us relax. "How about a cup of coffee?"

I salute again. "That'd be good right about now, sir."

His orderly fills two tin cups with the steaming hot liquid as Beckwith studies a map.

Poole takes his. "Thank you."

We move closer to the fire to warm our legs from the chilling breeze. I notice a group of men sitting under a tree guarded by 4th Iowa cavalrymen. One slowly stands, peering at me like he's sizing up a man he's about to fight. I know him.

He glares through narrow slits and grits his teeth. "I thought that was you, Tullos! I would've given my right arm to have caught your sorry ass for killin' my best friend, Lester. I'd cut you up for fish bait in that creek where you threw his body, you blue suited niggah lovin' turncoat!"

"Well, if it ain't Captain Tom Ford. You still makin' puppies with that black and tan bitch dawg you sleep with? You must be lonely. Or maybe not. You do have some of your pups with you."

The 4th Iowa men laugh hard and long, embarrassing Ford beyond repair. I don't like being so nasty, but that mouth needed to be nipped in the bud. A sergeant gets the prisoners on their feet.

Ford lunges as he's taken away. "I'll get you, Tullos, wait and see. I'll get loose, and I'll get you, you bastard. I know you're here to burn Bankston. You do that and I'll make sure you won't ever get to come home, boy. I know where you live, and I'll…."

I don't hear the rest as he's dragged away.

Captain Beckwith looks up from his map. "Who was that man, and what was that all about?"

"Please excuse that heated exchange, sir."

He waves off my apology.

"Nothin' and nobody really, sir. That's Captain Tom Ford, who's made it his business to hunt down men loyal to the Union. He chases men down with a pair of black and tan bloodhounds. He's hung several good men. He almost caught Mistuh Dotson, who caused a stir in Bankston before he took his family north. Ford tried to catch me before I left to join the Rifles. No worries, though. I know this county better than him."

"Well, Private Tullos, you won't have to worry with that bastard again anytime soon. He'll hang soon. Men, I know it must be difficult for you to invade your home county. But General Grierson and Sergeant McGugarty believe you men are faithful to the Union and willing to help end this war anyway you can. That true?"

We stand at attention. "Yes, sir."

"Relax, enjoy your coffee. It'll be the last you'll have for a couple of days."

Captain Beckwith shakes the hand of a man in plain clothes, who joins the small group gathered around the table. "For you men who don't know, this is the famous, or should I say, infamous, Chickasaw the Scout. He's from Chickasaw County, and like you two from Choctaw County, he's a true blue Union man. They tried to hang him in his own hometown once, but he escaped to serve his country. Privates Tullos and Poole, you're in good company with ole Chickasaw here."

Chickasaw bows. "Serving at your pleasure, Captain." He tips his rain soaked hat at Poole and me. The water drips off, and he smiles. "Glad you men are with us."

The captain looks back at his map. "Since you two men will guide us on this raid, I can free Chickasaw to scout in another direction. But I do value his insight as we complete our plan for Bankston and Greensborough. So Chickasaw, speak up when you need to."

Chickasaw nods and lights up a small cigar. "Yes, sir."

"This will be a fast movin' raiding party. You men know this county better than anyone in First Brigade."

Poole grins. "Yes, sir, Lummy and me, I mean Private Tullos and me, know every ridge, every creek, deer path, and swamp for miles around. Why me and Lummy—"

Beckwith pats the air. "Thank you for your enthusiasm, soldier. It will come in handy when you've been in the saddle for two days without rest, but right now, we don't have much time. Private Tullos, I hear you joined up with the First Mississippi Mounted Rifles earlier this month. Why'd you do that?"

"To get Missip's twentieth star back on the right flag, sir. With all due respect to your rank, sir, I'd appreciate my loyalty not being questioned."

Captain Beckwith looks at his officers who take a step forward. "At ease, men. I like this one, no nonsense and ready to do his duty. Here's a piece of free advice, Private Tullos. Living it ain't easy as saying it."

"Yes, sir. Good words, sir." I remember my good friend and Mexican War veteran, Mr. Wiley's good advice, 'Keep goin' forward, keep your trap shut, and let the officers be the officers.' So I do just that. I have no need to argue my thoughts and feelings with this man.

Sarge cuts in, "Yes, sir, I can vouch for this young man and his friend, Poole, here. They're ready to run straight at trouble when you say go."

Captain Beckwith stares at me for a moment, sips his coffee, and leans over a crude map.

"All right then, Private Tullos, the road goes due south from here to the county seat." He points to a spot on the map. "What is the name of that place? I can't see it. Orderly, where are my spectacles?" The captain slips them on.

"Ah, Greensborough. Sounds like a peaceful place. What's there?"

I nudge Poole, who's lived close to Greensborough most of his life. He runs his finger along the road on the map. "Comin' from this direction, there's a graveyard just north of town. Then you'll pass the crossroads for the Starkville Road and a brickyard. Then it's just a rock's throw to the county courthouse and the rest of town."

Beckwith looks up from the map. "What's in town?"

Poole studies the map. "The courthouse is right there by the road that goes south to Bankston, and the town spreads out east from there on a couple of streets. General Brantley's law office is next to the courthouse, with the school house, Baptist Church, and Jim Nolen's mercantile close by. The two streets that go east, and one a little north, have law offices, shops, and people's homes scattered about. That's about it."

"Can you draw me a better map, son?"

Poole nods and an orderly hands him paper and a pencil.

"Any soldiers you know of?"

"No, sir."

Beckwith rubs his unshaven chin and speaks to his lieutenants. "I'll ask about Bankston in a minute, but should we fire the town?"

I cringe, and Captain Beckwith sees Poole squirm a bit.

"I know this is a tall order for you two boys, but we're instructed to break down the governmental structure wherever we can to confuse the enemy's efforts."

I don't want to lose my family's land and marriage records housed in the courthouse. "Sir, there's an office for the Confederate government on the main street. The courthouse only holds land records and tax offices. It's of no value to the Rebs, sir. I sure would hate to burn that beautiful old building, sir."

He stares at me for a moment. "All right then. We'll burn Greensborough on our way back from Bankston. Don't burn the courthouse, but destroy all law offices, the post office, and anything that looks to aid the enemy. Do no harm to private homes or property if possible. These people will need to eat and live after we pass through. My order will be obeyed. I expect good behavior on your part, understood?"

The officers salute.

"These two men are not to participate in the destruction. They are to point out main objectives once you arrive and watch from afar." Beckwith turns to me. "I assume you know Bankston the best?"

"Yes, sir, I do. I grew up near there. It's where we got our mail and supplies. My Uncle Burrell used to work in the tannery and shoe factory. I've been in all those buildings several times. I know my hometown inside and out."

"Good. Tell me about Bankston."

I give him the layout and describe in detail each building that makes materials for the Reb Army. I draw a map that includes all the roads going in and out of town. He looks it over with his lieutenants, and they agree on the best approach. I fidget a little.

"Got ants in your britches, son, or is somethin' else botherin' you?"

"Meanin' no harm, sir, I hear your order to harm no civilian property. Does that include the town folks, as well?" He nods. "Will you keep that promise, Captain?"

Beckwith, a little impatient, says, "You sure speak your damn mind, don't you, soldier?"

"Sir, I've lost a wife and three brothers, one who was killed by the Home

Guard, and too many good friends. I know the cost, and I'm ready to give more. I just want it to be worth it."

Poole slinks back hoping I'm not about to get us in trouble. Sarge grips my shoulder.

Two lieutenants step up, but Beckwith backs them down. "Son, war is a terrible thing and has taken its worst toll on good folks like you and yours. I appreciate the sacrifice you two men are making and will make when you go back to your homes after the war. You want this war over as quickly as I do. Destroying these towns will speed that up. I have instructed these officers to do just what you ask without a shot fired, if possible. I'm not General Sherman, who burns everything in sight. But if resistance is met, we will do our best to wipe it out, you understand?"

I hand him my crude map of the town. "Yes, sir, thank you, sir."

He studies the map. "Now, if that's good enough for you, Private Tullos, tell me about the Rebels in the area."

"Yes, sir. The forces I'm aware of total no more than a hundred men and four cannons. Mistuh Wesson, who owns the mills, formed up several home guard companies. Most are either too old or unfit to serve in the regular army. You caught Captain Ford, so the Home Guard won't give us much trouble. Fast as we'll be movin', we'll be done and gone before they get out of bed."

Captain Beckwith leans forward. "You killed one of the Home Guard here, is that right?"

I glare at Sarge who shrugs his shoulders. "He needed to know the strength of your loyalties, son. So I told him."

"Yes, sir. He tried to rape and murder my ma and nieces."

Sarge adds, "The man came to Private Tullos's farm claiming that the authority of the Confederate government allowed him to take the pay he was owed out on Private Tullos' family—meaning the females, sir."

Captain Beckwith slaps his cup across the room. "Private Tullos, I hope you gutted that bastard like a fish and chunked his sorry ass into a deep hole where he'll never be found."

"I did somethin' pretty close to that very thing, sir. But they found his body. That's what the ruckus with Captain Ford was about."

"All right then." Beckwith nods at the map for me to continue. "If we go in the wee hours of the night, Captain, we'll surprise the sleeping town and easily finish our work. If trouble comes, we can swing west to Huntsville and up to Kilmichael which will put us back on the road to join General Grierson and the main column."

"Sounds good, Private. You and Poole, ready yourselves to join with 120 men of the 4th Iowa Cavalry. How far is it between Greensborough and Bankston?"

Poole steps up. "About ten miles, sir."

Captain Beckwith checks his map again. "Good. Chickasaw, any comments or suggestions?"

"It's a sound plan, Captain, with two good men serving as scouts." He nods at me and Poole. "Good luck, boys, and keep your powder dry."

Captain Beckwith announces, "That's all, men. The lieutenant here will get you two positioned ahead of the column. I'll be right behind you with the column if you run into any trouble you can't talk your way out of."

A lieutenant asks, "Did you bring your farmer's clothes like Sergeant McGugarty instructed?"

"Yes, sir, they're in our saddlebags."

"Good, put them on. Deal with whatever situation that comes, but you are not to engage the enemy. Diffuse anything that could lead to a local alerting the Rebels."

I rest my elbow on my pistol instinctively. "And if guns are pulled on us?"

Captain Beckwith snorts laughing, "Shoot 'em dead and run like hell back to the column. We'll take it from there. Make no mistake. You could get in harm's way. Just get the job done and get back to the column in one piece. That's all."

We salute. "Thank you, sir."

Beckwith stands and salutes. "Get ready, we leave tonight at 8:00 sharp."

Sarge walks us back to our horses. "Keep a clear eye and get back to the column in one piece. This is your home ground, but it's enemy territory. Don't forget that." He kicks the dirt. "We've come a long ways since the parole in Vicksburg, ain't we, Columbus Nathan Tullos?"

"Yes, sir. I wouldn't be here if it wasn't for you. You've been my guiding angel. Thanks."

Sarge kicks the dirt again. "I ain't never been called an angel before, but it sounds kinda nice." He slaps me on the shoulder. "I'm proud of you, boys. But before we all go to crying together, get the hell on back to your horses before I kick your asses!" He scratches his eye, but I know he's wiping a tear. He laughs as he walks away.

"What you thinkin', Lummy?"

I don't want to talk, but I know he needs me to. "That I don't want to do this, but I have to."

Poole and I finish caring for our horses—without talking.

Conviction. What a thing for God to put in man's soul to make him do the right and hardest things in life.

Poole snickers. "Ain't that the damn truth?"

CHAPTER 39

HOME GROUND NEVER FELT SO UNEASY

8:00 P.M., DECEMBER 29, 1864

So this is what bein' a stranger in my own land feels like.

I'M HOME, BUT I've never felt more uneasy riding on the very ground that raised me. Traveling this road not far from our farm doesn't make it feel like home. Not tonight.

Poole and I shed our blue uniforms for farm clothes—risky business at best. If captured, the Home Guard could either hang us as spies in the town square or just shoot us right then and there. No questions asked. Fortunately, I know every critter trail and sandy bottom ditch that could hide an ambush. Captain Beckwith assured us that we've traveled so quickly in such a short time, no Reb troops or guerillas could know we're here—yet.

Poole fits the description of a home grown backwoods farmer. We look like two hayseeds heading to Bucksnort for a drink or Bankston for supplies. But two men on horseback at night is suspicion enough for anyone looking for deserters or Yankee scouts. If we're seen, I have no fear that we'll get away. A little fear keeps a man from being reckless. Still, I can't find any in my heart.

I want to ask Captain Beckwith if I can visit my family, but I won't. We'll pass within a mile of the Tullos farm as the crow flies when we hit Bankston. There'll be no time for such things. I'm not here to be home. I'm here to free home.

"Boots and saddles, men, let's go!"

Poole and I head to the front as the column quietly falls out on the road south.

We salute Captain Beckwith. "Tullos, Poole, take us around Greensborough. We'll return after destroying the manufactories in Bankston, if practical. If attacked in Bankston, you men will lead us on another route to catch up with the main force. Understood?"

"Yes, sir." Poole and I trail about a hundred yards ahead of the column. Captain Beckwith and three soldiers hang back thirty yards or so.

Poole whispers, "So this is what it feels like to be a stranger on my own home ground."

I don't respond. I just keep my eyes open for any trouble.

CHAPTER 40

GHOSTS ON THE ROAD

10:00 P.M., DECEMBER 29, 1864

*A man doesn't have to tell all about himself
just to satisfy another's need to know.*

RAIN AND SLEET mixed with snow makes the road difficult to travel. We sneak along like a buck returning to his bed for the night, having roamed all day searching for acorns and chasing does. Five miles south of Bellefontaine at the crossroads that goes to Pigeon Roost to the east and Lodi to the west, we hear horses coming. I alert Captain Beckwith, who holds up the column. We ease out of sight. Twenty ghostly shapes slosh through the icy mud.

Poole whispers, "Dang, Lummy! They look like haints from a graveyard. Are they real?"

I put my finger to my lips and whisper back, "Oh, they're real all right. Act drunk."

We step our horses out from the shadows, rifles cocked. "Now what brings you fine gentlemen out on such a cold and rainy night?"

They stop short and pull their guns from underneath their jackets, where they've kept them dry.

The sergeant leans on his saddle horn. "Guess I could ask you the same thing, you dumbass farm boy."

We scared him.

I calmly nod though I don't like him calling me names. But with twenty rifles and shotguns pointed in my direction, I'll take the slur. For now.

I laugh in a half-drunk kind of way stumbling over my words. "Aw, no need for name callin'. We got nowheres to go, suh. We done spent what little silver we had on whiskey and whores in Bucksnort. You boys wanna go? We'll take you there for the small price of a bottle."

I fake like I'm about to slide out of my saddle and pull my pistol quicker than a copperhead strike. I point the barrel directly at the sergeant's forehead, cocking it quickly. He draws back, and I speak loud enough for Captain Beckwith to hear. He and his men have come up quietly behind the sergeant and his men, but they don't know it.

I ask, "You boys votin' for Davis or Lincoln this year?"

It's difficult to tell if they're Yankees or Rebels covered with slickers and blankets. But it's not hard to detect a Yankee trying to pull off a southern accent. I notice the U.S. brands on their horses, but that doesn't mean a thing either. Horses get stolen. Some switch sides more than once.

I laugh, trying to lighten the tense moment before he speaks. "Guess it depends on who's payin' the most at the moment, huh?"

The rest of the sergeant's men surround us, but they still haven't realized Captain Beckwith and his thirty soldiers have come up behind them with rifles trained on their backs. The sergeant hears a horse snort that's too far back to be one of his.

He understands his predicament and declares, "I'm Sergeant Parr of the 3rd Iowa Cavalry, and these are my men. Now, am I a prisoner, or are you boys votin' for Lincoln this year?"

Captain Beckwith rides up with hand stuck out laughing. "We're Lincoln men, Sergeant. Relax, and I'll give you good reason to come with us if you like. I'm Captain Beckwith, 4th Iowa Cavalry, better known as the Hawkeyes. Damn glad to run into you. You men look to be a horde of demon ghosts riding in this devilish weather."

Sergeant Parr sighs with relief, and his men put their weapons away. He explains that he and his men were out foraging but got turned around thinking this was the road back their camp.

Captain Beckwith explains the mission and asks if they'd like to accompany us.

Without hesitation Sergeant Parr says, "Well, hell yeah, we'll go with you." His men nod. "Burn a damn secesh town to the ground and chase pretty Reb gals around? I can't think of anything better to do even on a shitty night like tonight."

His men chuckle quietly but have the look of demons in their eyes. These men aren't just on a mission to end the war. No, they go beyond orders to pillage, plunder, and rape. I ain't having it.

I step my horse up within arm's length and look him dead in the eye. "You do that and this dumbass farm boy who had you hawg tied for the slaughter house before you even knew what happened will burn your ignert ass to the ground, do you hear?" I raise my Sharps carbine from his gut to his head.

Captain Beckwith quietly barks, "Private Tullos, that's enough! But he's right, Sergeant, there will be no burning of Bankston. Manufactories and public property, that's all. Any harm comes to the civilians or private property, I'll have your hide, you hear?"

Parr says nothing.

Captain Beckwith stands up in his stirrups. "That goes for the rest of you men, too."

They whisper together, "Yes, sir."

"Is that clear, Sergeant Parr?"

He answers, "Yes, sir, I get it." He glares at me, but I match it with my finger still resting an inch from the trigger of my Sharps so he can see it. I wink, and he growls, "What's it like being a damn Rebel turncoat?"

"No worse than being a man who can only get a woman by forcing her into bed, Sergeant."

I say nothing more because I owe him nothing. Not even an explanation. A man doesn't have to tell all he knows about himself just to satisfy another's need to know. Silence can often be a better weapon than running your mouth. I nudge Cloud forward, giving Sergeant Parr a glare.

We skirt the county seat of Greensborough without so much as a dog barking. The weather has turned colder and windier, and the rain has become steady sheets of sleet. Even the worst of drunks wouldn't brave the road to Bucksnort for a drink tonight except to get warm in a saloon. In Bucksnort, that'd be in a whore's bed.

Pa warned many times, keep your roosters in your britches when you pass Bucksnort or you'll catch a disease you can't explain to a new bride. I'm glad I followed his advice.

It's terrible weather to travel in but perfect cover for a detachment of cavalry slipping through the countryside. I shiver a little. Not because of the cold but for what I might have to do. I'm fully capable and willing to do it.

We have ten miles to make Bankston by midnight. That gives me a couple of hours to enjoy the peace of a cold stormy night when no one wants to talk much, not even Poole. I didn't think I'd be back home so soon. But I was asked to do exactly this—lead the Yankees to Bankston to destroy the factories.

It's probably not very smart coming back to Choctaw County with a bunch of Yankees. But we'll be in and out of Bankston before the first squirrel barks in the morning. The last thing I want is to cause more grief for my family. Killing Lester caused enough trouble, but it had to be done. I don't regret protecting them, but it caused quite a stir when they found my alligator tooth necklace on his body. Fortunately, Sheriff Platner was as glad to be rid of that bastard as I was.

Too much change in too little time. I want to tell Ma how George died but not in a letter. That needs to be done in person. George was a straight and true arrow when it came to his convictions. Ma said there was no talking him out of joining up with the 15th Mississippi Infantry. She said his darling new wife, Sarah, cried and pleaded to no avail. He was determined to protect home and family. Now he's buried on some forgotten battlefield in Tennessee, never to return home. Such conviction has to be honored.

It hits me again and hard. Damn! George killed and Amariah dead from some unknown disease. Ben murdered by that damn Dawg Smith. All were violent deaths. Dead because of a war they didn't start. How will Jasper and James see me now? Will they hate me because I fight for the blue? Will they call me a traitor? Would they shoot me if we crossed paths? They'd have to follow orders. Would that mean shooting a brother? It did in Vicksburg. If it happens, I'll take the bullet. War is hell on a family.

I can't blame the Good Lord. He didn't start this war. We did. I once told Mr. Gilmore how I wished we humans hadn't eaten the fruit in the Garden of Eden. Death came in a bite, and death has been biting back ever since. His response rings true even now. "Then each one of us should give the fruit back and apologize for thinking we know what's better for our lives than Creator." Mr. Gilmore possessed wisdom of the ages.

I think about what home means. Ben mentioned several times he never felt like he had a home growing up and didn't, until he and Dorcas made one together in Winn Parish. He always felt like Pa wanted us gone and rarely made it pleasant for us growing up. Maybe he and Pa have made peace now that their home is in the heavenly realms. I say a short prayer about that.

Bankston is close. We're nearing the wagon road to the Tullos farm and home. Home is as elusive as an old buck sneaking into the deep woods to hide from hunters. Home now has become where I lay my head each night—where I am in the moment. *Will I settle in Choctaw County one day with Martha? Lord?*

Until then, this horse and bedroll are my home.

CHAPTER 41

A LATE CHRISTMAS GIFT

JUST BEFORE MIDNIGHT, DECEMBER 29, 1864

Better to get a late Christmas gift than none at all.

WE'RE ONE HUNDRED and forty men on horseback moving quietly through forests familiar only to Poole and me. We lead the Third and Fourth Iowa Cavalry across icy Big Bywy Creek Bridge.

Poole snickers. "Sure could use a snort of Uncle Rube's fine moonshine right about now."

"That'd be good."

I expect to see no one in the darkness near my home, but lights of familiar farms flicker where people I know live their lives. Some of them work in Wesson's mills. It's their livelihood, and I'm about to make their lives more hellish than they already are. I trust the Good Lord will shorten the war because of what we're about to do, and the hell storm that will come with it.

We pass the road that leads to our farm and suddenly the bushes rustle. "Don't shoot, I'm a friend to the Union and here with information y'all might want."

I can't believe my ears. "Elihu?" I hold up the column, and Captain Beckwith trots forward, accompanied by two privates with shotguns up and ready to shoot. I signal all is well and turn back to Elihu who crawls out of a pine thicket.

Elihu rubs his eyes. "'Lummy, is that you? Well hell, boy, ain't you a sight for sore eyes?"

I turn to Captain Beckwith. "It's all right, sir. He's my brother, Elihu Tullos, true to the Union and makes the best muscadine wine in the whole county." I hop off my horse and bear hug him.

Captain Beckwith shifts in his saddle. "Private Tullos, we have no time for this. Get the information, and let's get goin'."

"Yes, sir! What'cha got, big brother?"

"Good to see you, little brother. Ma, the girls, and Seth are good. We're makin' it fine."

Captain Beckwith clears his throat.

"Oh yeah, Lummy, don't take the Trace except to cross it on your way to Bankston. The Home Guard has men watchin' the road all the way to French Camp. They know you're somewhere in the county."

Captain Beckwith asks, "Son, are you sure?"

Elihu laughs. "Yeah, everybody knows you're comin'. They just don't know when you'll strike. You're smart to come in this storm. You'll catch 'em in bed tonight. Take the Hamrick Creek Road, Lummy. You know the way from there."

I whisper, "The storm that carried me home."

Beckworth checks a map under his slicker. "Tullos, do you know the way?"

"Like the back of my hand, sir." I turn back to Elihu. "Is the Home Guard lookin' for us tonight in this weather?"

Elihu shakes his head and looks at Captain Beckwith. "Hell naw. Since y'all caught Ford, them boys ain't been worth a shit. Don't worry about them. They're probably drunk by now anyway. I took a load of moonshine for their New Year's celebration. You know them. They're already in it by now. Just go the roads I told you, and you'll be all right."

Poole whispers, "You got any shine on you now?"

"My friend, Poole, I knew you bastards would be comin'. Here's two jugs to chase the chill away. It ain't Uncle Rube's recipe, God rest his moonshine makin' soul, but it's damn good." He hands Poole the jugs. "Call it a late Merry Christmas gift."

He takes the jugs from Elihu. "Better to get a Christmas gift late than none at all."

Captain Beckwith clears his throat again, his patience wearing thin. "Private Tullos, keep the cobs in those jugs until I order them pulled. Mount up, let's go."

"Yes, sir, thank you, sir!"

Elihu snickers. "Damn, Lummy, I ain't never seen you take orders so easy. Pa wouldn't even recognize you, boy."

"In more ways than one, brother. Good to see you. Kiss Ma and the girls. Hug Seth for me. Gotta go."

Elihu takes me by the shoulders. "I'm proud of you, boy. Always knew you were the strongest of us all. I look forward to seein' Bankston tomorrow after you boys do your deed."

"I ain't looking forward to it, but it has to be done."

I turn my horse to lead the column, and Elihu slaps my leg. "You're doin' the right thing. Get it done and get on back home."

I nod and wave as Elihu slips away into the darkness.

CHAPTER 42

GOING TO CHURCH TO PLAN THE DEVIL'S WORK

MIDNIGHT, DECEMBER 30, 1864

Even the Devil goes to church. It's where he does his best work.

WE TURN WEST at Baptism Branch and rest our horses beside the McCurtain Creek graveyard. We go in the Baptist church house to get out of the weather for a moment. I build a fire in the wood stove and soon the warmth of the small building takes the sting of freezing temperatures out of our hands and feet. Over a hundred men crowd in. Some eat light rations and drink from canteens. I have no appetite for food or for what we're about to do.

I stand next to Poole. "Makin' the evil plans in the church house. I guess even the Devil goes to church sometimes."

"It's where he does his best work."

Captain Beckwith calls me over and asks Sergeant Parr of the 3rd Iowa Cavalry to join us. I don't like Parr, but I ain't in charge. Captain Beckwith explains his plan from the map I drew earlier today. I remind him where the principle targets for burning are located.

Captain Beckwith straightens up, rubbing his back. "Sergeant, since you boys are itchin' to see some action, and I possess the larger force, I order you to set the fires. My men will guard all entrances into the town. That'll make it easier to coordinate our efforts."

Sergeant Parr agrees and looks at the map. He asks a couple of questions of the captain who points at me for the answer. Sergeant Parr looks at me in disgust and asks about any possible resistance. I inform him of what I know.

Captain Beckwith motions Sergeant Parr and me closer. "You two must get along, get this thing done, and get out of there in one piece. Put your differences aside, that's an order. You can settle your issues when this mission is done if you just have to. I don't want to hear anything else about it. Get on the same side of this thing, is that clear?"

I wait for Sergeant Parr to speak first.

Captain Beckwith repeats gruffly, "Is that clear?"

We salute. "Yes, sir."

Captain Beckwith stares at Parr. "Private Tullos is under my command, Sergeant. He answers only to me. He is chief scout on this raid with Private Poole over there. You have no authority over them. You will follow his lead, and he will report as to your conduct immediately upon your return. Should you encounter resistance, fall back to my lines, and we'll assess what needs to happen next. But if I even hear of any harm done to civilians or their property, you best give your heart to Jesus right now in this church house while you can, because if you disobey my orders, your ass will be mine. I say that upon penalty of death. That's straight from General Grierson himself. Do you understand?"

"Yes, sir. I will obey my orders and do what's right."

Captain Beckwith grins and pats him on the shoulder. "I have no doubt that you will. Now, Private Tullos, bring in those two jugs and let these men have a sip of the Devil's brew before they have to do a demon's work."

I salute and walk to the church door. I step outside and check on my horse first. I need some air after having to share it with that bastard, Sergeant Parr. I do hope there will be no trouble. More than one man has been shot by friendly fire in the heat of battle, and no one's been the wiser. I don't want to die from a bullet in my back in my own hometown.

A layer of snow and ice forms on my coat. My horse puffs foggy breath like a locomotive pulling a hill. Numbness takes my hands in a couple of minutes. I put them under my slicker. On the trail I worried that if we ran into Rebs, I wouldn't be able to pull a trigger. But the weather isn't the only cold plaguing me tonight. My soul has lost its warmth.

I keep telling myself I'm doing the right thing. I'm glad Elihu reassured me. Sometimes doing the right thing doesn't feel like the right thing. I guess it doesn't have to. I just want it to.

The captain gave strict instructions that no damage or harm is to come to civilians, at all. We're only to destroy the cotton and wool mills, the shoe and cloth factories, the tannery, and flour mill. When I walked out of the church building, I overheard some men talking about looting and deflowering southern girls.

Poole steps out of the building. "You better get inside. Some of the 3rd Iowa boys are makin' evil plans."

I walk back inside with the two jugs held high. "Captain's orders, men, gather round." I walk through the crowd to where the flames lick the front of the open door to the cherry-red potbelly stove. I pull out my cup, and Poole hands me his. We get a couple of swallows in our tin cups and move away as the men take their turns getting liquor.

Poole and I stand back until the moonshine jugs are drained. Off to the side, I overhear words about looting and raping. I move to the stove where they make their plans. I stick my hands out to soak in the warmth of the flames.

The youngest in the group smiles up at me. "Thank you for the moonshine. It's my first taste. It made me feel warm from the top of my head to the bottom of my feet."

The biggest of the bunch drains his cup. "Yeah, good moonshine will sneak right up on you. I had an uncle once who'd never tasted good shine before. I brought him a quart jar for Christmas but told him to sip it slow and only a little at a time. He was up late one night with his head in a good book. He'd sip a little shine, read a few pages, sip a little more, read a little more, forgettin' how long he'd been sittin', reading, and sippin'. Finally, he told his wife, "Ain't nothin' to this shine except a little warm feelin'." So he got up from his chair to go to the outhouse. When he stood up, he couldn't straighten up. He started walkin' to the door bent over at the waist faster and faster until he ran his head right into his own front door."

The youngest one falls off his church pew laughing so hard.

I laugh with them. "That's dang funny. Remind me, where you boys from?" I look around at the shadowy faces lit up only when the fire flickers. They say nothing, so I ask, "Ain't it Biloxi, Red Lick, Natchez, maybe Meridian?"

They shake their heads. I know they're not from Mississippi.

The biggest one grins. "Them's all towns here in Mississippi, ain't they?"

"They are."

"You know we ain't from nowhere around here. I'm from Bluff City on the Missouri River, John's from Davenport across the state line on the Mississippi River, Alfred lives in Cedar Rapids, and Matt in Lancaster. All Iowa corn fed and hog raised."

I step closer laying my hand on my pistol. "Good. I want you all to get home safe and sound. I heard you talkin'. Understand this. Bankston is my hometown. These people are my neighbors and friends. I'll have words, and much more, with anyone who harms anythin' or anybody we ain't supposed to, you hear?"

One smart mouthed young buck stands up, grinning. "And if we do?"

I lower my head, peering from just under my eyebrows as I cock my pistol. "Strange and unexpected things can happen in a raid on a dark stormy night, boy."

He looks at the others for help. They shake their heads and shrug their shoulders. He turns to see if I mean what I say.

The biggest one says, "You're Lummy, the one who got us this moonshine, right?"

"Yeah."

He stares at the smart mouthed kid with piercing eyes. "I wouldn't want what we were talkin' about to happen in my hometown. I got family and sisters." He looks up at me and then at the kid. "I'm sure you do, too. Sit down before I sit you down." He grins at me. "We'll do the right thing. Count on it."

I nod and walk away. Sergeant Parr stops me. I bristle.

"I heard what you just said, and I have no reason to hold a grudge against you. You're right, and I'll control my men. Let's just get this thing done and get back to the main column."

He sticks out his hand, and I shake it with a good grip. The Devil may have showed up in this church tonight, but the Lord sent him packing.

I open the small door in the sermon podium at the front of the room. I find a long, leather bound ledger and lay it on top. I move the big black Bible to the side and open the ledger to dates recorded in the late 1840s and early 50s. I read where Uncle Roland Tullos represented New Zion Baptist Church as a messenger to an association meeting. My older brother, Ben, accompanied him. Ben and Dorcas became members in this church when they left New Zion in '47. They didn't stay long. They left for Louisiana the next year.

One entry talks about how boys from other churches are showing up for what the leaders believe are for less than spiritual reasons. It reads....

It appears the young ladies of McCurtain Creek Baptist Church have captured the attention of several young men from surrounding churches, especially two from New Zion who come from fine families named Tullos and Rosamond. Though we believe church is the proper and right place for young people of opposite genders to meet and mix, we must certainly keep a sharp eye on these young men to help them keep the purest of thoughts and motives in place.

I laugh so loud, everyone stops talking. I wave my hand. "I was just readin' in the minutes here about how the good brethren were tryin' to figure out how to keep my brothers' hands off their pretty daughters."

Poole yells, "And one of them was my cousin. Damn you Tullos boys, anyway." It's a good laugh before we tend to business.

Captain Beckwith gets everyone's attention before I step down. "Some of you are of the Bible totin' kind and some ain't. I heard from Sergeant McGugarty that Lummy Tullos is a prayin' man of sorts. You don't have to wear a collar to speak for the Lord. The best prayin' comes while a man plows his fields or aims at a deer when his family needs meat."

Some immediately bow their heads in anticipation of what they know is coming next.

"So, Private Tullos, since we're in the house of the Lord near your home, say a prayer for us and the good citizens we must disturb this most unpleasant of nights."

"Yes, sir."

"Make it short, son."

I lay out my hands with palms turned up. Every head in the house is bowed. "Lord, keep us safe as we do what we've been ordered. Help these men to remember their own families at home and how they'd want them treated if the tables were turned. Let not one shot be fired and no soldier be harmed as we destroy the mills and factories. Let us do so quickly before the good citizens can get out of bed. Lastly, Lord, please end this damn war that I know You must be sick and tired of. In Jesus' name, let us all say, Amen."

Men finish their prayers and mutter amens. They stand and put their hats back on. Captain Beckwith thanks me.

"Boots and saddles, men!"

CHAPTER 43

THERE JUST AIN'T NO OTHER WAY

12:45 A.M., DECEMBER 30, 1864

Not much I can do now but do the deed and pray for God's forgiveness.

AFTER FEEDING OUR horses and warming ourselves one last time, we dowse the fire in the potbelly stove. We ride into the dismal cypress swamp near McCurtain Creek where I stayed with Dan Creekwater this time last year. Funny thing, I was hiding then, and I'm hiding now. When this is all over, I ain't hiding no more.

Even in this weather, Dan will know we're in his woods. We're not a mile from his camp and like he used to say, "I can hear you white boys comin' a mile away." I'd rather be tracking an old boar coon tonight with him than doing this. I miss that old Choctaw and wish he was with me. But the less he knows, the less he can tell if questioned by the Home Guard after we're done.

We single-file it through shadows drenched by icy dripping trees. The silence is unnerving, being so close to people I've known all my life. It's more unsettling that soon I'll be party to the destruction of the town where I sold whiskey empties for candy as a child, got the mail and supplies for Pa, and slammed Kneehigh down on the hardpan dirt street before I left for Louisiana to find Susannah.

Our farm ain't far as the crow flies from here. Sleeping in my bed after one of Ma's fine suppers sounds good right about now. Elihu's singing and muscadine wine would do the trick.

Poole laughs. "Put that dream out of your head. But it does sound good."

I'm glad Poole is with me. If I make it home after this, I'll need a good friend who participated in what we're about to do if people find out we helped the Yankees. We both are well-known in these parts.

We shadow McCurtain Creek on the road to Bankston. We're close now, and the weather turns even worse. That's good. No one will know we're close until we fall upon the town. Even then, all will be asleep.

Captain Beckwith positions his men to guard the roads in and out of town. A detachment of twenty men remain with him in case of an attack.

Sergeant Parr and the 3rd Iowa cavalrymen stop where Captain Beckwith, Poole, and I wait.

He removes his hat even in the falling snow and sleet mix. "Hat's off for doin' this tonight, Privates Poole and Tullos. May it be the beginning of the end, or maybe better said, the start of somethin' new for you in this county."

I nod, and we move out.

The faint lights of Bankston flicker through the trees.

CHAPTER 44

THE FIERY RAID ON BANKSTON

1:15 A.M., DECEMBER 30, 1864

*Burning your hometown never makes for a good welcome
from the people you grew up with.*

DECEMBER 30, 1864, I sit on my horse in the middle of McCurtain Creek near a favorite swimming hole where families picnic in the summer. Poole and I have led the Union Army to the town where our folks shopped after harvest, sent off catalog orders from Wesson's Mercantile, and where we got our first pairs of shoes. I've brought Yankee destruction to my hometown, Bankston, Mississippi.

My horse drinks in the cold water as I ward off the cold icy rain. I'm miserable. Not only because of the cold rainy and icy weather, but also from the raw chill I have in my soul.

Captain Beckwith knows what's at stake if I'm seen destroying my hometown. Some callings cost more than others. If I'm recognized, I won't receive a very good welcome when I return.

Before we ride up the hill to town, Captain Beckwith reminds Sergeant Parr, "Don't fire unless fired upon."

Parr pats me on the shoulder. "In this weather, hell, Captain, our boys'll have the factories and mills burned to the ground before anybody gets out of bed."

Captain Beckwith introduces a man in plain clothes. I've yet to figure out his purpose. "This is Geoffrey Sims, newspaper correspondent for the Memphis Bulletin. He'll record what he sees for an article in his newspaper. Private Tullos, he'll ask you a few questions later, if you don't mind."

I stick out my hand. "If you use my name, make it Handerson, not Tullos."

The correspondent shakes my hand. "I won't use any names, just regiments and leaders."

I ask Sergeant Parr to send that message about my name down the line.

Sims starts to ask a question, but Sergeant Parr winks at me then whispers to him, "Let's get this damn thing over with. Then you can ask your questions, newspaper man."

The twenty 3rd Iowa Cavalry raiders move forward quickly but silently. I wade across McCurtain Creek to the town side of the stream near the tannery. The raiders thank me and whisper Handerson as they pass.

Suddenly, I want to lash out at their thanks, but I keep my mouth shut. Don't thank me, you damn northern boys. We wouldn't be in this damn mess if you'd just stayed out of Missip. I catch myself before anger takes hold. If we don't do this, then the war goes on, and Susannah's people still rot in chains.

"These boys didn't ask to come here on such a shitty night to do the devil's work. Hell, we started this thing back in '61. Damn." Heat rises in my cheeks.

Poole eases his horse up next to mine. "You got that right, brother. We are doin' the right thing, Lummy."

I hang my head. "It was bound to happen. So why not now, and why not us?"

Poole straightens up and holds his head higher. "Reason has to outweigh feeling this time, but it sure don't feel good. At least we're keepin' the whole town from gettin' burned to the ground."

I think about the old cause which was really no cause at all. The cause now, as much as I hate what I'm doing, is leading these men. My friends and maybe some family will consider us turncoats. I guess God can call a man to be a traitor in his own home county. Poole pats me on the back, and we ride on.

The weather returns to cold rain and stinging sleet. The trees offer shelter but not enough. We amble into town like we're supposed to be here. No one stirs. Five pairs of men dismount and gather around Poole, Sergeant Parr, and me. I point out the flour mill, the wool, cloth, and shoe factories, and the tannery down by the creek.

Five soldiers hold the horses as men scatter to their targets with unlit torches. The first gets to the flour mill, where a private lights the coal oil soaked strips tied around a fat pine knot. That'll insure the building will go up in smoke. Through the icy rain blowing sideways, ten torches move about rapidly in the darkness. They set fire to whatever burns easily and smoke creeps out of windows and doors.

Sergeant Parr leans over. "I hear the cloth mill produces a thousand yards of cloth every day, and the shoe factory can make 150 pairs of shoes per day?"

"And the flour produced in the mill rivals any made in St. Louis." It suddenly hits me. "Five hundred workers won't have jobs when they wake to smoldering ashes in the morning. At least those been pressed into service for objecting to the war will be happy."

Parr scans the town for anyone lurking about. "General Hood's gonna raise hell when he hears about this. Burnin' this place will shorten the war for sure."

My brother, George, served under Hood. He would've received goods made in Bankston had he lived. If Bankston had been destroyed sooner, would he still be alive? Too much thinking. I watch as fires light up the cold dark streets.

Poole leans over. "Yep, too much thinking."

Flames tower high, and it looks like daytime. A man runs into the street yelling and waving his arms. It's Mr. Wesson in his nightshirt.

I point at him. "There comes President Wesson, forbidder of liquor, presser of free men to work his factories, and forgetter of the Negro who makes all his machines work right."

Sergeant Parr laughs as Wesson runs about, cursing and swearing, threatening to arrest the night watch. "Why in the hell didn't you extinguish the fire?"

I pull down my hat. "Oh, hell, here he comes."

Wesson rushes to where we watch. "Just what's the meaning of these fires, suh? I don't know who you are, but I demand to know your purpose here with those torches." He skids to a stop in the mud when he sees we're Union cavalry. I elbow Poole to pull his hat down and our coats up to keep Wesson from recognizing us.

Sergeant Parr, in his best try at a southern accent, but the worst I believe

I've ever heard, answers, "It is a *ve-e-e-ry* cold night. We just wanna keep warm, suh."

We laugh, and Wesson stomps off. "Hell and damnation! You'd burn the manufactory just to have a fire to warm by?" There is absolutely nothing he can do to stop the destruction. Sims, the newspaper man, writes down notes as fast as he can.

It's over as quickly as it started, without one shot fired. I'm relieved. There is no resistance, except for Mr. Wesson screaming for the Home Guard to do something. They're nowhere to be found. Neither can the 500 employees working for him be found anywhere. That's not so strange. Who wants to die for cloth and shoes anyway?

Being the commander of the Home Guard, Wesson surely must've known there'd be a raid sometime soon. After all, his is the last of the mills still operating in Mississippi. The others at Woodville, Jackson, and the state penitentiary were destroyed some time ago.

I tell Sims, "Bankston has been the last best kept secret in Mississippi. The Yankees didn't know it was in full operation until my friend, Mr. Henry Pettus Dotson, sent word to the Yanks." I answer Sims's questions as we watch the fires take down the buildings.

Walls tumble down, and flames die to a smolder. I want to pray for forgiveness, but I'm not convinced that I should. The 3rd Iowa keep their word—no civilian is hurt, no private property is harmed. Sims seems happy with what he's recorded.

Sergeant Parr inspects the damage for his report to Captain Beckwith and returns to the spot where Poole and I wait. "Private Tullos, our men will stay until daylight since there appears to be no resistance. They want to rest up, dry out a bit, and maybe get a hot breakfast before we catch up to the column. You and Private Poole want to join us?"

"Yes, sir, thank you, sir." We're counting on our long hair and grisly beards to disguise who we are. We'd never live it down, or them let us live, if we're recognized.

I ask forgiveness and give thanks in the same breath. The Lord surely gave us the right night for this raid.

CHAPTER 45

AFTER
THE RAID

4:00 A.M., NEW YEAR'S EVE, 1864

A stranger in my own hometown—it's best that way.

THE RAID IS I over. The flour mill is ashes. The cloth and shoe factories smolder. The wool mill is a pile of burnt wood and crumbled bricks. The tannery still smells to high heaven. We're the only ones out on the cold windy street. I'm happy about that. Though I don't want to be recognized, I am proud of who I am and what I represent now.

Sergeant Parr again offered to let Poole and me leave now that the flames have died down. It's risky, but we did accept his breakfast invitation. We decide to stay in town. The men are careful to call me Handerson. I have only a little concern about being recognized by most of the town's people. I never hung around Bankston much, and it's been five years since I was here last.

Some will remember the day I slammed Kneehigh down on the street, but they wouldn't expect that man to return. My hair is long, my beard rests on my collar, and I can fake an Iowa accent now.

It's four in the morning, and the few citizens who came out for the show have gone back home. With all the excitement over, there's nothing left to stand out in the cold to see. We ride slowly so as to not scare the town's folk and to watch for Reb snipers lurking in the shadows. I keep my coat pulled up and my hat down as I pass a couple of bystanders carefully studying us. The Home Guard could have spies ready to report any familiar faces.

Sergeant Parr stops at the Bankston Hotel, dismounts, and ties his horse to the hitching post. "We'll stay here 'til daylight, men. No sense lettin' good bed sheets go unused. Be respectful or I'll have your hides!"

I stay in the middle of the pack as we enter the hotel. Sergeant Parr secures rooms despite the clerk's protests.

"And who do I make the bill out to, Sergeant?" the clerk says sarcastically.

Sergeant Parr writes in big letters, smiling. "That'd be Mister Abraham Lincoln, President of these United States of America, sir."

The clerk slams the ledger closed, angrily. "I'll be damned if I'm gonna let that son of a bitch or any of his stay under this roof!"

The clicking sounds of pistols cocking fill the room.

Sergeant Parr leans over the counter with the look of a mean dog with ears pinned back ready to fight. "You'll be damned if you don't. We still have plenty of coal oil torches left."

The clerk shies back from the desk and hands over keys to several rooms. "I meant no harm."

"Then none will come to you. I expect some food cooked to your finest customers' tastes in two hours. Handerson."

I step up quickly. "Sir?"

Sergeant Parr speaks loudly to ensure the whole place hears him. "You'll serve as a guard in the kitchen to make sure there ain't no devilment when these fine people prepare our breakfast." He turns to his soldiers. "Post a guard on the front porch."

He glares at the clerk. "We're tired, hungry, and could be easily provoked into a very bad mood if you or anybody causes any trouble, you understand?"

The clerk is defeated. He lowers his eyes and nods. "Yes."

"Good then, we'll stay 'til dawn and be on our way. Your hotel continuing to stand come daylight depends upon your favorable manners in the darkness tonight."

I hand my haversack off to Poole as they step heavily up the stairs. I check my pistol and make my way to the kitchen. Sims sits down in one of the padded chairs by the large fireplace to organize his notes. One of the 3rd Iowa boys steps out on the porch with a blanket.

I push open the two-way kitchen door to find two Negro women making biscuits. They're grinning from ear to ear. The older gray haired lady rolls out the dough while the younger one cuts out biscuits with an empty bean can.

Suddenly, the younger runs to hug me. "Suh, the Lawd done blessed us all with all you pretty men in them blue suits comin' here! What about you, farmer man? Your body says homespun, but your heart says blue suit."

"You're right on both counts."

"We been prayin' you'd come our way, Massuh. You can trust we'll fix you a fine set of eatin' vittles. Don't worry none about how the food's cooked. It'll be good, and it'll be safe. It's the least we two niggahs can do to show our thanks."

"Hold on there, ma'am. Ain't no niggahs here and no masters either, not anymore. You're two kind women made in the image of the Good Lord. I want you to shuck those names like corn husks."

They slink back from the tone in my voice with eyes as big as saucers.

I calm myself and pull them close. "What are your names if you don't mind me askin'?"

The older woman wipes her hands. "Rachel be my name, straight from the Good Book. Do you knows your scripture, son?"

"Yes 'um, I do, and you have a beautiful name."

I look down at the younger lady who looks very familiar. "And yours?"

She turns her head, embarrassed, "Ruth, from the Bible too, suh."

We pull apart from a hug that I've needed for some time. They get about preparing food. The younger of the two keeps staring at me. After setting the pans on the stove and getting the fire right, she whimpers as subdued as she can.

She bursts out, "I'm sorry, suh, but I know your voice, and when I cut your hair and trim off that beard in my mind, I know it's you."

I'm a little nervous now. "Whatever do you mean, little sistuh?"

Ruth runs to hug me again. "I heard the mens call you Handerson, but you're Lummy, my sistuh Susannah's lovin' husband. Momma Sophie told me all about you."

I calm her to keep the noise down. The older woman keeps cooking and smiling.

Still hanging on to me, the younger lady whispers, "I be Ruth, Susannah's little sistuh. I covered for her every time you two snuck off to love up on each other. I was so happy for her. I hate to tell it, but I snuck off once to watch you two down on Big Bywy Creek. You treated her like the lady she was."

I back away, still holding onto her shoulders. "Can't be!" Several moments flash through my mind of Susannah telling me about a younger sister I'd never met.

I get a little nervous. "You didn't see us swimmin' in the creek, did you?" She grins and nods her head up and down quickly. My face burns hot with embarrassment. "Well now, I don't rightly know what to say."

Old Rachel reaches for a pot but pops me on the butt. "Uh huh, bet that was a sight to behold, you good lookin' devil, you." I ain't good looking, but I can be the Devil when I want to.

The more I look at Ruth, the more I see the resemblance. I want to laugh and cry at the same time. I give her the whole story while she rolls out biscuits and fries eggs and veal cutlets. She cries and laughs at the same time— sad for her sister's death but happy Susannah found love, even if for only a short time.

Old Rachel smiles. "Son, the Lawd took the scales from your eyes and blessed you with his sight. Praise the Lawd!"

The food is ready too soon. I want to spend more time with these ladies, but I have my duty. I report to Sergeant Parr that our meal is ready, and the men sleepily shuffle down the stairs to the dining room. He relieves the porch guard and sends another out on the front porch with a blanket and a steaming hot plate of the best food we've had since leaving Four Mile Bridge. Ruth and Rachel serve us like kings.

Poole leans over between bites. "The young one sure looks a lot like...."

I elbow him as I reach for another biscuit. "She's Susannah's sister."

One of the 3rd Iowa boys keeps looking Ruth up and down like a side of beef. He leans over, "Lummy, I mean Handerson, what about the rump on that pretty little thing?"

I jab his side with my elbow, and he jerks like he's been stabbed with a knife. "Friend, that pretty little thing's name is Ruth, sister of my wife, Susannah, who is with the Lord now. Treat her with the respect she deserves, or I'll use this carving knife on your privates."

"Didn't mean no harm. It's just been so long, and she's, well dammit, so danged pretty."

"With that I cannot disagree, but these women have been treated like animals. We're here to change all that."

"You're right. Excuse my bad manners, Handerson."

Sergeant Parr nods and takes another biscuit. Ruth and Rachel smile through the kitchen door window. With no one else allowed in the hotel, I talk about my life in Choctaw County.

I study the ceiling, walls, and furniture. "I always wanted to eat in this hotel. My pa did a few times when he'd bring Ma to town after the crop was sold. He'd say, "Finest milk fed veal cutlets in the county." That's what I told those sweet ladies to fix for us. They go good with eggs and taters, biscuits and gravy, and cold milk. There'll be caramel pie for dessert."

A couple of men thank me but mostly with smiles and nods as they continue to eat.

Sergeant Parr compliments Rachel and Ruth and lays a silver dollar down for each of them. "A fine meal, ladies, thank you." They curtsey and shy back into the kitchen. "It's good to sit at a table with you men. Why'd you pick the name Handerson anyway?"

I finish chewing. "To honor a good friend who owns Handerson's Café in Vicksburg. Annie doctored me back to good health when a tree fell on me one time. I borrowed her name."

Parr stuffs a biscuit in his mouth, with gravy dripping. "Interesting."

I take my last sip of coffee. "Sergeant, I feel like a bear just jumped on my back."

"Get upstairs and rest. Poole, when you finish, relieve the guard on the front porch."

"Yes, sir."

I wink. "Don't fall asleep, brother. It could cost us our lives."

He finds a spot in the shadows with a steaming hot cup of coffee and lays his rifle across his lap.

I hug and kiss Ruth and Rachel on their cheeks. Why, I don't know. It just seems right. They hug me tight and say they'll have food ready to take with us when we leave.

"Rachel, I'll look you up after the war." I touch Ruth's arm. "Sistuh, take care and tell momma Sophie I'll be by directly for some of her good cookin'. Love y'all."

I ease up the stairs, find an empty bed, and collapse. The deed is done.

CHAPTER 46

SO CLOSE TO HOME, YET SO FAR AWAY

6:00 A.M., NEW YEAR'S EVE, 1864

It's a hollow feelin' to be so close to home knowin' I can't go there.

MY EYES OPEN with a start, but it's still dark outside. I hear voices, and the door to my small hotel room creaks open. I point my pistol and cock the hammer.

Sergeant Parr sticks his head in. "C'mon, boys, get up. We don't want the Rebs catching up with us."

I lower my pistol and lay it on my chest. "Be nice to have just one more hour in this warm, soft, feather bed, Sergeant."

He laughs. "Maybe they have one in the prison they'll put you in up north if we get caught. C'mon, let's go."

"Thanks, but no thanks." I'm stiff from long hours riding in the cold. I creak down the stairs to get the food Ruth and Rachel prepared.

I stop by the front door of the hotel. "Poole, get yourself another cup of coffee. I'll watch 'til you get back."

"Thanks, I think what's left in my cup is frozen."

I sit in Poole's rocking chair, hand on my pistol. Faint sun rays creep through the trees making the ice sparkle on the limbs. It's a beautiful scene, except for piles of rubble and burnt wood.

Sergeant Parr steps out on the porch of the hotel, hands me a cup of steaming hot coffee, and sits in the chair next to mine. He blows on the steam and slurps. "Good stuff for bein' so far off the beaten path. Your man, Wesson, must have connections."

"Well, Wesson, surely ain't a happy man this mornin', you think?"

Sergeant Parr grins. "I think. In less than two hours the 3rd Iowa Cavalry of these great United States of America destroyed 5,000 yards of cloth, 10,000 pounds of wool, 125 bales of cotton, 500 sides of leather, three steam engines, a machine shop, and 10,000 pounds of flour."

"I'm just glad it's over. The deed's done but not for people who'll suffer for our work."

"Yeah, I know it'll be hard. But Hood'll have a hissy fit when he hears about this."

Sims jots down the last details of the raid and results of our destruction. "What'd you say your name was?"

"Handerson, and that's all."

Sergeant Parr stands. "Handerson, finish your coffee and see about the food your friends prepared. We mount up in fifteen minutes. We still have work to do." Sims continues writing, following Parr inside.

I take a deep breath and doze for a second when someone in the shadows of the curtains by the door whispers sweetly, "Lummy, that you?"

Startled from my sleepy state, a dark pretty girl peeks out from behind the thick fabric. "Susannah, is that you?"

Dawn's light illuminates Ruth's face. I think I'm seeing Susannah's ghost.

"I'm so sorry, Lummy. I don't mean no harm. I don't wanna bring up tearful thoughts."

I hug her closely. "It's all right, little sistuh, you just look so much like her. It's just, I'll never get over my darlin', Susannah."

Ruth squeezes me tighter. "It can't be easy, big brother, but I just had to tell you goodbye. You come back when you're done soldierin'. We's family. Always will be."

"I will, little sistuh, I will." She pecks me on the lips and tiptoes back inside.

The men upstairs come down wearily. I go inside to greet them, and Ruth scampers off into the kitchen to get coffee for men who want a last cup.

My heart aches once again for my long lost wife. "Lord, heal this heart of mine that still hurts so badly." I step back out onto the long porch of the hotel and scan the town.

Smoke still rises from the ashes of burnt buildings. Structures that once housed factories have fallen in, and bricks are scattered everywhere. The flames must've been hotter than the Devil's Hell to do such damage. I doubt repairs can be made to put this place back together. I'm sorry for the folks who lost their jobs. Things will get even harder on them now. A dark heaviness fills my heart. My life looks like Bankston this morning—a bunch of burned down buildings with bricks scattered everywhere.

I close my eyes, and Martha's smiling sky blue eyes and long hair replace what I'm seeing. Little rainbows appear in the ice on trees that sparkle like stars. Hope chases the darkness away as the sun bursts over the horizon, and my heart is renewed.

Few people stir about, probably afraid with bluecoats still in town. That's all right by me. Fewer chances of being recognized by someone I once knew. That'd be bad, with my heart set on returning to Choctaw County after the war.

It's daylight now. People mill about looking over the ruins. They keep looking my way, not because they know me, but for the blue jacket I wear. I traded my farm clothes for my blue suit after breakfast, but I kept my homespun shirt underneath. I need something of home touching me as we finish our task.

Around the corner of the hotel comes a long, lean black man with hair as white as snow. The gathering crowd is too busy gawking at the buildings where they once made their livings to notice us clasp hands.

"Remember me, Lummy?"

His eyes smile, and mine want to pop out of my head. "Chat, I mean, Josiah. How did you... oh, it's so good to see you, my friend."

He puts his finger to his mouth as he takes the chair next to me. "Act like you don't want me sittin' here so's folks don't think me too sweet on bluecoats. Just had to say hello. I expect to see you when this is all over, you hear?"

I wave my arm. "Get on out of here, ain't got no money to give you."

The good citizens turn to look but turn back to the ruins.

"What're you gonna do now that the big engine is destroyed, Josiah?

You were the only man smart enough to figure out how to run the damn thing and keep it goin'."

"Couldn't tell it by Mistuh Wesson. Heck, Lummy, you know he couldn't stand no niggah bein' smarter than a white man. He had me train a couple of fellers to take over not long after you left. Said it was time for me to retire. I know he was embarrassed to depend on a Negro to make sure his whole town kept workin'. I don't care. He pays me a little pension, and with huntin', fishin', trappin', and sweepin' up his businesses, I make it all right. I won't miss sweepin' them factories no more, though. Too much floor, too much time, and never enough pay for doin' it. Cuts into my fishin' time too much anyway."

What little pension Josiah gets just went up in smoke—the first of many who lost their livings last night.

"I'll be all right, Lummy, you'll see."

"When's it all gonna change, Josiah?"

"Already did, when you started callin' me Josiah instead of Chat years ago. I best go. Glad you put on the blue suit, boy."

I whisper as he walks away, "Be seein' you one day, Josiah. And we'll go fishin'."

He stretches his right arm into the air like the church steeple in Port Gibson with the golden finger pointing to heaven. He strikes up a tune, singing about the Lord coming back soon.

I stick my head in the door. "Sergeant, we best go. The crowd's startin' to grumble, sir."

"Boots and saddles, men."

Ruth hands me the food bags, and I give her one last hug. We ride toward McCurtain Creek on a road back to Greensborough. I thank God I made it through the raid unscathed and unrecognized. By the whites, that is.

The colors in my life have changed—white to black and gray to blue. I can't do anything about being white. Creator made that choice, not me. But I could choose blue over gray. I am thankful to see all men and women, especially black, as equal human beings with the same rights, whether some dern fools can see it or not.

Poole rides up. "Got a biscuit in that sack? I'm still hungry."

I pitch him one of the flour bags loaded with biscuits and salt pork.

He pulls one out and throws the sack back. "We did do the right thing, didn't we?"

I'm ashamed for the suffering we've caused but feel a deep sense of joy that our deed will help put this war to bed. He starts to say something else, but I don't want to talk right now.

I bark, "Leave me be, Poole." He backs off. "Sorry. I don't mean any harm, but yeah, we did the right thing. It just don't feel like it right now."

He eats his salt pork biscuit.

We pass Bankston cemetery. I wonder what Great Grandpa Cloud would think about me destroying a tannery and shoe factory—the very trade that brought him from Scotland to Virginia back in 1665. Probably nothing, except to say he did what he had to do, and he'd expect no less of me. After all, we're Tulloses.

We water our horses in McCurtain Creek and gather around Sergeant Parr. "Private Tullos, what's the best way to catch up with the column and still finish our work?"

"Head to Lodi just west of Bellefontaine. We'll find the main column there."

Parr announces, "Check your weapons. We ain't done with the Devil's work yet."

The county seat of Greensborough is directly in our path.

CHAPTER 47

GREENSBOROUGH, GREEN NO MORE

8:00 A.M., NEW YEAR'S EVE, 1864

Just because a place has a peaceful name doesn't mean it is.

WE RIDE HARD north from Bankston to Greensborough. I'm surprised the Home Guard hasn't come down on us, or even some regulars, but no one shows. We ride into Greensborough like we own the place. Citizens run for the woods or into their homes, yelling and shouting, when they see our blue uniforms. No shots are fired.

Captain Beckwith shouts, "Get those fires started! I want us out of here fast."

I plead, "Sir, please don't let them burn the courthouse. My family's land deeds and papers are stored there. It has nothin' to do with the Rebs."

He eyes the ornate brick building. "It is a beautiful structure." He stands up in his stirrups. "Okay men, burn anything that looks to be of use to the Rebels, but spare the courthouse. Burn the law offices and that government building over there. That'll shut things down for a bit." He spits. "I always hated lawyers, Private Tullos. They took my grandpa's farm for a few dollars in taxes years ago."

The 3rd Iowa Cavalry, Poole, and I are spared having to participate. We stay just out of sight.

Captain Beckwith checks Poole's map. "Good work, Private Poole. Your map is correct."

Poole slaps my shoulder. "Remember when you hit Lester between the shoulder blades with that big ole rock and Sheriff Platner made you stay in that jail over there for a week?"

"Well, hell yeah, ain't made a shot like that ever again, except when I shot the hat off a Yankee at Vicksburg at four hundred yards. But that's another story."

"Those were some good days, huh, Lummy?"

I glance at the jailhouse. "Yeah, I had one of the best weeks of my life livin' there, eatin' good food, learnin' to read better, and findin' out how the law works. And I got paid a silver dollar for cleanin' up the jail and walkin' patrol with the sheriff to boot."

Poole sits up straight to stretch his back. "I wonder if we'll have fun like that again."

"Don't think so. The world has changed too much."

"Yeah, and so have we."

That, I lament. "Wonder where old Sheriff Platner is this morning?"

"Probably off tryin' to catch the Wood boys sellin' moonshine and not payin' taxes on it."

"Probably so. Wish I had a taste right about now."

We ride on to guard the road to Bellefontaine just north of town. I look back once to see Captain Beckwith instructing the 4th Iowa Cavalry on which buildings to fire. They rush around on horseback tossing torches with less discrimination than Sergeant Parr was allowed in Bankston. A good part of the town is on fire, and citizens race through the streets cursing the men in blue.

I ride up to Captain Beckwith. He looks to have a lot on his mind. "The Lord will hold us accountable for all we do in this world, Private Tullos. I pray he finds mercy for men like me and Sergeant Parr who have little choice but to obey orders."

We ride silently for a moment.

"You're a prayin' man, Tullos. What effect will this have on what we can't see, you know, in the unseen?"

This man has deep spiritual thoughts. I scratch the back of my neck. "Captain, can say what I wanna say?" He nods. "It's like throwing a rock into a pond. The splash is easily seen, but the ever so slight ripples can still be felt all the way to the edge. Our children will long live with what we do here, as will theirs. I'm countin' on the Lord makin' good out of somethin' bad here today."

"There was no good reason to burn Greensborough, except to slow the Rebs down, hopin' they'd stop and help the citizens put out fires."

"At the risk of bein' too bold, Captain, sir, your job is to get these 140 men back home. The good citizens? They know how to rebuild. The most important thing to me is that you kept your word, sir. Not a shot was fired, not a citizen was harmed. For that, I thank you, sir."

"You're a wise man. Private Tullos. I appreciate your words. Say a prayer for me tonight when you lay your head down."

"I'll say that prayer now, as we start for Lodi."

I fall back behind him next to the color bearer at the front of the column with Poole.

"Wait. Captain, sir, there's somethin' Private Poole and I have to do before we leave."

"Make it quick, Private."

We salute and turn our mounts around.

CHAPTER 48

GETTING BACK TO THE COLUMN... AND FAST

MORNING, NEW YEAR'S EVE, 1864

Ownin' up to what you done did is a good thing, even if it's only in your heart.

THE 4TH IOWA finished their work in less than fifteen minutes. As the flames leap high into the air, we're off and running. Poole and I make a dash for the courthouse.

"Poole, hold my horse." I run to the courthouse and pull from my pocket a piece of paper attached to the small Union flag Sarge gave me when I joined the 1st Mississippi Mounted Rifles. I nail it to the courthouse door with the butt of my pistol.

The twentieth star for Mississippi is now returned to the right flag. May it fly proudly over Choctaw County forever.
CAT & TRP

We both agreed to put our initials on the note. I'm sure the good citizens will spend their nights trying to figure out who they belong to. Probably not, but we had to claim responsibility.

We ride at half gallop until Captain Beckwith slows us to walk our mounts. We move north on the muddy roads still caked with sleet and snow. The miserable weather made the perfect cover for our good deeds done for the Devil.

Poole bumps my horse with his. "Feel better now?"

"Damn straight I do. If I was a brave man, I would've signed my name." I think about the message I left on the courthouse door.

Then it hits me. "What's the 'R' stand for, Poole?"

"Unh-uh, I ain't tellin'." He shakes his head, but I want to know.

"After all these years of huntin' and fishin' together, goin' to church and chasin' pretty girls, gettin' in and out of trouble together, you never thought to tell me your middle name?"

"You never asked, dumbass."

"I'm askin' you now, shit shoveler."

He looks around and whispers, "Rosey, the 'R' stands for *Rosey.*"

I rear back nearly falling out of my saddle laughin', but Poole gives me a look like he'll cut my throat if I do. "Why in hell's thunder did your folks name you Rosey?"

"Well it went like this, my daddy said. They had Thomas picked out already, but that left me short of a middle name. When my pa took me outside to see the family, my beloved uncle said, 'His cheeks are red as roses!' You can guess the rest."

"Huh, never knowed that. Rosey ain't such a bad name. I think I'll call one of my girl children that when I have a family. I always liked the name Rosetta. I'll call her Rosey for short, in honor of my good and faithful friend, Rosey Poole."

Poole punches me in the shoulder. "Say it again, and I'll hit you in the mouth with my rifle barrel. Keep it to yourself, you bastard. I hope your bad shoulder hurts tonight."

I rub a sore spot. "You're safe with me." We ride in silence, each lost in his thoughts.

Poole bursts out laughing. "Rosey! What the hell were my folks thinkin'?" We laugh long and loud. "The one thing that sticks like glue your whole life and the only thing a man has left when he goes under the dirt, and my folks chose Rosey? A child ought to have the right to change his name when he gets to a certain age."

I don't hear the rest. I think about the twentieth star on the little flag and our initials we left on the Greensborough courthouse door. Somebody'll figure it out someday. I only found out Poole's middle name today, and I've known him since before I can remember. Burning down a town is different. People will want to know who did it.

Poole sighs. "Ownin' up to what a man's done is a good thing, even if it's only in your heart."

CHAPTER 49

RIDIN' HERD ON HAWGS FOR HOOD

11:00 A.M., NEW YEAR'S EVE, 1864

Bacon cookin' smells better with the hide off.

WE MAKE IT to the small village of Lodi before noon. Captain Beckwith dismounts. "Privates Poole and Tullos, follow me."

Colonel Karge steps out of his tent into the drizzling icy rain. "How'd it go, boys, any trouble?"

Captain Beckwith clears his throat, and we all throw up a salute.

"At ease, men. Orderly, get these men coffee. They surely need it." Colonel Karge winks at Poole and me. We grin like schoolboys who for once didn't get a whipping after class.

Beckwith relaxes and begins his report. We listen for any detail he may have forgotten. He finishes with no stone left unturned.

Colonel Karge looks at me. "Son, it sounds like the captain and Sergeant Parr were perfect gentlemen in these towns."

Captain Beckwith and Sergeant Parr wait confidently but with a tinge of uncertainty. Maybe they wonder if I'm upset about the burnings. Maybe it's because they know I have a small amount of power over them with whatever I say next. That's power I don't want or need. It's of the devil to hold men hostage like that.

"Perfect gentlemen in everything they did, sir, and we enjoyed a fine southern breakfast at the Bankston Hotel, no less. Why, Colonel, sir, I even had them prayin' in the church like good saints on Sunday before we commenced with the Devil's, I mean, the Lord's work."

They all laugh, and I step back. Colonel Karge breathes in deeply and lets out a long sigh. "That's just what I wanted to hear. Good work, men. I'll give the same good report to General Grierson. I hate to tell you this, but we're movin' out in about an hour. Get your horses fed and watered... and yourselves, too. We'll place you men back down the line so if we run into trouble, at least you won't be first into action. But be at the ready, these damn Reb guerillas can come at us at any time in any place."

As we start back to our horses, the most God awful sound blasts down the road.

I look at Poole. "I know that sound."

Poole grins. "Hawg killin' day! Ham for supper!"

Colonel Karge steps out of his tent. "What in the hell is all that racket?"

I'm still close by. "Sounds like a thousand hawgs comin' our way, sir."

"What you bet that bacon is bound for General Hood's men just over the Alabama line?" He rubs his bearded chin. "We'll take 'em with us." He goes back into his tent.

Sarge steps up and looks us over. "Sounds like you boys did good. I'm proud of you." Poole and I salute. He returns the favor. "We captured more'n ten thousand feet of hog chitlin's for you southern boys. What do you think about that?"

I laugh trying to salute. "Hell, I wouldn't eat a damn chitlin' with your mouth, sir. But if I had to, they'd need to be...."

Sarge cuts me off. "Hand slung, stump whooped, and creek washed, right?"

Poole jumps in. "Damn straight. How'd you know that?"

"You forget I've been in these parts before but never ate any hog leavin's. Glad to see you boys made it back in one piece. How'd it go?" We don't have to answer, he knows. "It's what they call a bittersweet experience, ain't it?"

Lieutenant Holman marches up. "Boots and saddles, boys. We're about to escort a herd of hogs to safety."

Company C, along with 160 cavalry men, tries to keep the large hog herd going in the right direction. Five miles into the march, the officers find it too difficult. We quickly build a large pen and drive the hogs in. That done, the entire 1st Brigade is ordered to draw sabres and kill the entire herd.

My stomach turns. I can hear the screaming, smell the blood and shit, and see the dying in the pit I was dragged into at Vicksburg. I puke and choke. Poole hands me his canteen.

"Sarge, can Lummy be relieved of the hawg killin'? It's bringin' up old stuff."

"Not a problem, Private. Stand guard in those trees. This won't take long."

The hogs squeal louder than I've ever heard them holler. Pigs are smart. They know something bad is about to happen. Their time is up.

Cavalrymen rush in with sabres swinging and slashing. Soon hogs are lying everywhere, and men drag them into piles. They lay fence rails on the carcasses, dowse them with coal oil, and light the fire. The bodies burn, sizzle, and crackle as the fat turns into grease. The smell makes me puke again. Bacon always smells better with the hide and hair gone.

Poole hands me a rag. "What a waste of good pork. That'd feed a lot of hungry people."

I sip a little water. "Yeah, but at least Hood won't get 'em."

I remind myself that this is what it takes to end a war and what I signed up for. I don't have to like it. I look up into the sky and thank the Lord I'm alive. I survived this raid. If I can just get back to Vicksburg, I believe the Lord'll give me another glimpse of hope when I see Martha. I daydream about her for just a moment.

Poole wakes me. "Let's go, lover boy."

CHAPTER 50

NEW YEAR'S DAY FINDS A BRAND NEW WORLD

JUST AFTER MIDNIGHT, JANUARY 1, 1865

Walking out of an old year into a new brings light to darkness.

WE RIDE STRAIGHT through to catch the main column at Winona just after midnight. I'm having a tough time staying in my saddle, I'm so tired. The Bankston raid was over so fast it makes my head spin. So much destruction accomplished in such a short time. This kind of fighting is a far cry from the long days hiding behind log earthworks in Vicksburg waiting for an attack or an underground mine to blow. It's hard on the body in a different way. Both wear on my soul.

Men in other cavalry regiments nod as we pass. Those who once ridiculed us now salute us with respect. We've crossed some unknown boundary to be accepted as equals. They may not like former Rebs from Mississippi, but they *have* come to respect us.

It hits me as we dismount. "It's New Year's Day, Poole."

"Huh, didn't know it's today."

"Yep, it's 1865."

"The beginning of a brand new world, huh, Lummy boy?"

A gusty breeze suddenly blows through, nearly snuffing out the few fires for coffee making. The clouds part, and the stars shine very brightly in the darkness.

"Sometimes it takes walking out of an old year into the new to find light in the darkness."

Amen to that.

Poole brings grain for our horses. "Maybe we can get to Vicksburg without a brawl."

"That's wishful thinking at its best. You know they're comin' for us."

After a short break, Colonel Karge orders the 3rd and 4th Iowa under Colonel Noble to Grenada to destroy Confederate property there. No rest for those weary boys.

I want to go, but I'm ready to get back to Company C. The raid on Bankston is history, but I have a sneaking suspicion we aren't done yet. But the 1st Mississippi Mounted Rifles are ready.

Poole and I return to our company, giving us time to rest our horses and get some cooked food. Other commands continue to wreak havoc on the countryside—destroying railroads, burning warehouses and all manner of supplies, and engaging the enemy wherever they can.

Sarge sits on a log next to our fire. "You've got a couple of hours to sleep. We leave at 7:00 a.m. on the Lexington Road." I lay my head back on my saddle.

I blink twice, and Sarge is rousting up to leave. "Boots and saddles, boys!"

We pass through Lexington town in Holmes County at 10:30 a.m. The good citizens hide in their homes and barns, but we don't even stop to forage. We're so tired. We've been in the saddle more hours than not. Poole's head bobs like a fishing cork on a slow moving stream. He's sound asleep.

I shake him. "Poole, wake up. I've got a feelin'."

The words hardly leave my mouth good when shots start blasting away in front of us. Poole almost jumps out of his saddle. I grab the reins before his horse bolts.

"Wha-what? What's goin' on, we under attack?"

"No, not yet."

Sarge throws his hand up to stop Company C. We turn our horses to form a line facing the shots with rifles aimed, waiting for the order to fire. Though cool in our spirits, we're a bit jumpy this dark, cloudy morning. For some reason, so am I.

Word races down the line to ready weapons, but by the time it makes it to the end of the column, it's all over. It's just a skirmish enjoyed by the 7th

Indiana Cavalry amounting to little. A few Reb guerillas took some pot shots but were chased away with one good volley.

I'm glad. I want to make Vicksburg without a fight or killing another man. Sarge starts the column again at a slow walk.

I punch Poole's shoulder as he wipes dust from his eyes. "Sorry to break up your slumber, Sleepin' Beauty. You sure need all you can get."

Poole grumbles, splashing water on his face. "Dang, I was havin' a dream about one of the pretty girls I met in Vicksburg. She had red auburn hair and green eyes and was wearing a beautiful blue dress. Want to hear it?"

"Sure," though I really don't want to get caught up in one of Poole's stories right now.

"I was a knight in shining armor. She was a prisoner in a really tall tower owned by some evil king. I was on my way to... hell, Lummy, you don't give a rat's ass about this, do you?"

"Sure I do. I love hearin' a good story, especially dreams. As the fire breathin', stump jumpin', pass the collection basket preachers say, I can interpret that dream."

He laughs. "Guess I need to go to those brush arbor revival meetin's more."

"Couldn't hurt you none. Anyway, the story you dreamed is one Miss Stansbury read to us in school. You were half asleep then, too, I'm sure. Your empty pine knot, that being your worthless brain, made you the hero in your dream. The evil king with the tall tower is President Jefferson Davis, and the castle is the Confederate State of America. The pretty girl is Mississippi, and you're the knight in gleaming bright armor to rescue the beautiful damsel in distress dressed in blue so she can return home. What do you think?"

Poole looks at me like I've lost my mind. "What do I think? I think you're full of horseshit. I only wanted to kiss the girl in the tower and squeeze her big ole...."

"You've got lots to learn about women, boy. *Lots* to learn."

As if *I* know anything about women.

"Would've been nice, though."

"You got that right. That's a good 'un. Sorry you missed the end. Pick the dream back up next time you sleep."

Poole stands up in his stirrups. "Holmes County. Hey, you were born here, right?"

"Yep, but we didn't stay long. We bought land in Choctaw County that same year, 1835. I don't remember anythin' about the place, of course, but Lexington looks to be a pleasant town."

Sarge barrels down the line in a good trot. "C Company, follow me. Lieutenant Holman's got us a mission."

My stomach flips. Here's trouble, and we're runnin' straight at it.

Poole whispers, "And there ain't a damn thing we can do about it but go."

CHAPTER 51

FIGHTIN' WITH THE RIGHT FOR THE RIGHT REASON

JANUARY 2, 1865

If you can't fight with 'em, then you ought not fight for 'em.

SARGE MARCHES C Company to Colonel Karge's tent. We stand at attention as orders are read by 2nd Lieutenant Edward E. Holman of Company C.

"Men, a Rebel lieutenant from the Fifth Texas Cavalry was captured yesterday and reports that eleven thousand Confederate cavalry with artillery wait at Benton to stop us from reaching Vicksburg. This has not been substantiated, but we will take no chances. Company C of the First Mississippi Mounted Rifles will forthwith communicate with Colonel Osband, commander of the Third U.S. Colored Cavalry on our left flank. You are to deliver the message that all regiments are to converge at Benton as is feasible."

I like the way these young officers use educated words with gentlemanly manners. It speaks well of their upbringing and training. It's a far cry from the Flower Boys I tangled with back at Camp Moore. They had fine educated upbringings in good families but thought they were owed position and status in the Confederate Army. They found out quickly their daddies were nowhere to be found when the lieutenant made them drag a ball and chain around for their disobedience.

I need to keep my mind off the coming dangers. It's not for fear of fighting but the possibility I may miss my chance to live a long and peaceful life. That's what all any of these men want.

"Boots and saddles!" C Company mounts up, and Lieutenant Holman leads us west to find Colonel Osband.

We've not been on the road long when Private Franklin Strahan grumbles, "Why in the hell are we goin' to help out a bunch of niggahs? I ain't against 'em, but I sure as hell ain't for 'em. I ought to not have to fight with 'em. It's beneath a man."

Sarge rides up. "Want a reason why you should?"

Strahan smarts off. "What, Sarge? You gonna give me shit shovelin' duty? I'd rather do that than fight alongside a bunch of field hands."

He sneers and laughs, but his friends see Sarge is getting red-faced. They don't laugh. Strahan turns just in time to catch a punch just under his chin that knocks him off his horse.

"Talk to me like that again, soldier, and I'll send you on to Vicksburg in chains where you'll shovel horseshit from daylight to long after dark and then pull latrine duty in the contraband camps all night until this war is over. Do you understand me, Private Shit Shoveler?"

Strahan wipes blood from his busted lip. "Yes, sir."

Sarge rides to the front with Lieutenant Holman.

Strahan remounts, rubbing his chin. "I'll get that bastard before we're done, watch and see."

He jerks around, hearing pistols and shotguns cocking.

I ride up beside him. "Just try it, please. We'll decorate these woods with your guts. Best take your ass whoopin' and learn from it. We fight because we volunteered to save the Union. Those Negro men volunteered to help save their people. You got that?"

He glares with gritted teeth. "I still ain't fightin' with no niggahs!"

Fire burns in my eyes. "I don't give a damn what you do. But if you come after Sarge, it won't be a black man you'll be worryin' about."

Strahan looks around, but keeps his mouth shut.

Enraged, Poole barks, "Damn you. If you can't fight with 'em, then don't fight for 'em."

Sarge yells back the last word. "Well said, Private. Enough of this! You men who disagree, bow your necks and bear it, you hear?"

Poole snickers. "That's what your old Pa used to say, Lummy."

"Yeah, but it didn't make me smile back then."

We're only two miles from Franklin when we see movement through the trees. 2nd Lieutenant Holman spurs his horse into a run believing we've found Colonel Osband's brigade. We race to make the bend in the road but stop with a start, horses skidding and sliding in the mud.

Holman throws up his hand. "Stop! It's Reb cavalry! Hundreds of 'em!"

The Rebels' mounts slip and slide trying to stop. We nearly smash into their column. The Confederate general leading the pack looks as mean as they say.

I turn Cloud around. "Dang, I know who that is! I've seen his picture in the newspapers."

Sarge yells, "Get the hell out of here! That's General Wirt Adams himself And the whole damn Reb Cavalry."

None of us like the idea of running, but we're outnumbered fifty to one. We retreat in good order, quickly escaping Adam's fifteen hundred cavalrymen.

We run our horses until we're sure General Adams isn't chasing us. From the sound of the fight at Franklin, he's got bigger fish to fry than our forty-one man detail. We flank Adam's line to find Colonel Osband. His 3rd U.S. Colored Cavalry is attacking a strong Reb force. The fighting is intense. They drive the Rebs from a church surrounded by tall shrubbery and capture a bridge over a small creek. The Rebs regroup and push the Colored Cavalry back. Then General Adams brings up his full force.

We deliver Colonel Karge's message to Colonel Osband. Bullets zip through the trees and ricochet along the ground. Lieutenant Holman calmly reads the order to Osband. We dismount quickly and form up, rifles in hand behind Holman. We're ready to join the fray as quickly as ordered.

But that order never comes.

Colonel Osband crumples the paper. "You men stand ready in reserve until we see how this plays out. Then report back with my reply."

The 4th and 11th Illinois Cavalry regiments deploy on both flanks of the brave Negro troops, extending the blue line to face General Adams's main body. The 4th Illinois dismounts. They move from tree to tree, chasing retreating Rebs who find cover in a house across a creek. The 3rd Colored Cavalry charge valiantly and retake the bridge. Though outnumbered, they drive off the enemy and hold the bridge. The fighting is fierce, some hand to hand. Blood lays in pools.

As the Rebels retreat, the 3rd U.S. Colored Cavalry men shout, *"Remember Fort Pillow!"*

When General Forrest's army captured Fort Pillow in Tennessee, they shot the Negro soldiers down like dogs. Both blue and gray condemned the action. Men of the 3rd U.S. cry out in victory and for the loss of dear friends.

Colonel Osband smashes his fist into his hand. "I *knew* they could do it if just given the chance! That's *my* men, fighting for freedom like our grandfathers did." He pounds his fist on the table. "Show 'em what real men look like! Let them witness chains falling from men set free. Give 'em hell!"

The Rebel attack is in check within the hour. Osband orders us back to the main column, fifteen miles to the east. We're to inform Colonel Karge that Osband's men will join him shortly by way of Ebenezer on his way to Benton.

We start to mount up when Colonel Osband asks Lieutenant Holman, "Is there a Bible scholar amongst your men, Lieutenant?"

He looks around. "I'm not sure, sir."

Poole yells out, "Sir, Private Tullos here has been known to talk Bible with the best of the Baptist preachers we grew up with and has done a little preachin' himself." I want to slap Poole.

Osband steps over to where I sit in my saddle. "Personally, I'm a Methodist, son. But hell, churches are just men's creation of what they think God wants. They stamp a name label on it believing they're right about everything about God. Anyway, we sing a song back home called "O Thou Fount of Every Blessing" that has a line that goes like this."

In a fine, clear tenor voice, the colonel sings a line, "Here I raise my Ebenezer. Do you recollect from your studies something about a rock and the name Ebenezer?"

I dismount and rub my chin. "Yes, sir, I believe I do. I don't think it's in the New Testament, sir, but surely it's in the Old." I pull out the little Bible

Mary gave me. I thumb through the pages until find the word Ebenezer in the first book of Samuel.

"Here it is, sir. I do remember this."

"Tell it."

I run my finger down the page, summarizing the story for the Colonel and his men. "Sir, the Israelites had been fightin' for the last few chapters before we get to the Ebenezer story. They'd lost the Ark of the Covenant to the Philistines but somehow get it back. So Samuel the prophet made a sacrifice to God." A good number of the Negro soldiers gather to listen.

"Here it is. On the approach of the Philistines again, God thundered with a great sound that confused the enemy, and long story short, sir, the Israelites beat the pants off of 'em, like your soldiers here just did."

"Continue please."

"Then Samuel raised a great stone as a memorial, calling it Ebenezer, to remind the Israelites that God gave them a great victory."

Osband looks into the sky. "Read the verse that mentions Ebenezer."

I read as loudly as I can. *"Then Samuel took a stone, and set it between Mizpah and Shen, and called the name of it Ebenezer, saying, 'Hitherto hath the Lord helped us.'"*

The colonel lowers his head. "The town of Ebenezer is down the road a few miles, but I believe this spot will do. Sergeant, find a large rock or something we can raise in this place so that every time a Reb comes by, he'll be reminded of how an outnumbered bunch of colored boys, by God's own hand, whipped the hell out of one of the best Rebel cavalry and sent General Wirt Adams howling with his tail between his legs. Today, God used the 3rd U.S. Colored Cavalry as his great thunder to confuse those who've kept the ark of freedom from Negroes. Men, you soundly defeated the gray clad Philistines. I'm proud of you."

The Negro troops cheer, *"Hallelujah!* The Lord has come! It's the year of Jubilee!"

Two black soldiers come forward, struggling with a large round rock they found. "Suh, me and Jeremiah here found this worn-out grist millstone in the creek over there. Will it do?"

Colonel Osband smiles and pulls out a piece of paper. "It surely will." He scratches out a short message and hands it to me. "Give this to them."

I hand it to a sergeant who looks at it and then back at Colonel Osband.

"One of you who can write, scratch that message on the stone. Make it quick. We don't want to be here any longer than we have to."

The Negro sergeant yells, "Isaiah, where you at, boy? You can write, can't you?"

A short private rushes up. "Yassuh, I knows my letters and can make 'em look real pretty." He scratches the words Colonel Osband wrote on the paper on the stone.

Sarge yells, "Mount up, men!"

Osband raises his hand. "Hold on there. Your men need to see this." Company C, First Battalion Mississippi Mounted Rifles, stands fast. I want to know what will be etched in the millstone. As we wait, a lieutenant rides up with the casualty report.

"Sir, good news. Our losses were only one officer and three enlisted men killed, seven wounded, and only two missing."

"It's never good news to hear about any of my men gettin' killed. Who was the officer in question?"

"First Lieutenant and Acting Adjutant Seward H. Pettingill. I'm sorry, sir."

Colonel Osband winces at the loss. "All the more reason to raise a stone to these fine fallen soldiers." He wipes a tear, clears his throat, and asks the lieutenant, "Do I understand you to say we did more damage to them than they did to us?"

"Indeed we did, sir. The enemy left one major, one lieutenant, and fifty enlisted men dead on the field, besides the seven we took prisoner."

Osband's face brightens. "*That* is good news and doggone it if that wasn't the hardest fought battle we've been engaged in yet. Now, let's get the hell out of here before General Wirt Adams tries to win his money back in this poker game."

The men laugh, and the lieutenant yells, "Boots and saddles! Let's go!" By the time Colonel Osband forms the column, Isaiah has finished scratching the message into the stone. Every man passes the stone, which reads....

The 3rd U.S. Colored Cavalry
defeated General Wirt Adams
in this place on January 2, 1865.
Here I raise my Ebenezer

As Company C forms up, the Colonel quotes, *"The Philistines were subdued, and they came no more into the coast of Israel; and the Lord was against the Philistines, all the days of Samuel."*

I salute the Colonel. "Sir, you didn't need me to read that passage or tell the story, did you?"

He shakes his head. "I've longed for the moment when these men could prove themselves and give God the glory for it. Thank you, Private."

He salutes the Rifles as we turn east.

Poole grins. "That's probably the greatest event I'll see in this war."

"Yeah, ain't it somethin'? Former slaves fight to set other slaves free."

He slaps my shoulder. "And beatin' the hell out of the Confederate cavalry."

CHAPTER 52

FOUR MILE BRIDGE, A WELCOME SIGHT

JANUARY 3-5, 1865

Home is where you lay your head at night.

WE CATCH UP with Colonel Karge at Benton, where most of the expedition converges after destroying their targets. We make our report of the battle at Franklin to Karge's delight—the Third U.S. Colored Cavalry engaged 1,500 of General Wirt Adams's Confederate cavalry and defeated them soundly. We rejoin the rest of the 1st Mississippi Mounted Rifles for the night.

The rest of this expedition is uneventful. We march to Mechanicsburg, then Mills Creek, twelve miles northeast of Vicksburg where we find good forage and receive rations sent from Vicksburg. I'm tired but itching to see Martha. We make Vicksburg at 2:30 p.m., January 5. Cheers erupt all down the line.

We're ordered into camp at Four Mile Bridge.

Poole complains, "I was hopin' to sleep in a feather bed tonight."

"Tonight, home is where your head hits the pillow, if you got one."

"They should have given us a parade or a medal, just somethin' for what we did on this raid."

"You want a parade for burnin' down your own hometown? It's best we just slip in and out of here quietly. There's a lot people mad as old wet hens, who'd love to twist our heads off for what we just done." No medals for me. Don't want 'em, don't need 'em. I still want to walk through life not hearing my own footsteps.

I take care of Cloud, get my belly full, and find somewhere warm and dry for the night. I could sleep for a week.

Sarge yells, "Company C, on me!"

Poole grumbles, "I could fall asleep sittin' here."

"You could sleep just standing there. Let's get this over with."

"Men, I'm proud to say we traveled four hundred and fifty miles to capture six hundred prisoners and eight hundred horses. We freed a thousand Negroes, some of whom have already enlisted. We destroyed twenty *thousand* feet of bridge and trestle work, ten miles of track, twenty miles of telegraph, four serviceable train engines and ten bein' worked on, ninety-five railcars, over three hundred army wagons, thirty warehouses filled with quartermaster, commissary, and ordnance stores, large cloth and shoe factories, several tanneries and machine shops, a steam pile diver, twelve new forges, seven depot buildings, five thousand new arms, seven hundred very fat hogs over which I still shed tears." We all laugh. "Three thousand bales of cotton, grain, leather, wool, and other Reb property in unknown quantities of great value."

It's hard to believe that one short swath through a state could result in so much damage.

"You Mississippi men will especially appreciate the quality of our commanding General Grierson. Many times he allowed poor and starving families to help themselves to bacon, salt, sugar, flour, and molasses to ease their suffering before burning the rest. That's a far cry from General Sherman. Grierson's good works will be remembered."

The men cheer loudly. I'm thinking there won't be much cheering from hungry mouths soon.

Sarge quiets us down. "I'm proud of you men. I don't give a damn what that pissant armchair officer said about us. We're the First Mississippi Mounted Rifles, and we'll give hell to anyone who says different, am I right?"

We yell together, *"Yes, sir!"*

He points at me. I know what he wants. The men bow their heads. I stretch my arms out with palms up. "Lord, thank You for a safe and successful raid that took no life from Company C. Forgive for our wrongs but bless us for doing right."

"Amen!" Men shake hands and hug, not for doing a good job, but just to be alive.

Sarge clears his throat. "Eat and get some sleep. Everybody hit the sack by nine o'clock."

Fortunately, there are plenty of tents and small cabins available. I want to see Martha. I look down at my clothes and the men around me. What an awful sight. We smell like a hog pen, too.

I walk to the cook fire and start to ask, "Do you think...?"

An older cook cackles, "Boy, get downwind of us. I can smell you through the smoke of this fire. Pe-*e-ew!* See them big cast iron pots over there? I'm boilin' up hot water so you men can scrub your stank off. Here's a bar of lye soap with your name written on it. I can't make you look pretty, but I can make you smell better. Bring me your clothes. I'll wash 'em."

I check on Cloud. She looks more tired than I am. I feed and water her, brush her down, and throw a blanket over her for the night. Cloud's been the faithful horse I needed and the quietest of friends.

I retrieve the farm clothes from my bag. I strip off the muddy stinking blue uniform and lay it all on a sawhorse near the wash pots. I wrap a blanket around me. I want to wash before I put my farm clothes on. The cook dumps my uniform in a wash pot.

"Damn, son, that's about the longest pants legs I ever saw. What are you, six foot six?"

"Yes, sir, to the inch, and hope I'm done growin'. It ain't easy findin' clothes for a dern camel's legs."

He laughs and hands me a cup of hot coffee. It's cold out here. It's hard to tell if steam's coming from the coffee or my mouth when I blow on my cup.

"My ma back in Choctaw County always said it took half again as much homespun to get me covered than any two of my brothers."

He hands me a pot of hot water, soap, and a towel. "It ain't no fancy bath at the Prentiss House Hotel, but it'll get you clean."

"You know the Prentiss House Hotel?"

"I cooked there several years before the surrender. One of the colonels liked my cooking, so I hired on with the Yankees. Pay's better."

"So it was your good cookin' the Twenty-Seventh Louisiana Regiment men smelled and couldn't afford every day when we stayed in the hotel?"

"It must've been torture. I saw y'all cookin' your rations on the street while I served up tasty meals set with china on a fine table cloth."

"I'd given my right arm for a meal from your kitchen back then." I finish drying off and hurriedly put on my farm clothes.

The cook hands me a plate of food and refills my cup. "Sit on that bench by the fire while I finish dryin' your clothes."

"This may not be the Prentiss House, but it damn sure is appreciated."

Less than half an hour later, the cook hands me my dry uniform neatly folded. I tip my hat and give him a couple of dollars for his trouble.

"Thank you much, son."

With all my tasks done, I fall into our tent, exhausted. Poole snores lightly. I may not get a week's worth of sleep in one night, but I will try.

CHAPTER 53

BACK IN VICKSBURG

EARLY MORNING, JANUARY 6, 1865

The best order a soldier can receive is to go see his girl.

MORNING ALWAYS SEEMS brighter when you wake to the sun shining in your heart. Poole and I sit with the other men of Company C, sipping coffee, having just polished off a fine breakfast of fried salt pork, hot biscuits, and boiled potatoes. We sit like men who drank through the night and suffer hangovers. A bugle sounds, and Poole covers his ears.

Sarge stands up. "Form up in five minutes. Lieutenant has our orders."

We gulp down the last of our coffee. I straighten my clean uniform. Some men were just too tired to do anything but eat and sleep. Not me. The rag bath and a clean uniform this morning suits me just right.

Sarge reports, "Forty-one accounted for and ready for action, 2nd Lieutenant Holman, sir."

Holman smiles as he walks the line with Sarge to inspect each soldier. "I want to commend you men for a job well done. You performed your duties throughout this expedition consistent with the best practices of Union Army mounted infantry. I am thankful that our losses were slight, but more action would have been welcomed."

We respond, "Yes, sir."

Lieutenant Holman continues, "The First Mississippi Mounted Rifles will board a steamer for Memphis early morning, January ninth. That gives you two days to clean your uniforms and weapons, have your mounts in fine order, and get your asses into town for some rest and relaxation. You've earned it."

We throw our hats and cheer. Except I don't. I just brushed mine clean this morning.

Poole slaps my chest. "That gives you two days to love up on Martha."

Lieutenant Holman raises his hand. "But men, we already have a problem."

We all look at each other, puzzled.

"Private Tullos has reported this morning in a clean uniform smelling of the finest lye soap the army can buy. He therefore will beat you to all the pretty girls." Men playfully push and shove me, but Poole comes to my rescue.

"No worry there, sir. Private Tullos's eyes are set on a pretty cook who serves the best apple pie you ever ate at Handerson's Café. Trust me, brothers, we still get first shot at the pretty girls."

I yell, "But *do* stop and try the pie at Handerson' Café."

Sarge shakes my hand. "The best order a soldier can receive is to go see his girl."

"Thanks, Sergeant McGugarty, sir."

Ainsworth, just trying to be a part, squawks, "The only piece of pie I want is...."

Holman stops the man short. "That'll be enough, soldier. I expect you men to be gentlemanly with the ladies of this town, and be careful where you lay. My grandfather told me more'n once that if you lay down with dogs, you get up with fleas. Is that not correct, Sergeant McGugarty?"

"I believe it is, sir."

The lieutenant removes his hat. "Men, I'm asking you to be good soldiers who can have a good time but keep the respect the Rifles now hold in this Army. Do *nothing* to tarnish it."

A clerk rushes out of Holman's tent with a small table and chair. He opens a metal box.

Holman checks inside the box. "Sergeant McGugarty, I want you to join these fine soldiers, but not until they receive one month's pay."

We cheer again. "Have them back for evening roll call January 8."

Sarge clicks his boots together. "Ye-e-es, sir, and thank you, sir."

I finish my chores in an hour. I even spit polish my boots. I pat Cloud on the neck and head to town. "Poole, find me quick as you can."

"Don't worry. I know where you'll be."

I'm now on a mission greater than the one we just completed. That was for just a time. This mission will last a lifetime.

CHAPTER 54

HEARTS ARE LIKE BUTTER AND MELT JUST AS FAST

NOON, JANUARY 6, 1865

*One of the prettiest sights a man can see is flour on the face
of the woman he adores.*

CLOUD'S IRON SHOES *clickety-clack* on the cobblestone street. I leave her at the army stable and trot over to Handerson's Café. I feel like a young boy who just discovered girls are something special. I never want to lose that feeling.

I peek through the restaurant window. Annie is talking with customers. She waves really big, and I open the door to the café. I'm nervous as a long-tailed cat in a room full of rocking chairs. I remove my hat, check my hair, and brace myself for Annie's hugging attack. She races over to kiss me square on the lips. Restaurant patrons turn from their meals, surprised. I'm just glad she doesn't dip snuff anymore.

Annie announces, "He's soon to become my new brother-in-law. Ain't he somethin'?"

I half wave, fully embarrassed. Annie has announced wedding plans before I've even asked for Martha's hand. The crowd still stares.

I throw my hands up. "Y'all know Annie, spillin' the beans before they even get done."

Everyone laughs, and several offer congratulations. Then I see Martha's face, red as springtime roses. She waves me into the kitchen where she hides behind the door.

She grabs my hand to lead me to the stockroom. I grin at the flour on her nose and cheeks.

"I'm sorry, Annie—"

She puts a finger to my lips. "I hope you came for that very purpose, Columbus." She pulls me down to kiss me. I'm stunned but not surprised. She stares into my eyes. "I got your letter. I prayed for you every day hoping God would bring you back to me."

I lift her up so we can see eye to eye. "I meant every word, Martha. I'll love you takin' my last breath. All my breaths are for you, and yours are for me."

She blushes like a schoolgirl kissed for the first time.

I set her back down. "One of the prettiest sights a man can see is flour powdered on the face of the woman he loves."

So like in the story books, I get down on one knee and ask Martha to marry me in a café stockroom surrounded by potatoes and cabbages with the smell of fresh bread and pies baking. I look up into her eyes, and she smiles like an angel of the Lord. "Will you?"

"Yes, Columbus Nathan Tullos, I will marry you."

I yell like the place is on fire. I don't know where it all came from, but I couldn't hold it in. Annie, the children, Beau, and Poole burst in the door behind me.

Annie laughs. "Y'all all right?"

Martha announces, "We're engaged to be married."

The small crowd explodes with joy and laughter. The children run to me and their mother with hugs and kisses. The children wiggle all over me like a bunch of puppies. I haven't been this happy in a long time—a very long time.

CHAPTER 55

COBBLESTONES MAKE A FINE FOUNDATION

EARLY AFTERNOON, JANUARY 8, 1865

The longest walk often is the shortest distance.

MY SOUL WARMS in the afternoon sun, walking the cobblestone streets with my arm around Martha. I show her the prayer garden in the Catholic Church where I spent many meditative moments. We sit on a bench surrounded by statues of the saints who witness our love.

"Martha, could we have the priest here at St. Paul's do the ceremony? I'm not a Catholic, but he's the best spiritual guide I've ever had in my life."

"Sure, Columbus, but maybe not the long ceremony? I don't understand most of it."

"I'll ask him to do a simple service."

She nestles her shoulders into my chest. I wrap my arms around her, and we sit quietly. I don't want to leave. She whimpers a little. I sense the reason why, but she gets it out. "Columbus, this'll be the last cry I'll have to let the children's father go. I'll see him again, and we'll always be friends, won't we?"

"Yes, just like I will with Susannah. It'll be all right, Martha. First love never leaves a heart. Because the Lord is good, those two will always be with us and, oh, what a reunion it will be someday." I cry my last tears.

I leave Martha at the café and trot down the street to get a room in the Prentiss House Hotel. Poole and I wander around town while she prepares the café's dinner meal. We're back for supper, but Annie won't let me or Poole pay a dime for anything.

She whispers, after I make my first fruitless effort to pay, "There once was a woman in a flour sack dress livin' on a riverbank not far from here who didn't know where her next meal was comin' from. A fine gentleman dressed worse than her shared his last bit to keep her alive. I seem to have forgotten his name for the moment, but I'll never forget his kindness. Ever. So count yourself lucky, you get the return on his blessin', Lummy Tullos." She winks and hops up to greet a customer.

Poole sips his coffee. "I'd like to know that story."

"When J.A. and me crossed the river after the surrender, we found her just a bag of bones and half out of her mind from being raped by Reb deserters. They forced her to watch Obe being murdered. We shared tins of beans we'd found in a Yankee trash dump. She ate like a starving animal. We left most of the money we'd found on dead soldiers in Chickasaw Bayou. She's just returning the favor, that's all."

Poole snickers. "And there ain't a damn thing you can do or say about it."

"I know that's right. We might as well enjoy the blessing."

MARTHA AND I finish picnicking with the kids up on Sky Parlor Hill our last afternoon together before I leave. I have to be at roll call by five o'clock and can't be late. Lieutenant Holman wants no stragglers when it's time to board the steamer, come morning.

Annie and Poole take the children back to the café. We find a secluded spot, and she starts to cry.

I reassure her that all we've promised each other is good and of God. "We will be together once this war is over, Martha."

She sobs a bit. "I've lost one husband. I don't know if I can bear losin' another before we're even wed."

I gently squeeze her hands. "Soon as I return, we'll marry and begin the life we both long for. I'll write often as I can, my dear Martha." I hand her thirty dollars.

She pushes it away. "No, Columbus, you need that."

I press it into her hand and pull her close. We kiss. "I need to know that you and the kids will be all right."

"Thank you, my sweet man."

I don't want this moment to end. I walk her down the hill to the café, hug the children, and say my goodbyes to Annie and Beau.

Poole and I leave to get our horses. "It feels like I'm wearing lead boots."

Poole puts his around me. "It ain't the lead in your boots that's heavy. It's the gold in your heart."

CHAPTER 56

A PAINFUL BUT HAPPY GOODBYE

5:00 P.M., JANUARY 8, 1865

Some announcements won't wait.

IT'S A LONG walk to the army stable to get Cloud. I wave big as we turn down Crawford Street to get our belongings at the Prentiss House Hotel. I saddle Cloud, and we start for Four Mile Creek camp. Poole and I arrive just in time to hop off our horses, grab our rifles, and line up for roll call.

Sarge yells, "You better be on time, Private Tullos, or I'll have your hide." He grins. "But dang, ain't no barn door to nail it to." The men laugh, and he whispers, "Did ya have a good time with your pretty sweetheart in the blue skirt?"

"Can I just get it over with? Some announcements won't wait."

Sarge barks, "A-tten-*tion!* Private Tullos has news to report."

"Seein' how you men are my brothers, though that's a stretch the way some of you don't behave, I have an announcement." A few chuckles filter through C Company.

Poole shakes like a kid on Christmas morning waiting to open a gift. "That boy done—"

I cut him off before he steals my thunder. "I'm now engaged to the prettiest gal in Missip, Miss Martha Brock. Sorry, boys, you're too late. She said yes!"

The men cheer, Sarge shakes my hand, Poole bear hugs me, and one man from the back of the line yells, "Has she got a sister who ain't hitched yet?"

"Sorry, she's done been took." The men congratulate me, happy to hear good news in a time of so much death and destruction.

After supper, I lay in my tent, exhausted from the continuous talk and back slapping. I see a star through a small hole in the tent. It blinks. "Thank you, Lord."

What am I going to do about a ring?

Not to worry. The Lord provided when I married Susannah. He'll provide another when I wed Martha. I wake at 5:00 a.m., and we're at the steamer by seven.

Waiting for the order to board, a faint figure in a blue skirt appears through the fog carrying a flour sack. Martha.

Poole grabs Cloud's reins. "Go."

I wrap my arms around her. "Thank you for comin', dear. It means everything to me."

She stutters through her sobs, "Please come back, my dearest. I will be right here waiting for you every day." She cries and hands me the flour sack filled with food and sweets.

I hold her tight. There's really nothing I can say to ease the pain of my leaving. "Granny Thankful told me once that if your heart hurts when you leave, you know it's been good."

"That pain won't leave until you come back, Columbus."

"Me, neither. It's the good kind of pain."

Sarge gives the order, "All right men, get them nags on board and stow your stuff where you can."

"Martha, I have to go."

Sarge yells over the noisy men and horses. "Private Tullos, give her one more for all of us and get on board, son. We gotta go."

Everything stops. I plant a long passionate kiss on Martha's red lips. C Company cheers. Martha covers her face, smiling.

"Martha, my pa once told me, 'The sooner you get goin', the sooner you'll get back home.' Think of me often. Tell the kids more about me, and look for my letters in the mail." I hug her like I can't turn loose and take Cloud's reins from Poole.

I turn for one last word. "Martha, I love you with all my heart."

She tries to say it, too. Her tears say it better.

WE ARRIVE IN Memphis January 12. A few men came down sick on the trip up, and the company surgeon doesn't know what the problem is. I'm fine, but Seneca looks a little peeked, as Ma used to say.

I walk Cloud down the gangplank. I've become useful again like this cobblestone landing and will be more so now that the Lord has put Martha and the children in my life.

"Please don't let me get sick, Lord," I pray.

Poole stands beside me, admiring the cobblestones. "I remember when you held Kneehigh above your head just before you slammed him down on that hardpan street in Bankston. You've changed. Let these stones make a strong foundation for you and Martha now."

I whisper, "Thanks, I will." I look to the sky. "Lord, help me live in your grace and give it to every man I meet. And stay alive."

Poole elbows me. "Me too, Lord, amen."

"And dang it, would you please find Poole a girl, Lord?"

Poole slaps my shoulder. "A double amen to that."

CHAPTER 57

THE NEXT MISSION

JANUARY 26, 1865

Boredom kills the spirit just the same as a bullet to the body.

WE MARCH FROM the river landing to Camp Karge near White Station Depot. Sarge gives us a few days' rest. We're not allowed to go into Memphis. Men complain about not getting to take advantage of legal prostitution. Sarge is saving those boys from the heartache of losing money and getting a disease.

I rest easy now that the raid is over. I completed my work and will ride out the rest of my time with the Rifles. I'm a far cry from the day Mr. Dotson showed me the enlistment advertisement in the newspaper. His work is finally completed—through me and the Rifles. He did it well. So well, Captain Tom Ford went after him with his hell hounds. He would've been killed, or jailed at the very least, had he not escaped to Illinois with his family. I hate to say it, but I hope Captain Tom Ford has met his maker by now. I'm at peace with what I've done and can move on to what's next.

One day back in camp, our company doctor, Sam Bell, races through camp looking for the men who feel sick. He checks Seneca. "Get him to the ambulance, quickly." The ambulance rushes Seneca and several others to Memphis for treatment. Sarge reports later that Seneca died of typhoid fever in Adams General Hospital. My heart aches.

Poole asks, "Wasn't that where Martha's husband died?"

"Yeah."

Fortunately, the doctors contain the small outbreak, and the rest of us escape the deadly disease. Ainsworth takes the news of Seneca's death pretty hard. He writes a letter to Seneca's folks in Winn Parish to let them know how he passed and about his faithful service with the Rifles. I say a prayer but not over his pine box. Too risky.

Rumors that we may go on another raid fly through camp. Colonel Osband had requested that when we returned to Memphis, the 1st Mississippi Mounted Rifles come under his command. He was so impressed with how we handled ourselves at Franklin he wants the Rifles in Second Brigade. Tell that to the knothead officer who said our Battalion is worthless.

Besides resting and eating well, there's not much to do after drill and roll call except wait. Some men play cards or roll dice gambling away what little money they have left from squandering it on useless items and alcohol. Poole and I stay away from those so bored that they look for trouble without even knowing it. I read my little Bible and any newspaper I can find. I write Martha several letters, but soon I run out of things to say. Not much to write home about. I did write Ma a letter to let the family know that I'm all right and that I'm engaged to Martha. That news must've created quite a commotion. She had Mary write me after the burning of the mills at Bankston.

Pensacola, Mississippi January 1, 1865

Happy New Year, my dear son. I pray this letter finds you well and in good spirits. We had hoped you would visit on your trip to Bankston. Elihu was so excited to see you in the blue suit. What you men did in Bankston caused quite the stir. The Home Guard was chastised for not putting up a fight. They were all drunk in Bucksnort that night. Mr. Wesson was beside himself. As much as I hated to see those buildings burn, son, you did the right thing. You carried out the mission Mr. Dotson started. Don't worry. Folks here will survive. Josiah and Ruth told me they saw you. No one else recognized you, so no need to worry about that. We're all fine and looking forward to the day you come home, hopefully with a new bride. I hope I'm not jumping the gun, but we're thankful God has brought you a good woman. We can't wait to meet her.

We love you and stay safe, my son, Ma

Poole laughs when I read her letter out loud. "Mothers always know. *Always.*"

"She knows me too dang well." I stuff the letter in my haversack to read again and again.

An aide trots into camp with orders in hand. He unfolds the note. "Lieutenant Holman, Colonel Osband requests your presence at a mission briefing in one hour."

Holman turns and grins at us. "Please inform the Colonel that I will be there promptly."

Poole grins. "We're going on the expedition. It'll be better than hanging around here tryin to avoid trouble.

"It'll make time go faster. And hopefully, help end the war."

Holman isn't gone long and makes a beeline for us sitting around the cook fire. He's smiling.

We stand, and Sarge calls, "A-tten-*tion!!* Company C, front and center!"

Lieutenant Holman speaks calmly with determination. "Men, we have been ordered to go on an expedition, leaving January 26, into Southeastern Arkansas and Northeastern Louisiana. Colonel Osband requested Company C personally for this expedition. You men should be proud. With the new recruits trained and ready, we now number fifty-seven officers and men. Our orders begin now for this mission. First, don't leave camp. There are too many listening ears waiting to alert the Rebs before we cross the river. Second, I want your horse, rifle, and gear ready to go at a moment's notice. And third, prepare well, drill hard, eating regularly, stay away from alcohol, and turn in early each night. I trust you men to do that and prove again to Lieutenant Henry Noyes that he don't know horseshit about the First Mississippi Mounted Rifles and in particular, Company C."

We laugh and cheer. Lieutenant Holman pats the air. "Excuse my poor but extremely appropriate language men. Please follow my lead on this. Be the good soldiers I know you are."

Sarge yells, *"Attention!"* We salute the man who has encouraged us greatly.

Poole hustles to get his gear in order. "Better than sittin' around here bein' bored to death."

"Ain't that the truth? Boredom can kill the spirit as quickly as a bullet to the body."

AT NOON, JANUARY 26, 1865, Company C of the 1st Mississippi Mounted Rifles waits in line along with the 7th Indiana, 5th Illinois, 12th Illinois, 11th New York, 11th Illinois, 3rd U.S. Colored, 2nd Wisconsin, and 4th Illinois Cavalries to march to the river landing in Memphis.

Poole shivers with excitement. "Hope this trip will be as good as the last."

I scratch Cloud's ears. "The best thing is we're traveling away from Choctaw County."

Sarge yells, "Shut the hell up in the ranks. I need to hear orders as they're passed down." He points his finger at me and Poole. We salute and keep quiet.

Finally at 5:00 p.m., the call comes, "Move *out!*"

My stomach's jittery. Call it nervousness or being anxious, doesn't matter. Those feelings have always been a warning before something bad happens. I keep my thoughts to myself as we leave to go board a steamer.

We reach the cobblestone landing to see fourteen transports waiting for us. I've seen a lot of steamer boats in my time on the river. Each one has a name and must have a story to go with it—I'd like to name one, Martha. Sarge leads us up the gangplank of the *Ida May.*

I yell at Poole, "How 'bout we rename this one Rosey, after you?"

He raises a hand gesture that would shame his mother.

I can't resist. "Yeah, and that's how many friends you had before your dawg died!"

He can't help but laugh.

CHAPTER 58

A FAILED
MISSION

10:00 P.M., JANUARY 26, 1865

Some things are meant to happen, some are not.

WE START SOUTH for Gaines Landing in Arkansas—a busy stop between Helena and Vicksburg.

I ask, "What's so important about this place we're goin' to?"

Sarge squints to see a bobcat racing across a sandbar. "It has the only year round road into the interior in this part of the country that serves as a gateway to Texas for immigrants and merchants. It's long been a staging point for Rebs harassing Federal steamers. They attack boats as they start into the hairpin turn, then move quickly across the narrow sandbar to attack the boat again on the other side. Steamers traveling north catch the most hell pulling against the current."

"I bet that gave the Union Brownwater Navy hell."

Sarge grins. "Yeah, it did, but it's ours now."

I try to rest but can't sleep, so I wander the deck in search of coffee. I lean on the rail, watching the dark shore. Poole comes not long after with his own steaming cup and hands me one of two salt pork biscuits he sweet-talked the cook out of. We eat and sip our cooling coffee, enjoying the quiet. We watch dark eddys and whirlpools pass. The clouds part, and the moon shines like daylight. A deer drinks at the edge of a sandbar. It's a good time of night.

I study the flotilla of fourteen steamers. I like our boat's name, the *Ida May*. A deckhand passes by carrying feed to our horses.

I ask, "Why is this boat named *Ida May?*"

He sets his buckets down and scratches his chin. "I think for the owner's niece, but don't hold me to it. I've been on this old gal since '56. You'd think I'd know by now."

"Thanks, anyway."

The deckhand picks up his buckets but sets them back down. "There's a better story than that, though, if you got time."

"We're goin' nowhere, tell us."

"Stephen Foster rode this very boat back in November of '58."

Poole asks, "Who is Stephen Foster? A politician or somebody?"

The deckhand grins. "No, bucket head. Stephen Foster is a famous song writer who brought his wife, daughter, and niece on our boat to enjoy some rest and recreation. We'd never had a famous man like him on our boat."

Poole asks, "Any songs we might know?"

"Let's see, 'Beautiful Dreamer' is his newest, but he died before it came out. You know 'Camptown Races' and....?"

Poole interrupts, "The boys sang that one in camp." He elbows me. "You heard it, too."

I nod.

The deckhand grins. "One of my favorites is 'Oh, Susanna.' Yankees sing it goin' south, and Reb prisoners sing it goin' north." He starts with the chorus, then sings each verse in a sweet tenor voice.

Poole elbows me. "Did you know about that song?"

"Yeah, a fellow named Dale sang it when we took his hack down Big Sand Creek from Carrolton to Greenwood back in '59. I changed Alabama to Mississippi and sung it from then on. I sung it to Susannah a hundred times if I sang it once."

"I guess it hurts a little hearin' it again, even though you got Martha now."

"You never really get over your first love."

"Can you truly leave Susannah to be with Martha?"

I sing the last chorus with the deckhand. "I believe I can. Susannah came to me in a dream and set me free from our earthly bond sayin' our ties are eternal now. It's more than coincidence that I ride the same boat as the man who wrote the song."

"I agree. You can feel good about where you've been with Susannah and can do the same about where he's takin' you with Martha."

"That's why I sang the last verse with him. It helps me move on."

The deckhand chimes in, "But my all-time favorite is 'I Dream of Jeannie with the Light Brown Hair.' My girl back home in Cincinnati has the same name and same color hair. I sing it to keep her in my heart." He breaks out in song taking his feed buckets to the horses.

We walk to the back of the steamer to watch the paddlewheel plow the rich brown water. We reach Eunice, just six miles above Gaines Landing. Lights glow in the windows of the few buildings along the shore. The little village reminds me of Desoto across from Vicksburg. The engines slow, and the steamer swings around to begin making port. I get a sick feeling in my gut as we start for the riverbank. Suddenly, the *Ida May* makes a sharp turn. We grab the rails to keep from falling.

Poole yells, "Look out!"

The steamer *Landes* looms large in the darkness. I push Poole back as the steamers collide. The collision sounds like cannons firing, and the boats stall for a moment. The *Ida May* lists like it's taking on water. Fortunately, we're close to the riverbank. She makes for the landing and banks up hard.

Sarge rushes through the crowd of men. "Get your gear and mounts, and get off this damn boat. It could be sinkin'!"

We disembark quickly, leading our horses and carrying our saddles. Company C gathers up, and Sarge takes a head count.

He turns to Lieutenant Holman, "All present and accounted for, sir."

The damage is too severe for the *Ida May* to continue. Colonel Osband sends the rest of the big steamers ahead. Fortunately no one's hurt badly—just a few minor cuts and bruises.

With the *Ida May* damaged, Company C is stuck in the nothing little town of Eunice. But not for long. After breakfast, we march six miles to Gaines Landing. In two days, and to our disappointment, we catch a steamer back to Memphis where we wait at Camp Karge for Colonel Osband. The expedition returns February 13, and the men look more exhausted than we did after the Grierson raid.

Poole complains, "I sure wish we'd made the raid with them boys. Sittin' around here, doin' nothin', ain't worth a damn."

Two men from the 3rd U.S. Colored Cavalry stop to beg a cup of coffee. They collapse near the fire. I bring them each a cup and a salt pork biscuit. A few men walk away, unwilling to sit with Negroes.

Poole whispers, "Ignert asses, every one of you."

I wave at him to stop. "Ignore them. We don't need trouble with the men we eat, sleep, and ride with."

I ask the two Negro soldiers, hungrily choking down the biscuits, "How'd it go? We didn't make it. The *Landes* slammed into our boat, the *Ida May.*"

One finishes chewing, takes a swallow of coffee, and in fine English, says, "Yes, we heard. Don't worry, you didn't miss much. Worst damn country a cavalryman ever rode through. Don't get me wrong now, we done a heap of damage to Harrison's men. But it was tough going all the way to Looseana and back. It was mud up to our horse's knees and roads a snake couldn't slither through. Anyway, we captured forty four prisoners, destroyed large amounts of corn, cotton, and meat, burned several mills, distilleries, and storehouses. We cleared a path all the way to Natchez and the Tensas River that could be held with just a hundred men, the Colonel said." He takes another bite, and his friend picks up the story.

"Yeah, we gave the Rebs hell but sure wish we could've fought 'em outright like we did at Franklin. Y'all were there. You saw us whip them niggah haters."

Poole slaps his knee. "And cheered you on, wishin' we were right beside you."

The other soldier chastises his friend, "Now you know we've stopped using that word."

He nods and continues. "But the best part was when we set four hundert and forty nig—, I mean, *Ne-e-egroes* free."

His friend laughs. "That's better."

"And two hundert of 'em have already put on the blue suit."

I pour more coffee. "Ain't that somethin'? Any casualties?"

"One man killed, two captured, and seven were left sick. I hate to think what they'll do to captured Negroes in blue suits. Won't be pretty, I can tell you that. Maybe they won't find 'em."

We sit silent for a moment, and I start a short prayer. "Lord, you know the names of the two captured soldiers and the sick left behind. They were only doin' what you called them to do, settin' people in chains free. Put your hand of safety on them and shine down Your light of mercy into the Rebs' hearts to not harm them, in Jesus' name, Amen."

The two soldiers whisper, "Amen," thank us for the food, and trot off for their camp.

I watch them until they're out of sight. "Ain't it somethin' that the very men President Lincoln emancipated New Year's Day of '63 now fight and die to set their own people free?"

Poole throws his last bit of coffee into the fire. "Does that mean we're makin' history?"

"I doubt anybody'll ever remember we even walked the earth. But yeah, these are glorious times. Wearin' the blue suit makes it so much more."

CHAPTER 59

MY FOURTH SURRENDER

APRIL 12, 1865

Jesus surrendered three times before his resurrection. I'll need four.

SARGE COMES RUNNING from the sutler's stand just outside of camp with a Memphis newspaper in hand. He's laughing and jumping around like a kid at his own birthday party.

He throws his hat into the air.

"The war's over, boys! Ole Bobby Lee surrendered at Appomattox in Virginia three days ago."

Men in every camp cheer and start talking about what they'll do when they get home.

Sarge calls, "Form up and take a knee. I know you're glad as I am this damn war is over. You're ready to go home, but we ain't done just yet. The surrender doesn't mean the fighting is over. This may be the most difficult time. There's two kinds of Rebs now—those ready to surrender and those who ain't. The ones who ain't are the meanest. For some of them, it never was about the Cause, just the joy of fightin' and killin'."

Poole shakes his head. "And we got to go home to men like that."

I raise my hand. "Like a snake with his head cut off. He can still bite you."

"Exactly, our mission now is to go on short patrols, receive surrendering Rebs, and help the good citizens. Point is, don't let your guard down. There's folks who'd still love to put a bullet in your head. Stay alert."

We mumble, "Yes, sir." The news that we can't go home yet throws a cold wet blanket over the joy of Lee's surrender.

Sarge hands me the newspaper. "Keep your eyes sharp and your trigger fingers ready. There's lots of work yet to do. Then we can go home."

I whisper, "Hallelujah."

"What do you say there, Lummy boy? It's finally over."

I glare at Sarge like I did in the Tullos graveyard before I left to enlist. "I've done my part. Now I can go home."

"Damn straight you can, soon as the army musters you out."

Men hug and backslap, yell and throw their hats into the air. I stew in my darkening thoughts.

Sarge yells over the celebration, "I'll come see every one of you fellers. We'll have a good ole time."

I don't hear anything after that. I slip away from the crowd and return to my thoughts. Poole follows me. I wish he'd leave me be, but I don't want to hurt his feelings.

"We made it, brother. Feels kind of strange, don't it?"

"It does." I rub the back of my neck. "This is my fourth surrender."

"Fourth? What do you mean?"

"I surrendered to leave Susannah and join the Reb Army. I surrendered at Vicksburg and got paroled. I surrendered leaving Choctaw County to enlist in the Union army. Now I can surrender all my pain and anger, go home, and live life again. Surrender. It's a tough word to get my soul around. Jesus prayed in the Garden three times to have the cup of wrath taken away. He surrendered each time to do what he had to do. I did the same, didn't I?"

Poole kicks the dirt. "Yeah, and he did a whole lot of surrenderin' to stay in the tomb three days. He had to get over it, just like you need to do. But look how that turned out. He came out of the grave a brand new man. You needed to surrender three times to get the resurrection coming for you, and the fourth—"

"Maybe you're right. I hadn't thought about it that way. I bet that ole Devil did some serious surrenderin' when Jesus whooped his... I mean, defeated him."

Poole snickers. "Yeah, and you're gonna do a whole lot of surrenderin' before a lady in a blue skirt takes hold of you in the holy arms of matrimony!"

"Marryin' that fine woman? I'll be happy to surrender 'til the day I die."

"Damn straight, and for the best of reasons."

Sarge sticks out his hand. "You kept your word not to kill another man. I'm proud for you, son. Fair warning, it'll take a little time to get you mustered out. General Lee surrendered, but that doesn't mean all the Rebs know it yet or will follow in his footsteps. Be patient. We'll get you men home soon as we can."

I look up into the sky. "Lord, will this ever be over?"

Sarge steps closer. "Lummy, you've walked a hard road these past few years, but you made it. You're gonna go home."

"It's hard to believe."

Sarge kicks the dirt. "You joined up for all the right reasons, son. I have to believe your sweet wife in heaven is smilin' for the good you've done and…."

My face heats up. I hear screams, smell burnt powder, stiffen like I'm about to fight. I'm losing control, and I can't stop the words from blasting out like grapeshot. "Yeah, the good I did was killin' men on both sides and burnin' down my own damn hometown. I hate the destruction, I hate the killin', I hate the anger, and I hate what it's made me into. I just don't want it no more!"

"Get it all out, son. It'll take some time, but it starts today. That's why the officers make us stay a while longer—to get this war out of our hearts."

Poole squeezes my shoulder. "And the bad stuff we brought with us when we signed up."

I shake my head. "I'll leave as much as I can here when we're done."

"Give yourself a chance, son. There's more good in you than bad. I saw that when you paroled out of the Reb Army. I ain't changed my mind one bit since."

"I have my doubts, but I'll try."

Sarge turns to Poole. "You boys should be home before July to make a crop."

Poole exclaims, "July? What the hell?"

I lay my hand on his shoulder. He quiets down. "Whatever it takes, Sarge. We'll do it."

Poole agrees, embarrassed by his outburst. "Sorry, Sarge."

He salutes. "Like my daddy used say, 'Son, just hoe your row to the end.'"

We salute. "We're good for that, sir."

Poole whispers, "Sorry, I don't know where that all came from."

I kick the dirt this time. "Trust me, I know exactly where all that came from. We'll leave it all here when they let us leave. Best thing we can do is do what we're told, stay out of trouble, and save our money for when we get back to Choctaw County. Can't we do that?"

Poole looks like he's about to cry. "Yeah, we can, if we do it together."

I slap him on the back. "That's the only way I know how. Let's get somethin' to eat."

WE ENJOY CELEBRATING Lee's surrender for a few days. The cooks serve good food and lots of it. They make all kinds of cakes and pies, and Sarge relaxes our duties. But then the news comes. News as bad as the news of Lee's surrender was good.

President Abraham Lincoln is dead.

Murdered in a Washington City playhouse.

He was shot in the head by a coward named Booth who wouldn't surrender. Ole Abe made the greatest of surrenders—his life for what he believed. It's like buckets of cold water have been thrown on our celebration.

Men cry over Lincoln's death.

Some call him a saint for saving the Union and setting slaves free. Some say he set the slaves free to get re-elected and call him a blood thirsty murderer who never should've let it come to war. Either way, it's easy to judge a man whose boots they've never marched in. No matter, it won't change the fact that the Union is preserved, and Negroes are free.

We settle into dull army life with no war. We stay at the ready, but no threats come. Early May, Jackson is captured for the fifth and last time.

Poole grins, "You finally get your wish. They hoisted the Union flag with Mississippi's twentieth star over the capitol for good."

And in my heart, forever.

CHAPTER 60

MUSTERED OUT

JUNE 26, 1865

Cresting a mountain means it's all downhill from here.

WE LINE UP with horses, equipment, and arms in front of tables where men in chairs scribble on papers. They take us three at a time. I stand ready with Sergeant Michael McGugarty and Private Thomas Poole who've walked this road with me.

A lieutenant announces, "The First Mississippi Mounted Rifles will now be mustered out and disbanded." Some men left already having served longer commitments. We're three of the last to go. Our turn couldn't have come any sooner. It's a good day, except for two things.

Seneca didn't live to muster out, and Ainsworth didn't wait until his commitment was over to leave. He deserted a month ago, taking his rifle and accoutrements. If they catch him, they may shoot him. I don't understand it. He was so close. There are many things I'll never understand.

I told Poole some time back that we should save our money. We didn't have to. None of us have been paid since the end of February except for what we got when we came back from Grierson's Raid. It's not because they don't have the money. It's just a good way to keep us from running off before they let us go, like Ainsworth. I guess he figured the trade was even if he didn't wait around to get his last pay.

I'm owed four month's pay at sixteen dollars a month and two hundred dollars of the bounty money I've yet to receive. That is, less any equipment I may have damaged or lost beyond what is reasonable. And if I want to keep anything. I look hard at my Sharps carbine. It sure would come in handy for deer hunting and protecting the family.

Poole holds up his Colts Revolving Rifle. "She's been faithful as my horse. Think I'll keep her and my rifle."

Sarge laughs. "You should might wait 'til you see what it'll cost you to keep 'em first."

I agree. "Poole, I told you they put a thirty dollars stoppage on my pay because of my Sharps carbine. I don't know why. Maybe it's just a misunderstandin' or a test."

Sarge says, "Yeah, that's all it is. Nothing personal, except it keeps men from running off. It's pretty dumb to desert just before a man's mustered out."

The clerk calls out, "Tullos."

I walk up to the table. A short, stocky man looks over my horse and equipment. I think about my Sharps carbine. I hate to turn it loose. If I keep it, the quartermaster will take thirty dollars of my bounty. That's a lot of money when a good squirrel gun costs less than ten bucks and much more practical back home. I still have the ten-gauge shotgun I left with Elihu, though it's too big for squirrels, rabbits, and such. It'll take down a deer and a flock of ducks in a hurry, though.

The clerk notices me staring at my Sharps carbine. "Son, you're lookin' over that rifle like a fine woman. You gonna keep her? Says here a thirty dollar stoppage was put on your pay because of that gun. You get the money back if you turn it in today."

A lot is wrapped up in this decision. It's not just about giving back a rifle. It's about turning loose of the old life, taking hold of the new. I want to know where I stand with the Army.

"What do I get when I'm all settled up with the Army?"

The clerk fumbles through a few papers. "Well, let's see here. You owe seventy dollars and ninety-one cents for either clothing in kind or money advanced and forty-three dollars thirty-one cents for other things listed here."

"I'm being charged for items I thought I wasn't supposed to pay for."

The clerk kindly says, "Didn't read the fine print like they told you to, did you, soldier?"

"I guess I didn't."

He talks in a low voice as he calculates. "Well, I'm gonna make this your lucky day. Let's see here. You were last paid February 28, so we'll make that four months' pay we owe you, which is sixty-four dollars. Take that away from the hundred and fourteen twenty-one you owe the Army. That leaves debt of fifty dollars and twenty-one cents."

He looks up. "The pistol was yours when you enlisted, and I assume the Rebel holster was a gift from some officer who didn't need it no more."

"That's right."

"The uniform and belt, boots, hat, drawers, and such, you can keep. You've paid for them. We'll take the fifty dollars and twenty-one cents out of your remaining enlistment bounty. I'm sorry, but the balance of one hundred forty-nine dollars and seventy-nine cents will have to be sent by mail to an address you give me. But you will get it."

I understand how slow the Army works. It's not worth arguing over like other men are doing.

"Please send the money to Handerson's Café in Vicksburg in care of Martha Brock."

He writes that down. "It'll take a week or so, at the most." He scribbles a few more lines and hands me a piece of paper with his figuring. I'm still holding the Sharps carbine. He pulls back the paper.

"I forgot, what about your weapon. Gonna keep her?"

"Can I take a look at the figurin's?" I see how the fifty dollars and change I owe works out, but I don't see anything about my horse, Cloud, and the equipment that goes with her. I start to speak, but he holds up his hand.

"I told you, son. This is your lucky day. I fixed it so you keep your mount and saddle, but I can't do that with a weapon. What are you gonna do?"

I look it over for the last time like I saw Susannah in her wedding dress for the first time. I rub the smoothness of the stock like I did when I softly stroked Susannah's arm.

Then it hits me hard. Susannah was God's perfect gift in hope for new life in this world. What I hold in my hands is no more than an instrument of death. She set me free to be with Martha. Now I must take that gift and turn away from anything that holds me back from moving forward with Martha. I thank Creator quietly.

"When I first walked up you said I was lookin' over my Sharps carbine like a fine woman. Well, I got a fine woman, but what I don't have is a ring to put on her finger for the weddin' we'll have when I get back home."

The clerk smiles. "That's a wise decision, son. Exchanging this weapon for a wedding ring will bring new life into this world. Sorry, son, call me sentimental, but that's a good story I'll tell the grandkids someday."

I hand over the rifle quickly, and he hands me thirty dollars. I take the paper that verifies I'm fully mustered out and squared up with the Army. I thank the clerk, turn, and don't look back. I'm leaving this all behind. For good.

As I walk away, the clerk says, "Good luck, and may God go with you."

He already is.

CHAPTER 61

TWO MORE SURRENDERS

JULY, 1865

Life is just a series of surrenders and resurrections.

I TAKE THE thirty dollars for my Sharps carbine and buy a wedding ring in a store in Memphis. It's a beautiful band with several small gemstones scattered across the top. It cost twenty-five dollars, but Martha will be so surprised.

Poole slaps me on the back when I show him the ring. "Vicksburg bound!"

I hop on my horse in one leap. "Damn straight."

Fortunately, soldiers get one free pass home which leaves me enough money to eat on while we travel south. We book passage on the first steamer going south and arrive in Vicksburg in three days. I'm antsy as a kid waiting for a pie to finish baking.

Poole pushes me. "Get goin', I'll get your stuff and Cloud."

"Be back in a bit." I race up the street from the landing as the clock bells strike nine. Martha will be at the café. I stop at the door, straighten my uniform, take off my hat, slick my hair a bit, and slip in quietly. Annie jumps up, but I put my finger over my lips.

She points to the kitchen and silently mouths, "Glad you're home, boy!"

I push open the door gently. Martha is kneading out dough to bake bread. She wipes the sweat from her brow with the back of her blouse sleeve and sprinkles a little flour as she continues to work the dough.

She stops and turns. "Columbus!" Martha throws out her arms. A cloud of flour dust follows as she wraps her arms around me. We kiss long and good.

I let her go slowly. "Let me look at you, Martha."

She tries to fix her hair but keeps making flour clouds and laughs, "I must look a fright."

I hold her cheeks between my palms. "You never looked so good."

She's so happy she's shaking. It's time to make our intentions solid.

"Close your eyes." She furrows her brow. I say a little softer, "Just close them, Martha." I take her left hand. I pull the band from my pocket and slide it on her ring finger. As I slowly push it, a huge smile forms on her face that looks to burst any moment. "You can open them."

Her eyes pop open like a newborn's for the first time. She squeals like a little girl getting a new doll for Christmas. Annie and Beau have been standing outside the door, trying to listen.

Annie bursts in. "What in the hell is goin' on?" Martha holds up her new ring. Annie puts her hands on her hips and laughs. "You never cease to amaze me, Columbus Nathan Tullos."

She gawks at the ring as Beau shakes my hand. Annie blurts out, "We better get you two hitched, and quick, before you do somethin' I would do."

We agree that since we've both had big weddings, a quiet ceremony with a few people will do. We hurry over to St. Paul's, and the priest agrees to perform the ceremony like we want. "I'd be offended if you didn't ask me. I never told you I was a Baptist before I went over to the true church." We laugh. "I'll get you wedded and make it legal."

We step out on Washington Street. Martha stops in front of a dress shop. "I hope you don't mind, Columbus, but I ordered a new dress for our wedding. I promise it won't be too much. I've been taking in extra sewing and been savin' my pennies to pay it off."

I put my finger to her lips. "How much?"

She looks down. "Twelve dollars. It's too much. I'll just tell them to cancel the order."

"You'll do no such thing." I take Martha's hand and ask for the lady in charge. "I will pay for the dress in full when it's completed, and I don't want to see it yet, not even on a pattern cover."

"It'll be ready in four days if that's acceptable."

" Yes, ma'am, I'll have the money by then, thank you."

Martha melts with happiness. We step outside into the sunshine and find a bench in the shade to rest a moment.

I put my arm around her. "Every woman should get married in a pretty new dress."

We sit still, enjoying the river breeze.

"Martha, there's somethin' I need to do. It's somethin' I promised myself right here in Vicksburg when I wore the gray suit. I need to do it before our wedding."

"You need to go somewhere quiet to cleanse your soul."

"How'd you know?" I think. "Poole, that ole rascal."

Martha smiles. "He loves you like a brother."

I smile back. "He does. Granny Thankful used to say that tree roots don't grow in a crooked line for nothin'. They wander and grow towards what makes them grow. Time on the sandbar will do that for me. Solitude, silence, and stillness can cure a lot of soul sickness."

She pulls me close. "You're a good man, Columbus."

"I'll be gone only three days."

CHAPTER 62

THE SANDBAR

JULY 27, 1865

Finding God in the wildest of places calms the wildest of souls.

I LEAVE JUST before dawn. I stop by the café and kiss Martha goodbye. "Come back a renewed man, Columbus. You need this time, and it won't be your last."

I throw my army haversack into a pirogue I borrowed from one of Beau's Cajun friends and set out for a long sandbar five miles south. The river is smooth as glass, and flocks of white birds roost in old dead trees. I don't have to paddle much, mostly just float along going nowhere in no hurry. The peaceful stream calms my troubled soul.

I remember the poem I wrote in the trenches of Vicksburg about the island of white birds. I'm thankful the Lord saw fit to allow me a little more time on this earth before I fly away to that final place of comfort and peace. I have good reason to live now. I didn't in those desperate days.

I pull the pirogue up on the sandbar. I stick a beaver stick into the sand at water's edge. The river is falling, but I want to know how much each morning. I make camp in a stand of cottonwood trees with a few willows mixed in. It's hot, but the breeze winding through shady limbs cools my skin and my spirit. I sit on a log for a couple of hours watching the current. Mid-morning heat waves dance across the white sand. Sweat rolls down my back and legs like tears. The cleansing feels good. I drink from my canteen.

It's my first time on a Mississippi River sandbar. I've spent my best times with the Lord in places like this. But here, it's the broad expanse of the river and the forever horizon of a cloudless blue sky that draws my soul closer to the Great Soul who fills me. It's my passion, finding God in the wildest of places.

The Catholic priest once said, "Isn't it so human to think we can build something to match his creation. We can't. There's no harm in helping people focus on God with stained glass and paintings, but window dressings can only take our souls so far. We're so busy building something for God that we miss being with God in his creation. Worshipping God happens in the soul, anytime, anywhere."

I think to myself, everything in that building, even the worship the priest leads, is touched by man. Not out here. There's nothing out here except that which has been touched by Creator. I'm in the right place.

Today, I build no shrine. I won't waste my time, or his, thinking I can create anything that'll match what I see out here. Sitting with Creator in this place is enough—no distractions, rules, or fuss. No stained glass window could ever match the beauty of this river.

The Great Alone is here. All who have ever known him are here.

A large gray bird glides just above the water inviting me into the stream. I check for any boats. I shed my clothes and walk quietly to water's edge. The warm sand feels good on my feet. I remember standing at the edge of the spring fed pool behind New Zion Baptist Church as a kid, ready to be plunged into the "watery grave of baptism" Pastor Dobbs called it.

"I need to do that again. I need to be cleansed of the anger, violence, hate, of all hurt, pain, killing, of all death, loss, and destruction." I scream, "I want to be free!"

A great gray water bird squawks like it's puking up its shad dinner and flaps wildly over the gently rolling stream. Yeah, I just squawked and need to puke up the past.

I sit in the clear water on the sandy bottom. Strange, it's usually coffee-milk brown with silt. A steamer deckhand said he'd seen six feet down in late summer after the snowmelt floods from up north have come and gone. The cool stream feels good washing against my back.

"Lord, wash me clean—heart, mind, body, and soul, in the name of the Father, the Son, and the Holy Ghost." I lie back and stay under for a few moments. My soul begs the Lord for purification as the cool waters cover me. Take it all away, Lord. Don't just let me know it. Let me feel it. I rise from my watery grave, leaving many things in the current to be carried downstream and out to sea. They won't be forgotten, but I have a better perspective on what they mean for my life. I am cleansed, pure, and a new man.

The day before I left, I told the priest my plans. He blessed me and gave me a small box.

"Don't open it until the right time. Then—and only then—you will know what to do with it."

I take it out of my haversack. Inside the box are a piece of communion bread and a small vial of wine. I know exactly what to do with this.

There's a note inside I read first. It's a poem of a sort penned by the priest dated 1859, the same year I left to find Susannah.

The greatest cathedrals are mountains above a plain.
The grandest chandelier is the sun glittering in sky of blue.
The most meditative light is the moon breaking through clouds.
The sweetest praises come through birds in flowering trees.
The purest baptism is found in the living waters of a river.
The most sacred ground is inside where you walk without shoes.
The clearest word of scripture is found in the Book of Creation.
The best prayers are never spoken aloud.
Humans are most like Creator when they co-create with Him.
Humans are closest to Creator when alone with the Great Alone.
Human's most trusted friends live in forest, water, and sky.
The most spiritual moment is blending with the Universe that surrounds.

I sit still, drying in the sun and thinking about how I can be a better man. I hold the bread and small vial of wine in my hands. "Show me the true meaning of this, Lord."

In a blinding flash lasting less than a second, the veil between the seen and the unseen parts. I see all who have or ever will take communion sitting with Jesus. I nearly faint. I eat the bread and drink the wine. Now I understand. Creator is timeless. Creator is everywhere. Creator moves between the seen and unseen as freely as wind through the willows, as do those who worship him.

I ask the wind, "Who is a man if he cannot face his inner most thoughts?" Not much of one.

I have to be here to do this. I can't run, hide, or let meaningless thoughts muddy my mind. No, here I must face me. Here I accept myself. Here I admit my guilt and find mercy.

THE RIVER FELL a half foot last night. I pen a poem. It's been a while, but it's the right time.

Sandbars of My Soul
As waters of the Great River recede,
Sandbars of my soul rise, the sun to meet.
For what lay hidden for ages gone,
Now is sung in a sun bleached sand song.
My soul begs for a pure and cleansed soul,
A confession, only a gray coated bird shall know.
A mournful cry drifts over bar of sand so alone,
Awaiting mercy and peace, from the Great Alone.

I sit under a great old cottonwood, meditating on how life unfolds and Creator's timing. A large yellow leaf floats gently to the ground. It's summer, when leaves should be green and full of life. Who knows the time for the falling of a leaf? Only the One who created the leaf.

I take out my paper again as I study the irregular shape of the old cottonwood tree. The ancient giant has seen sun and rain, snow and wind, flood and drought, blight and insect. Though bent and twisted, it still stands. I marvel that it has survived. I write down the wisdom Creator gives to carry back as I begin the life I've always dreamed of.

A Great Old Tree

A great old tree grows where Creator plants it.

A great old tree weathers sun and storm with equal patience.

A great old tree stands firm in the storm quietly scarred.

A great old tree survives flood and drought in silence and stillness.

A great old tree never complains or exacts revenge from anyone for life endured.

A great old tree listens to the wind never telling it which way to blow.

A great old tree slows the wind just enough for it to be sure of its own path.

A great old tree stays the same no matter how infrequent come her visitors.

A great old tree spreads its branches to shade all.

A great old tree is content with simply being a great old tree.

A great old tree stands only as long as it serves Creator's purpose.

A great old tree is still of great use even when its time has come.

I STAY ON the sandbar three days, eating nothing, like Jesus in the desert. This last night, I lay under the stars enjoying a gentle breeze, enough to keep the mosquitoes away. I stare into the endless sky searching for my soul.

Poole asked me on the night we burned Bankston when the rain clouds parted for a moment, "Lummy, What do you see when the stars come out after the storm?"

"Eyes. Eyes of the men I've killed." That's all I said then. I look deep into the dark expanse tonight. No eyes of the dead stare back. I only see the starlight in Martha's eyes now.

Darkness surrenders to bright sun rays, like a perfect Easter morning. I put my clothes back on, eat a little, and paddle the pirogue upstream to Vicksburg. My muscles feel good straining against the gentle current. The soft sounds of the flowing stream speak words I can live by. The wind whispers, In your failings you will find Creator's perfection. I don't have to be perfect. I can't be. I just have to let Creator make me so. That could take years. I believe Martha will walk with me.

I glide up to the Vicksburg landing and leave the pirogue with the man I borrowed it from. I race up the street to Annie's café and check my reflection in the window to see if I'm even halfway presentable. I'm not, but I go in anyway.

I make a beeline to the kitchen and hold Martha close. "Life is just a series of surrenders and resurrections."

She smiles. "Then let's surrender to each other before the priest."

CHAPTER 63

WEDDING DAY!

AUGUST 7, 1865

Some short moments make eternal memories.

THE WEDDING IN the prayer garden at St. Paul's Catholic Church is a short but an eternal moment. Poole stands as my best man. Annie is Martha's matron of honor, holding baby William in her arms. Martha's son, John, stands as a groomsman next to Poole and Beau. Margaret holds a bouquet of flowers, and two year old James, holds a little satin pillow with the ring.

Martha is simply beautiful in her new dress. When we're pronounced man and wife, I kiss and hold Martha like I'll never let her go.

The priest finally clears his throat. "Uh hmm, I hear there's cake and coffee waiting at Handerson's Café."

I stare into Martha's eyes. "I'll never let you go."

The reception is just perfect, and several of Fanny's patrons come to present gifts.

I don't want this moment to end.

CHAPTER 64

HOME, WHERE I'M SUPPOSED TO BE

AUGUST 15, 1865

Home now is who I'm with

MY ENLISTMENT BOUNTY came just in time to pay for Martha's dress and buy a new wagon. We head for Choctaw County on my thirty-first birthday. I put a short letter in the mail to let Ma know we're coming. The eastern sun on my face reminds me of all that I can look forward to now. It's the best birthday gift.

Poole hands me a small package. "Happy birthday, boy."

I untie the twine and unfold the paper. It's a small silver cross. I look up, but no words come.

"I got it from the priest. It'll keep your soul goin' forward." I put the cross where the gator tooth has hung for some time. "Don't need this kind of luck anymore."

I hand the tooth to John. "Son, it kept me from danger. It'll do the same for you."

"Thank you, Pop. I'll wear it every day."

I whisper to Martha, "Pop?"

"They've been calling you that for some time now."

"I never heard...."

"You have now, Columbus Nathan Tullos. And you best get used to it. You're a father now."

I hug and kiss her. The kids laugh and yell. Martha's face turns bright red. "Oh, Lummy."

It's the first time she's called me that. There's no doubt now. I'm where I'm supposed to be.

IT'S SLOW GOING but lazy traveling gives us time to become family and make plans. The children jabber continuously about getting to live on the farm.

I can barely contain my own excitement. "You boys will get to run and swim, fish and hunt, and work with the animals and in the fields. You girls can do any of that you want, too, if you like. Margaret, you'll find Mary and Emaline to be wonderful cousins. You'll share everything with them, learn to sew, dance to Elihu's singing, read novels, help run the farm, and do everything farm ladies enjoy." Suddenly I'm embarrassed. I lean over to Martha. "I really don't know how to act."

"You're doing fine, darlin'. Just remember, they're kids. They'll figure things out. Just keep lovin' them the way you're doin'. The rest'll fall in place."

"I can do that."

When we reach the turn off that goes to Poole's place, he and I take a moment away from the wagon.

"Poole, I don't know what say."

"There ain't nothin' to say, brother. We made it together. This isn't no goodbye. It's just, see you later, my good friend."

"Yeah, there's only a few miles between us."

"And a fishin' hole between us where we can meet and sip a little shine."

Martha clears her throat. "I heard that."

I hug him close. "I couldn't have done any of it without you. I'll see you soon, brother."

I drive the wagon thinking about all that's happened. The war is over. At least the killing is, I hope. These are still dangerous times, and there are dangerous men unhappy that the South lost the war. They don't understand that no matter who won, we all have won. Doesn't matter what they understand or don't, I'm disappearing to the life I've always wanted.

CHAPTER 65

A NEEDED FAREWELL

AUGUST 23, 1865

A reunion with the living and the dead brings heaven and earth together.

THE RECEPTION WE get at the Tullos farm is nothing short of grand. Ma instantly falls in love with Martha and the children. Elihu takes John to see the farm animals. Mary and Emaline whisk Margaret away to play, and Seth walks little James to see the chickens.

Ma cradles baby William in her arms. "Get used to it, this one's mine."

Martha looks around at the farm, sees the fine crop of corn growing and the gently rolling hills that surround with tall pines swaying in the breeze. "I'm home."

I shift in my rocking chair a little. "You are."

"Don't you feel it, too, husband?"

"I'm happy to be home, but I ain't all the way here. Not yet. I need us to do somethin'. I need to think on it for a bit first. I'll tell everyone when it's time."

We settle in over the next few days, and life becomes normal. I don't say anything else to anyone except Martha about what I need the family to do.

One night after the little ones are in BED, I ask Elihu for a sip of muscadine wine.

He pours a cup, but Martha takes it. "So this is the famous wine Lummy's talked so much about."

Elihu glows at the compliment. "Yes, ma'am, it is."

She takes a sip. "Umm, boy that's good! Lummy will need his own cup."

Elihu jumps up to fetch another. "Yes, ma'am!"

Ma shakes her head. "This girl's fittin' in ju-u-ust fine."

Elihu hands me a full cup. "Okay, Lummy, what's on your mind? You rarely, if ever, drink unless somethin's on your mind."

I take a sip. "You're right. Y'all know there's nobody happier to be home than me. I'm here in body, but my heart ain't arrived just yet. My soul's wanderin' somewhere between here and Winn Parish. It won't settle until we do somethin' special as a family."

Ma folds her hands. "Tell us what you need, son. If it'll help the healing, we'll do it."

"I know that, Ma. I just waited until we all got acquainted good."

I hesitate, but Martha gently nudges me. "Go on darlin', it'll be fine."

"I want to have a farewell celebration for all who've passed on since I left home." Tears blur my eyes. "We've all lost too many not to give them a proper send off from family who's left. I hope it ain't too much to ask."

No one speaks. Finally, Seth whispers, "I'm so glad I got family to be with in times like this."

Ma perks up. "You're right. After the words are said, we'll have a big dinner to celebrate. Like Granny Thankful used to say to those passed on, 'Thanks for being with us today, because we know heaven ain't never far away.' We'll do the same."

CHAPTER 66

A REUNION
YET COMPLETE

AUGUST 31, 1865

A reunion ain't complete until all attend.

ON THE LAST day of August, 1865, family and friends gather in the Tullos cemetery on the hill above our farm. I'm so happy Rebecca and her husband came. Jasper and James are here. Mr. Allrice and Sophie, Susannah's younger sister, Ruth, George's wife, Sarah, and Pastor Silas Dobbs all join us. And of course, Poole.

The breeze lays lazy this warm afternoon. Seth quotes the Twenty-Third Psalm. Elihu sings several hymns as we remember the lives of those so dear. Mr. Allrice says a prayer that takes us up close to heaven. I want to do the main talking, so I asked Pastor Dobbs to give the closing benediction. Earlier, I'd asked my brothers, John A. and Seth, to gather twelve large flat sandstone rocks. They sit in a wheelbarrow next to me.

I rub my hand across the stones. "It's only by grace and mercy we stand here to honor our loved ones gone before us. They may not be here on this earth, but only a thin veil exists between us. Death came on a hill far away, but life comes on a hill near home. Even on a day like today, God is still good."

All say together without my asking, "The Lord is good."

Pastor Dobbs leans over. "You've done this before, haven't you?"

"In my heart, too many times, Pastor."

Pastor Dobbs announces, "Young people, remember what you witness here today. Bring your children and grandchildren to this place so they will know their ancestors."

I stand silent for a moment. "I thank God for Amariah who gave his life for his country with the 1st Mississippi Light Artillery Company C and his sweet wife, Amanda, who followed him, heartbroken at his death." I take the first stone for them and plant it on a flat spot in the center of the cemetery.

"I honor George Washington with the 15th Mississippi Infantry Company I, who was still true to his convictions when he fell at Franklin, Tennessee." I place another stone. "I honor Ben's strength to take his family to begin a new life in Louisiana. I miss him still." I place a stone. "I thank God for Mistuh Gilmore treating me as a son and Mistuh Wiley's advice that kept me hopeful in the worst of times." I place a stone for each.

"I honor Granville who lost his young life at Vicksburg and Edrow, who we affectionately called Hog Fart." The children laugh, and the adults grin. "His life simply faded away on the march after the surrender." I place two more stones. The monument begins to take shape.

"I ask God's mercy on all those killed in this war, especially my friends and those killed by my own hand." I look into the sky. "Forgive, Lord." I place a stone for each, blue and gray.

I stare into the blue sky for a moment. "Lord, forgive Dawg Smith and Lester like you forgive each of us every day." Ma shudders, and Sophie hangs her head. "I say with no regret, there is no stone for them."

"For my former wife, Susannah, and Martha's former husband and the children's father, Henry, bathe them in the warmth of your eternal sunshine, Lord."

Martha's son, John A., sets a stone for his father, and Mr. Allrice places another for Susannah.

Ma and Elihu nod. "And last, I honor Pa, who brought us to this land years ago. Good and bad, he made us what we are today. Archibald was a hard man. Some even say he was mean. He wasn't perfect. He'd be the first to tell it. But I'll give no attention to his imperfections today. Today, my daddy rests with his fathers." I place the final stone on top of the shrine.

Elihu softly sings "Amazing Grace."

"These twelve stones will forever remind us that these good people blessed our lives. Let us never forget them."

All say, "Amen."

Pastor Dobbs steps before the group. "A reunion with the living and the dead brings heaven and earth together." He takes a handful of dirt and scatters it in the breeze. "Ashes to ashes, dust to dust. The Lord giveth, and the Lord taketh away. Blessed be the name of the Lord."

We repeat, "Blessed be the name of the Lord." Pastor Dobbs ends with a short prayer.

Ma steps into the circle. "Now then, let's feast to celebrate our loved one's new life in the Promised Land." She points to the spaces between every person in the circle. "I am so thankful for all who came—you I see, and you I don't. Let's do this every year."

Everyone claps, and the ladies lay out the food.

Pastor Dobbs offers me his hand. "Good service, brother. Can I call on you to fill in for me at Mt. Pisgah Baptist when I'm away sometime?"

I can see Mr. Gilmore asking me to speak at Prayer Meeting for the first time in Winn Parish back in '59.

"Not too soon, Pastor."

"I understand, but you never know when the Lord may call. But right now He's calling me to eat some of your momma's good fried chicken."

I lean back on a big pine and watch the children play. The women laugh and talk as they prepare the meal, and Elihu, Mr. Allrice, Poole, and Seth sneak off to turn up a small jug. I soak in the peaceful moment.

A familiar looking man drives up in a carriage. Out bound a couple of children and their mother.

"Mistuh Dotson. Didn't know y'all were back from Illinois."

He waves to all and makes a beeline for me. "Lummy Tullos, just the man I wanted to see."

I shake his hand firmly. "It's been too long, H.P."

"You did well, Lummy, very well. I know it had to be tough to burn the Bankston manufactories and Greensborough, but that was planned long before you volunteered with the Rifles." I nod. H.P. rubs his forehead and continues, "We shortened the war by a fair amount, destroying Wesson's efforts to supply General Hood and the Confederate Army."

"It just wasn't easy knowin' people living here lost their jobs."

"Rest assured, they will be better off in the long run. And don't worry, no one knows you were a part of the destruction except Josiah and Ruth."

"Yeah, but the afternoon before we raided Bankston, that hound runnin' Union hatin' bastard Tom Ford saw me. They took him prisoner, but he escaped a few days later. Didn't he almost catch you before y'all headed north?"

"He almost did, but we escaped. Your friend, Dan Creekwater, got us to Union lines. Said he'd catch Ford himself. I imagine Captain Tom Ford's hanging from a tall cypress somewhere in McCurtain Creek swamp by now." H.P. nods over to food table. "Elihu asked Dan to be here today." H.P. heads to the food table, and I sit next to Dan on the ground.

Dan bites into a chicken leg and shakes his head almost unnoticeably. He whispers, "Be careful. Two black and tan hell hounds and their demon owner still run loose."

I calm my angering spirit. "Damn. Tom Ford ain't dead."

Dan looks up from his plate and whispers, "No need to worry. His time is short."

I start for the food table when bushes rustle in the shadows. A man steps out from behind a large pine.

I lay my hand on my pistol under my jacket but relax. "Sheriff Platner, how in the hell are you?" I walk to the shade where he leans against a tree.

He laughs, breathing hard. "Too damn old to be pullin' these hills, Lummy boy."

I search his eyes. He has every right to take me to jail for killing Lester last year.

"Glad you're back, son." He tips his hat. "H.P., good to see you, too."

H.P. nods in return, "Sheriff Platner," and takes his food to sit with his wife and children.

Platner catches his breath. "Good words you said back there. Heard every one. You've gone through a lot since you left six years ago. Elihu told me everything. The boy's too honest for his own good."

Platner takes off his hat and wipes his brow. His wrinkles match the graying hair that lays flat against his head from sweat. "I'm retiring in a few days."

"What are you gonna do?"

"Fish, love on my wife, and play dominoes. That's what a worn-out old sheriff should do."

"Sounds good to me."

Sheriff Platner takes hold of my arm. "I always knew you were a good'n, Lummy. You've done well, son. I'll say this and shut up. If I had a son, I'd want him to be...."

A gunshot erupts. "I told you I'd find you, Tullos!"

I jerk my pistol, but Elihu jumps in front of me. "Tom Ford, what do you want?"

"I want justice for Lummy killin' Lester and for that niggah lovin' Yankee ass, Poole, who helped him burn Bankston. I'm gonna kill 'em both, right here, right now."

I move away from the crowd. Ford's pistol barrel follows me.

Sheriff Platner steps out of the pine shadows, pistol in hand. "Not if I can help it."

"Sit down, old man. Your days of protectin' this bastard are over."

"Not too old to blow your ass off that horse straight into a damn buryin' hole, boy."

Ford dashes into a thicket firing his pistol and screams, "I'm comin' for you, Tullos. Get ready. I'm the law now, damn you!"

I turn to Martha, who's crying into a handkerchief. "This won't be over 'til he's dead in the ground."

She jerks my arm and pulls me close. "Then dead in the ground it'll have to be."

A TALE OF TWO COLORS

BLOOD of my BIRTH

A SHORT STORY

THE STORY OF RAINY MILLS

PART I

"PICK IT UP, Ratliff!"

Ratliff reached for the torn black vest with one hand, sneaking the other up his hip for a hidden knife.

Rainy snarled, "Stick it in your mouth."

Ratliff sneered, "I ain't doin' it."

"Taste my blood or taste yours. You decide."

BORN AT NOON on a day so dark you'd think it was midnight, his mother had nothing more to wrap his tiny shivering body in except the borrowed black dress she wore to her husband's funeral. Thomas Mills died the day his murderer violated her. Nine months later, she stood in a storm at an orphanage door, mustering up the courage to do the right thing.

Thunder clapped as the wind whipped her frail body. She peeled back the cloth for one last look. Lightning webbed across the sky. For a moment, her son's face glowed like an angel's.

She whimpered, "Lord forgive me," as she gently placed the basket on the doorstep with the cooing infant wrapped in bloody black lace. She hammered her fist against the old wooden door. With a last kiss blown, she turned to leave.

The old preacher who ran the place snatched the door open before she could escape into the torrents of rain that pelted her pale cheeks.

"What's this?"

"I can't take care of him. Please take him in."

"I've got more mouths than I can feed now."

She thrust out a gold locket, a gift from her husband on their wedding day. "It's all I've got." In a few words, she shared her story.

The old preacher's mouth cornered a sad smile. He couldn't turn her down. "I'll take the child. He'll get the locket and his story when he decides to leave."

She pulled her drenched blanket tighter. "Thank you, kind suh."

"What's this child's name?"

"He ain't got a first name, but my husband's last name was Mills."

The old preacher picked up the basket. "You choose a name for him. It's not for me to do."

His mother gazed into the swaying trees and then up into the pouring rain that washed away her tears. "Rainy. That's it. His name is Rainy Mills."

Without another word, she slipped away into the darkness. The blood trail told the old preacher she wasn't long for this world.

He sent for the sheriff.

When the sun peeked through the clouds the next morning, the sheriff found Rainy's mother at the bottom of a gully where she had tried to climb her way back up the muddy bank. When he brought the body to the old preacher, he couldn't help but hang his head and kick at the mud.

"Poor girl. She was clawin' at the last bit of life she had left. It just wasn't enough."

The old preacher buried her in the graveyard with the other paupers.

AS THE BOY grew into a young man, the old preacher never spoke of Rainy's family or the circumstances of his birth. That time would come soon enough. Rainy clung to hope that one day his mother might return. On his darkest days, he sat beside an unmarked grave for hours, not knowing why he was drawn there.

In Rainy's eighteenth year, the old preacher called to him, "Rainy, my son, I can hear the angels coming for me. I'll soon cross the Jordan River. There are things you need to know before they take me to glory. I cannot go to my grave with you not knowing about your folks."

Rainy shivered like he did in the cold rainstorm the day of his birth.

"That grave you sit by? That's where I laid your mother to rest."

Rainy had no words.

The old preacher propped himself up on one elbow and told Rainy a story that made him smile, cry, and seethe with anger. Finished, the old preacher asked, "Hand me that box over there, would you?"

Rainy took the tattered box with faded, painted-on flowers from the shelf and blew dust off the lid. The old preacher removed the top and pulled out a black dress trimmed with lace and a gold locket on a chain.

"This is all I have that says anything about who you are. You were wrapped in this dress when your mother brought you here."

Rainy held it close to his cheek. He laid it on his lap and noticed red specks on his hands.

"What's this?"

"The blood of your birth. I couldn't bring myself to wash the garment."

Rainy trembled as he opened the locket and read the inscription.

Love you always, Epsie
Thomas Mills
August 7, 1830

"Epsie was my mother's name?"

The old preacher nodded but said nothing.

"And Thomas was my father's name?"

Rainy looked up, hoping for more information.

The old preacher sighed. "Besides the fact you were born that same year, that's all I know."

Rainy studied the old preacher's face. "Not true. You do know more."

The old preacher closed his eyes. "I won't lie to you son, I do, but—"

"Then tell me. Who murdered the man who should've been my father?"

"Some things are best left in the past. You've got the best classical education, a fine trade as a gunsmith, and lots of good living ahead of you. Don't spoil it hating a man who's probably dead anyway. Don't let it poison your soul."

Rainy clenched the black dress and held up the locket. "My soul was poisoned the day of my birth. Look at me. I have no memory of my father or mother. All I have is a locket with their names and a funeral dress stained with the blood of my birth." Heat rose in his face like a steamy summer sunrise. "Was there no justice for my folks?"

"No, there wasn't." The old preacher coughed and spit. "The murdering rapist and the judge were friends. It seems the judge liked other men's wives as much as your father's killer did."

"What's his name?"

"Leave it alone."

"I've got to know."

"What you're thinking could get you killed."

"That's on me."

"He's a dangerous man."

"Enough! Tell me. Who murdered my father and raped my mother?"

"John Ratliff."

"How did my father die?"

The old preacher winced. "Ratliff was good with a throwing knife."

"And the judge?"

"Son, you don't want to go there."

"His name?"

The old preacher shook his head.

"Now!"

"Judge Jeremiah Waters. He's retired now."

"Where?"

"Shreveport, Louisiana, I believe. As for Ratliff... he went to Fort Smith some time back."

"Arkansas?"

The old preacher nodded.

Rainy ran his thumb across the engraving on the locket and gripped the tattered black dress like he was trying to squeeze blood from it.

"Don't do this, Rainy. Let it go."

Rainy gritted his teeth. "How can I? I hold in my hands the only two things left of my family and my life. Ratliff and Waters took the rest. I mean to take theirs."

"Son, revenge isn't the way."

Rainy chuckled. "Oh no, preacher, this is not revenge. You taught me better than that. No sir. This is balancing things out, making them even again. It's the reckoning."

"That's the Lord's work."

"Yes sir, and He's gonna use me to get it done."

"God has His own avenging angels."

Rainy squinted with a glare. "Yes He does and I'm happy to be one."

The next day, Rainy buried the old preacher beside his mother's grave with the sheriff's help. He whispered as he tapped a wooden cross into the ground, "The law didn't help my folks back then and I sure as hell don't need the law to help me find Ratliff and Waters now. Avenging angel? That has a nice ring to it."

Rainy gathered his belongings and tools of the gunsmith trade he'd acquired, and watched Natchez disappear around the bend from a steamer northbound for Vicksburg. Before he left, he laid a single rose upon his mother's grave.

FOR THE NEXT ten years, Rainy worked as a gunsmith in Vicksburg, trying to forget about John Ratliff and Judge Jeremiah Waters. Drinking, wearing fine clothes—always black, visiting houses of ill repute, and gambling could only medicate the sickness in his soul. Healing wasn't to be had. Practicing with a pistol soothed his nerves a little. He figured a man who sold guns ought to know how to use them—and well. He got good with a six-shooter, but the wound in his soul continued to fester.

Often, he sat by the big river staring over into Louisiana, trying to forgive his father's murderer and mother's rapist. Though peace never came, Rainy finally decided to put it all behind him until a gun customer on his way to Fort Smith bragged about a friend who'd violated over twenty-five women.

The braggart snickered, "He even left a bastard son behind in the children's home down Natchez way." Rainy thought to himself, John Ratliff.

Over time, Rainy had saved enough money to buy a few guns to peddle and still have a bit of jingle in his pockets. He gathered his things and thanked the gun shop owner who'd helped him make his way. He bought a horse and walked him onto a ferry to cross the Mississippi River. Repairing guns and selling a few to ne'er-do-wells along the way would get him into the right places with the wrong kind of people to find Ratliff.

Rainy edged his mount next to the braggart's and made him an offer as they crossed the river. "It'll be safer if we travel together."

The braggart squinted. "You headin' to Fort Smith?"

"Yeah, I've got business there. I'll provide the whiskey, if you agree."

The braggart spit. "I got no problem with it. I like rye whiskey though."

Rainy purchased several bottles when the ferry landed in Louisiana. When they made camp the first night, the braggart turned up a bottle and boasted of his exploits. Then he spoke of Rainy's blood father with a sickening pleasure in his voice.

"Yeah, I tell you, ole Ratliff ought to run a damn cathouse the way he loves the ladies."

Traveling west, Rainy's companion told story after story confirming the rumors of lawlessness across the Arkansas River in the Indian Territory. Men like his father's killer could hide just beyond the law's reach there. It'd be the perfect place to end Ratliff's worthless life. They stopped for a drink in Fort Smith.

His drunk traveling companion asked, "Where you goin' now?"

Rainy peered over his shot glass pretending to sip. "To sell a few guns before moving on, I reckon. You?"

"I'm headin' across the river to meet up with my friends in Skullyville. That's Injun land, you know. They come to the agency in town to get their government dollars. The Choctaws say it means Moneytown because it sounds like their word for money. There ain't hardly a cent to be had there, 'cept what we take from 'em." He chuckled. "The Injuns don't say nothin' and the law's too scared to come after us." With that, he passed out and slid from his chair onto the floor.

The barkeep yelled as Rainy left, "What about your friend? You can't leave him like that."

Rainy turned and glared with his hand on his pistol. "He's not my friend."

AT DUSK THE next day, Rainy tied his mount to a post in front of a run-down shack that posed as the only saloon in Skullyville. He eased through the batwings like a copperhead on the scent of a barn mouse. The dimly lit room smelled of unemptied spittoons and stale beer—a place where men didn't want to be known.

Rainy tossed a quarter on the bar. "Whiskey, please." He tipped the barkeep another quarter. He needed all the friends he could buy in this place.

Three men sat in a corner, cards in hand. A man with gray whiskers blew a smoke ring that traveled halfway across the room. He sat up to get a better look at the young stranger.

"That's a pretty fancy vest you've got on there, sonny."

Rainy knew it was Ratliff the moment he opened his mouth. He gritted his teeth but didn't look up from his shot glass. "It is."

"Don't think I've ever seen you around here before."

"You haven't."

The man with gray whiskers tipped back his hat. "You seem familiar. Do I know you?"

The man looked familiar to Rainy as well. Too familiar—like looking into a mirror.

"You don't know me at all, and never will."

"A mite testy, ain't you, boy? Guess I would be, too, wearin' a vest with all that sissy lace." He elbowed his friend, laughing. "Makes you look prettier than the lady sittin' on them quarters you tossed on the bar." Ratliff leaned back in his chair, dropping his hand next to his pistol. "Where'd you get the cloth? I might want to get one made just like it."

"You should know. My mother wore it to the funeral after you raped her and murdered my father."

"Well, boys, looky here. Chasin' the ladies finally paid off. My son's come to find me after all these years. How's that fine lookin' momma of yours?" Ratliff cupped his hand on the side of his mouth and whispered, "She had the best lookin' backside you ever saw, let me tell you."

Rainy slammed his fist on the bar. "You couldn't be so lucky as to call me son, Ratliff!"

"Cool down before you burst into flames, boy. Come on over and take a chair. Let your old pa buy you a drink. It's been what, twenty-five, twenty-six years?"

Rainy tightened the grip on his shot glass. "Twenty-eight to be exact you sorry, no good, violator of women. Only a gutless yellow cur could do such a thing."

Ratliff pulled his pistol but Rainy wheeled around and hit him square in the forehead with his whiskey glass. "Drop the gun or I drop you."

Ratliff blinked in disbelief, wiping blood from his wounded brow.

"Do it now. Slow as honey dripping from a beehive in a black locust tree."

Ratliff eased his pistol from its holster and let it drop.

"Kick it to me and get down on your knees."

Ratliff kicked the gun and shook his head. Rainy cocked his pistol.

Ratliff grinned, his yellow-stained teeth catching the dim light. "You want me down on the floor like I had your mother?"

Rainy could take no more. He squeezed the trigger. Ratliff went to his knees, howling like a bit dog.

"You shot my knee!"

"That could've gone easier for you." Rainy ripped off the black lacy vest and threw it on the floor. "Pick it up, Ratliff!"

Ratliff never broke eye contact with Rainy, snatching the dress as he snaked his other hand up his hip. A throwing knife lay hidden in his belt under his coat.

"Stick it in your mouth."

"I ain't doin' it."

"Taste my blood or taste yours. You decide."

Ratliff spat and slung the lacy vest across the greasy dirt floor.

Rainy reached for the vest and Ratliff saw his chance. He snatched his knife and buried the blade in Rainy's thigh quick as a rattler strike. Rainy grimaced but made no sound. He hesitated at the shock of the wound and Ratliff lunged for his knees, toppling him over. Rainy yanked the knife from his hip just as Ratliff knocked the pistol from his hand. Ratliff pounded the knife wound like a pugilist, sending Rainy into agony like he'd never felt before.

Ratliff wrestled himself on top of Rainy, forcing the knife from his hand. He grabbed the blade's handle and inched the edge toward Rainy's face. Ratliff snickered as he drew a thin red line above Rainy's ear. Rainy screamed. Ratliff yanked the knife up to strike a death blow.

Rainy threw a knee into Ratliff's ribs, knocking him across the floor. He scrambled to his feet and head-butted Ratliff. Rainy picked Ratliff up over his head and slammed him down on the floor—hard. Rainy pinned Ratliff's shoulders with his knees. He took a deep breath and reached for the tattered black vest. He held it close to his cheek, exhaling the foul air of the room.

"You murdered the man who should've been my father. Then you violated my mother. You have put me in a most uncompromising position. I now must end the life that began mine."

"Don't kill me. Your father wasn't supposed to be home. I didn't want to hurt your mother. I just wanted to... It all went wrong when—"

Rainy backhanded Ratliff's jaw, splattering blood and spit across the floor. "It all went wrong when my father caught you attacking my mother. I knew you'd be a coward, even now."

Ratliff grabbed for the knife but Rainy knocked it away. One of Ratliff's friends picked it up and stepped toward Rainy.

The barkeep leveled a double-barrel shotgun at him. "Take another step and I'll decorate that wall with your guts. This man needs to finish what he started. I'm makin' sure he does." Ratliff's friend dropped the knife and backed away.

Ratliff whimpered, "What are you gonna do?"

"Leave you like you left my folks, without a breath between 'em."

Rainy crammed the black vest made from his mother's funeral dress into Ratliff's mouth.

"This is the last thing you'll taste in this world." Rainy shoved the vest deep into Ratliff's throat and covered his nose with a hand until he could breathe no more.

"Taste the blood of my birth as yours grows cold."

Rainy sat on Ratliff's chest until the light in his eyes went out. He stood, surveyed the room, and gathered his pistol and Ratliff's knife. No one rose to challenge him. The deed was done and he was exhausted.

The barkeep brought him a glass of whiskey with the scattergun in the crook of his arm.

Rainy held the glass high and held it there a moment. Then he slowly poured the whiskey on the floor. "For Thomas and Epsie Mills. May they rest in peace."

The barkeep cocked the rabbit ears on the shotgun and turned to Ratliff's friends. "This man's had enough. He's evened a score you men had no part in. You'll be stayin' here at least an hour after he leaves. Drop your guns and belly up. First drink's on me."

Rainy downed a second drink the barkeep offered. "Thank you, kind sir. I'll go now. I apologize for the trouble and the mess."

Rainy yanked his mother's blood-stained funeral dress from Ratliff's lifeless throat. He held it close to his cheek for the last time then dropped it on Ratliff's face.

Limping toward the batwings, Rainy whispered as he stuck Ratliff's knife in his belt, "Even avenging angels get wounded sometimes, I reckon." He flipped the barkeep a double eagle.

"Make sure the blood of my birth covers his face when they lay him in the dirt."

The barkeep nodded and followed Rainy to the door with the shotgun trained on Ratliff's former friends. "Good luck, son."

Rainy slipped away into the same darkness from which he was taken by the preacher that day so many years ago.

Rainy patted his horse as he mounted. "Let's go see us a judge in Louisiana."

ANTHONY WOOD grew up in historic Natchez, Mississippi, fueling a life-long love of history. Not long after high school, he lived and worked in Alaska for several years. He returned to the South and ministered for nearly three decades among the poor, homeless, and incarcerated. Leading an effort that planted five urban churches inspired him to co-author *Up Close and Personal: Embracing the Poor* about his work in Memphis, Tennessee. He also authored a number of articles and stories about inner city ministry.

Anthony is a member of Turner's Battery, a Civil War re-enactment group, the Civil War Roundtable of Arkansas, sits on the Oghma Communications Board of Directors, and serves as secretary for the White County Creative Writers' group. His short stories and poetry have won multiple awards and have been published in *Saddlebag Dispatches, The Vault of Terror,* and *The Avocet: A Journal of Nature Poetry.* One of those stories, "Not So Long in the Tooth," won a Will Rogers Medallion in the Best Western Short Fiction category for 2021.

When not writing, Anthony enjoys roaming and researching historical sites, camping and kayaking on the Mississippi River, and being with family. Anthony and his wife, Lisa, live in North Little Rock, Arkansas.